The 53rd Parallel

a River of Lakes novel

CARL NORDGREN

Light Messages

Published 2014, by Light Messages
www.lightmessages.com
Durham, NC 27713
Printed in the United States of America
Paperback ISBN: 978-1-61153-076-6
Ebook ISBN: 978-1-61153-077-3

As with all my life's work, this book is dedicated to my wife, Marie

INTRODUCTION OF CHARACTERS

The River
> The River flows in all Four Directions, through all the characters' lives, in Ireland and Ontario.

This Man
> A great 17th century Annishinabe hunter and warrior who lives on in the lives of the Ojibway who respect the ancient ways.

Brian Burke
> This great big man is an Irish ghilley blessed and cursed by his dreams and passions. With his wife Deidre he is the father of Tommy, Katie, and Patrick.

Maureen O'Toole
> A girl one moment, a woman the next, her rich black hair and bright blue eyes captivate. She's from Northern Ireland, just outside Derry, and a foot soldier for the IRA. Maureen is the smartest person in the room.

Kevin Coogan
> He has a shop in Dublin where he sells musical instruments. Even as a young man the IRA entrusted him with important responsibilities. Maureen is one of his recruits.

Eamon Burke
> Brian and Eamon are cousins who grew up brothers. Eamon is a couple of years older and the only man in the West of Ireland bigger than Brian.

Deidre Burke
   Married to Brian, the mother of his three children.

Joe Loon
   An Ojibway, the elder of his clan of some of the last 'off the Reserve' Ojibway living on the River. He is a dreamer of visions.

Naomi
   Joe Loon's wife.

Albert Loon
   Joe Loon's nephew, though raised as a son. The father of Mathew Loon.

Mathew Loon
   A young boy of the Ojibway village, Albert Loon's son, Joe Loon's grandson, and Simon Fobister's close cousin.

Simon Fobister
   A young boy of the Ojibway village. His father left his family when Simon was very young. His mother is Joe Loon's daughter and Joe Loon has helped raise him. He calls Mathew Loon Big Brother, Mathew Loon calls him Little Brother.

Nokomis
   A title of honor for the matriarch of the clan, and Albert Loon's mother.

Old George Fobister
   An older Ojibway man, long a loyal member of Joe Loon's clan.

Sean Russell
   The leader of the Irish Republican Army leading up to World War II

James and Stephen Miller, the pulp mill brothers
   Grandsons of the owner of Atibiti Lumber Company Chapter

THIS MAN RIDES THE MOOSE

WITH SO MUCH LIGHT ABSORBED in the full rolling clouds of fog floating over the River's lake and shrouding the fir and birch forests it seemed like dusk all day. At the far end of the lake, where the current collected its force to return to the River's channel, some of the clouds were smoke.

A large animal was swimming in the middle of the lake, lost now in a fog cloud, then seen as a shadow before it emerged. It was a big bull moose, his heavy muzzle held just above the water's surface, his dewlap submerged, his large ears folded back, a massive rack of antlers trailing a stalk of broken reed behind.

The drifting silver white clouds just above hid the sky. The big bull's bulk was hidden under the water and his neck cut a modest wake.

Following the moose at some distance, veiled in a great curtain of cloud, then appearing, and only slowly closing the gap, was a gracefully rounded long-nose birch bark canoe paddled by This Man. Before his people were called Ojibway by the French voyageurs and then Chippewa by the English fur traders, they called themselves Annishinabe, for they were the Original People, the First People, and This Man had been a great Annishinabe hunter, and a courageous warrior.

He was dressed in light buckskin leggings and jacket. A heavily beaded pouch draped over his shoulders and crossed at his chest, bandolier-like, repeating the floral pattern painted on the bow of the canoe. He wore a bright red wrap around his head and his hair fell with the extra cloth over his shoulders. The tip of a foxtail was woven into his hair above his right ear.

This Man paddled once hard to glide, paddled twice hard to

glide. The first glide revealed the image of a fox carved into one side of the paddle blade, and with the next stroke and glide the image carved on the opposite side of the blade was revealed—a rabbit dashing away.

This Man paddled to a rhythm that he began to hum deep in his chest as he followed the moose across the lake. He drew close enough to hear the moose snorting a heavy breath, then kept that distance and followed the moose across the lake.

The moose approached the thickest cloud as somewhere a loon cried and the fog clouds captured the trilling wail of high tremolo calls and kept reviving them as they echoed everywhere. When he saw the moose approaching the thick cloud This Man paddled faster to close the distance. He paddled right up behind the moose as the broken bit of reed washed free from the antlers and swirled first in the moose's wake and then twirled in the paddle's whirlpool.

This Man pulled hard with his paddle one last time, then dropped it as the canoe darted alongside the moose. This Man looked up to a break in the fog where he could see blue sky. He heard a song floating muffled from the shore; it seemed to be from another world, and he stood and sang a welcome from his world. When the clouds broke and he could hear the song more fully he raised his voice to join the others.

It was The Path of Souls song.

Just as they disappeared into the cloud, This Man leapt from the canoe onto the moose's back and he sang louder still.

Chapter 2

"IT'S A GRAND DREAM."

IT WAS THE SUMMER OF 1939 in the West of Ireland on the shores of Lough Mask, where the River drained the lough. Sportsmen from England and Europe escaped there from the threat of war for the world-class salmon and brown trout fisheries of the River and Lough Mask and Lough Corrib, though the recent depths of despair had diminished the flow of visitors.

Brian Burke was the ghillie Lord Clarendon had hired to guide his fishing of these waters, and Clarendon was attended by his manservant as well. It was their first day out; they had been fishing the River all morning. Clarendon listened to Brian's suggestions carefully, respectfully, and quickly understood the River's clues as Brian framed them for him. He cast his flies with accuracy and handled his line effectively; the fishing had been superb.

They were taking a leisurely break before they fished Lough Mask. Lord Clarendon, full of his morning pleasure, sighed, and, enjoying his contentment, sighed again as he sat on a camp chair set in place for him by his manservant who brought him his favorites from the wicker hamper. Brian stood apart, near shore, studying the storm clouds passing to the north of them, then admiring the two largest trout his Lordship had caught that morning.

Brian was still a young man, tall and big. Clarendon was no bigger than the average English Lord firmly planted in his middle age. He showed such genuine delight in the morning's events that Brian decided it was the moment he had been waiting for, to tell him of his dream.

Brian's Irish voice boomed over all.

"So you'll find me tellin' this dream every day, keepin' it polished, yeah. Yourself, now I wonder this, have you ever had a dream deserved a daily exercise?"

"To be honest with you, I've always found it annoying to listen to others talk about their dreams. My wife is incessant, telling me such nonsense as delivering meat pies on horseback to the villagers then realizing she's hopelessly lost." With a flip of his hand he continued, "And once she starts it's too late to stop her. I find it's to be avoided from the start."

"Women befuddle easy, you're right there. But the grandest dream ever, you'd want to hear that now, knowin' it will be as glorious a story as this mornin' has been, an' take but a moment to tell you, an' then we'll be findin' you more monsters like these."

Clarendon got up from his chair and joined Brian's up-close admiration of his catch.

"The fishing's been marvelous. It appears your reputation as the best in the West is well earned, young man."

"Makes sense they'd give the best fisherman the best ghillie, yeah." Brian stooped down to pick up the largest brown, to pose it, to appreciate the heft of it.

"As I was watchin' yourself bringin' in such a beauty as this one here, an' she's ten pounds, I'd wager the day's wages on that, an' that's none too common these days. As I was watchin' you, I was thinkin' a fisherman of such quality needs to hear a dream made of the same stuff."

"Very well then, proceed with your night-time fantasies."

Brian laid the fish down with the others.

"Oh no, no fantasy this, not at all. It's one of them dreams offerin', nay beggin' to come true since the—"

"You've my permission. Proceed."

"It captures everythin' you were feelin' this mornin'." Brian picked up the second of the biggest trout, slightly smaller than the first, but it had fought with a heroic determination. "Like when this beauty first rose to your fly, and your heart felt that low down tug, a taut line connectin' you to what it is we need connectin' to so we don't ever lose track of what it is we're made for."

Clarendon smiled as he clapped Brian's arm.

"You Irish play with our language in such an original manner. I find it highly entertaining, if you don't mind my saying so. And you really are remarkably accurate with your description, yes."

"An' am I right thinkin' yer feelin' it again, yeah, that it's so strong in you now, just the discussin' of it carries its own delight?"

"I was told you were a most amusing ghillie as well. It appears you are all of that."

Brian frowned, confused at that description, as Clarendon smiled and returned to his camp chair where his man was refreshing his tea and adding a bit of cheese and biscuit to his plate. He sighed again as he settled to show all was right with his world. When he looked up Brian was holding both of the two biggest brown trout, one in each hand, the solid bodies swaying a bit as they hung in front of him.

"And you say all of that is there in your dream? In what fashion?"

"I'm dreamin' I'm servin' it up, all that brilliance you feel, I'm servin' it up to hundreds an' hundreds of rich American businessmen."

Clarendon looked to his man to see if he had followed it, but he shook his head no, so Clarendon turned back with confusion.

"I'd say that sounds as bizarre as delivering meat pies."

Brian took that as an insult but hid the feeling by studying the fish, and waited just a moment so the scowl dancing on his lips wouldn't be heard in his voice. When he was collected again, he looked up.

"Nothin' bizarre about it." Brian laid the fish back, wiped his hands on his trousers, and reached into his back pocket, unfolding the tattered magazine article he retrieved.

"This is from the February edition of *Wilderness of the World.*"

Without direction the manservant retrieved the pages. Brian showed how the torn parts fit together and pointed out the pictures he wanted Clarendon to see before he handed it over.

"It's a bit worn, yeah, I carry it with me always, but there's pictures, you see, of the most beautiful forests an' rivers and lakes in

Canada, in County Ontario an—"

"Ontario isn't a county, it's a province."

"An' still so wild there's red men who hunt them an' trap an' the Hudson Bay Company is still there to trade with 'em, for beaver an' mink pelts, just like in the pioneer days we see in the American Western filims."

Clarendon examined the photographs quickly then handed the pages back to his man for their return to Brian.

"Yes, lovely Canadian forests. I dare say it looked just like that here a few centuries ago before your people cut down all the trees, but what does this have to do with your dream?"

Brian could sense he'd lost the best moment but decided he could still recover.

"The land in those pictures is so cheap they're practically givin' it away so someone like meself, an' maybe someone like yourself, so we can come an' build a fishin' lodge to create jobs for the red men who live in these woods. Ojibway Indians is what they call 'em."

Clarendon motioned he needed more tea, and his man came for his cup.

"What are you suggesting?"

"An' when I see just how cheap this land is, it's wilderness forests with moose an' wolves an' waters filled with huge pike and trout. Well now, it appears to me in a dream just beggin' to come true that I—"

Clarendon stood and walked to where his waders were laid out, distancing himself from Brian's enthusiasm.

"As I say, this entertaining quality you Irish possess, it never ceases to bring a smile to anyone who appreciates good story telling."

Again Brian bristled.

"I'm askin' you to respect a man's dream here now, and let me tell you about this loveliest little cove with a bit o' beach where we'll build a spectacular fishin' lodge."

Lord Clarendon turned with his waders in hand, and his man brought the tea to him there.

"Yes, yes, I'm sure it would all be quite charming, but if you're suggesting I should consider being your banker, I can tell you quite firmly I'm really not interested."

Brian followed him.

"Picture a lodge where a sportin' man such as yourself would be proud to sip a tea in the mornin' an' a whiskey at the evenin' as you tell your stories about the great places you've fished an' the adventures you—"

"I don't like being directed and I must request you be decent enough to make it easy for me to say no." Lord Clarendon traded with his man, waders for tea cup. "Any further and you'll only be embarrassing yourself."

"Only one thing more an' I'll leave off, for ya see we'd only need to start with five or six cabins, an' the Indians can build 'em, so we'll have cheap labor. It's log cabins we'd be buildin', so most of the materials will be free, yeah, an' when we see what a fine job I'm doin' keepin' the first cabins filled with the Chicago factory owners, many of them sons of Irishmen who would love a bit a' ol' sod at the end of a day, we can add more cabins."

After sipping his tea, Lord Clarendon handed the cup back to his man and began putting on his waders.

"Perhaps you aren't feeling it here in your little corner of the world, but there's a Depression going on and a war that's getting closer to enveloping the whole world every day. There are few rich American businessmen taking holiday these days and I expect fewer soon."

"It won't please me to point it out to ya, but if we hain't feelin' your Depression, it's only that we've grown numb from livin' our own since the day yer people stole our island from us, an' cut down our beautiful forests, an' so here's the bet I'd be makin' with you. Your Depression will be over well before ours will be."

Lord Clarendon was struggling with his waders and it took a moment for his man to realize it and put the cup down, so his help was too late to keep his Lordship from tripping a bit when he turned suddenly at Brian's last comment. When he collected himself, he was a British Lord.

"I was feeling good, no, I was feeling *grand*, much to your credit, but now you've got me... I don't know, what have you got me?"

His man offered, "Peeved?"

"Peeved, thank you, yes. I've come over here to relax and get away from business grabbers, to fish the waters my ancestors—"

"We all know who yer family used to be."

Lord Clarendon pulled his waders up over his chest.

"You know who we *used* to be? Do you know that it *used* to be this land was productive and cared for a damn sight better than is happening now. How rude of you to force me to say these things in defense of my family name."

"I hope your family cared for it. You not only owned it, you owned nearly every bit of everythin' was around it. An' now I'm to understand when we have nothin' else to give, then you're declarin' our language is for your entertainment?"

"So you tell me your dreams and expect that I will give you my money, what, out of pity for your plight?"

The Lord delivered this line with his man blocking his view as he helped buckle the last shoulder strap on his waders, so he didn't see how his words brought Brian to his full height and red fierceness to his face.

"Hear this clear, an' that is if I ever saw you lookin' at me with pity, I'd put a stop to that right away, so."

"Now you're going to become the radical Republican, are you?"

Brian snorted his laugh of disdain. Behind his back the folks from his village and the neighboring ones referred to him and his quick and ferocious temper as the Red Bull Demon, and it was the Red Bull Brian was becoming even as he struggled against it.

"Me a radical Republican? Never thought so, unless you're sayin' so's the whole world become Republican for believin' you had no right takin' our island from us in the first place, let alone keepin' it for... how would you say it? For so bloody long."

"Some important lines are being crossed here now. This is not what I expect from someone in your position, and it will be fully reported to the game steward."

"So the reason you're the man I must be askin' for the money I need for this dream is simple. When you take what's mine, at some point I'll be knockin' on yer door an' askin for it back." He tried to control his anger for one more attempt. "You know how much my fee for services is, or how *little* is more like it, an' you can see how long it would take for me to save what I'd be needin'. But I'd be payin' you back in just three years, if ya'd rather lend it than be investin' it."

"You know the difference between a loan and selling shares, so I have to take you *seriously*? You have no right to continue haranguing me when I have explained I don't want to hear another word about this silly dream of yours. Now let's get back to the water."

The British Lord stepped forward boldly though with waders on there was just a bit of waddle to his walk. In any case, he expected the Irishman to retreat the half step that would clear the path down to the shore.

Instead Brian leaned forward just enough, and there was even more size advantage than first expected, so their shoulders collided and his Lordship nearly fell, staggering two steps back. Brian's rapidly rising anger burned brighter than Lord Clarendon's frustrated indignation, but before his Lordship realized it, he had collected himself and turned to Brian.

"I think you should re-examine this behavior immediately, or you'll find I am quite prepared to withhold your fee altogether."

Brian loaded up a hard right, and threw it. It was the sledgehammer punch he had thrown many times with devastating effect when the Red Bull Demon raged within. But it wasn't a pub brawl with nothing to lose, and so he continued to fight hard against it and he was able to stop the punch in the last instant, a foot short of Lord Clarendon's jaw. Lord Clarendon would have crumbled from the blow, he knew it, and he shrank from the threat.

But Brian's rage kept building. He knew he must walk away.

"Keep me fee money. Take it home an' put it back in the Bank of feckin' England with the rest of our patrimony. Ya feckin' Brit."

Brian turned to Lord Clarendon's manservant.

"You were watchin', and I never laid a finger on 'im..."

The man stepped back, and nodded yes without meaning to.

"So you won't be tellin' falsehoods about what happened later."

The man looked away, and Brian walked up the bank to the road as his Lordship sputtered threats. Brian climbed into the fishing lodge's panel van, slammed the door behind him, started it, and pulled away, leaving his Lordship and his man stranded at the riverside.

❄ ❄ ❄

That same day, in County Tyrone, one of the Six Counties of British Northern Ireland, a dirty and dented Ford Talbot chugged down a quiet country road weaving a route through the moors, headed east and south towards the Dublin road. It was raining softly.

Kevin drove. He was a quiet man and a serious one. Though he had served the Irish Republican Army for years, and been a unit commander the past two, he had just turned thirty. While he drove he was intently questioning his passenger, Maureen O'Toole, his raven-haired, blue-eyed recruit—she appeared a lovely girl one moment, a beautiful woman the next.

Maureen answered his questions but was distracted, watching to see if the car following them would finally pull off onto the upcoming side road. It had been following their route for some time now, staying well back at times, even disappearing in the road's turns, but always reappearing in the straight-aways. Theirs had been the only two cars on the road for some time.

"Comin' a bit closer now, Kev, but I still can't make 'em out."

"Are you going to answer my question?"

"Ask it again."

"Do you understand that you are as important as any one of them waiting for you?"

"You're askin' do I think I am as important as the boys in London. I don't see myself that way, no. They're the heroes, yeah. But I am proud to be a servant to the heroes of our cause."

"That's what I'm saying. Russell wasn't eager to permit a young girl into this particular operation."

"I'm twenty my next birthday."

"And so that makes you just nineteen and he's after me to be sure you are looking at this full in the face. You need to acknowledge to me you understand that smuggling in the makings is no different than making them, and making them is the same as setting them off."

"You can tell Russell this girl'll place 'em too, if that be needed." She turned to look straight at him. "And I prefer it when you call a thing what that thing is, Kevin. It's makings for bombs and the bombs are for killin' the enemy."

They drove in silence for a moment, the wipers flipping back and forth across the streaked windshield, before Kevin asked the next question.

"And those who die in the blast of bombs you're making? It's enemy soldiers if we do our jobs with an exact effect. But that's hard to deliver and there will come a day when others will be too close and they'll be caught in the blast, civilians is what I mean, and they will be called 'The Innocents' in the headlines."

"And so you're tryin' to talk me out of it, Kev, is that it?"

"That, or making sure you know what you are doing before you get all the way in it. We've never taken it to London like this before. There's some who are against it. I've told you my misgivings because I need to make sure you know what you are doing."

"Haven't I been beggin' you to get all the way in it? It's what I have to do, so."

"Lady Girl, what I'm trying to tell you is you *don't* have to. Right now you can tell me to turn around and I'll take you home and Russell will thank you for what you have done already and what your da—"

The car didn't turn off on the side road.

"The car's still back there."

"And you don't have to worry who might be following you. Unfortunately, there's lots of girls whose da's were murdered by Black n' Tans. But they sit home trying to forget it, permitting themselves a smile as they sit with their mums and wait for a lad to come calling for a River walk."

Maureen stared back at the car quietly for a few moments, watching it come closer, then fade back again before she could see any details of the driver, and her throat choked from fighting deep emotion.

"There's time for walks... later... an' them who can forget is better off than me, Kevin, I understan'... but this time is for mindin' me da's memory by gettin' 'im his due."

"No, Lady Girl, you have to be doing this thing we're setting off to do, not for revenge, but for true Fenian causes."

"Not for revenge? Not for revenge." She stared forward now, and they drove along quietly for a mile. When she faced Kevin there was a tear falling across her cheek, but Kevin didn't hear it in her voice.

"I want the Brits out of the Six Counties as much as you or Russell or anyone. It was Derry where they murdered me da, in front of us, Kevin. In the house he was born in, in Derry." Her tears were falling now, but still her voice had held steady.

"Your da was a brave man and I understand righteous anger. But your da always told me to keep personal feelings under control, that's what I'm saying. I'm saying anger clouds the mind, and what you are setting off to do requires full composure and great discipline."

"If you don't want me angry then don't talk to me about sittin' at home an' smilin' with me mum, Kevin, because when I sit with her... When I share a smile with me mum it carries the memory of that last moment Da was alive. When *she* had to look away. I knew she wouldn't be able to look him in the eye, so I did it for her, I held him in my eyes so he could see his family loved him and we were proud of him but she couldn't watch... So I did... She was lookin' at me as that bastard put the pistol right there an' shot me da... An' Kevin, what she tells me now is she doesn't know what was more frightful to see, me da's murder, or me fillin' up with hatred as I watched it happenin'. So you see, Kevin, I can't smile at me mum when she cries til mornin'... I will find the men who did this to him, and I will kill them. In the meantime, I will carry on his work."

They drove in silence. The car followed them. Maureen saw another side road ahead. Kevin checked the rear-view mirror.

"Then I'll let Russell know there's no doubt. You're all the way in."

"I have lots of reasons to deliver the bomb makings to the boys in London. Assure Russell I'm all the way in."

Maureen saw the car behind them finally take a southward fork in the road and she turned back to Kevin.

"An' God bless the innocents, so."

❀ ❀ ❀

The fishing lodge's van was parked in front of the main street dry goods store in the village of Cong. It was parked in the exact spot Barry Fitzgerald's horse and cart would stop twelve years later in the filming of *The Quiet Man*, when the shop would be turned into Cohan's Pub for the movie. This night Brian stood at the bar in the pub across the street.

As the story of Red Bull Brian and the British Lord spread, men from town had joined earlier drinkers and paid for his drinks all afternoon and into the early evening.

"Any closer I'd felt his mustaches. As me demons was pullin' my right arm back and loadin' it with all their might, I was sure they was intendin' I'd be throwin' it full square to his jaw."

"Ah me Bri, I'm quiverin' each time I hear it. Here, let me get you anodder."

"An' his grandfather bein' the very landlord who failed at the Big House. Dat's feckin' perfect, feckin' beautiful."

The pub door opened and Brian looked up with a smile to see who'd be buying the next round. It was his cousin Eamon who'd come looking for Brian. Eamon Burke was a couple of years older than Brian, perhaps an inch taller and nearly two stones heavier. They were easily the largest men in the pub and celebrated by their village as the two biggest men for miles around. Eamon joined them, shaking his head at their high spirits.

"No singin' at the lodge tonight, lads. Just fury over Jimmy's van gone missin' an' a British lord spittin' threats at your man here."

"Eamon, join us, we've just moved to the whiskey."

"I'm here fetchin' the van, Cos, an' they're callin' for you as well. Finish that an' let's go see what we're facin'."

Brian sipped but didn't finish, then wiped his mouth and smiled to the crowd.

"You can fetch the van, Cos, but you hain't fetchin' me. Not to go apologize to no feckin' Brit."

"Right, so. But if I'm to take care you need to do me a favor, Cos, an' tell me your version of the story. A moment with Brian, lads, he'll be right back. I'll just be askin' himself for some advice on how to proceed."

Eamon led Brian outside behind the van. Brian leaned on the back door, his arms folded across his chest. Eamon stood facing him.

"He was laughin' at my dream, Cos, an' it all starts with how one man respects another man's dream."

"No, it all starts with a man earnin' a livin' for his family. I set you up at the only fishin' lodge in all the West with anythin' like a steady business an—"

"Innish Cove is a grand business opportunity. You've said so yourself many times."

"You've named it."

"I'm still thinkin' of a name for the camp, but the cove I've been dreamin' of, that's Innish Cove."

"I've said it's a grand dream, yes I have, but if the choice you'll be offerin' guests is bein' your London bankers or your punchin' bag, well then I start to feel a little different about it. There's no song in what happened today, Cos, but I did see Gardai arrivin' at the lodge as I was leavin'."

"What will they arrest me for? Abandonin' a man in the middle of the best trout fishin' he's ever seen? He said so a dozen times. He caught two trout over six pounds and one a' them was nearly eight."

"He says you swung at him, an' if he hadn't ducked at the last instant, you'd a broke his jaw. He's declarin' an assault."

"He may be a lord in England, but he's a lyin' coward in Ireland." Brian stood. "So I will go with you, yeah, an' I'll tell him to repeat his story with his man who saw it all standin' there in front of me."

Eamon knew that would be a mistake.

"You're right. No need in you joinin' me. I believe this will be handled best with you sittin' in your cottage awaitin' the outcome."

"I'm tellin' ya' his man saw it all, an' if you can find anyone who ever knew me to throw a punch an' miss I want to meet 'im. I stopped." Brian stood. "You can fetch for 'em all ya want, but I'm makin' plans for a new life now, Cos, an' he was laughin' at 'em."

"Hangin' out at the pub tellin' the lads all about yer dreams hain't the same as makin' plans."

"Don't talk like this is just idle fantasy, Cos. I'm doin' this for my family an' for yours. Not a one of us is meant to be just another generation of famine survivors."

"Your family needs your wages more than your dreams, more

than ever now since there hain't many around these days, Bri."

"So I got to get us out of here."

"You need guests who trust you an' you need to be takin' your money home an' not leavin' it in there—"

"I've not paid for a drink today."

"An' ya need to be takin' care of your woman again so she don't get so run down as the last time."

Brian looked for further signs of what Eamon meant by the last time, and as he seemed confused, Eamon shook his head.

"So you didn't know."

"What are you sayin'?"

"About your poor Deirdre."

"What about her?"

"You didn't know your wife's with child again."

"What? Sure. Of course I know."

"Did you know before I just told you now?"

"Whatta you sayin'? I'm a great da."

"No one questions Tommy and little Katie love their da, but Deirdre is always tellin' me missus that you're never home attendin' to her."

"If that's her contention how is it she's with child again?"

"When she came by last night to tell me missus, she said she hadn't told you yet."

"She shouldn't be tellin' none our business."

"She don't need anger, Cos, she needs you lookin' after her. She didn't appear tip top last night when she came 'round for a cup. She told my Marie she's scared she's carryin' again so soon."

"That's the way women talk. She's stronger than you think. I'm the one was lookin' after her after we lost the last baby, an' she never was as bad off as the midwife was sayin'."

"I'll talk to Jimmy for you an' see if I can settle things with him. Maybe he'll make a big show out of sackin' you an' then he can hire you back after Clarendon leaves. Jimmy don't like the man neither, his father was struck more than once by them when they was the landlords at the Big House."

"Jimmy knows I find his guests more brown trout than anybody else he's got."

"Give me the keys, and no more sellin' shares to guests, Bri. Promise me that."

"But who else do I have?"

"You need the wages, Cos."

❊ ❊ ❊

Late that night Brian sat at the table in his cottage in the light of an oil lamp, close to the small peat fire. He leaned over a piece of paper, a thick stub of pencil in his hands. On top of the page he had written the words "Plans for the Canadian fishing operation to be named the Great Lodge at Innish Cove, Brian Burke Proprietor and Host," and below that he wrote "Ojibway Indians as ghillies" and "trees for log cabin construction" and "Chicago business men many Irish" but the rest of the page was blank.

Their bedroom door opened and Deirdre stepped from darkness into the glow at the light's edge, her bare feet sounding soft, her voice hard.

"When did you come in?"

"A while ago."

"Why didn't you come home for supper?"

"I'm home now."

"You were at the pub all night."

"An' all afternoon."

"Your guest left off fishin' early?"

"The day he had, I'm guessin' he's still shakin' with excitement."

"He paid you the full wage?"

"Not yet."

"We need wages, Brian."

"You'll wake little Katie if you keep huffin' at me."

"Oh, no, don't you tell me how to be carin' for these children."

"An' I'm carin' for these children and theirs to come with what I have in front of me here, so leave off an' get yourself back in bed."

"I've got another child growin' in me."

Brian pushed the table away and pivoted in his chair to face his wife.

"I've been told. Eamon knew, his missus knew, what's next, the whole feckin' village knows an' then you tell the father."

"You haven't been home now, have you?"

"I sleep next to you every night, how the hell else would you be carryin' again?"

"That's the only time you're home, to crawl on top of me."

"I'm just sayin' you ought not be tellin' others before you tell the father... or are you tellin' me somethin' else now?"

Deirdre entered the full lamp light and took one more step to slap Brian. He caught her wrist and held her arm but as Deirdre began to swing with her other arm he pushed her away, hard. She stumbled back, slipped and fell, and hit her head on the wall, but that was just a glancing blow for her back took the full force flat on the hard floor. Her cry at the shock was lost as her breath was knocked out of her. Her body twisted as the pain demanded.

Brian saw he'd hurt her and rushed to her side.

"Oh, here now, I'm sorry, Deirdre."

He tried to lift her to her feet but she couldn't rise, for a second wave of pain twisted her back.

"No, hooo, no... jest... hoo... let me lie here for a moment."

Brian cupped her head, and she lay there, then a smaller wave of pain jerked her up and Brian caught her head when the spasm released her. He had felt how cold the floor was so he wrapped his arms around her the next time she flinched in pain and he carried her momentum forward.

"Lemme get you into bed. Can you get up?"

He picked her up as she winced and whined and twisted to relieve more pain. He carried her back into the darkness of the bedroom.

"I've a... baby growin' in me Bri... ya can't hit me when you feel like it."

"I didn't hit you. It was that Red Bull Demon in me who pushed you; he's been dancin' round all day. You're not bad hurt, are you?"

"Of course I'm bad hurt."

He placed her gently on the bed, then knelt at her side.

"Do I need to get someone?"

"Let me lie here... hoo... let me see."

The worst pain didn't return and slowly she was able to relax her body on the bed.

"That wasn't me, you know that. I'm the man who is goin' to

get us outta here, Deirdre, that's who I am. I'm the man who will make this dream come true an' some folks today was laughin' at it an' since then the Demon has been testin' an' tauntin' me."

"Just let me rest here." She folded her arm over her face. "Without havin' to listen to your nonsense."

"You want me to leave you?"

"I want you to leave me alone and let me rest."

Brian patted her shoulder, stood, and left the room. He returned to his paper, picked up the pencil, and underlined everything he had written.

❀ ❀ ❀

A week later Maureen was in a Customs line waiting to claim her luggage—the two large trunks she had checked into stowage on the Dublin-to-Holyhead ferry. Three young British soldiers stood by and she had casually allowed them to admire her when she passed to get in line. She cocked her hip when she turned back to catch their gaze. Then she smiled and offered a wave that beckoned them to her.

"I wasn't sure if you soldier boys are lookin' serious or lookin' bored."

"See 'ere now, birdie, it's what a 'ighly trained British soldier has been 'ighly trained to do, to look 'ighly trained."

"You have to be trained to be serious, do you?"

"That's 'cause otherwise, deep down inside, we're just like you Irish. We're all of us just lookin' for a little bit a' fun."

"A little bit a' fun? Just so happens I'm on my way to London to join my girlfriends for a little bit a' fun."

"Lookin' for a bit a' fun in London are you?"

"An' did I say there's three of 'em?"

"Four Irish lasses enjoying Londontowne, without an escort?"

"An' those other three, they're the pretty ones."

"Listen to this birdie sing."

"We got a leave comin' Tuesday."

"So I've got an offer for you highly-trained British soldiers. If you'll fetch those two trunks for me right over there, those two big ones an' mind 'em careful, they're heavy with everythin' dear to me. It took one Irish lad to carry 'em, may take all three of you."

"Ah now, birdie, you give me a chance and I'll be 'appy to show you what one good British soldier can do."

"If you'll help me get 'em loaded on me bus, I'll write our address out for you an' as soon as you get into London, we'll find out what the British Army means by a little bit a' fun."

"An' 'ow do we know you'll give us the proper address?"

"I don't see anyone queuin' up to offer a better deal, so... It's those two trunks, right there. Careful with 'em. Me friends back home warned me to watch out for British soldiers. Whatta you think they meant by that?"

Chapter 3
THE RIVER FLOWS NORTH

THAT SAME DAY FOUR OJIBWAY fished the River that drained the great sweep of northwestern Ontario wilderness, collecting and carrying the waters north to Hudson Bay. They were two men and two boys, and they fished the River where it opened up to a massive lake that the Ojibway call Kaputowaganickcok, "The Lake where the Funereal Fires Burned on Shore." They worked from a large wooden freight canoe, hauling in their gill net.

Joe Loon was the elder to his family clan. The younger man was Albert Loon, Joe Loon's nephew, though adopted and raised as his son after Albert's father never returned from a hunting trip when Albert was a young boy.

They hauled and folded the net between them while Mathew Loon, Albert's nine-year-old son, and Simon Fobister, Joe Loon's seven-year-old grandson, pulled walleyes from the net and slipped them into the wet burlap bags at their feet. It was proving to be a good haul.

They reset the net above the shoal below Top Rock Hole then headed back to their village a couple of miles north where the River had carved out a quiet bay. Joe Loon paddled from the stern, Albert from the bow, and the boys made plans for the last hours of daylight as they paddled from opposite sides in the middle. Together they found a steady pace and cut through the waters briskly, easily.

They paddled across the waters their ancestors had fished for over 200 years, driven there from the East not by European settlers but by Iroquois and then driving the Dakota they found here further West out onto the Great Plains after a hundred years of forest battles and ambushes.

They turned wide of a large island when no one recognized the two boats pulled up on the shore of the island's southern point. Without seeing the boats' owners, they knew they belonged to the white man.

The village wasn't far from the island and Joe Loon guided the freight canoe in line with two others and next to the smaller birch bark canoe the children had named Nigig, Otter, for the elders described Otter's grace as the model for the children as they learned to handle the light craft. Back from shore at the edge of the forest were two large canvas miner's tents, a smaller tent, three full-sized birch-bark wigwams, and one small wigwam. Joe Loon's clan, the Ojibway of these Keewatin forests, had kept camp here since late in the spring and had for generations.

Joe Loon was greeted by his wife, Naomi. Albert's widowed mother stood with her and as the oldest woman of the clan she was the Nokomis. Albert shared his wigwam with his wife Sarah and their three children and his mother. Simon Fobister and his mother, Joe Loon's only surviving daughter, lived in the wigwam closest to Joe Loon's wigwam. Simon's father abandoned his family when Simon was very young.

Old George Fobister, no older than Joe Loon but called Old George since he was a young man, lived alone in the smallest wigwam. Louis Assiniboine and his wife and two children slept in one of the tents, Sam Turtle and his family in the other. Simon Fobister and Mathew Loon were the oldest boys of the clan's eight children.

All of the children appeared from the bush to greet the returning fishermen and were followed by the rest of the clan.

"Ahneen."

"Ahneen."

After they unloaded the canoe Joe Loon put his hand on Mathew's shoulder and waited for everyone's attention.

"I have an adventure for a boy who will soon become a man."

"Yes, Grandfather."

"The white man camps at Many Tall Women Island. You will go there now. You will sell them fish for their meal."

"They will speak the white man's words to me, Grandfather. I do not understand many of their words."

"The elders tell stories of the days our people traded with the white man before we knew their language. Take them four fish and bring me their largest silver coin that will trade for many good things at the Hudson Bay Post. Then you will have your own story to tell your grandchildren."

Simon stood tall next to Mathew.

"I will be in this story with Big Brother."

"Yes, you will be in the story with Big Brother."

The boys put their arms over each other's shoulders and followed Joe Loon as he retrieved three walleyes and a northern pike from the day's catch.

"You will take Nigig," their grandfather told them. The boys loaded the fish in the birch-bark canoe and before they climbed in and shoved off Joe Loon called to the spirits to watch over them.

❊ ❊ ❊

Simon paddled Nigig from the bow, Mathew from the stern. As they found the rhythm to their strokes that created the greatest speed, Mathew allowed himself a sharp bark of joy. Simon smiled to hear it.

Just behind the boys This Man paddled his canoe. He had heard Joe Loon's call, waited for them when they left the bay, and followed the boys into the open water. Soon the island was in sight and This Man kept pace with the boys as they approached the island and found a place to beach their canoe, out of sight of the white man's camp. This Man paddled in to shore and beached his canoe next to Nigig.

"What do we do next, Big Brother?"

"We will arrive at their camp quietly. We will watch them before we let them know we are here."

"Why?"

"We will watch them so we will know what we must do to bring them into our story."

"Grandfather taught you this."

"Yes."

"This is what we will do."

The boys ran through the forest at a fast trot, cutting between fir trees, leaping over logs, and ducking under branches, the bag of fish bouncing over Mathew's shoulder, Simon behind but staying close.

This Man ran just ahead.

They slowed in the same step when they saw the trees opening at the far shore line and a few steps later they heard a voice ring loudly. The boys had visited this island before; they had explored it in play many times, and they knew a small, rocky bluff just ahead would let them look down on the campsite. This Man and the boys followed a barely-worn path to the top of the bluff. They crouched around a boulder and then crawled closer to the edge, Mathew behind a stump, Simon behind Mathew, This Man standing behind a tree, watching the boys as they studied the camp just below them.

Two men near the cook's fire were speaking loudly.

"I didn't mean to start an argument with you. I'm just trying to get you to acknowledge that they won't build the next mill anywhere near here, that's all. I'll bet you a week's wages they'll build it closer to Dryden."

"I don't want to bet with you."

"Because you know I'm right."

"Because I know they sent us here to do a job for 'em. So let's do it right, eh?"

"If you thought I intended to do otherwise, you don't know me."

A white woman stepped out of the tent and walked to the fire. She was holding a big bowl of batter and was beating it with the spoon she had just retrieved from the tent. There was a frying pan over the fire. The boys had seen one or two white men every time they went to the Post, but very few white women, so they were curious and watched her closely. She poured the batter into the pan, but not nearly as much as their grandmother poured when she was making fry bread. This white woman poured just a thin layer and the boys were curious so they studied her.

After a few moments she wrapped the frying pan handle with a towel, grabbed it with both hands, and stood. When she flipped the pan and sent the disc of batter up into the air, Simon's hold on

Mathew's arm tightened, and when the flying disc turned once and she caught it in the pan Simon cried softly, "Yaway."

"Quiet."

She returned the pan to the fire then turned, looked up at the bluff, and waved to the boys to come on down. They scooted back, looked at each other, then smiled.

"We will meet a white woman. We will find out what she is cooking. This will be a good story to tell the others."

"You are the oldest."

This Man stayed on the bluff to watch over the boys as they stepped into the opening of the camp filled with three white men—another had been resting in the tent but he came out when the others called to him to see the Indian boys. The white woman stood in front of the men. She smiled at the boys when they stepped out of the forest. They looked only at her. Simon took Mathew's arm again and whispered to his cousin.

"I must taste that flying bread."

"It was like the moon flipping to show its other side."

"I thought this would be a story about selling fish to the white man. It is now a story about the white man's woman and the moon bread."

The woman's smile broadened as she listened.

"What a lovely sound your language makes. It's the song of the forest. Where did you boys come from? I saw you sneaking up when I was in the tent. You got anybody hiding back there with you?"

The Ojibway boys stepped forward. When the woman turned to check on her frying pan and waved the boys to follow they stayed with the men, to tend to business, but stole glances at the woman. Mathew placed the sack of fish at his feet and opened it enough for the men to see inside.

He spoke one of the first English words taught in Joe Loon's village.

"Fish."

"You brought us fish, eh? I thought you come to swipe some of my wife's pancakes. You think they're here all alone?"

Mathew repeated the word fish then spoke to the men in the forest language.

"You get these fish. You give us a big silver coin for Grandfather."

"I have no idea what you're saying, boy."

"That ol' Swede at the dock was telling me there's still a couple of villages of half-wild Indians back in the bush that have never lived on a reserve. These boys must be from some camp of that sort around here somewhere or other."

"Been sent here to sell us these fish, eh? Show him some money. Let's see what he does."

The white man reached into his pocket and pulled out three coins; one was a big silver dollar, the one minted in 1935, the coin's reverse design sculpted to show two Ojibway men paddling a birchbark canoe, and that was the side displayed when he opened his hand to offer the coins to Mathew. Simon looked from it to Big Brother.

"That is the silver coin Grandfather wants."

"It makes him happy each time he sees it."

"Yes, but we could take the smaller coins and bring back some of the batter for the moon breads. What would Grandfather say if we did that?"

"We must taste the moon breads first."

Mathew stepped forward and selected the two smallest coins, then continued on past the men to the cook fire where he hunkered down to study the pancakes stacked on a plate and the biggest one that nearly filled the frying pan.

"Yaway, Little Brother, these moon breads smell good."

Simon pointed to the cook fire by puckering his lips out ahead of him and thrusting his chin so the white men would know he was following Mathew, then stood next to him, his hand resting on Mathew's shoulder.

The woman clapped her hands in delight.

"Look at them. They're adorable. I wish I had a camera."

"They're sure interested in your pancakes."

"Fix 'em up all they want. Give 'em a big pat of butter and plenty of syrup."

Mathew smiled when he realized that the bottle was pouring what looked like the sweet goodness of the sugar bush on the moon breads. His grandmother would often pour a bit of it on his *manoomin* for him. The boys accepted their plates and took their first bites.

"Yaway, Big Brother. This is the best taste I have ever had in my mouth."

"We must bring some back to our people. That would be the best end to this story."

❈ ❈ ❈

Simon pulled Nigig up on shore while Mathew retrieved their packages: a big jar of batter, a block of butter, a cup of maple syrup. They were first surrounded by the children, but then all the people of the village gathered to hear of their adventure. Before they were through telling them, Nokomis had uncovered the bowl of batter to dip, then lick, her finger.

She smiled. The children loved that smile and followed her when she turned to set a frying pan on the fire.

"I must grease the pan while the moon bread is floating above me?"

"No, Nokomis, you grease the pan first like you always do." And the boys practiced their stories of their great adventure selling fish to the white men as the children gathered for the moon bread feast.

Chapter 4

THE RIVER FLOWS EAST

MAUREEN HELD A BAG OF GROCERIES as she waited at a bus stop in a neighborhood in the Richmond district of London. A grandmother said good morning and smiled as she passed by. A bus pulled up, but Maureen explained she was waiting for a friend so the bus driver smiled at the lovely lass and drove away without her.

Maureen followed the grandmother to the corner and stopped to study the post office down the street. The grandmother was crossing the street and Maureen nearly called out to stop her, then caught herself and stayed silent. The grandmother raised her arm to wave to her husband who was waving back as he skipped down the post office steps. A sudden blast behind him shattered the doors to splinters and shards in an explosion that whip-ripped the grandfather's waving arm off at the shoulder and threw him out over the stairs and he bounced down to the sidewalk. There was enough force to the explosion that the grandmother was knocked back and fell to the street.

An alarm rang and kept ringing. Maureen ran to help the grandmother to her feet. She studied the bomb's effect after the grandmother pulled away from her to stagger to her husband and throw herself on top of him, wailing just like her mum had at her da's wake.

Chapter 5
AND THE RIVER FLOWS SOUTH

IT WAS A COUPLE OF WEEKS LATER in the first days of autumn, the grasses turning yellow and brown, when Brian took the bus to Donegal where his friend Aidan promised an introduction to a fellow who had been operating a bed-and-breakfast fishing operation for a number of years. The B&B owner showed his interest in learning more about Brian's plans for his fishing camp in Canada as soon as Aidan made mention, and said he'd be eager to meet Brian so he could learn more about it.

They met in the B&B owner's favorite pub. He paid close attention as Brian told him all about his dreams and his plans. Just as Brian approached one of his big finishes Kevin entered the pub with Maureen at his side.

After the London bombing raid, a radical move of bringing violence to England for the first time, all IRA operatives were listening carefully to the reaction of the people in the countryside. Maureen and Kevin were just starting their own trip to towns and villages to purposefully prompt conversation by carrying a newspaper with the bold stacked headline "IRA Bombing Kills Constable 83-Year-Old-Grandfather".

When they realized that this big man standing at the bar had captured everyone's attention with the story he was telling, Maureen and Kevin sat at a table where they could listen.

"Now for the best idea yet. It's a formula that can't fail to produce for me. Just as soon as I've worked out any early problems, as soon as I know I'm ready for what's to come, I'll be invitin' famous men to the camp, to come fish at the Great Lodge at Innish Cove, an' as my guests, for free, yeah. You're Ernest Hemmingway, an' you get a letter from the best ghillie in the West a' Ireland an' now he's promisin' a wilderness adventure in Canada that can't be matched anywhere else. I'll include pictures of my red men holdin' great big pike or crouchin' over a massive rack of a moose, an' we'll promise a real gentleman's comforts in a magnificent lodge as da top notch."

"From what we know of him, he just might come."

"An' I send letters to Teddy Roosevelt—."

"Ah, I believe Roosevelt's been dead for a number of years."

"An' so you can help me make the list of the famous American outdoorsmen, an' I'll offer 'em each a free week in the wild woods, with the Irish country lodge's comforts a gentlemen appreciates, an' then our payin' guests, when they return home an' talk about the trip they had to an earthly paradise where they was fishin' with a big man—"

"Innish Cove becomes just the sort of place to come to if you'd like to be seeing yourself as that sort of a man. And you can charge extra for that experience."

"Exactly right. Aidan, you finally found me someone who gets me dream."

"It's your Indians makes this special. Nice touch, them."

"Americans love Indians. Being Americans they had to kill millions of 'em before they figured that out, yeah, but they especially love Ojibway, which is what Hiawatha was. So we throw in a little somethin' like this here." Brian stood up at the table to recite.

"Should you ask me, whence these stories? Whence these legends an' traditions. With the odors of the forest. With the dew an' damp of meadows. With the curlin' smoke of wigwams. With the rushin' of great rivers. With the frequent repetitions an' their wild reverberations as of thunder in the mountains." He acknowledged the claps and table slaps with a tip of his head. "We give 'em the poetry of the wilderness an' great fishin' an' huntin', they can sleep in a bed Hemmingway slept in, an' we'll put some true Irish craic right in the middle of it all."

"Can't deny it, the power in your presenting it all is grand."

29

"Lots of businessmen in Chicago got Irish in 'em, so we play strong to them. I spend the first winter after we build the camp livin' in Chicago and sellin' as many of them sons of Ireland business owners I can meet." Brian paused. "You're seein' the potential."

The B&B owner slowly sipped the last of his whiskey, then wiped his lips to hide the smile that was forming. He admired confidence. He distrusted over confidence.

"I do, I do, and I think we should do this, this Great Lodge of Innish Cove, you and me, and we should make it grand."

"Yes?"

"Absolutely."

"It's the Great Lodge at Innish Cove."

"Sure it is."

Brian took the B&B owner's hand, and shook it.

"You'll be makin' my dream come true and that demands a drink." Brian signaled to the publican. "I'm buyin' the house here, Johnny boy." He waved all to join him at the bar and said to his friend. "Ah Aidan, you done me right."

"Yes, Aidan, this introduction to the great Brian Burke, well, I won't forget it was you who brought me this opportunity."

Brian didn't like "the great" so much but set it aside.

"I figure it's five thousand pounds to get started an' I commit to you here I won't spend any more than I need to. Yourself, you get a third of the business for your money, or if you'd rather it be a loan, I figure I'll pay it all back plus interest in five years."

"Ah, I see. Well… I was thinking something more like I'll put up the money, and I'll hire you to go over and find your Innish Cove and build the Great Lodge of your dreams, but I own it."

"You own Innish Cove?" Brian laughed. "Then you weren't listenin'."

"Indeed, Brian, I always listen carefully when people are asking me for my money you see, and what I heard you saying is no one else is interested in investing in your dream. If I heard that wrong please correct me here." He barely paused a half beat. "You see, if this feckin' Depression makes for a good time to be buying and building on the cheap, it means there's little money available for fishing expeditions, so it'll take longer to get the business going strong, which means it will take more money than you are projecting."

"I am proposin' it as an investment."

"I'm willing to take on all the risk, you see, and I want you to run it for me. That sounds like a great deal at a time there's blessed few with steady employment, am I right there lads? An' after we see just how it's going, we'll sit down then and talk about you getting your fair share. Maybe a five percent interest in five years, maybe fifteen percent in ten, we'd have to discuss that further. I think that's fair."

Brian stared at the man, felt his cheeks beginning to burn red, and tried to force a laugh that came out hard.

"Aidan said you were a slice a' fun. Your man here is playin' with me, Aidan."

"Listen, Brian, who pays for the party tells the band the tune to play, 'specially when everyone else has declined your invitation. If this were to fail—"

"Don't you be sayin' so."

"It's possible, no offense meant to you, and then I'm out all me money, and when you say it will need no more than five thousand, I'm thinking it will likely need two or three thousand more, and that's a lot to put at risk. If it fails I lose it all, but you get two or three years of good wages and plenty of stories of wild Canadian adventure to tell your lads back in Cong."

Brian thrust his hands in his front pants' pockets and grabbed a fistful of the bottom of each to hold and hide his fists.

"But it won't be failin' an' it's my dreams an' plans makes that so. Your money don't mean a feckin' thing without me an' me plans."

"Your dreams are grand, they are truly magical, but a dozen versions of your plans are just as clever. And to do any one of them others, well, I could do this without you, Brian, but it appears you aren't able to do it without me. It's that plain, it's that simple. So let's not argue, let's make this the beginning of a great adventure together."

He held out his hand and Brian reached out to knock it aside, then returned his hand to his pocket, startling himself by the swiftness of his move and afraid of what was building behind it. He stared hard at the B&B owner as he growled, "Aidan, tell your man here to quit feckin' around or let him know who it is he's feckin' round with."

"I don' think he's kiddin' ya, Bri, but be careful now, he's already warned you what a dung-heap dwellin' creature he is. I don't argue he's not deservin' a thrashin', but he's got a room full of witnesses."

Maureen and Kevin had been sitting at the last edge of the crowd, but when she saw the big man's fury brewing at what seemed like betrayal she stood and stepped forward, afraid the big man was getting close to delivering that thrashing. She called out to the B&B owner.

"You should see it's time for you to leave now and not a one of us'll be sorry to see ya go."

"Yes, but then it's none of your business now is it, so let's have your fella there go back to telling you sweet things and leave this to those who know better."

The B&B owner turned back to Brian. "All I've done is offer you the first real chance to make this lodge happen and you're threatening me with—."

"I'd take the girl's advice an' get out of here now."

Maureen took another step forward.

"To see one of our own fail one of our own shames me, but it's your shame from now on that your friends here all saw you called out by a girl."

He tried to ignore her.

"My God, I'm offering a piece of the business when there's a piece worth having."

Maureen was surprised she was so determined to make this big man's case for him.

"You're offerin' to take his best an' make him earn some sliver of it back. You'd be stealin' his dream."

The B&B owner drained his glass as he shook his head, put the glass down hard, and called back over his shoulder as he departed. "It's ourselves that is keeping ourselves down now if we're listening to a girl's prattling and calling it wisdom."

Brian relaxed his fists, and took a deep breath. Maureen smiled up at him.

"It sounds like a grand dream, mister."

Maureen returned to her table.

❉ ❉ ❉

Later that evening, Brian and Aidan and two locals sat at a table hosted by Kevin and Maureen. First Kevin had asked Brian questions about his dreams and plans for his fishing camp while Maureen watched and listened, delighted by the vivid pictures this big man created as he told stories of the beauty of that foreign land. They both wished him well with it, then Kevin asked if Brian would share any opinions about the IRA bombings in London.

Brian nodded.

"My first thought was bombin' London could be the act of desperation as easily as an act of confidence. My next thought was what can possibly be gained by killin' an 83-year-old man."

Kevin's question came as Brian felt inspired by the drink that led to another drink and then the next, and he had been enjoying the excitement of Maureen's interest in his dreams about the Great Lodge at Innish Cove. But it was the pub regulars sitting on either side of Aidan who leaned forward to take over the table talk.

"Me granda is 83."

"Big Johnny Flannigan, yer da's da."

"I hain't heard anyone call 'im Big Johnny Flannigan in years. He's 83 next mont'. An' hain't quite so big anymore."

"But we got a soldier as well."

"No, they got a constable."

"You got a British uniform on an' you're the enemy, that's the only way to see it. The only way to see it."

Brian recollected his thoughts.

"What's been shapin' in my head, the strongest notion anyway, it seems less an opinion an' more… Maybe it's a confused confession."

"A confession?"

"Perhaps."

The table was quietly attentive and waited while Brian worked through some of the confusion with another sip of whiskey. He collected his first words while he stared at his glass.

"It's a safe bet you're in the presence of the most violent man any of you will ever meet."

The table was quiet.

"Aidan here will tell you 'tis so."

"Now Bri."

Brian looked from his glass to Aidan.

"You've seen the Red Bull Demon start the game and me jumpin' in to play it full on. Yeah, I know that's what you call me when I'm safely put away, the Red Bull Demon."

"Whatta you askin' of me here, Bri, because I don't—'"

"The truth an' nothin' else. Like the offer your man made this evenin'. You saw what I was turnin' to do. Didn't it make this lady girl interrupt her evenin' from across a room to prevent it from occurin'? I'm givin' ya the pass to admit your fear of what I become in the grip of my Red Bull rages. Go on, tell 'em what I've done."

Aidan was uneasy.

"Tell 'em."

"Let's put it this way. There's plenty of poor sods who wished someone had stepped in the way Miss Maureen did tonight. There's three pubs where they won't let Brian return to that I know of."

"An'…"

Aidan shook his head, still not comfortable with Brian's demand. "An' he spent more n' a few nights in lock up after particularly ferocious beatings… An' I've been sittin' in the pew behind 'im when he's been called out from front of the church twice I remember."

"You're avoidin' what it is I done. Tell 'em."

"Those pubs are where the beatings were so severe that… well, we know between 'em that four was sent to hospital. An' I seen him get so angry with a donkey he punched it so hard in its throat it was brought to its knees."

"He'd stepped on my foot."

"And I'll never forget about Tag."

"Poor ol' Tag."

"Brian was ragin' one day and his dog Tag just happened by, so he kicked Tag against a wall… We had to put the poor creature down the next day."

"The most recent be dogs and donkeys more than men, ya' see, because now men know to hide when they see the Red Bull a snortin'."

Aidan signaled he was finished by sitting back and drinking deeply. The table waited for Brian.

"I try to control it, I feel the Demon comin' on and takin' over, and I try to stop it... It's terrifyin' to me how hard it is, how quickly I can lose so much to it. I can't ignore the damage I do to others, an' I'm sorry for it all, past and future, I am." He drank, paused, and went on, "But that's not what matters here."

He tapped the newspaper.

"What matters here is this truth. You must understand each time the Demon's violence is released there's a terrible damage done to *me* as well an' I can see it just as plain as the damage I do to the victim... Each time, every time, my violence leaves me a bit darker. My anger goes deeper, each time. That's why I fight it so... What I'm sayin' is I hate the feckin Brits for what they done to my people an' would give my life to get back our Six Counties. But my bet is this. The more Brits I killed, the more I'd hate the Brits."

❋ ❋ ❋

Brian and Aidan found a cot for the night, and took the first bus the next morning back to Cong. Brian said good-bye to Aidan at the bus stop, walked the road to his cottage, then began to run when he saw people milling about in the yard and road outside his door. As he approached, Eamon came to meet him.

"Doc says she'll be fine, Cos, an' he thinks the baby is fine."

"What happened? Why wouldn't the baby be fine?"

"Deidre fainted, she must have fallen hard, she has bruises on her back and shoulders."

"When?"

"Soon after you left, as she was preparin' the meal. She's in bed. Doc said she should stay there 'til the baby's born, Bri. That means you got to be here to take care of her."

Brian nodded and entered the cottage on those words.

Chapter 6

HUNTERS FROM WIISHKOONSING

Later that year, Joe Loon and Albert sat at the fire. It was one of the first autumn nights so cold it smelled of the winter creeping slowly but steadily down from the North. Across the fire sat four white hunters from a place far away, a place they called Wiishkoonsing. This was the second year the hunters from Wiishkoonsing would spend nearly two weeks moose and bear hunting in these woods, guided by Joe Loon and Albert.

They arrived that afternoon, flown in by bush plane, a rust red Fairchild 71-C. A tent was erected for them at the edge of Joe Loon's village, and the plan was to head out early the next morning.

The hunters from Wiishkoonsing brought a brand new five horsepower Johnson outboard motor to give to Joe Loon. It lay on the ground next to him and Albert saw how pleased Joe Loon was to have this gift. The last time Joe Loon had bartered for a canoe, years ago, he had waited until he found one with a square-end stern that offered a motor mount. Before he had ever seen an outboard motor, he dreamed he had a canoe that traveled up the River by its own force, and when he saw a white man's boat with a motor he knew he would have one someday.

Joe Loon spoke to Albert in the language native to this place.

"We will hunt Big Birch Ridge in the morning's sun. You will hunt North Slope. We will hunt South Slope. Naomi saw many bear this summer feeding on the blueberries. If it is time to kill a bear, it would be good to kill one of them."

"The boys will leave then to set up the camp at Red Rock Wall. We will meet them there in two days."

At the same time the hunters from Wiishkoonsing spoke of the previous year's hunt.

"So Gary, how often do you lie awake at night thinking about that monster bull moose you missed last year?"

"'Bout the only time I think about it is when you're bringing it up, Ernie. Mostly I think about how Joe Loon likes to keep the old bulls around. I could swear after I missed the shot he said something sounded like thank you."

"Sure, nice try."

Albert had spent four years in a Jesuit-run residential school until the brothers grew tired of chasing after him each time he ran away. Some English had been beaten into him first, just enough to make it possible to guide these hunters.

"We sleep now. We leave with the first sun," Albert said to the hunters from Wiishkoonsing.

❄ ❄ ❄

The next morning, the forest's early winter chill not yet chased by the sun, Albert showed the hunters bear sign where a fallen tree trunk had been shredded so the bear could eat the beetle larvae burrowing throughout its soft decay. Ahead of them was a thick cluster of birch saplings, and Albert knew that behind those trees the bear was slowly making his way up the ridgeline as yet unaware of their presence. Albert was nearly certain it was a male.

He signaled quiet, crouched, and trotted noiselessly into the birches, then waved the hunters from Wiishkoonsign to follow. This Man was there, studying bear scat, obviously fresh.

❄ ❄ ❄

Simon and Mathew paddled the freight canoe north down a broad River channel as it gradually opened up to another of its chain of lakes. For such a long trip the hunters from Wiishkoonsign wanted to camp with comfort so the cots and sleeping bags and blankets and tents loaded their canoe.

Simon turned back to look at Mathew paddling at the stern. "When we arrive at the campsite that will be the farthest North I have been on the River."

"It is the same River."

"It is the same River, but it is changing."

"I like the stories about the giant moose that live where we will make the hunters camp. Grandfather says the antlers are the biggest in that place because the earth there has special powers."

"This place is where the white man dug in the mountainside for gold when Grandfather was a boy."

"We are looking for a clearing on top of a north point. Three stones are stacked and Old George says we will laugh when we see them. There is a large clearing for a camp. We will find it just before the sun sets."

❋ ❋ ❋

Albert Loon stopped and studied the forest ahead. The large boulders turned this ridge into a slope of small, shallow caves and hidden places. Just past another rocky point he saw the head of a black bear, bobbing in and out of view, nearly fifty yards away. Albert retreated behind some trees to his right for an unobstructed view of the big bear eating nuts at the edge of a small grove of hickory trees.

The bear's size was convincing: it was a male.

Albert waved one of the hunters from Wiishkoonsing forward, the same hunter who missed the big bull moose, and if it had seemed Joe Loon was shaking his head no as he approached to shoot the moose last year, Albert seemed to be nodding yes today. The hunter studied the bear for a moment, requested and received Albert's permission to proceed, said a prayer that his aim was true, levered a bullet into the chamber of his 30-30 Winchester as he raised it to his shoulder, released a deep breath and sighted for the lung shot, the biggest target for a one-shot kill. The left lung was most available and he aimed and gently squeezed the trigger. The gun barked, the bear jerked, and then began running down the ridge towards them, at great speed at first, apparently unhurt, but then stumbling at twenty yards before he collapsed, and tumbled once, and didn't get up.

They approached cautiously with Albert leading the way.

Albert crouched over the bear, removed a small buckskin bag from around his neck, and placed it on the bear's chest. He began to softly sing to the bear's spirit as he stroked the bear's head.

This Man stood over them.

Two hunters from Wiishkoonsing watched, appreciating the peace.

"My brother..." Albert put a pinch of the bag's contents on the bear's brow, his chest, and tossed a bit to the spirits in the wind. "Please forgive me, my brother. You have given your life so my people will eat. These hunters from Wiishkoonsing will tell many stories about your spirit. My brother, I will be happy when I see you have returned to these forests. I will rejoice to see you young again."

❄ ❄ ❄

The boys raised the tents and set up the cots, they collected firewood for three nights, and should have then prepared their meal. Instead, in the last light they scrambled up the face of the rock bluff above the clearing, a bluff that didn't just beg to be climbed but to be raced to the top. When the boys reached the top they found ruins of a small mining camp.

Simon asked, "This is where the white man took gold from the earth?"

"There was gold in some of these holes. In some holes there was nothing."

One shack had fallen in on top of itself and another was absorbed by young forest growth. Behind them, solid timbers framed a mineshaft opening into the side of the mountain face. The boys peered inside, took tentative steps, and found two small wooden barrels stacked just inside the shaft. Simon tapped one and then rolled it out of the cave when he found it contained a liquid.

"What would this be?"

"There is no smell of the gasoline."

Mathew removed the plug and smelled it.

"Yaway, Little Brother. Smell this."

"I know this smell. This is the whiskey."

"This is filled with the whiskey. We must hide this until Grandfather can destroy it. This would make too much trouble for the men who like the whiskey."

"Let us take it down to the River and pour it out. Grandfather would be proud of that."

"And then we will keep these barrels. The white man makes good barrels."

❀ ❀ ❀

Simon and Mathew sat in front of the fire at the outpost camp.

"Big Brother."

"I am listening."

"In some holes there was nothing?"

"Yes."

"Before we discovered the whiskey, you said in some holes there was nothing."

"Yes."

"Holes are empty. In all holes there is nothing."

Mathew and Simon looked at each other, their eyes smiling, then they both laughed.

"Ah, that is right. In all holes there is nothing… But if I fall into a hole, it is still a hole. And in that hole there is something." And they laughed again. "We should have saved more of the whiskey, Little Brother. It fills up the holes."

"That is why my idea was a good one. First we pour it out. Then we keep a small amount to drink to know what the whiskey is."

"I would like to drink more whiskey and fill up all the holes with the stories my Little Brother tells me by this fire."

Chapter 7
A DUBLIN SPRING, 1940

MAUREEN AND KEVIN FOUND the small apartment on Pearse Street where they were to meet with senior IRA leaders. Kevin introduced Maureen to two men, and as everyone settled the older of the two asked Kevin how much Maureen had been told about this mission.

"What you told me to tell her and nothing more. That it's secret, a deep secret, that Russell himself is behind it, and that by meeting with you she has committed herself to say yes to whatever is proposed."

The older man got up from his chair and sat next to Maureen on the couch. "It's the last moment you can retreat, young lady. But once you've heard our plan, understand you have to take on the role we have for you."

"I understand."

"Understand that how Russell's putting it is we are looking at a mission could change Irish history an'—"

Kevin interrupted as he spoke to Maureen.

"When I think about it, and how it could change history across the Continent, around the world, I want you to know it's not just another bombing raid."

It appeared that only the older leader would talk as the man sitting across the room lit a cigarette and sat back staring at the smoke. "Kevin has some concerns. But the die is cast. We are going forward with this mission."

He took Maureen's hand. "Your countrymen offer condolences

for what the Brits have done to you an' your family. Your da was a true Fenian an' a fine man, an' we won't stop until we can identify which Black 'n Tan it was who murdered him. He'd be proud of your work in London."

Maureen was clear. "I'll never forget the face of the man with the gun. When you find him, I ask you to allow me to confirm it and to complete the execution."

"If operational circumstances allow it, it will be handed to you to be done."

"Da never leaves my thoughts as I do my duty, thank you. An' in return I am ready to do whatever you ask of me. I pledge my oath here and now."

"An' when a duty kills someone's grandfather?"

"I regret that occurred an' I've prayed for forgiveness every night since." She stood from the couch and found the place in the room where she could speak to all the men. "But I am a soldier fightin' in a just war. The Church says that even in a just war innocent civilians get killed."

"You're ready to provide us another service."

"I've said yes, an' I'm here to find what it is I've said yes to."

"Russell arrived in Germany three weeks ago. His plan was to meet men in Berlin—military leaders and their biggest industrialists, to convince them that Ireland can be of great service to Germany right now."

Maureen looked at Kevin when she spoke.

"But we are to be neutral. I heard de Valera declare that again on the wireless just last week."

"And Russell has decided otherwise an' so he's workin' the German military for a coordinated attack in the Six Counties. At the same time, he's workin' their industrialists for money so we can buy guns and ordinance, so we can step up with a new series of skirmishes an' keep the Brits busy on every front."

"You keep sayin' Germany, but what the people in the cottages will be hearin' you say is that IRA has thrown in on the side of the Nazis."

"A nasty bunch, there's no doubt, and none of us is happy about it, but it's what the Brits have driven us to. The play we're after is that the Brits will be smart enough to realize they'll be needing all resources to defeat the Germans so they can't be fightin' us at the same time. We'll finally have the top hand an' the bargainin' power on our side of the table, and all the Brits have to do is leave our island and we'll leave them alone."

"But we've thousands of our boys enlistin' in British regiments and already fightin' the Nazis."

Kevin answered, "Irish lads have always fought for British pay. That's never affected IRA policy before."

The older man decided Maureen was ready.

"Maureen, hear this clearly. Because your concerns are legitimate, it is and will remain just the four of us in this room and Russell who knows about this, and that's how we intend to keep it. But we have to move now if this is going to happen at all. We have a berth on a freighter to Copenhagen tomorrow. Russell will have someone meetin' you there, quay side. Your contact will be looking for this yellow scarf an' when you're asked if you're from Connemara, you'll answer 'Yes, it's the Wild West'. He'll take you on to Berlin to meet with Russell. If Russell has raised any money, well, his problem is they'll be looking for him at customs."

Kevin added, "But they won't be looking for you."

"He'll have a plan for you to bring the money home along with any word about attack plans."

"What time do I board?"

❄ ❄ ❄

Two months had passed after baby Patrick's hard birth and Deirdre was too weak to get out of bed. If on some days she was better than others, most days she wasn't. Tommy, ten now, had come home from seminary school to see his brother born and when the Brothers learned the news of the hard labor and poor condition of the mother they allowed Tommy to remain at home to assist with her care. Tommy read to Deirdre from *The Lives of the Saints* and any tabloid Brian brought home, and he helped care for five year-old Katie. Patrick lived in his mother's arms, or wrapped tightly at her side.

Women from the village looked in on the family once or twice a day to check on them and, Brian knew, to make sure he was caring for his poor invalid wife. At first they approved when they found him home and attentive since Deirdre's faint, for he was working as a ghillie or taking other odd jobs to maintain their larder then dashing home without even a pint on the way. But then one woman wondered and soon others grew worried about the deepening depth to his despair as he stood at the door to their bedroom and watched his wife grow weaker and weaker, fading midst her children.

As was becoming their habit, Eamon and his wife stopped by with a stew pot. She went inside and left the two cousins outside Brian's cottage.

"Ah, Eamon, she's gettin' worse an' worse every day, an' ol' Doc's no help as far as I can see."

"Them children are tirin' her out, Cos."

"Sure they are. Or maybe not, I ain't seein' much clearly these days. But it makes no difference for you can't get 'em away from her. I tried."

"They're all livin' right on top of her, all in that bed all day."

"An' she won't have it any other way is what I'm sayin', goddamn it. She knows she's leavin' us an' it's how she wants to go, yeah, so you don't do me any good goin' on about it... She tells me every night about what it's like to be slowly dyin' an' she wants 'em all she can. When they aren't 'round to hear she's taken to callin' it her last wish."

"Well, I told you when you weren't, so I should tell you when you are—you're doin' all you can now, Cos, an more than most would."

"Don't know if you can ever catch-up when you start out so late in the game."

They were quietly loading their pipes with some last bit of tobacco Brian had when Eamon's wife joined them.

"She's askin' for you, Brian."

Brian nodded his thanks for their help and entered the cottage to attend to Deirdre.

Eamon's wife placed her hand on her husband's arm.

"Go fetch Doc. An' I'm thinkin' Father should be alerted."

❄ ❄ ❄

Brian knelt down next to the bed at Deidre's shoulder and

stroked her hair. Tommy stood next to him, Katie sat on the bed next to her mother, and baby Patrick was in Deidre's arms.

She was pale, worn. Her face was damp. She smiled, her lips cracked.

"Tommy, take Katie into the other room for me and stay there until I call ya back."

Katie hopped off the bed and Tommy led her out of the room, and as soon as the door closed Brian spoke.

"This is my doin'."

"This isn't your doin'."

"I saw how hard you hit the floor the night I threw you down."

"You didn't throw me down. You were defendin' yourself from me slappin' at ya and I tripped and fell, and in any case we don't know that has any play in any of this... I was sickly weak after I lost the last."

"An' you got better, an' you'll get better now, an' I'll be makin' up for my mistakes every day, for you, from now on, every day, for you."

Deidre patted Patrick's head as he began to fuss.

"And if I don't get better—"

"You will."

"And if I don't, you'll promise to take care of these..." She began to cry, and Brian sat next to her and held her close.

❀ ❀ ❀

When Brian heard the doctor's bleak diagnosis he didn't leave the cottage for a week. But they were desperately short of money, the village had no surplus to share, and there were few jobs to be had, so he regretfully accepted a guiding job when Eamon told him of one.

He was out on the River showing his fisherman a best hole for browns the afternoon Deirdre died.

Eamon was looking in on his cousin's family and found Tommy lying asleep at the foot of the bed, Katie sleeping next to her mother's body, and Patrick asleep in his dead mother's arms. He sent a boy to find Brian, but more than two hours passed before Brian was alerted, and by then the whole village knew. As Brian trotted down the road to his cottage he felt condemned in their looks. The next night, at the wake, it occurred to him as if he had just arrived to find his cottage filled with the judgment of mourners.

He and his cousin stood outside. It was a soft rain that fell.

"You can't tell me they're not all thinkin' it, whisperin' it. I can see it in their shiftin' eyes as I draw near."

"No, Cos, you're seein' sadness for her an' for you an' the little ones. It's sadness for your loss. Everyone saw how well you tended to her at the end."

"Yes, that's right, you've said it again. You can't help but say as such, it's true, so you say it the same way, every time."

"What's that?"

"That I tended to her at the end, yeah. That I tended to her *death*. That's what you're sayin'. But before that—what was it you were always tellin' me? That I was drivin' her to an early grave. How many times did you say *that* to me, Cos? Those exact words. An' that's what I see in everyone's eyes. That it's my fault."

"It won't do anyone good for you to be thinkin' like you are, so."

"So then that's the pity, isn't it?"

"Deirdre dyin' is a pity."

"Deirdre dyin' was a pity."

"A deep sadness for us all."

"And the pity that remains is how none can look at me an' not think about the role I played in drivin' her to an early grave. An' that you predicted it, that you talked about it, together. There's the lastin' pity of it." Brian's tears mixed with the rain on his face as he demanded, "Didn't it come true as you said it would… that I would drive her to an early grave?"

"Was as much her weakness from childbirth."

"An' so I am now understandin' this, that it's with your pity that I will live amongst you from now on. That is as it should be, my crime is deservin'."

"Even if it is pity you're seein', it's up to you to turn it into somethin' else."

"You want me to turn a village's pity into somethin' else."

"Into somethin' better."

❋ ❋ ❋

A few days later, Maureen sat alone in a lobby of dark paneling and large portraits of serious men with great mustaches or mutton-chop sideburns, some in military uniforms, others in suits, all of their wardrobes mostly grey or black. One of the large double doors opened and a man appeared, bowed precisely, then beckoned her to follow.

In the board room over a dozen men stood in small clusters of conversation, some in Nazi uniforms, some in business suits. Maureen had never met Russell but had seen a photo of him; when the closest group turned at her approach she did not find him there. She looked past to the others as an elderly man took her hand.

"If all da Irish veman are as brave and as lovely as you, my young Fraulein, I understand vy da British ver never eager to depart."

She pulled her hand back. "They hain't left yet, sir."

"Quite so, quite so. And perhaps ve can help."

"Perhaps."

As the men settled in their chairs at the great table, Maureen determined Russell was not among them.

"Excuse me, gentlemen, but I must not be in the proper place. I don't see my man."

"No, this is vere you should be. He's been delayed a brief moment."

"I'll just wait outside 'til he calls me in."

One of the officers spoke in German to the others. "I said let's not engage in such foolishness." Then he spoke in English. "Captain, go tell Mr. Russell to join us. It is clear we have a voman we can all trust amongst us."

❄ ❄ ❄

Maureen sat in a corner of the boardroom alone with Sean Russell away from the big table where two angry German voices were taking turns making their case. Maureen focused on Russell's plans for her to smuggle the black valise that sat on his lap into Ireland. Behind his round glasses his face was drawn. She thought he was very tired, or sick, or both.

"It's two things I'm good at, sir. When I don't want someone to find somethin', I can put it right under their noses an' still they'll miss it."

"To keep British soldiers from examining your trunks, you ask them to load a bus with the makings." He started to chuckle, but it turned to a dry cough.

When he stopped Maureen replied, "If you were there, you'd have seen it was the smartest play."

"And the other thing?"

"I am loyal to the end. You can trust me, in every way. On me da's honor, you can trust me, to keep any secret, an' if you don't want me to know what's in this bag, on my oath, I won't look."

"No, it seems if you are the one risking bringing it home, you have a right to know what's in it."

He fished a key out of his pocket, handed it to her, and she unlocked the latch. It held stacks of British pounds, and Maureen smiled up at Russell, but he was not happy.

"They're still refusing the joint attack in the North… and while there's enough here to purchase some arms, it's not as much as I hoped. Some keep promising more while others keep standin' in the way, an' it's a political argument I don't follow. The one thing they all agree on is how difficult it is to acquire British pounds right now, so they have that as a built-in excuse for so little… But it's a start."

He closed the valise and took the key from Maureen to lock it.

She held the valise by its handle and placed it on the floor beside her. She didn't let go of the handle. "How much longer will you stay?"

"Seems those negotiations have been less than satisfactory as well. I've suggested they get me to the west coast in one of their U-boats where I can flag down a fishing boat. I believe I need some time at home. I am a bit worn. As soon as I'm feeling better, I'll push harder to leave."

"I understand your plan to get the bag into Ireland, but then who do I give it to?"

Russell removed a pack of cigarettes and a lighter from his pocket, and offered a smoke to Maureen. She declined.

"You get the money safely in Ireland. Then you keep it, hide it, make sure it is safe. When I am ready to retrieve it, I'll send someone around… They'll have this."

He placed his lighter in her hands.

"Note the scratch on the base. Look at it closely. When someone places my lighter in your hands again, you will give him the bag. Until then, I want you to tell everyone we never even met. Tell them you never found me, understand? Even Kevin. The only people who know about this money are in this room. Ryan isn't even aware of it."

"Ryan?"

"He's in Berlin as well, working his own angles."

"So we'd go public that Nazis are providing support if it meant a joint attack in the North. But if all they'll do is give us money, well, that connection can be kept secret, so it should be kept secret."

Russell's smile was brief and was colored by his sadness.

"Kevin said you were bright. You'll be the first woman leading a brigade someday was his prediction."

"It's Ireland I serve, an' them that serves the cause. I'll do as you say."

Chapter 8

FOG AND SMOKE

THIS MAN EMERGED from a thick fog bank riding upon the moose's back. The moose wasted no energy trying to shake him and continued its course, swimming powerfully from fog cloud to open water.

The lakeshore had been hidden in fog all day, but now the outline was seen as a hazy silhouette. When the moose swam through the next wisps and rolls of fog, a tree-lined ridge appeared above the clouds and well back from the shore. A glowing light diffused by low, thick clouds marked the shoreline. These clouds were fog and smoke, waves of white and black smoke rolling out from shore to mix with the silver-white fog from the River's lake, and the moose's nostrils flared open wide, and it snorted once and tacked left, away from shore, away from the smells of the smoke.

The wind picked up. The fog on the lake was pushed from behind and the smoke on the shore was swept into the trees. This Man could see the shore clearly. There were four funeral pyres, each large enough for many bodies, and there were many mourners, full villages of mourners, all along the shore.

The moose paralleled the shore, swimming in open water now, and This Man rode on its back, singing The Path of Souls song, the same song the mourners chanted.

And the sound that they made and the spirits that they called upon floated above them in the smoke of their fires.

Chapter 9
TIME TO HIDE

MAUREEN RETURNED WITH THE MONEY secretly, without incident, following the plan she proposed to Russell and one he immediately endorsed. It meant she was to avoid Dublin to report in until she traveled to Derry to hide the valise behind the cottage where she lived with her mother.

She gave Russell a sketch of her yard and marked where she would bury it so he could find it if anything happened to her.

After she buried the valise, she took the bus to Dublin to lie to Kevin and the others as Russell had instructed. Later, alone with Kevin, when he asked again about the trip, she repeated the lie that she hadn't found Russell. Only then did he believe her. They agreed to meet two weeks later at a regular rendezvous point, and so she wandered a market morning in a small village near Letterkenny, expecting to find Kevin waiting there, but he wasn't.

She sat in a tea shop then strolled the market again, and just as the vendors began to break shop and she was giving up she spotted Kevin; their arcs intersected near the last of the potato bins. He nodded for her to follow him down the street, away from the thinning crowds. She felt he had bad news.

"Russell's dead."

"What?"

"We'd been hearing rumors for two days. Timmy came by last night to confirm."

"I've heard said when you find Timmy standing at your door

he's come to name the dead, the recent or the next. How'd they get him?"

"It wasn't the Brits, no. It appears he died on his way back from Germany in the Nazis U-boat that was bringing him home. Seems they buried him at sea."

"Was Nazis killed him?"

"First word is, it doesn't look like foul play."

"Buried at sea means no one has seen his body. Why are we sure it's not a rumor?"

"We got word from Ryan. He's in Germany. He had it confirmed by their military."

"So then no one knows... what's our next step. So what's our next step?"

Kevin studied Maureen as he answered, "Timmy says lay low for a wait-see. The story about Russell is spreading fast. Folks are furious as they're figuring Russell coming home in a Nazi U-boat can only mean the IRA and the Nazis are collaborating. And if we're collaborating then we're supporting them that's shooting at their sons."

"I haven't heard anythin' about it here."

"Folks were spitting with anger talking about it on the bus coming in. I heard some say they'd end their support of the Cause if it's true."

"It's why you warned the leaders."

"Looks like it might be even worse than I imagined."

"So it's time to teach me a new lesson. I'm not sure what you mean, 'lay low for a wait-see.'"

"It means Timmy himself is heading to Boston for now, to talk to the boys there and keep them in line, and Johnny Boy, he's going to Chicago. And if Timmy sounds like a man staying gone for a while, Johnny Boy sounds like a man not planning on returning at all. Seems they're all looking for similar cover." Kevin stepped away from Maureen, then turned to study her. "You know, Lady Girl, I don't think I've ever seen you do such as that."

"Do what?"

"Take a misstep and lose your balance."

"My balance?"

"You were headed in one direction and slipped when you changed it."

"I don't know what you're sayin' here Kev."

"Just now, when you said, 'So then no one knows.' You were going to say something more. Your voice was going one way, but then your words took you another."

"What does that even mean? So no one knows if there were plans for an attack in the North was the question was comin' to me, but I realized as I was askin' that there was a better question to ask, so I did."

"Well, what Timmy says is the only reason he could think of why I should contact him again before he leaves is if I learned anything more about those plans, or about any money, from yourself."

"What I've told you is all the truth to tell, Kevin."

"And I know I've never seen you hold in what you've got on your mind to say until just now. So listen clear, Lady Girl. I'm saying some are thinking a young woman as clever as yourself wouldn't have failed at the mission in Germany. And that you know more than what you've been saying. I'm telling them the daughter of Donovan O'Toole can be trusted to the very end of the line. But if they're right, if there is truth you haven't told, this would be a good time to say so, yeah."

Maureen believed she could trust Kevin with the full story, and that he would take responsibility for the money from her. But she never considered it, for she had sworn an oath to Russell. And they hadn't seen his body.

"I never found him. Your man in Copenhagen had a train ticket and a promise a man would approach me when I got off the train in Berlin, but nobody contacted me at the station. I waited there, wearin' your yellow scarf, it feelin' more an' more like a noose around my neck, if you need to know. So, when three days go by an' no one has yet approached me, an' just enough travel money to get home is what I had left, this clever young woman was clever enough to know it was time I came back, that I do you no good wanderin' penniless around Germany."

"Then it's the best outcome of all. If we're laying low just on rumors we tried something, perhaps a successful operation with the

Nazis would have been the death of the Cause."

"With so much left to be done."

"With so much left to be done."

"There's been rumors before. Are you certain Russell's dead?"

"Timmy says Ryan's convinced."

"There's no reason I can think of to rush to certainty. About whether he is dead, and about whether the Nazis are innocent."

"You're right. But that doesn't change the fact that ceasing all operations and keeping low for now seems right in any case. Whether the Brits win this fight or lose it, they'll be so weak when it's over we'll have our best chance ever of getting them out full stop."

"Does leadership hold it against you that you were against Russell's plans?"

"That's got no consequence when we're in danger of losing the people. In the end that's all we've got, and so it makes for a confusing time. Timmy says O'Hearn is so upset no one told him about Russell's mission that he's making threats about leaving and taking others with him to start their own organization. He says he wants to purify the organization."

"I can't say I blame him—he was senior to you and Timmy, but he didn't know."

"Russell wanted to keep him out of this. He knew he'd try to stop it. So maybe the only way to keep us from getting ripped apart is to just fade away for a while."

"I'm not sure I know what that means, or how I do that. You haven't taught me that."

"Never thought I'd need to. Let's meet in Castlebar on Friday, at the market, and see if the people in the countryside are as upset as the folks in the city. If I'm not there you need to cut and run, for so have we all."

❀ ❀ ❀

Maureen sat on the beach as the sun set on the Atlantic. Waves were breaking and a cold wind cut. She tended a fire at the base of a great rock, and she cast a large shadow behind her on the face of the stone. Two days before she had waited for Kevin in Castlebar all day. The last bus came and left without a sign or a message from him.

She came to this spot the night after Kevin told her Russell was dead. She slipped away from her cottage at two in the morning in case she was being followed, and traveled here to hide the money safely away from her cottage. She wasn't sure she wasn't suspected of something that might lead to her cottage being searched.

When it was full dark and the beach had long been abandoned, she slipped between two cottage-sized boulders set well back from the high tide's reach. Behind them, hidden from view, she dug up the valise.

❄ ❄ ❄

As the driver tied her bike to the front of his bus, Maureen climbed in, carrying the valise in a rucksack. Traveling by bicycle from village to village was the safest way to travel, she decided, for only another bicyclist could follow her. She settled into her seat in a middle row on the last bus to Westport on her way to Leenane.

❄ ❄ ❄

It was early the next morning when she left the stillness of a small bed and breakfast and cycled along the narrow, stone-walled roads to the Maumturk Mountains. A car passed from behind, then another, and she grew anxious each time one approached and relaxed as they passed.

❄ ❄ ❄

Maureen climbed a ridgeline among the peaks and severe cliffs. The rugged mountain plains between the peaks held large pools of rainwater stained bog-brown. Wind whipped around her and half-wild sheep scattered when she approached. She continually scanned above and below for witnesses but found none.

Two thousand feet above the sea, at the base of the highest peak around, Maureen had a full view of the coast line, the Connemara bogs between the mountains and the water, and the distant mountains of County Mayo to the northwest.

She opened her rucksack and pulled the valise from it. With a fist-sized rock she struck at the lock, and after repeated blows it broke open. It was her first view of the money since Russell had showed it to her. It looked to be more than she remembered.

She counted the first stack of twenty-pound notes and placed it on the ground, securing the notes in the strong wind with a flat stone. She counted two more stacks. When she'd counted £3,000, with more pound notes in the valise, she stopped.

She returned the money to the valise, the last bit uncounted, and stood to study her mountaintop. Thin clouds scooted past just above her, the sky was a brilliant blue, and the highest peak glistened from a large vein of white quartz. In the rocky point above her a second large quartz deposit glowed. Maureen discovered she could align both quartz outcroppings with the tip of the highest mountain peak behind them, all three in a line.

On this bearing she found a large boulder, cracked at its base and open at the ground where she could reach deep under the big rock. She carved up a sod of alpine grass and placed it aside, then dug a hole. She pushed the valise down in as far as it would go.

Then she retrieved it, opened it, and removed five twenty-pound notes. She stuffed them into her pocket, then pulled two out of her pocket and put them back into the valise.

Maureen returned the valise to the hole and covered it in a foot of earth and rock. She patted the sod in place, removed a sandwich from her rucksack, and leaned against the rock to eat. Looking up she saw the rainbow gradually advancing before lowering clouds, vanishing, then reappearing, vivid and bold. It stretched across the bogs below and slowly faded away.

She spent the rest of the afternoon exploring her mountaintop, leaving secret markers to be certain she could find this spot, for she didn't intend on returning for quite some time.

Chapter 10

WILD RICE

WHEN FADING SUMMER DAYS and cool autumn nights dance together, it is the Moon of Manoominike-Giizis. This is the time the Ojibway harvest manoomin, the wild grain they eat as soup and cereal, that they use to thicken stews of venison or moose or bear, that they stir with the sweetness of the sugar bush and blueberries to make a confection, and that they trade to the factor at the Hudson Bay Post who calls it wild rice.

Albert Loon stood in Nigig's bow and poled the canoe along the shallow bay. His wife, Susanna, sat behind him. Their six-year-old daughter knelt at her mother's feet, watching her use the two knocking sticks; with one Susanna would bend a stalk so the grain heads hung over the floor of the canoe, and with the other she gave the stalk a tap. Some grains dimpled the water's surface, but the little girl watched most cascade around her as a pile of manoomin kernels grew between them.

Susanna's pace was Albert's to match as he poled to glide a quiet path between the plants.

This Man sat in his canoe, hidden in the thickest growth, and sang a song of honor to the Great Creator.

"We receive the gifts of Gitche Manitou. Because they are your gifts, we take only what we need. Because they are your gifts, we leave more than we will take. Everywhere we look we see the gifts of the Great Creator. This is a song your children the Annishinabe are happy to sing all the days of our lives."

Chapter 11

THE FAMILY PRIEST

TOMMY STAYED HOME with his family after his mother's funeral. One morning a month after the funeral, Uncle Eamon waited for him outside the village church where Tommy attended morning mass.

Eamon took Tommy by his shoulders and held him in front of him. "Tommy, it's time you returned to the Brothers."

"I'd like to go back."

Eamon patted his shoulders as he released him.

"Then we've settled that in a quick. I'll get you on the bus in the mornin'."

"But Da needs me here."

"If we ever figure out what your da needs, I'll be here to get it for him. You need to go to school."

They walked the road out of the village to the cluster of cottages where both families lived.

"You have a notion what Da needs?"

"You're the one the Brothers are trainin' for this sort of thing. What do you think he needs?"

"The Brothers would say it must start with an understandin' that whatever it is he thinks he did wrong, the Lord forgives him."

"That's what the Brothers teach, and they're right to do so. But I'm thinkin' it's his own forgiveness that's needed here. And it's never been clear to me which comes first. That's why you're on the bus in the mornin'. We'll be needin' a priest in this family. I'll tell your da it's time for you to go."

✳ ✳ ✳

A week after Tommy returned to seminary, Katie and baby Patrick were both sleeping in Brian's bed, as they often did when Tommy was at seminary, and Brian sat close to the fireplace for the last warmth of the peat turf. Outside a cold rain fell, and inside there was a damp chill. Brian had wrapped his neck with the wool scarf Deirdre had knitted him when they were courting.

Brian clutched a crumbled collection of papers in his left hand. His other held a small round bottle of the local poitin. He took a sip against the chill and placed the bottle on the floor at his feet, then picked up the last paper that was laying there. He read it, as he had read the others. Then he crumbled it into his left hand with the others and picked up the bottle for another drink.

Brian mumbled a few words as he put down the bottle, and laughed bitterly, then mocked a genuflect as he leaned forward to feed the papers into the fire, one at time, each one adding a brief, bright flame, until all the papers that had held his notes and ideas and plans for the Great Lodge at Innish Cove were nothing but ashes.

Brian took one last drink, returned the bottle to the cupboard, and found his way through the dark to his bedroom. He felt for the children to move them aside, too late realizing his weight was coming down on Katie's leg.

"Ouch, Da. That hurt."

"Sorry, Katie, just tryin' to move you over here a bit."

"But Patrick made it wet over there."

"What?"

"He wet through his nappy again."

Brian roared "Feckin' hell!" and kicked the bed in anger and then felt Katie recoil in fear. He immediately stepped away from the bed, his heart pounding, his head pounding; he retreated to the door and stood there, trembling, afraid himself at such quick fierceness in him, from him. From the dark Katie spoke, a soft whisper Brian could barely hear.

"I moved him to a dry spot. I'll clean the bed clothes in the mornin'."

Brian took a deep breath, then another, and he clenched and unclenched his fists.

"I moved him out of his pee."

"Ah, thanks, sweetheart. I am sorry if I scared you just now."

"I'm sorry Patrick peed your bed."

Brian was breathing more easily now.

"Has he cried?"

"Not a sound."

"Nothin'?"

"None."

"You go back to sleep. I'm out here... takin' care of you."

"Thanks, Da."

"Good-night, Katie."

Brian returned to the hearth, and fanned and fueled the dying coal to a heat-generating glow. He straightened up and retrieved the bottle from the cupboard, realized there really wasn't much left, and decided to finish it all.

Chapter 12

CRIES

IT WAS TROUT SEASON, the spring of 1942, nearly two years since Deirdre's funeral. Brian stood on shore as the British gentleman cast the river. Brian's eyes were moist and framed in fire-hot redness.

"Excuse me just a moment Mr. Evan."

The fisherman shook his head.

"It's Devon, not Evan. Mr. Devon."

"Mr. Devon, yes, that's right. But I've got to relieve meself an' that grove up there will serve me fine." After a few steps Brian turned, "But let me make sure I'm clear. It's that fold of current along the far bank, that's what you need to be workin' along this stretch of the River."

"I understood you the first time, I understood you the second time."

"Because it's the hole between them two big rocks what's makin' the water roil, an' that's where the big brownie is a sittin'. Not five yards to the right nor five yards to the left, but just in that bit of current right along that bank there."

"Thank you, I appreciate the completeness of your directions."

"I take pride in doin' a job right."

Brian entered a small oak grove in the field above the River, emptied his bladder behind a tree, walked back around to the front of the tree, and removed a bottle of poitin from a pocket inside his coat. He took a good drink, leaned back against the heavy trunk, licked his lips to enjoy the entire sweet aftertaste unique to each batch, then closed his eyes. He smiled, first his mouth, then his whole face. As he slowly shook his head back and forth, the smile went away.

His eyes still closed, he raised the bottle to his lips for a second portion as Mr. Devon entered the grove looking for him.

"You must think me an idiot."

Brian made it a deep drink, then opened his eyes and showed a harder smile.

"I will if you try to say it's me been keepin' you from catchin' trout."

"Look, at the proper time I can understand a little drink. But this is inexcusable."

Brian took a quick sip to show he could, then wiped his lips.

"It's so very important to me that you understand."

"If you think this is accomplishing something, I don't know what it would be."

"I've been trying to accomplish you catchin' one of them brownies swimmin' around in the River. I'm bringin' you to their doorstep all day."

"But this seems a deliberate effort on your part to be rude to me. What have I done to you to deserve such treatment?"

"We can't have you bein' the only Brit I've taken out who doesn't catch a fish. Say, how 'bout I hook one for you an' you just reel 'em in, an' we can tell ever after wonderful tales of your heroic battle."

"I am sorry for you and whatever your troubles may be, but I'm being irresponsible if I don't tell the full story of your gross impertinence to the steward."

"Ah, Jimmy himself, he knows the full story. It begins Brian Burke is the best damn ghillie in three counties an' he knows the story always has the same happy endin', with a couple of nice brownies floppin' on the bank of the River and the proud Brit starin' down at his good fortune."

"I can't imagine any self-respecting British gentleman would allow your drunken disrespect, or is it mockery?"

"Fact is, they're usually too busy catchin' trout for me to have a chance to slip away. It's the likes of yourself makin' the bottle needed who also make it available for relief."

"The likes of me? Where's the fault in my behavior?"

"You got yourself the finest piece of split bamboo in your hands. I took one look at your flies an' wanted to feast on 'em. But your holdin' it back when it wants to fly, an' you're forcin' it when you hain't collected the energy first. You're yards short on half your casts, an' when you do reach the pools your presentation is scarin' the fish. But the fact you can't catch any fish is my fault now, because you Brits enjoy feelin' insulted when an Irishman drinks in your presence without beggin' your bye or leave."

"I imagine you're just carrying on so because we both understand what happens next."

"You tell me what happens next."

"What happens next is that you're through. I will make sure of that."

Brian made a dash at Mr. Devon, a man trained and drilled in hand-to-hand combat as a British officer, and Captain Devon was stone-cold sober, so it was easy to sidestep the mad rush of the Red Bull Demon and then flip Brian over his hip and into the base of a tree where Brian heard something pop but was so stunned he didn't understand it was his own shoulder. He jumped to his feet but then the pain came hard, and both his brain and his gut were so completely defeated by it he had to lean against the tree, then slowly drop back down to his knees.

Mr. Devon stood back.

"I didn't mean to hurt you. I am sorry. I had no time to choose your landing site."

"Get the feck outta here, or I'll be comin' at ya again."

Mr. Devon turned to leave. He looked back once as he walked along the bank of the River and saw Brian sitting against the tree, holding his left arm tightly to his side, trying to relieve the sharpness of the pain in his left shoulder, replacing it with a steady, throbbing ache.

Brian sat there for some time, watching clouds go by, listening to the wind in the oaks, feeling his heart pumping in his ears, feeling foolish. Feeling defeated. When he stood to get to his feet, though he never let go of his arm, the worst pain returned and it took long moments of hot, sharp jaw-clenching burn before he found a new way to hold his arm for some relief. He slowly walked through the trees down to the River, following the path Mr. Devon had taken to the fishing lodge, practicing the story he would tell Jimmy, flinching again as his shoulder spasmed.

❊ ❊ ❊

Brian and Jimmy were talking in the gamekeeper's cottage. Jimmy was a humble old man. Brian still held his left arm close to his body with his right hand, and he tried to ignore the deep ache and frequent flashes of pain.

"So why pretend indignation of a sudden, Jimmy? We have our understandin', so long as your guests are catchin' trout an' I'm keepin' it under control."

"My understandin' was some guests actually enjoyed a big wild Mick ghillie playin' tragedy as a comedy, takin' on the role they expect us to play for 'em. As long as they was catchin' limits regularly they was fine laughin' at your sideshow."

"Whatta you sayin' here Jimmy? No one was laughin' at me."

"But when it's barely a trickle a' Brits is comin' over in the first place, Bri, an' them that does is lookin' for a respite from violence… An' this fella here, Bri, he hasn't struck me as anythin' but fair in all my dealin's with him. But he makes the second you take a swing at."

Brian's anger was rising, and he held his arm tighter as the ache and pain was spreading with his anger.

"An' I'm sayin' no one was laughin' at me."

"No? Okay, but we have very important things to talk about an' I deserve a break here, Brian, so calm yerself. We get few guests and you've gotten your share, even as you're late one day and failin' to show up at all the next, 'cause I know what you're facin'."

"No feckin' pity fer me either, ya hear."

"An' after I took you back even though you swung a punch at one of me best guests."

"Years ago, Jimmy, an' you wanted to take your own poke at him, you admitted that. Anyway that hain't got nothin' to do wit—"

"With you drinkin' all the time now? Not just some of the time, not just most of time, but now it's all of the time?"

"I'm like the man whose wife divorced him after thirty years when he came home sober for the first time, yeah."

"They think there's a charm to you when it's a quick nip in the afternoon tea, Brian. But a drunk hain't that charmin' to most people."

"You put up with it for yer own benefits, not mine. I'm the best damn ghillie been around in your sorry old lifetime—you says so yourself."

"Truth be told, the rest are either too old or off fightin' the Nazis, so it's yourself I been stuck with."

"An' so it is."

"But not anymore, Bri. Until you get the drinkin' under control, I'll take 'em out meself if I have to, but I got no more work for you here."

"With my three children to feed."

"An' I got a wife who is expectin' I will be lookin' after her in our old age—"

Brian shot out of his chair but held the desk to stop himself, and his shoulder flashed so hot his stomach cramped hard and his head buzzed.

"Now, I meant nothin', Bri. I'm sorry for what I said, but I'm too old for you to be threatenin' me, even when you're drinkin', you can't be that foolish." Brian stepped back and supported his shoulder again. "This job here, Bri, this is all I got, an' I just can't be riskin' it. If you leave now an' quietly, I'll pay you for a full day today an' for tomorrow as well an' that second bit I'll be takin' outta me own pocket."

"Pay me what you owe me, old man, an' I'll forget you offered me charity."

Tommy had returned home from seminary two days before to see for himself the state of his father and the condition of Katie and little baby Patrick, for Eamon had called the Brothers to tell them that Tommy was needed. With Tommy home and a few extra pounds in his pocket, Brian decided to try and drink away his shoulder's pain at the pub before he returned to the cottage. Drink helped, and more drink helped more, so he stayed and drank until the pub closed.

He walked the road away from the village to his cottage. Just before he opened the door, he took a last sip from a bottle and returned it to his pocket. As he stooped to step inside, baby Patrick cried.

Since the day of his mother's funeral and for all the days thereafter, Patrick had been absolutely silent except for a soft sort of cooing sound when taking a bottle. Everyone who stopped by noted the quiet baby boy. First they called him "a brave little Paddy" and Brian hoped they were right. But as soundless days became weeks and then month after month, some grew afraid that the constant quiet found about "poor Patrick" just wasn't natural. They began to call it "Patrick's deep quiet". Some became uneasy in his presence.

For Brian, the guilt he felt over the death of Patrick's mother had settled in with the silence of their son. He found this final mute testament of his neglect and abuse was a companion to his guilt.

Then one day as Patrick was struggling to learn to walk he tripped, he hit his head on the chair as he fell, and he began to cry. Brian was surprised by the sound, and as he held his son in his arms to care for him, he realized just three days before he had awakened early to attend Mass for the first anniversary of Deirdre's death; the day Patrick cried was the anniversary of her burial.

Once he started, Patrick's cry continued, but it brought Brian some relief for it gave him a role to play, a role that comforted him as he comforted the child. Night after night as Patrick cried, lying on his father's chest, Brian sang to him and called him "brave little Paddy". He patted his back until Patrick's deep sleep brought them both peace. And many nights he put Patrick aside, sleeping deeply, and picked up Katie to quiet her fears and wipe her tears.

Only after the children were both asleep would Brian retrieve the bottle.

Why one night was different than all those before, Brian would never fully understand. Why was it that one night, just two days before Brian injured his shoulder, that the baby's cry no longer sounded like a son's sad song asking for his father's comfort? Instead it seemed to carry a hard condemning wail that scratched and tore at a widower's guilt.

It might simply have been fatigue. In order to bring comfort to his children, Brian had been in constant struggle with the Red Bull Demon that fed on his guilt and pity, and the fight was exhausting.

And earlier that day he'd had no choice but to borrow some money from Eamon for the first time, and he asked for it, knowing his Cos had little. And he asked for it knowing much of it would go to buy another bottle.

But on this night, after months of comforting Patrick's cry every night with a song or a story and his loving arms, Brian popped the baby on his butt, harder than he meant to, and Patrick stopped crying.

The next night Patrick's cry seemed fiercely resistant and Brian slipped again, spanking him hard, and his baby son stopped crying.

So the third night, when Brian entered the cottage, his shoulder's pain growing in intensity, he ignored Tommy's questions about why he was so late and he yelled at Katie.

"Make him shut up."

Katie had her eighteen-month-old brother in her arms, rocking him, and Tommy was at her side, singing a song. They didn't know it was the searing shoulder pain that twisted their da's face and darkened his brow, but the look of it frightened them. When he roared again to quiet the baby Katie said, "Da, I don't know how, Da."

The fear they showed of their father angered Brian more and he reached out to grab the sobbing baby boy from Katie's arms, the pain in his shoulder sharp and hot.

"No, Da!"

He held the little body against his chest, first to try to position his shoulder for the least pain, and when little relief came he popped the baby on his butt, but this time Patrick's cry added a scream that drove the pain in Brian's shoulder through his whole body. Brian clenched the child in a quick jerk chest to chest, to shake even a bit of the power out of him, trying to get even a moment of relief from the baby's scream, or from his pain, so he could think about what came next, but the baby cried a new fear, and the children pulled at their father's arms to get at their brother. Tommy's pull wrenched his father's shoulder, and Brian's painful fury exploded and he pulled away from his children and roared down at them.

"I'll take care of my son."

Katie froze, Patrick screamed, and Tommy dashed to the door and out into the night while he called to his sister, "I'll get Uncle Eamon." His voice acted as a release for Katie who ran to grab the back of her father's shirt as he carried the baby into his bedroom. Brian pulled away and slammed the door shut against her pleas.

Brian pinned his baby boy on his back on his bed, on Deirdre's bed, where she had lain dying slowly and surely, and Brian knelt in front of the baby, his shoulder throbbing, his head throbbing, both burning hot, and he leaned over as close as he could, nearly nose to nose and he roared, "Shut the feck up!" trying to blow all the sound out of the room.

Patrick stopped crying. He froze. All that moved were his eyes' frantic search of his father's face.

Brian held his breath in the moment of quiet, hoping this worked, hoping that his guilt for his dreadful neglect of Deirdre's care would stop feeding his demon, wishing his neck and back and head and shoulder would stop hurting so much that he was getting sick. On the five-count the baby boy screamed his cry, and Brian picked him up by the front of his night shirt and threw him down hard on the bed, too hard, he knew, even before Patrick's head jerked with a snap in his neck. Brian picked his son up so he wouldn't do it again, and Patrick's hottest cry yet burned to cinders anything still alive in Brian's heart and soul.

Katie pounded on the door. She fell to her knees, continuing to beg and plead as she beat her fists against the door.

Then she heard the sound of muffled blows and Patrick's terror-filled shrieks, all to the beat of her father's demonic voice. "Shut... the... feck... up!'"

And she froze when Patrick's cry stopped, and the hitting stopped, and her father's roar became a sound she'd never heard before.

※ ※ ※

Katie was sitting on the floor staring at the bedroom door when Eamon arrived. As he entered the bedroom Tommy appeared at the cottage door, breathing hard, then walked to the bedroom door and tried to block his sister's view while he watched.

Eamon found baby Patrick curled in a ball under the pillows shaking and moaning in pain. When he pulled the pillows back he saw bruises were already forming, and Eamon turned to where Brian was sitting on the floor in the corner of the room, crying. Eamon took one step into a hard-booted kick to Brian's side and they both felt his ribs break.

Eamon carefully cradled the baby in a pillow as he picked him up and then stood over Brian. Tommy was standing at the door crying. Katie was crying, still sitting on the floor behind him, her face buried in her arms.

"These children are mine now. You leave here an' you don't *never* come back. If I see you in the mornin', I'll set the Gardai after you an' I'll make sure you're sent—"

"Take care of 'em."

"Shut up. God damn you, just shut up. You're nearly beatin' the life out of your own son is what it appears to me, an' you're tellin' me what now?"

"I do love you, Katie… Tommy, I love you, son… I'm so sorry for what I did is what I'm tellin' you."

"I don't care where you go, just take all them feckin' plans of yours with you so then you have nothin' to come back here for, 'cause these children, they're mine now. You'll never see them again."

Eamon turned, and led Tommy and Katie away. After a few moments, Brian got up, the pain in his side and the pain in his shoulder nearly blinding, and he collapsed in the bed, where he cried well into the night. Before sun up he shambled about, bent and broken, to collect a few things. He left under the last cover of darkness and was as far down the road at dawn as a beaten man could travel.

Chapter 13
GRASSY NARROWS

THE NEXT TWO CANADIAN WINTERS were bitterly cold, so cold they forced Joe Loon's clan and the other Keewatin tribes who still traveled the River and lived in these forests to move to Grassy Narrows Reserve as their winter camp. There they lived in the cabins that the Grassy Narrows Ojibway and other neighboring clans had been paid by the government to build on the banks of the River years before. The cabins had wood-burning stoves and a couple had fireplaces as well, making them much easier to keep warm when it was 30 below night after night.

The second of these bitter winters, Joe Loon sat in a one-room cabin on a pillow on a tree-stump stool and repaired one of his snowshoes. Naomi sat on a pillow on the floor next to him, boarding a mink pelt. Stretched and framed furs of beaver and mink and muskrat, along with a fox and a fisher, hung on the walls, and in one corner were stacks of furs ready to be traded at the Hudson Bay Post.

The only light in the room came from the kerosene lantern. The corners of the cabin were in shadow. In one corner was a mattress, where Joe Loon and Naomi made their bed. It was piled with blankets, highly valued commodities so far North. The rug Naomi spread out on the floor when the family ate their meals was rolled up on top of the mattress, out of the way. In the other corners were propped two fishing poles, a rifle, a bow and quiver of arrows, an ax, and a two-man crosscut saw.

70

On a small shelf next to the stove were a couple of sacks and three or four boxes of food staples, and on the floor a sack of flour.

Simon Fobister's bed was up the ladder to the cabin's shelf-like loft. He looked down at his grandparents from his bed.

Joe Loon stood, placed his work aside, and looked up to Simon.

"If you will come with me to check the trap line tomorrow, you must sleep now."

❄ ❄ ❄

Later that night Joe Loon and Naomi lay under blankets and furs in the dark.

"Tomorrow I will check the long leg of the trap line, so I will spend the night at Gone Again Waters."

His wife reached under his bed clothes. "Is this the long leg? Ohhh, see how it gets longer, Husband."

"Longer and longer, Wife."

"I will catch it in my trap, Husband."

❄ ❄ ❄

In pre-dawn, Simon Fobister climbed down the ladder. Naomi was fixing the first meal. Joe Loon sat on the stump in front of the stove, the door open. He was staring into the fire.

"I have dreamt this now for four nights."

He put a small log on the fire. This Man stood in the darkest corner.

"It is a big dream. Now I understand this big dream to be true in all of the Four Directions."

Simon Fobister stepped forward to stand at his side, and Naomi turned from her work.

"Tell us your dream, Grandfather."

"I camp on the shore of Kaputowaganickcok. I stand at the place where the funeral fires burned those who died of the white man pox. The spirit of one who died appears before me there. This spirit tells me the white man is coming. I do not want to laugh at the spirit when I tell him the white man is always coming. Though I try to hide it, the spirit hears the laughter in my voice. He becomes angry with me. So angry that he goes away."

Joe Loon closed the stove door.

"The next night I dreamt I am camped there again and the spirit returns. He tells me to be quiet. He tells me to listen to him. He tells me the white man is coming to help our people. He tells me the white man is coming who will help protect this place for our people. I tell this spirit that a white man coming to help will be a strange sight to see. That I do not need a spirit to find this white man. He becomes angry with me again and he goes away.

"The third night I dreamt I have returned to camp on the same shore and the spirit is waiting for me there. He says that there will be another white man coming, and then he goes away though I was quiet.

"Last night was the fourth night I had this dream. I am camping there and many more spirits come, ah gee, so many of our people died from the white man pox and now the spirits of all the men who burned are standing there. Behind them, I see the spirits of the women who burned and they are holding their babies. Their children stand around them and so many old men and old women. They all speak to me with one voice."

This Man began a soft lament as Joe Loon paused to prepare to speak clearly.

"They tell me that the white man is coming who would help our people and the white man is coming who would destroy our people. The spirits tell me that all the clans who live on the River should fear the white man who will be against us. But that all the clans who live on the River must invite the white man as a brother who comes to help us.

"They tell me the white man who gave them blankets did not mean to give them the white man pox. They meant the blankets as gifts. They say the white man who comes to destroy us will not know that is what they do. If we do not stop them, they will turn our River against us. If we do not stop them, they will make the River a poison and this poison will kill everyone. The babies will become sick. The old people will die. They will destroy our forests. After our forests are destroyed and our River is poisoned, the white man who did this will not let us live with them. Our people will be so sad, many of us will want to die. The spirits tell me I must watch for these men. They tell me I must not let them poison the River."

Simon and Naomi were silent. Joe Loon placed his hand on Simon's head. This Man stopped chanting and stood behind the boy.

"This dream is so big, you must remember it with me. For these spirits did not tell me when the white man will come. They did not tell me which white man will come first. They only told me we must protect the River now and always. You must help me watch for them."

"Yes, Grandfather."

"Now and always."

"Yes, Grandfather. Now and always."

Chapter 14
THIS MAN AND THE FRENCH TRADER

THIS MAN STOOD ON THE SHORE of a narrow bay where a reedy creek drained into the River's lake. He was waiting for the French trader and his Ojibway wife who approached in their canoe.

It was 1761.

Behind This Man, an Ojibway village of twenty or thirty families' wigwams lined both sides of the bay.

The French trader's canoe touched shore. His wife was a daughter of this village. They would find their six-year-old son already there. Lately, the boy spent as many nights in his cousins' wigwams in the village as he did in his bed with his parents at the trading post cabin, as there were no other children at the post.

The canoe was filled with supplies. The trader left them in bundles in the canoe, taking only the two new flintlocks which he carried in the crook of his arm, and the bottle of brandy he directed his wife to bring. She followed him, and This Man walked with her, past the sniffing dogs, into the center of the village where the trader found the wigwam of the chief.

Many villagers had collected in their wake, for the French trader always brought gifts. By the time the trader was attended to by the chief and elders, then the tribe's warriors, they were surrounded by all the people of the village.

Their son stepped away from his cousins and friends and stood with his parents.

The French trader had for many years been a voyageur, and one of the first European trappers to return regularly to this fir forest River basin, often times alone, well before a trader's cabin was built, well before he married the young daughter of a warrior who was now an honored tribal elder.

The trader and his son were fluent in both French and the forest language. His wife had learned only a little French, as her husband enjoyed speaking the language of the Ojibway people.

At the fire ring outside the chief's wigwam, the French trader handed the flintlocks to his son so he could bend down to fill each of his hands with ash from the night's fire.

"I come to speak of a sadness in my heart. I tell you my family is in mourning now."

The French trader poured some of the ashes on his head, and rubbed some on his clothes.

"I come to tell you that your Great French Father across the great water has grown weary. He has been fighting the evil English for too long. Your French Father is so tired he has fallen asleep. While he slept, the English enemy stole many of your French Father's greatest treasures. The enemy has stolen this land that you have shared with your French Father. The English enemy now forces your French brothers to leave this place, to return to our homes across the great waters to the East. This is the reason for my great sadness. This is why I mourn. Soon great distances separate us."

"We will mourn with you."

The chief scooped a handful of ashes and slapped them on his shoulders and rubbed a hard line down his jaw.

"The French Father has been kind to his Ojibway children. He has always been generous with his gifts."

The chief reached for the nearest flintlock, held by the tribe's best hunter who handed it to the chief.

"With this firearm, Red Wolf keeps our wigwams filled with fresh meat. When the thieving Dakota hear its thunder, they grow afraid and hide in their wigwams like women.

They no longer raid our villages to steal our women and children."

"I give you these last gifts before I leave my brother. Here are two more firearms. In my canoe I have more powder and many leads. There you will also find many cooking pots. There you will find the very best knives with the big steel blades. Here I place in your wigwam the last of the brandy."

The French trader took the bottle from his wife and handed it to his son who placed it at the door of the chief's wigwam.

"These gifts are given the day you depart?"

"Behind us is an empty cabin, for soon the English will arrive. The day will come that your French Father will wake again, and he will take back his treasures from the English. Then we will return to this land to live with you again. Until that day, your French brother will remember his Ojibway family when I pray to the Chief of all Chiefs, Jesus the Christ."

"You have warned us of your enemy, the English. Now they are our enemy. We will do battle with them. We will drive them out of the trading post before they light their first fire."

"Your French Father loves you just as you love your children. You will not ask your children to fight your battles for you. You are proud when your children grow up to fight by your side, but you will not ask them as children to put themselves in the path of your enemy for you. If my Ojibway brothers drive away the enemy, your French Father will be very grateful. But I love the people of this village. So I ask you to be careful, for these English are a treacherous people."

"You take the daughter of the Loon clan with you across the great water?"

"She will wait for me here, with her people. This is her wish. And our son will grow up in this village as your son. This is why my sadness is so deep."

"When you are gone, your son will be my own son. But you are welcome to build your shelter here to live the rest of your days with your brothers. It would be good for you to tell us your wisdom about how to fight this English enemy."

"I will sleep here tonight and tell you all I know of the English at your council fire. I must leave at daybreak. My honor calls me to one last duty I must perform for my chief. When that is done, I will find my way back to you."

Chapter 15

A TIME FOR PEACE?

ALL THROUGH THE REMAINING WAR YEARS Brian stayed exiled from Cong as he traveled spiraling circles around his village, from Galway to Oughterard or Clifden, to Westport to Castlebar or Sligo, with only an occasional side trip to Dublin, then back to Galway to begin another rotation. He was in one place a few days, the next a couple of weeks. With so many able-bodied men away earning a soldier's wage fighting in the Irish regiments of the British Army, odd jobs were usually available, and Brian accepted any dry bed he could find. But when a bottle was offered, or he had what was needed to purchase one, a hard night of drinking would send him out on the road again.

Maureen spent the war living with her mother in their cottage just outside Derry. She recovered the valise from the mountain top eighteen months after she buried it there and at two in the morning to hide it from her Mum, she buried it again in the spot she mapped for Russell under two feet of dirt and clay, a large stone covering the spot at the far edge of the yard behind the cottage.

She found a job working as a cook's helper in a large hotel and a year later became a cook's assistant. At first her wages didn't cover their meager living expenses, so once or twice a year under cover of darkness, she uncovered the valise and removed a few pound notes. Each time, she diligently recorded her actions on a slip of paper she kept in the valise, noting her situation and her use for the pound notes. She also noted her efforts at finding former IRA contacts, like the day she ventured by bus to Dublin to look for Kevin's music shop but found it closed, permanently it seemed. She also noted how she asked in the nearby shops but no one knew where he had gone. And each rumor she heard of renewed IRA activity was recorded as well, but nothing occurred to support any of the rumors.

As months passed and the war went on there was no sign of the Brotherhood under any name. And when the months became years, she tore up the pages of notes of actions and transactions and threw them to the wind.

※ ※ ※

One day while war waged across the world, Simon and Mathew paddled Nigig across two lakes linked in the River's complex chain, portaged the canoe to a landlocked lake sitting up in a ridge valley, then paddled to the far side. Simon sensed it was a good day for him to take the stern, for his Big Brother was not as excited as he was to be making this trip. They left after the midday meal and paddled all through the remaining daylight looking for the small wigwam that sat on a bit of open shoreline.

The wigwam marked the foot of the path that led up to the top of the highest ridge peak for miles around. The path started up an easy slope but half way up it became a steep climb to the top, to the ancient and sacred place. The boys of the River clans and many of the boys from Grassy Narrows Reserve were brought to this place by their fathers and elders to pray for the vision that would guide their lives as men.

Simon Fobister and Mathew had helped the elders repair the wigwam the year before when a Keewatin boy from Grassy Narrows was preparing for his vision. As they worked together, Old George told a story about his time there, and the dream vision that would set him on his path.

"In my dreams I was a young man setting out to hunt all alone. I came to a shallow bay where a bull moose was feeding. He saw me and ran back into the forest. I stalked him for many days through the forests and swam after him when he crossed the River until after many days I finally got a killing shot. I killed him with just one arrow right through his heart. When I returned to my village with my kill, I had become an old man. I gave away all the best pieces of meat to the others and I kept the poorest portions for myself. When I told the elders this was my dream, they helped me understand I was to live my life without a family so I was always free to serve my village with the best portions I have."

In just a few weeks it would be time for Mathew to climb the path to the top of the cliff. He was fourteen now. Simon's time was still a couple of years away. They made their camp for the night at the foot of the path.

Night came, and they were lying on their backs, watching wisps of smoke rise from their small fire. The great milky sweep of stars that formed the Path of Souls arched across the sky.

Simon knew Mathew was anxious.

"Big Brother. I have been very lucky."

"How is it you have been so lucky?"

"I was living with Grandfather when he had his dreams of the White Man Coming to the River. You and I are both his grandsons. But I was there."

"Why does this make you so lucky?"

"I was there so he asked me to care for this dream with him. I have dreamt of it since then myself. In my dream the white man who will destroy the River comes wearing robes of wolf hides."

"In Joe Loon's dream they do not mean to harm us."

"Yes. But in my dream I show the white man that the Keewatin children are dying of their poisons, but they do not understand, or they do not care. They throw their wolf robes over them and pretend they do not see me."

"Some say Little Brother has had his vision."

"This I why I am lucky. That Joe Loon has asked me into his dream."

This Man stepped from the darkness to sit in the firelight between the two boys who were still and quiet, lying on their backs, studying the stars. Mathew sat up and looked at his cousin. Simon turned and smiled.

"I am afraid Little Brother."

"What is Big Brother afraid of? I will fight it with you."

"I am afraid to be alone on that mountain for four days and four nights."

79

Simon turned his head to look up at the peak, a silhouette framed by stars.

"You will not be alone. We have heard the elders speak of this."

"Tell me again."

"They say on the first night the Great Creator will send an owl to call out to all the spirits that Mathew Loon is here. The second night the spirits of your ancestors will find you."

As Simon began to list the nights of Mathew's search for his dream vision, This Man looked to the stars and raised his arms and opened his hands, and though faint at first, barely distinguishable, the Northern Lights started to emerge out of the black sky, glistening white and green, green and white. Mathew saw the delight in his cousin's eyes, looked up, saw the First Lights, and settled back again.

"And on the third night Waussnodae will dance across the heavens for you, and you will know your ancestors join this dance for it is a dance of great joy."

The boys were quiet for a long time, watching the lights grow as waves shimmered and shrank then grew wider and broader with a soft trace of blue rippling at the edge. Simon stretched his leg to touch Big Brother's foot with his.

"The fourth night your vision will come."

"This is my fear. I am afraid my vision will not come."

"The elders say it comes when you are ready."

"And if it does not come at all the elders say this means I choose for myself how to be a man. I am free to walk any path. That too is my fear. For how will I know if I choose the right path?"

Again the boys were quiet. A log popped, sending sparks to the heavens to join the show. Mathew sighed.

"I have never liked the sound of the owl calling down the valley. It is a sad sound."

"That was when you were a boy. When you hear him from the mountain top, he will be telling the world Big Brother is a man."

❄ ❄ ❄

The night in May of 1945 when the war for Europe ended, Brian found himself caught up in the celebrations at the very pub in Donegal where the B&B owner had offered him the deal years before, and for the first time in years Brian found himself entertaining drinking companions with his long-lost dreams and plans for the Great Lodge at Innish Cove. As he told his stories and his dreams and the bits of plans that came to him in the midst of the great exultation of the evening, he found himself believing in them again. The next day, as the world declared life should begin again, he decided to resurrect his plans.

He knew he needed to break the cycle of his heavy drinking to have his plans taken seriously by anyone who might want to invest. To do that, he broke the cycle of his travel by heading south to the pier in Cleggan where he took the ferry to Inis Bo Finne, the Island of the White Cow. There he hired himself out to the island's commercial fishermen when the mackerel and pollack were in season, and he worked as a turf cutter the rest of the year. Both jobs earned a decent wage for the island economy, and both were hard labor. And most importantly, he knew the island's small villages of Fawnmore and Knock offered little of the temptation found so easily on the mainland.

He left the island when he had a pocket full of savings and the confidence an evening's pint didn't lead to a second and third and then the whiskey. He decided to begin again in Donegal, at the pub where the story of the Great Lodge at Innish Cove was most alive. He was telling the story of the near miss with the B&B owner and how the lady girl stepped forward that night with a flash of steel and a touch of spice.

"I saw her come in. You couldn't help but notice her. She was stunnin'. But I had forgotten her as I'm back sharin' the schemes I have for the place. Well, just as I begin an understandin' that me man standin' there in front of me has his own schemes to steal this dream away from me, an' as the Red Bull Demon begins loadin' a thunderous right hand an' poor ol' Aidan Howley, poor ol' Aidan, he's dancin' all round tellin' me to take 'er easy here Bri. Well then right in the middle of what's soon to be a terrible dust up the lady girl is standin' there between us an' we're all wonderin' what she means to do until she shows herself to be a powerful righteous woman, a righteous woman indeed, who tells this fellow to feck off an' he curls his tail round his scrotum an' scoots out of here. An' to top it off, the fellow she's with, he buys me drinks the rest of the evenin'."

"So what's your plan for gettin' the money you're needin'?"

"I've near enough now for transport to Chicago where I'll room with some of me da's family an' look for somethin' promisin' success. When I have the capital, I'll head north to Kenora, in Northwest Ontario. They call it a frontier town, where the great wilderness starts. I need to begin my serious study there. So if you know of anyone payin' a man's wages, I'd be obliged."

❋ ❋ ❋

When it was clear the war was ending, Maureen grew hopeful again. Kevin said they would just lay low during the war and emerge after to take advantage of Britain's certain post-war weakness. She became alert again, eager to see a face that would recognize hers, that might approach with a furtive whisper of a Republican call or a message from an IRA unit. She decided to make another trip, to look for any movement or trace of one, to listen for any rumors or hints of organization.

Kevin often referred to the Cork Brigade, so she traveled there, again recording her use of funds, but found nothing. She headed back to the West, listening for anything that sounded like the IRA's renewal.

Finding nothing she headed north, stopping in Donegal at the pub where Kevin had taken her, where a woman could come comfortably alone. She heard little about the IRA during her travels and increasingly what she did hear was the story of its demise. She pictured the valise buried behind her mother's cottage and after years of presuming she was simply holding it for others, she finally allowed herself to wonder who the money belonged to if the IRA no longer existed.

When she entered the pub she immediately saw Brian, and there was a smile in the memory of that night. As an idea began to form her smile brightened.

He looked much older nearly six years later, but so had she until her smile refreshed her.

"Of course the lodge hall will include a grand Irish pub. Americans lovin' all things Irish, I figure we'll make it look an' feel like this very place ya got here, Johnny boy. You need to take a picture of it for me before I go."

The fellow drinking next to Brian, a new companion, waved to another as he spoke to Brian.

"I think you better be hirin' me an' Padraig just to drink wit' your guests at night an' provide what Americans call the local color."

"I'll be writin' to let you know when I'm ready for you."

"After you write to Mr. Ernest Hemmingway, or was it John Wayne?"

Brian turned to find it was Maureen standing in front of him.

"Tis a pity how much of the best of Ireland is always takin' themselves over the ocean to prove what they can do."

"The most bounteous blessin' on us all lads, it's herself, the lady girl of me story. Here's the very beauty what scared the beast. I told ya she was dazzlin'."

"If I introduced you to someone who can invest in your Garden of Eden across the sea, what are my chances of joinin' the adventure of it?"

"Ah, Lady Girl, my guess is you'd be welcome in any adventure of your choosin'."

❀ ❀ ❀

Brian and Maureen settled in at a corner table, away from the others who couldn't help but look their way. When Brian returned with a second pint for him and a second half for her, he thought she had moved her chair closer to his.

"You gotta respect me on this point, Brian Burke. I've never been comfortable lettin' anyone knowin' I have so much money."

"You can rest easy, Lady Girl, an' if it appears an insult then I'll be beggin' your pardon in advance, but I assure you I've not been takin' your offer seriously enough that I'd tell anyone. You want me to believe you have the exact outstandin' sum I'm lookin' for, an' you'll give it to me, but there's no story attached tellin' how it comes to pass that a simple Derry girl has such a sum."

"Good luck is rare enough, it has to be held accountable?"

"It should have a name, yeah."

"A name?"

"Or enough of a description so's I get to see where bad luck might be lurkin'."

"It's a silly convention, this needin' to know where money comes from. Surely it came from someplace else before that an' before that as well."

Brian's smile had been growing.

"It's the story that makes it real for me."

"Maybe it just fell from the sky."

"I could believe yourself fell from the sky, but believin' in angels is different than believin' angels would offer me quick riches on earth."

"There's plenty of stories of men of faith rewarded."

"In the Bible, sure, but naught in Connaught."

"Then you can just ask me to marry you."

Brian's first look of surprise quickly became disappointment.

"I see… Now I get it. Your game is to spend the night havin' fun at the expense of a fool an' see if you can keep him buyin' an' keep him flatterin' as you go about makin' him out a fool."

"Don't be silly. I'm sayin' you'd have your answer for the lads. You can tell them the money came from the dowry."

"You're sayin' you're not playin' with me?"

"Sure I'm playin' with you, but all to good purpose."

"An' what might that good purpose be?"

"To get to knowin' each other quicker. If we're startin' off with a laugh, I can already reach over an' touch your arm." And she did. "But I'm altogether serious when I say you an' I should begin talkin' about how much fun we could have if we was playin' the same game, all together so."

"That's what you're doin'?"

"I've heard your Eden in the New World wilderness story twice now. I said Amen the first time and it sounds even better these years later. So I've got the money your dreams need an' the Good Lord knows how I love this crumblin' bit a' island and will always be true, but if we could go live an adventure with your red men in the forests, why would we stay? Make me your business partner if you're not ready to talk about gettin' married."

"First you tell me where your money came from after it came from where it came from before."

"So you don't want to marry me?"

"You're dazzlin' me an' me head is swimmin'. But I'm still in mournin'."

"It's been five years you said."

"A respectable distance by any measure from poor Deirdre's demise, God rest her soul in Heaven above. But I'm still in mournin' for me children an' that starts over again every day I ain't with 'em."

"Ah, the first I hear of the children. Tell me about 'em."

"I don't talk about them. There's no fun in that story, so let's leave it there for now." Maureen took a sip of her Guinness.

"You confessed to me that night, sittin' at that table right there. Remember? About what violence can do to a good man's soul."

"I don't remember callin' myself a good man an' surely wouldn't now. I've done things since that I'm most ashamed of an' won't confess until me oldest boy himself can serve as my confessor."

Maureen waited for more, but Brian was quiet.

"Just the same, I'll even the score an' confess what I did to get this money, where the money came from."

"I just want to hear it, an' we'll move on from there."

"An' it's just this once. If you accept me as your partner, you accept what I did to get the money, an' we don't ever talk about it again."

"Of course, Lady Girl."

"No. Put the "Lady Girl" aside and tell me you swear to it."

"I swear to it."

"Where I come from an oath means somethin'."

"A place called Ireland?"

"An' you'll forgive me."

"An' I'll forgive you? It's not my place to forgive you. But I'll only be acceptin' your money an' yourself as my partner if I accept what you did to get it."

"Of course." Maureen edged her chair closer and leaned in close to Brian so she could talk softly. "You see, I spent time in London, before the war started. I went there to do what some will think was a terrible thing. But understand, I was young."

"You're young still."

"I was just 18, or 19, when an older man came along. He seemed so wise, an' he had some ideas. An' it seemed I fit right in with some of his schemes."

"I have no idea what you're sayin' here."

"He was rich. I liked that, because my family was threadbare an' crust poor even before Da... died. So when this older man asked me to come live with him, in London... He did regular business in London, and so he had rented a flat. He asked me to stay there an' take care of it for him, an' if I did, he'd take care of me. He'd not only take care of all my expenses and pay me a wage, he'd buy me dresses an' take me out to fancy places to make me feel special if I would..." She sipped from her glass to study Brian's face, but he was only confused. "If I would treat him special. All I had to do was be nice to him when he visited me in his flat, you know, do what he likes to make him smile. When he made his offer, I found it very easy to say yes."

She saw the dawn of understanding.

"Jaysus, I've heard of such but always figured it was just more story than actual occurrence."

"There was lots a' times he didn't come around for weeks an' weeks, an' for those occasions he'd leave me an extra stack of pound notes to live on. An' then I figured out all I needed to do was ask for more an' he'd give me more. My scheme was to save all of it I could, so when he wasn't 'round to take me out to restaurants I lived tightfisted, miserly, beans and bread. I know how to live on the cheap, I'd done it all my life. And I'd keep a look out for part-time jobs to earn."

"It was that fellow you were with the night we met. I could tell there was somethin' between you."

"Kevin? No, it wasn't Kevin. Kevin's more like my older brother, or uncle. This other fellow, let's just call him my first business partner."

"So in your first partnership you managed a flat in London for the amusement of your partner?"

"Sure, an' it taught me to be a very good partner. An' provided me with the investment capital your dreams need to come true."

❋ ❋ ❋

After meeting for three straight nights—Maureen first appreciating Brian's dream, then shaping and reshaping his plans, with Brian's delighted thanks—Maureen decided it was time to close the first phase of her plan, to find a cover for getting out of Ireland with the money and make something extraordinary of it.

"I have a proposition for the man with the grand dreams."

"Each one you've made has been worth me listenin'."

"I'll buy us two airline tickets, Dublin to New York, New York to Toronto, then we'll find how to get to Kenora, by bus or by airplane, once we get to Toronto."

"I'm learnin' to like it when you're the boss."

"I leave now to retrieve enough money to pay for our travels and we'll meet again in Dublin. When we arrive in Kenora we'll need hotel rooms for a fortnight. But only by bein' there can we get serious about makin' plans. We need to talk with the proper people, we need to see the land an' explore the place a bit, an' collect the information we'll need to mount a proper plan."

"I get no response at all?"

"Response to what, now?"

"Me sayin' I like it when you're the boss."

"I'm good at it."

"There's few men would accept a young woman as boss in a venture like this, that's all I'm pointin' out."

"That's the fault in others."

Brian found his smile deepening.

"As I am sayin' yes I'm askin' for two days an' maybe three before we depart. I need to go get... a blessin', I guess, from my family. I can be ready in three days."

"We'll be gone but a fortnight."

"What's excitin' about you, Lady Girl, is you give this the feel of a true start. An' if this next step is the first real step, well, I got to visit my village before I take it. Nothin' may come of it, but my family needs to know this has begun."

"I'll get a room at the Clarence Hotel an' expect you Thursday. If I can't get us tickets for the flight on Friday, we'll have seats on a flight to New York by Saturday."

"I'll be there Thursday."

❊ ❊ ❊

When Brian got off the bus at Cong early the next afternoon,

87

it was his first time back since the night he was banished from his village. His stomach churned and his legs were weak. His plan was to walk directly to Eamon's cottage and knock on the door. He would offer his apologies to any and all who presented themselves, and if he wasn't told to leave, if anyone was still listening, he would tell them about his trip and the plans. And then he would ask for their blessing for this endeavor. He knew his dreams of forgiveness were too grand to consider real.

Over his shoulder was a sack filled with the gifts for Tommy, Katie, and Patrick that Brian had collected the past years during his travels. There were nights he dreamt his children were again in his care, and the next day he made a point of finding a gift for one of them. He'd leave the bag of gifts at the doorstep of Eamon's cottage if nothing else.

He walked around the village, stepping over the tumbled down low spots on the stonewalls so he could cut across fields to get to Eamon's cottage. He crested a hillock that bordered Eamon's land and there was Katie, collecting wildflowers, not thirty yards from him.

She looked up and saw the big man standing there. It took a moment for her to recognize her father, then she froze when she did, a look of terror on her face that dropped Brian to his knees. With his movement she turned and fled, spooking the milk cow grazing nearby. Brian stood, but when she looked back to check on him, he realized his getting back up must look like he was going to pursue her. She shrieked and he sat back down, so heavy he felt he'd never get up.

He had imagined anger and had even wondered what hate on a child's face might look like. He hadn't expected full-on terror though, and the hot fear of it unnerved him.

He sat, fighting his sobs. He hoped Eamon would come out when Katie calmed enough to explain he was there. Still sitting, he picked the flowers in his reach and with each one he told Katie he was sorry.

His cousin came around the corner of the cottage and slowly walked up the slope, following the path Katie had made in the tall grasses and stopping where Katie had stood.

"I'm only surprised you haven't tried somethin' sooner."

Brian was grateful he came out.

"You told me to stay away."

"I'm surprised you have."

"How's Katie?"

Eamon answered first by shaking his head. "Katie and Patrick begged me to keep you from comin' any closer."

"I come to apologize."

"Sure you have."

"I've come to apologize for what I did, Eamon."

"Tell me, Brian. Tell me what you did."

Brian slowly got to his feet and looked his cousin straight on.

"I haven't pretended for one moment it was anythin' other than what it was. It was an evil act of a cowardly man, the most despicable thing a father could ever do."

"An' so I cast out the evil-doer."

"Yes, an' I thank you for that."

"Do ya' now? You thank me for sendin' you away?"

"I don't know if the ancestors had it all figured out, but I've come to understand somethin'... that I had to be cast out, for reasons you may not even know."

"So you're a wise man now."

"It's for the good of the village, to restore peace, yes. But I've learned that evil-doers are exiled for our own good as well... Because it is our only chance to change, to fight the evil in us. If we have any chance of defeatin' it, we have to go away."

"I did it to protect the children from a violent man."

"Yes, yes, yes. It starts with that. But when you cast out the evil-doers, it's easier for us to see what we did... an' I found I had a deep desire to cleanse my soul an' purge the Red Bull Demon. If I was here, I'd be around those who can't help but see me as the man who does what I did, an' they'd treat me like they always see the Red Bull Demon in me, an' that calls to the Demon, an' makes 'im harder to exorcise, makes it harder to change."

"An' so you're a changed man now? A good man?"

"Not yet a good man, no. But I am a different man now than I was then, for now I try to be a good man."

"So the world can breathe a bit easier."

Brian smiled, but his cousin didn't smile back.

"I brought 'em some… things. Will you give 'em to 'em?"

"I'm not sure you understand how badly you injured that baby boy, Brian. There was much took a long time to heal an' some things that hain't healed yet."

"Not healed yet?"

"He has spells still, Brian, an' there's a weakness to him that lingers, somethin' fragile still. An' Katie, she has the night terrors, not just bad dreams, mind you, but she wakes up screamin', an' if a week goes by without Patrick's spells an' Katie's terrors, that just makes it sadder when they return."

Finally Brian's tears began to fall, and Eamon saw them.

"An' Tommy?"

"I'm afraid some parish is gonna get a very angry priest."

"I was gettin" a different picture about Patrick, about all of 'em."

"If your friends have been tellin' you any different, it must be they know you couldn't stand to hear the true story. Just leave the bag an' I'll show it to Tommy next time he's home, an' we'll decide what to do with it. You can move along an' I'll get word to you if anyone wants to see you."

The cousins approached each other.

"I came because I want you to know I'm goin' to Canada. I got the plan. Well, actually I got a partner who is real smart at makin' out plans an' she has money, too, so we're goin' over for a couple of weeks to check the details and scout for Innish Cove."

"*She's* got money?"

They met and Brian handed Eamon the flowers and the bag of gifts.

"Katie was pickin' these when I frightened her. Yeah, she's got money an' she's a real smart lady, the sort who knows how to think two steps ahead."

"You're married?"

"She's asked me, twice."

"She's got money, an' she's asked you to marry her, an' you've said no?"

"I'm ready to take her on as a business partner, but I can't start a new family until I mend this one. One thing I was hopin' to have a chance to say was anytime you change your mind, an' are ready to give me another chance, hell, I ain't ever expectin' forgiveness, Eamon, but maybe just a chance to come around… I know you'd see I've purged the Demon an' I'm not that man anymore."

"I hope you'll find peace in Canada, Brian."

"I won't be findin' that anywhere but here, we both know that, Cos, so if you'd offer up a blessin' for me trip."

"God bless this trip of yours to the wilderness of Canada, and God bless Innish Cove."

"Thank you." Brian gestured to the bag Eamon held at his side. "Can't be any harm comin' from seein' a bag of treasures their da collected in his travels."

Eamon opened it and looked inside while Brian described the jumble.

"It's not really so much. Some posters from fairs an' carnivals from all over the island, an' handbills from plays in Dublin an' Galway… a bottle of pink sand, lovely, yeah, from the beach at Rinvyle Point… two dolls made by travelers who helped me out of some tough times, near Limerick… I found a copy of *The Imitation of Christ* under a bush by the side of the road one day an' picked that up for Tommy. Tell him I've been readin' it some… An' another book, *Hiawatha*, a poem about the Indians I'll be livin' with. An' a box with a half dozen flies I tied when material was present… It saddens me to think I don't get to teach the boys to fish the River."

"I'll show it to Tommy next time we see him."

"An' letters as well, for each of 'em, in the bottom of the bag, an' there's one for you, too, Cos. Apologizin' to each of you, to all of you. An' I better tell you before you just decide to toss it all on the rubbish pile, there's more than just a few pounds tucked in each envelope."

"Tommy'll decide."

"Thanks for takin' care of 'em, Cos. At least keep the money for that."

"A fair gesture."

"I have dreams about 'em. I hain't askin' you to tell 'em that, I just want you to know. I dream I'm still their da, an' I'm sittin' at the table smokin' a pipe an' listenin' to 'em laughin' just outside me window."

"You've always had dreams."

"If you can tell 'em I came because I love 'em. An' tell Katie she's a lovely lass, an' I'm sorry I frightened her so."

Chapter 16

DREAMS OF IRISH AND INDIANS

ON A BRIGHT AUTUMN AFTERNOON, a week after Maureen and Brian had arrived in Kenora, they were passengers in the Norseman bush plane owned and flown by Dutch Acker. They had been following the River's chain of lakes all day, heading north. Maureen started the trip by hiring a different bush pilot each of the first three days, to learn from many, to hear a range of informed opinions. After their first day with Dutch she changed tactics and booked him for the rest of the week. This was the beginning of their second day together.

Brian's bulk filled the co-pilot's seat and more; Dutch commented he'd never had a larger co-pilot. Maureen sat behind Brian on the plain bench seat of metal frame and canvas that ran along the plane's fuselage. Once they had leveled off after taking off from the municipal dock on Lake of the Woods, Maureen pulled a large leather case from under the bench. She removed and examined the spreading maps and charts and checked her files for notes. The bench and the open floor around her were soon covered with her research. When she found what she was looking for, she unbuckled her seat belt to stand, crouching, with one arm leaning on the back of Brian's chair, the other on the pilot's chair. Then she could look out the windshield to see where in the wilderness Dutch was pointing.

"It's a pretty spot. The impression your guests would have when they first see that, well, they'd think they've come to the right place, no doubt about it, so I wanted to take a look... Ahh, sorry, there's a big downside, that ridgeline is pretty steep, and closer to the lake than I remembered. There would be lots of weather conditions when I really wouldn't want to be trying to fly in or out."

Maureen sat back to check her maps and then returned with one, holding it out in front of the two men, pointing to one of the River's biggest lakes, farther north. "So it's Rainbow Lake next, eh?"

Dutch said, "Got it". Brian turned to smile up at Maureen. "You said 'Eh'?"

"It's contagious, eh?"

The plane banked slowly and vibrated loudly. As he continued following the main River channel flowing north, Dutch kept his eye on the first dark clouds just beginning to collect at the distant western horizon. He knew a storm front was approaching, but it was forecasted for late in the evening and nothing major was predicted. These clouds were showing up sooner than expected.

So he wouldn't have to yell over all the sound, Dutch leaned a bit towards Brian who was studying the shoreline. "The cove you've marked on your map is just beyond that point. We won't see it until we get over this ridgeline. It's the only sand beach on Rainbow Lake and probably one of the biggest sand beaches for miles around—that I know of anyway. I know this is farther north than you wanted to go. I don't get jobs that take me this far too often, but I recollect it is lovely."

Maureen stood and again crouched between them.

"I was sittin' back there thinkin', Dutch, that you sure bring a helpful understandin' to what we are doing here."

"Happy to help."

"And then I was thinkin' that as we build the Great Lodge at Innish Cove, Brian Burke proprietor, we might want to have our own floatplane operation as well. If we get just halfway to our full plans in a couple of years, we would keep a couple of planes like this one plenty busy just attendin' to our own guests and supplies."

"That's if your camp's successful. No one's ever tried this far north. We flew over so many great lakes to get here, folks figure you don't need to go this far."

"That's just one reason we'll be successful. Bein' so far north makes us even more exclusive, even deeper into the wilderness. We can promise them they will fish all day an' not see any other boats but those with their friends. Lady Girl here has all sorts of schemes to make it more attractive still."

"Well Dutch, I'm bringin' it up here now so that if Brian does decide to build a bush plane business, I want you to know we would want to talk about doin' it with you."

"I'll take the compliment and leave it at that for now."

The plane crested the ridge. Just as Dutch promised, they got a full view of the expansive lake. Across the lake was the cove, half enclosed by a curling finger of rocky point dotted with stunted pine. The golden-brown sands of the beach were hidden behind the pines until they had flown halfway across the lake; there was a small, but brilliantly white stand of birch just above the beach in front of the deep pine green, and there was a rising forested ridge behind it all, green trees stepped up and up and up into the most dramatic ridge crest of rock line they'd seen. Brian began to shake his head, and Maureen leaned on his big shoulder so she could speak softly in his ear.

"It's beautiful."

Brian was quiet; she studied his smile and watched his eyes flash with his excitement. She squeezed his shoulder. "You could build from that point west all way 'round the eastern tip of the cove, an' that's a hundred meters, wouldn't you say, Dutch—from the rocky bluff to that fingertip of forest, a hundred meters?"

"Close enough."

"You could site fifteen cabins in those trees, each one hidden from the others."

Brian was still quiet. Dutch stole a glance and saw Brian was not just quiet, but speechless.

"Like I said, I haven't been this far north very often, a couple of times a year might be about right. But if I remember right, your maps will show your guests could fish three lakes upriver, and two more downriver without ever leaving their boats for a portage. There are nice, wide River channels connecting all of them in a row. And you can see Rainbow Lake is plenty wide—I can take off and land regardless of wind direction."

Brian leaned forward in anticipation and Maureen enjoyed the view of the great lake and its many islands, clusters of small ones, a large one out alone.

"I've seen but one boat since we crossed the second ridgeline north of Lake of the Woods."

Dutch was lining up his approach and gave Brian more to think about.

"What you're looking at is the heart of some of our last great wilderness. Nothing but Ojibway around here, at Grassy Narrows and White Dog Reserve to the southeast and a good number still living off the Reserve back in the bush... There's a Hudson's Bay Post near Grassy Narrows, and that's it."

Finally Brian spoke.

"Let's set her down at the beach."

"I'll land in this open stretch here, then taxi into the cove."

"Whatever you do, Dutchman, I need to stand on that beach—now."

❄ ❄ ❄

Joe Loon and Simon were scouting a new leg for their trap line for beaver along the Little Drive In channel when the Norseman passed overhead. The course it took suggested a landing near the Shore Where Many Burned For Many Days, so they abandoned their search for new trap sites and turned their canoe to follow the plane's path.

Just before the plane's sound attracted their attention, Joe Loon caught a glimpse of the western horizon, noticing the first dark clouds gathering. "We will go see who the plane is bringing to our River. We will go now for this storm will be building faster than it first appeared. The winds will be strong."

❄ ❄ ❄

The bush plane landed on Rainbow Lake and turned to taxi towards the cove. Brian leaned forward in his seat, eager to see around the rocky point, and Maureen, who sat back and buckled in for the landing, came forward to her regular position affording her best view of the cove. Dutch angled his approach so the full expanse of golden sand would be suddenly seen and fully appreciated as they entered the cove.

"I know this is farther north than any of the camps, and that means the trip in will be more expensive for the guests and for supplies, but I can tell you that you'll not find a beach like this anywhere on the River, and the fishing, I've been told, is the best there is anywhere."

Maureen, still crouched between the men, squeezed Brian's arm.

"When you first saw it, what was it you were thinkin'?"

"It's a dream comin' true."

"It's Innish Cove."

"But we're not there yet. We're close, yeah, but we're not there yet."

❋ ❋ ❋

The River's Little Drive In channel opened into Kaputowaganickcok. The wind stirred just a slight chop. First the trees on shore where the channel was narrow hid their view of the western sky but when they cleared them and entered the open water Simon and Joe Loon could see the storm building behind the far west ridges.

Albert and Mathew, paddling Nigig at a steady pace, were halfway across Kaputowaganickcok when Joe Loon and Simon came up behind them in the outboard-powered freight canoe. When the canoes met, they stopped to talk.

Whenever a strange white man arrived on the River, they watched. When more than one white man arrived and acted as if they might stay awhile, they watched carefully. That this plane was headed to the cove where Joe Loon's dream was set was reason to act. Albert touched the freight canoe with his paddle to hold them together as they drifted, the breeze stronger than the lake's soft current.

"This is the first time a white man has come to the sacred place since the Dream."

Albert shook his head.

"The plane passed overhead just as I noticed the dark clouds building."

"Simon saw the dark clouds before the plane came."

"I have seen this plane at the Hudson Bay Post. Three or four times. The pilot of this plane is the one with snow-white hair. He is always wearing dark glasses so we cannot see his eyes. But he has a laugh that you can trust."

"I will go ahead but will wait for you before I approach them."

Joe Loon started the motor, opened the throttle, and his bow cut just a bit of spray as the wind picked up and the soft chop kicked up into small waves. He headed towards the cove.

❊ ❊ ❊

As the plane taxied across the cove to the sand beach, Brian got out of his chair, opened the door, and climbed down to stand on the Norseman's starboard pontoon. He called out "Hello, Innish Cove!" and Maureen laughed as she opened the fuselage door, climbed down the ladder, and stood on the port pontoon. When the pontoons touched the beach the pair leapt from pontoon to sand in the same moment, and Maureen moved to Brian for his embrace, but he hadn't noticed her expectation as he turned and headed for the top of the beach, the edge of the forest sitting on a shelf just above the wide, long sweep of sand. He stopped there and turned to look out at the cove protected by the rocky point, then he looked up the beach where it ended in a forested shore. Maureen stood next to him, studying him studying the cove.

"Tell me what you're thinkin'."

"From where the beach meets the beginnin' of the bluff, there as a boundary to the point there, and the ridgeline behind…"

Maureen reached down and scooped up a handful of sand.

"And the beach."

"It's grand," and Brian turned and stepped up onto the shelf, entering the forest through the birch grove that served as a door into the thick jack pine and spruce forest. Maureen turned to Dutch and waved, then followed Brian.

❊ ❊ ❊

The winds were kicking stronger as the canoes crossed Kaputowaganickcok, and Joe Loon knew that the plane's sounds had masked the sound of his small motor. Now he turned off his motor to glide to a stop just behind the tip of the rocky point. He could see in the cove; he couldn't be seen. Albert and Mathew were still behind, paddling hard for the final distance.

Joe Loon arrived at the point just in time to see a white man with snow-white hair climb out of the plane, walk up the beach, and stop at the edge of the birch trees in the pine green forest.

"Grandfather. He has flown here to stand at the Trees the Women Watered with Their Tears. This must be a white man from your dream."

"We will find out."

The wind suddenly gusted and danced along the fir trees setting them a swirl and that gust was followed by another and another.

"What does this mean, that they arrive as a storm is coming?"

"We will watch and see."

When Albert caught up with Joe Loon, they saw the white-haired white man sitting at the top of the beach next to the birch grove. He wore sunglasses, and Mathew told Simon, "My father says this Snow Hair is a good man."

"Let us go ask him why he is here."

❀ ❀ ❀

Brian had been weaving his way through the trees keeping the cove in sight, attempting first a broad survey, determining the depth and breadth of this flat forest shelf between beach and ridge. He discovered that it ran wide and long between beach shore and the foot of the ridge that started on an easy slope before it grew more severe with each step up. And he found it was home to deer flies and mosquitos, and he swatted them without being distracted. Maureen followed, catching up when Brian stopped to note another cabin site by counting it out. He was up to eight cabins and two dozen swats when she caught him again. She had been looking out at the cove between the trees and spotted two canoes headed towards the plane.

"Bri, look."

"How grand. Innish Cove has its first visitors."

"Might be good to look at it from the other end."

"What? That this is their home an' we're the visitors? Ah, yes, you are the smart one."

They turned to work their way back to the beach.

❋ ❋ ❋

The two canoes pulled up next to the plane. With a smile Dutch reached out his hand to Simon but since Simon couldn't see Snow Hair's eyes he was uncertain of this man's purpose so he looked past him as he stepped out from the bow.

"Proud fellow, eh. So whatta you boys up to today?"

Joe Loon walked the length of the canoe then stepped out onto the beach. Simon stood next to him, and Joe Loon nodded to Snow Hair. Albert spoke for them all from Nigig's stern.

"This is Joe Loon. He is chief elder of the Loon clan. He does not speak the English words. I will speak for him. I am Albert Loon. Joe Loon is my uncle. Here are grandsons of Joe Loon."

Joe Loon told Albert to ask why Snow Hair kept his eyes hidden from them but before he could they were surprised when the biggest white man they had ever seen charged out of the bright white grove of birch trees. This big man was followed by a woman with raven hair, so very black as their own that for a moment Mathew thought she was one of their people.

Simon took a step closer to his grandfather. "Yaway, Grandfather, this white man is as big as a bear."

Mathew said, "He comes from the Trees Watered by the Tears of our Sorrows."

When Brian saw Joe Loon and Albert and the boys, he called out, "Greetings, neighbors!"

Dutch called back, "Seems only the one there in the canoe speaks English."

Brian and Maureen joined them as Albert spoke.

"Joe Loon would like to know why you have come to this place."

Brian gained a moment to collect his thoughts by nodding with a smile to each of the Ojibway. Just before he spoke, Maureen answered.

"This big man, he has been dreamin' big dreams for many years. This beach here an' this cove, an' that lake out beyond that cove an' these forests, they are the world that makes up his big dreams. This big man has been on a great journey to find this place so his dreams can come true."

Then Brian took over.

"You an' your people are always in my dreams as well."

After Brian explained to Albert that he was going to buy this land and build a fishing camp, he waited while Albert translated for the others. Dutch had been watching the wind pick up and he left the group to climb a rocky outcropping at the edge of the beach where he would get a better view of the western sky behind them, though the ridge still prevented a far view.

"This woman tells us this big white man has traveled a great distance from his home for he has dreamed of this place for many years. She calls them big dreams. She says our people are in his dreams. He says he will buy this land and he will make this a place that many of the White Man Who Fish will come here to catch fish. He would like to meet all of the People who live on the River to tell us of this big dream."

Joe Loon looked at Brian as he spoke to his people. "What is this we are hearing? That this big man is here because his big dreams bring him here from a far off place. This must be a white man from my dreams. He is so big, he looks like he would be a good fighter. I hope this is the white man sent to help our people, for I do not want to fight him. But what does this mean that he would bring the white man to this sacred place? "

"He says to tell you he dreams he will build many cabins at this place and in the middle will be a great meeting lodge. The White Man Who Fish will come stay in his cabins. He tells me our people will make more money guiding for the White Man Who Fish than we do catching fish in our nets."

"Grandfather, this is Where Our People Cried as Our People Burned. They must not build cabins for the White Man Who Fish on ground that is sacred to our ancestors."

"All the Keewatin clans must hear this big white man's dreams. I must think about this for four days. Tell him our people will meet him at this place in four days. On that day when the sun is at its highest, we will be here to listen to his big dreams."

Dutch returned from his weather observations.

"Maureen, tell your partner we should be getting out of here now if we're to make it back to Kenora without taking a risk."

"Hear that, Bri? Our fellow here says we need to be in the sky carl nordgren

right now or..."

Brian told Albert he would return in four days, then he reached out his hand to Joe Loon. After they shook hands, Joe Loon said to the others, "You must shake this big white man's hand. It is as big as a bear paw."

After they all shook hands, Dutch boarded to prep the plane while the men and boys and Maureen pushed the plane off the beach, turning it as they did. Brian and Maureen scrambled inside, and Brian sat next to Dutch as he started the engine to taxi out of the cove.

"Or what Dutch?"

"Or we could be spending the night right here, and we won't find much overnight comfort for us in the plane beyond protection from the rain."

After the plane was airborne and Dutch had a clear view west, he saw the storm was rolling in much faster and apparently larger than forecasted, so he headed south with a constant eye on the storm's leading edge. He was still well ahead of it. But they had come much farther north than he had planned, and it was gaining on them.

After takeoff Brian sat next to Maureen on the bench seat in the plane's fuselage.

"We'll want to buy the whole cove, bluff to point an' to the top of the ridge line behind."

"You want Joe Loon's approval first. Without them, there's no business. With them, it's your Eden in the wilderness."

They passed the first row of ridges and as they approached the second, the storm front was closer. Soon the mild turbulence just ahead of the front caught up with them, just rattling them a bit at first, but it grew in intensity and within minutes was shaking the plane. They crossed the third ridgeline with the clearance Dutch favored, but the next two ridges were taller, the last much taller.

The engine's roar and the plane's rattles were amplified, and now the bouncing began as the clouds gathered. Brian had to call loudly for Dutch to hear him.

"The storm's caught us, yeah?"

Dutch had removed his sunglasses.

102

"Not yet, but it's getting close."

Brian stepped up to stand next to Dutch for his own view of the storm.

"We have to stay below those clouds, and if the ceiling gets any lower or the visibility any worse, then crossing the ridges becomes a problem."

The plane was caught in a sudden downdraft and dropped sharply; Brian knocked his head against the plane's ceiling before he fell over the co-pilot's chair as Dutch regained control, checked, then recovered some lost altitude.

"It's time to sit this out."

"Like you say, the safest place to fly, with all these lakes as landing strips."

"It's an easy decision when you ask would you rather be a day late or thirty years early, eh? In the back you'll find some life jackets. Get 'em on, but then get back, I need your weight up front with me for best handling."

Brian turned and was rocked back hard against the fuselage, but he smiled at Maureen who smiled back and reached out to help steady him. He took a step then her hand for support but still fell past her as the plane bucked again. He crawled back to sit down next to her.

"I'm never going back to Ireland," she said.

"We're safe. Dutch is looking for the right lake to set her down."

"No, I mean, that cove, that is exactly what I imagined when you told me your dreams, Bri. Let's stay here and make it come true."

Brian released her hand to scoot to the far edge of the bench where he could reach the supplies in the tail section, stowed behind cargo netting from floor to ceiling. He found just one life vest.

Maureen called out loud.

"That's Innish Cove, you said so. And it's got a golden beach."

"An' the grandest people livin' right there, like they were waitin' for us to come."

"That Joe Loon fellow, he's the last puzzle piece. I could feel he had a deep regard for us being there. So I'm sayin', let's commit to it all. Right here an' right now, eh. Let's never go back."

Brian sat back holding the life vest.

"We have to go back, don't we?"

"Not if you don't want to. I don't want to. I'm staying here, whatever your decision is."

Maureen pulled the map case from under the bench so it rested between her feet. When Brian had caught up with Maureen in Dublin at the start of the trip, this brand new map case had been waiting for him in his hotel room in the middle of his bed. Next to it was a note from Maureen that read "A magic box, to make your dreams of the Great Lodge at Innish Cove come true".

Later that evening she told him, "When we get to Kenora and we place the proper maps and notes and plans inside, the case will work its magic."

Maureen emptied the case of all the papers they had collected in their exploration and piled them on the bench between them. Then she placed the empty case on Brian's lap.

"I want us to be man an' wife. I want us to start a new life right here, as our own family, with these Ojibway Indians, with Chicago businessmen an' Texas oilmen as our guests."

She reached in the case and pulled up the false bottom and Brian had a brief glimpse of the British pounds before the plane bounced, bounced again, then dropped, deep and fast, and Maureen was thrown off the bench. Brian caught her as they both fell to the floor, and maps and charts and British pounds spilling out of the tumbling case flew all around them.

Dutch gained control and called out as Brian and Maureen found some balance.

"Get up here, Brian. I got to land my baby now."

The plane was bucking up and down and back and forth as Maureen and Brian leaned over to attend to the mess and bounced off each other again.

"Now Brian!"

Brian handed Maureen the life vest. "Put this on."

"I got this. Go."

"Okay, but put this on."

As Brian slid back between the seats, a sudden gust spilled him on top of Dutch and then dumped him back into the co-pilot's chair. It was raining hard, and the wind was howling. Quick drops followed sudden bucks, one after the other.

"There was just one vest. Maureen has it on."

"Sorry, I was sure—" He was cut short by another sudden drop. "That lake right there. That's where we'll set her down."

Dutch turned to the east, a hard port bank. Below them the thick fir forest canopy swayed and swirled and twisted in the powerful winds. Dutch fought to make a hard, tight turn back west and into the wind as he lined up the approach and the plane rocked constantly.

"I got the wind, you got reef duty."

"Reef duty?"

"There's reefs all through these lakes. Some are just under the surface of the water. On a sunny day you see 'em from the air as shadows in the water, so you can plan a landing to avoid them. Not now. But you know how to read waves, so look sharp for places where waves are breaking over rock and point it out to me right away. Don't assume I've seen it."

"Got it."

The plane dropped again.

"Lots of ways it could be a very hard landing."

In the next drop Dutch lost fifty of the three hundred feet he had planned to maintain above the trees as the lake opened just ahead.

"Maureen, brace yerself. The Dutchman has the angle he wants an' is approachin'. I'll count you down from lucky seven... six... five... four..."

A sudden wind shear sent the plane plummeting down and down until its pontoons crashed into the tops of the dense fir trees twenty yards from the edge of the lake. The plane still had enough forward momentum that it skied across the canopy as top sections of trunks and limbs bent and snapped and fell away into a natural ramp of boughs and branches that delivered the Norseman to the water in a hard, whiplashed, but controlled, landing.

While Dutch throttled back and released the pontoons' rudders to direct the taxi, everyone was still stunned, and quiet. When Dutch turned the plane and taxied towards the closest shoreline best protected from the winds, Maureen called out from the back.

"What just happened?"

Dutch was quiet, in disbelief. When he considered what had occurred, he shook his head. Brian looked back to give Maureen a smile.

"We was fallin' from the sky an' God decided to reach down an' catch us."

"Sitting right over the pontoons it sounded like claws reaching to grab us."

Dutch said, "Let's get to the shore there. We should make sure we got no punctures in any of the pontoons."

❄ ❄ ❄

The left pontoon was dented from the trunk of one of the trees they'd skied over, but neither was punctured. Dutch anchored the plane just offshore in a bay that got all the rain but deflected the winds enough that the plane gently bobbed in the heavy downpour. Night had fallen, and Maureen was in the pilot's seat, curled in a ball, facing Brian in the co-pilot's seat. Dutch had made a pallet on the floor of the fuselage from a blanket and the life vest. The beating of the rain against the plane had been loud but was softening and was finally comforting.

Maureen looked up at Brian. "Let's go ahead an' declare right now our first cabin is built before summer's end."

"You're sure?"

"I'm sure nothin' back in Ireland is half as promisin' as this is right here."

"My children are back there."

"We'll invite 'em to visit. Once they get here, they won't want to go back."

"We'll be a long time before we'll know if all that's so. It's my fear gettin' 'em here for a first visit won't happen anytime soon."

"Marry me or make me your partner, but let's decide right now to make these dreams of yours come true."

"I can't marry you, Lady Girl. Have no doubts I imagine it a sweet life... but meetin' with the solicitor to begin the plannin' of our partnership to purchase Innish Cove—I think that's the right move."

"I've met with two. I know which one I'd recommend, but I got meetin's set up with both to see what you think."

"Here's to the partnership."

They shook hands as Brian added, "We need the blessin' of the red men first. You're right, we got no business without 'em bein' a big part of it with us."

"We'll put the land purchase in motion, then come back an' help them understand how the fishin' lodge will be good for their people."

The next day Joe Loon motored his canoe to a bay in the River where a shoreline clearing was home to two wigwams and a tent. Two Ojibway women and a man appeared at the shore to offer greetings. Joe Loon asked them to come pow wow and listen to the Big White Man, for he must be a white man from Joe Loon's dream and they needed to discover which one.

Brian and Maureen visited both solicitors; the first talked about how he would handle the formation of a partnership to buy Crown land and build a fishing camp. It was the second solicitor, the one who had most impressed Maureen, who delivered the disappointing news.

"I've spent some of my own time looking into this for you, and I'm afraid the other gentleman is giving you false hope with his ideas of a schedule. What I have found out is that your acquisition of land in that sector won't be processed this year. It's not likely anyway. I've dealt with these Ministry officials many times before. Sure, they say they want to help create jobs back in the bush for the Indians. But by the time they get their surveyors in there, and then each department signs off, and there's groups within each department that will want to review it, it's going to take some time. And you're both foreigners so that will take additional paperwork. I would be leading you astray if I didn't tell you we could be well into winter before you have a clear title, and even then you're likely going to have to settle for a long-term land lease."

❉ ❉ ❉

Albert Loon sat in Nigig in the middle of one of the River's lakes, holding onto the gunwales of the small motor boat that rocked gently next to him. The young Ojibway man at the motor held Nigig steady and listened as Albert told the Ojibway elder in the bow about the Big White Man's dream and where he wanted to build cabins. The elder looked away and shook his head no, the single feather tied in his hair waving back and forth.

❉ ❉ ❉

In the chapel of a small seminary school in the West of Ireland, Eamon and his wife sat in a pew with Patrick and Katie between them. They were surrounded by the parents of the teenagers and nearly twenty-year-old boys Tommy sat with in the front pew. Tommy waited his turn to deliver a homily on The Seven Christian Virtues he had been working on for nearly a month.

❉ ❉ ❉

On a commercial side street in Dublin two men approached a music shop and entered. Kevin was in the middle of giving the long-abandoned shop a good cleaning before he would display new merchandise. "Back in business I see," one of the men said as Kevin joined them in his back room. The visitors told him some of the old guard had started meeting regularly, and they were talking about becoming fully active. Then they asked if he had heard rumors about Maureen O'Toole living in Boston with her contact from Germany with a bag full of the Nazis' gold.

❉ ❉ ❉

Many of the Keewatin Ojibway who planned to meet with Brian arrived at Joe Loon's village the day before the pow wow. The village grew as they erected tents and temporary wigwams, bending saplings into small round house frames they covered with reed mats, blankets, or fir boughs. Albert applied fresh paint to the buckskin draped over the wall of his wigwam. The Loon clan totems he refreshed were first painted long ago.

That evening the men sat in a circle around Joe Loon's fire. Many wore their heads dressed with feathers, bits of tail, or red-cloth turbans. Some bore chest plates of quill and bead or necklaces over buckskin vests.

Two drums pounded the same heartbeat. Two men shook rattles of dried hide and pebbles. As they changed to a new song cycle, one man carefully placed a bundle on the ground in front of him and unfolded the covering to remove a pipe carved from a deer's antler.

This Man stood up from the circle and began to dance All Four Directions of The Great Creator.

❄ ❄ ❄

Before Dutch flew Brian and Maureen back to the sandy shore for their meeting, he showed them there were now six life vests in stowage. When they were airborne and well on their way, he apologized again.

"That flight back was the most danger I've ever put anyone in. I am so sorry."

"Don't know it was anyone's fault we were in danger, an' if God assisted, it was still your skill made us safe."

"I'm haunted by the whole series of mistakes I made. I should check for life jackets each time I leave with guests. I should have gotten us out of there sooner. And I certainly should have landed us sooner. Or maybe I should never have taken off in the first place. I feel like I owe you something."

Maureen smiled when she heard that.

❄ ❄ ❄

When the plane passed overhead, more than a dozen canoes and boats had been pulled up on the beach and thirty or more Ojibway were waiting to hear Big White Man's dream. It was mostly Keewatin men who gathered with the older boys, but there were also a few of the older women and the young girls they had brought with them. There were also two boats of White Dog Ojibway, and three boats from Grassy Narrows, and two Metís who had been traveling through when they learned of the pow wow and stayed.

Another canoe was arriving with two more Keewatin men from the back bush as the plane taxied into the cove.

At breakfast the day before, Maureen mentioned this gathering to the hotel diner waitress who had befriended her. She advised Maureen that it was a sign of respect to bring tobacco to any gathering or ceremony with Ojibway to give to the elders. "Most folks around Kenora don't care enough about them to know much about these sorts of things. You're lucky we met." Maureen gave her a nice tip and loaded two cartons of cigarettes and a half dozen containers of snuff into the map case. As they were leaving the plane, she gave the tobacco to Brian and he approached Albert.

"If you would show me how to share these gifts of tobacco, you would be doin' me a great favor."

"You must start with the chief elder."

"Joe Loon?"

"No, he is the elder of his clan. It is Gegiwejiwebiniing who is chief elder of all the Keewatin people."

"Who are the Keewatin people?"

"Everyone knows we are the People who live in on the River in these forests."

Albert told Brian that the snuff was the preferred gift and led him to the chief elder, the man who three days earlier shook his head no when Albert met him out on the water. Next they honored Joe Loon, then the rest of the elders, then he showed Brian who he should approach next until the last cigarettes were gone.

As they settled into a large circle where a flat grassy ledge split the beach from the edge of the forest, Albert introduced Young George Fobister to Brian as the best interpreter. Brian sat next to Young George.

The women formed in a small cluster near the men's circle, and Maureen found a place near the women but close behind Brian. The drums pounded, rattles shook, and the men chanted songs.

Young George leaned close to Brian and Brian to him so they could speak softly, respectfully. "There are many spirits we honor when we pow wow. We ask them to be present here now before we begin and we wait until all have gathered. They will bring wisdom to guide us."

After the song cycle was repeated Joe Loon was ready to speak. Young George translated his words for Brian.

"He calls you Big White Man From an Island Far Away Who

Has Visited this Sacred Place in His Big Dreams. He is telling them you and Raven Hair Woman traveled from an island far away to tell us about this Big Dream. He is asking us to listen for what this Big Dream will tell our people about who you are."

Young George did not translate all of what Joe Loon said, however. When Joe Loon spoke of his own dreams, of the white man coming to destroy the River and of the white man coming to save the River, Young George knew this was not for the ears of the strangers. So Brian wasn't told that Joe Loon also said, "I know this Big Man Who Dreams of this Sacred Place is a white man from my Dreams. It was the spirits of our ancestors who died here who told me he was coming. I was standing here when I was told he was coming in my Dreams. This is where I saw him. This is why I am certain. His Big Dreams bring him to this place. This is why I am certain. I pray they are here to help us for I can see this Big Man and his Raven Hair Woman are strong and they are clever and they would be good friends. But I do not know if he is the white man who has come to help us. This we need to find out."

The song cycle was repeated, and the chief elder nodded to Young George.

"It is your time to speak," he said to Brian.

Brian looked around the circle and then found Maureen and smiled to see her. She nodded at his smile.

"I thank the men who traveled here today to hear my dreams about this place, this cove, this lake that is your home. The place I come from is a lovely island that lies far across a great ocean of water. On that island I am a fisherman. I do not trap or hunt, but like you I fish the waters there for my livelihood.

"An' even though my island is far far across the ocean I have heard that the Keewatin Ojibway are the best hunters an' the best fisherman in all the world. I have read this in magazines..." Brian wished he hadn't burned those magazine pages the night he burned his plans. "... an' I tell you that you are in my dreams, that when I dream of this place you are here. An' because you are the best hunters an' the best fishermen I want to make my dreams help you and all your people."

Brian waited as Young George translated and wondered if his

full meaning was conveyed for the men did not seem impressed with his compliment; the response was little more than one man leaning to whisper with the man next to him.

As Brian told the men his dreams and Young George translated, Maureen watched for any reaction, but there was little show of emotion.

"Next spring, when the ice melts away, we will arrive to live here an' build the first of many cabins. We will pay five dollars each day to every man who helps us build our cabins. We ask the men who work for us buildin' these cabins to bring your families here with you while we are workin' if this would please you. We will provide all the men who work for us with good food for them an' for their families, an' you can build your wigwams here or we will give you tents for shelter."

When Young George translated Brian's plans to build cabins on this cove, Maureen heard low moans and groans from the women's circle. She wondered if Brian heard it.

"The year after that, the next summer, we will hire our first fishin' guides an' pay 'em ten dollars a day when they guide. In five years we will have many more cabins so many more Americans will come to fish here. Every man sittin' here with us today will be able to work as a guide if this is what he would like to do. An' we will have many jobs here for your womenfolk as well."

Brian had not heard the women and was growing more confused that there was still so little reaction. He looked at Joe Loon who turned to the chief elder sitting next to him. An eagle feather and a red-tailed hawk feather were tied in his hair. His magic hung around his neck in a small beaded pouch. This Man sat just outside the circle at the right side of the chief.

Young George translated the chief's question for Brian.

"He asks of you to tell us what you know of this place."

Brian hesitated a moment, not sure what was being asked. "We will follow Ontario's laws for purchasin' the land, but we will always follow Ojibway customs of carin' for it."

Young George translated Brian's answer and the chief's response.

"He did not ask you this. He says the Keewatin clans know the white man will say one thing and then what they do is very different. No, he asks what is it that you know of this place."

"That it has been in my dreams for years. An' now that I see it, it is even more lovely than I dreamed. I plan to get to know it very well over the next thirty or forty years, livin' here with your people, learnin' from your people."

Again, Young George translated both ways.

"You must know what happened here during the days of our ancestors. He will tell you."

"Yes, please tell me."

"This was the time his Grandfather was a boy. That was when the white man came to Keewatin Mountain. You must travel two days north to arrive at Keewatin Mountain. The white man came to take the gold from the mountain. They say they discovered this gold so they could take it. His grandfather was called Wenjimaadob. They told Wenjimaadob to bring his brothers and the other men of his village to work for them in the gold mines. They would pay them with important coins and with gifts. This was during the time all of the People still lived on the River and in the forests. The men from Wenjimaadob's village and from other villages came to work in the gold mines for the white man for his important coins. The white man fed them good food. The white man gave them many gifts of friendship. The Hudson Bay would take the important coins for the best goods.

"Then the first winter came. Before the people left for their winter camps, the white man gave the people many blankets. The white man gave them as gifts. When the people slept under these blankets, many of them got the white man pox. Their skin began to boil and make many sores. Soon many of the people who lived near Keewatin Mountain began to die. The old women died. The babies who were not yet named died. Even the strongest men were dying of the white man pox from the blankets."

Maureen saw the oldest women, eyes closed, shaking their heads slowly, and heard their soft moans.

"A Nokomis named Weegibance was holding her dying daughter in her arms. Her daughter was holding her dying child in her arms. That was when Weegibance had a vision that if they did not defeat the white man pox, all of the People would die. In her vision she saw that only fire would defeat the white man pox. That is why she told everyone who had the white man pox to come with her to this place where we sit. She told them the only way to save our People was for them to gather their dead family members and all of the People who had the pox. They got in their canoes and they paddled for two days until they came to this place. It took many canoes to hold all the dead and dying. Even more canoes than are on the shore today. Nokomis told the People to build four large funeral fires here to burn the bodies of the dead. After all the dead were burned, the others who had the pox knew they must walk into the fire so the flames would devour them and that would end this terrible curse. The old Nokomis, Weegibance, burned herself last, after all the others. This was what they did to save our People."

Some of the old women began to rock and cry.

"The ash from the fires covered the beach. These birch trees were watered by the tears Nokomis cried as she watched so many of her People throw themselves into the fire. She heard their screams. She watched every one of the People burn. She knew soon she would be lying in those flames."

Brian heard Maureen whisper, "Good God, we can't..." but the rest of it was lost as a song cycle began, and the people chanted their grief, for everyone gathered had ancestors whose ashes had mixed with this earth and whose spirits were there now.

Before the song cycled again, Joe Loon gestured to show that he wanted to speak. The people were ready to hear his words.

"Since that day Weegibance stepped into the fire and saved our People, we have kept this place sacred. To honor the deaths of our ancestors, we have kept this place sacred. We have kept this grove of birch trees sacred to honor the tears Nokomis shed for all those who died from the white man's pox.

"What I ask you now is this. Do you see that a new time is coming? A time for us to honor the way our ancestors lived in these forests. Not just how they died."

Joe Loon paused so the men might ask each other, answer each other, and begin to frame a communal understanding of what Joe Loon asked of them. Brian waited for Young George to tell him what

Joe Loon said, but instead Young George spoke the forest language with the man sitting on his other side. Then Joe Loon showed he was ready to speak again.

"A good death honors a good life."

He paused so all his people could remember loved ones whose deaths had been good.

"When dying has pain so big that our songs and dances do not change it, that is a sorrow for the People. The People who laid themselves down in the fires here lived good lives before they died. When the terrible fever came upon them, their bodies burned for many days before they laid themselves down in the fires. Their suffering filled these forests. But before that they lived good lives. Before the white man's blankets brought them such painful death they lived true lives."

Again he paused, and Brian was growing anxious.

"I will not forget the sadness of Nokomis dying in these fires, but it is time to remember the courage she had when she was alive."

The old women had stopped their mourning sounds to listen carefully to what Joe Loon was saying. Maureen was growing anxious.

"It is a good thing that this man I will call Big Brian has brought his Big Dreams to this sacred place. Big Brian comes here to build cabins for the White Man who Love to Fish. I see that it will be good for the Keewatin clans to live with the White Man who Love to Fish at this sacred place. When they come to fish the River a good thing will happen. The spirits of our ancestors will be here whispering to them that they must protect the River from the white man who comes to destroy it. I believe this is what will happen when the White Man who Love to Fish lives with us on this sacred place and fishes the River with us. They will see the River and know it must be protected from those who will come to poison it. I say to you that Big Brian is the white man who has been sent by the Great Creator to help us protect the River. I say to you we must help him build his Dream right here."

Brian ached to learn what Joe Loon said. He felt it was for him and that the others were beginning to agree. This Man had been sitting, but now he stood behind Joe Loon.

"I hope Big Brian will give us a new name for this place. His Dream tells of a good memory for those who died here."

The people gathered there that day agreed with Joe Loon's wisdom. And when Brian and Maureen learned they had the support of the Keewatin Ojibway they excused themselves from the group and stepped away to be alone for a moment.

Maureen wanted them to embrace, but only took Brian by the arm. "It's the power of the right dream comin' true."

"My dreams. Your plans." Brian nodded to where the Ojibway were gathered. "An' now Mister Joe Loon."

They returned to the circle and listened to the magical songs and musical conjuring until Dutch told them they had to leave to beat nightfall.

Chapter 17

A NEW YEAR

IT WAS NEW YEAR'S MORNING, 1950. Maureen had just settled at a table in the diner at the Hotel Kenora. Since Brian and Maureen had been living at the hotel for the winter they had eaten in the diner every day, sometimes two meals a day. Her favorite waitress with the friendly tobacco tip approached with a menu and the makings for a pot of tea.

"Happy New Year."

"Happy New Year. Bri been down yet?"

"I've been here since we opened this morning, and I haven't seen him. There haven't been many, for that matter. Must have been lots of New Year's Eve partying going on."

"Brian was buyin' his share at the hotel pub, sorry, bar."

"You two have earned a celebration."

"An' we hadn't yet celebrated, not really. Not like last night, anyway. It took so long to get that land deal done that once we signed it, we felt so far behind, we just doubled our efforts preparin' for buildin' in the spring."

"So last night was the full razzle dazzle?"

"I'm not sure what I'm agreeing to if I say yes."

"Here he comes. I know it's going to be a Happy New Year for the two of you—you deserve it. Good morning, Brian. What can I get you?"

Brian sat down, heavy and tired, and he growled, "I hain't hungry. Tea's fine."

The waitress left.

"Someone's startin' the new year off regrettin' his razzle dazzle."

"What's that supposed to mean?"

"Seems to me I should be the aggrieved party this mornin'."

"Yeah, I knew you'd have that all worked out that way."

"Was yourself made the unwanted advances."

Brian was able to stare blankly at her smiling face.

"Unwanted? You've been wantin' my advances for weeks, for months even, an' there's no denyin' what I'm sayin'."

"You ready to get married?"

"No."

"An' that's been my answer every time you've knocked on my bedroom door at midnight askin' for a kiss."

"So then quit leadin' me there. Please just quit leadin' me there."

"Leadin' you?"

"You know what I'm talkin' about. I can see the smile in your eyes each time you see it's workin' on me that way."

"You just need to be told what you're lookin' at. It's me showin' you all the reasons you should ask me to marry you."

"Yes, it's clear by now that's your view of things, that I won't understand a situation 'less you've told me what I'm lookin' at."

The waitress returned with a cup for Brian, and while Maureen began to prepare his tea for him, she gave him a hard look.

"The minute you're truly believin' I am manipulatin' you to my advantage is when I sell you my stake an' I'm out of here. So unless you're ready to trigger that now, you can't even be makin' fun that way. I need to be boss when I need to be boss. Same for me as for yourself in that regard. That's the partnership we both agreed to."

Brian mumbled, "Sure, but then what you were doin' to me last night had nothin' to do with our business."

Maureen pushed his cup into his hands.

"Brian, try this out, just for now. Imagine for just a moment that we can live any life we want here. That Ireland is past."

"An' you consider we don't need to make a common decision on that one. You can decide one thing about that, me another."

"Can't you imagine Joe Loon tellin' you to let go of your misery if it's what's keepin' you from acceptin' the gifts Gitchi Manitou is offerin'?"

Brian hit the table with his fist, rattling his cup so that tea sloshed over the edge, rattling the cup again when he stood.

"An' you're sayin' our partnership is business only so I'm sayin' you got nothin' to say about me an' me children."

He turned and left the room. When the waitress checked with Maureen, she ordered two eggs, bacon, and toast.

❋ ❋ ❋

It was well into the summer. Above the beach at Innish Cove, spread along the flat table of forest, three work crews were felling trees.

The string of long, cold winters had continued and the ice hadn't gone from the River until early May. Then the spring was the wettest in memory, raining day after day, so Brian and Maureen and Joe Loon and the men of his village got a slow start building cabins. Brian and Joe Loon struck alternate chops with their axes against one tree. Albert and Mathew chopped another. Two Ojibway men stepped back from the third and called out as the tree began to fall.

Maureen and Simon worked behind them, Maureen with a hand ax chopping away branches from felled trees, and Simon with an ax shaping the ends of the logs.

The first cabin was built, and another half dozen trees had been felled and stripped in the small clearings their work created. Three tents and two birch bark wigwams were set up in the middle of the clearing above the beach.

Albert called out his warning, and they all looked up and stepped back as another tree crashed to the forest floor.

Maureen found herself standing close to Simon.

"My ancestors in Ireland lived like the Keewatin Ojibway live here in your forests. It was long ago, but my people had our tribal time. We were called the Celts."

"Celts were Indians?"

"Celts were Indians. When the Brits came, they thought Celts were the Indians. They took the land they wanted an' treated the whole island like it was their private reserve."

"Celts did battle with the Brits? To defend their land?"

"Some still do."

❄ ❄ ❄

The first two cabins were small but still took days to build for Brian and Maureen learned that the men were great workers when working but that they were in no hurry. They deeply enjoyed the labor, and their delight and the easy mastery of the skills needed fascinated Brian and Maureen. But often their greater interest was in talking, or watching the children playing at the camp, or taking a canoe out to work their nets, or they disappeared for days scouting new trap lines for the winter.

So it was days later that the third cabin was built, twice the size of the first two, and the day it was completed Simon led Maureen away from the work and into the forests. They hiked the steps of the forested slope to a high ridge above Innish Cove. Before they reached the top of the ridge, they found a flat shelf covered in a low sweep of blueberry bushes displaying white and pale pink blossoms so thick a special harvest was promised. As a breeze swept through, first blossoms fell. When Maureen examined the bushes more closely, she found the first small buds of young green fruit, some just beginning to darken to blue. She knew Simon was studying her study of the plants.

"It's that the practical is also beautiful. That's what always made God a loving Creator to my way of viewin' it."

"Gitchi Manitou gives many gifts to my people."

"He gave the Celts plenty. You need to do a better job protectin' yours than the Celts did protecting ours."

"Joe Loon says Big Brian is here to help protect this place. Gitchi Manitou sent dreams to Big Brian to lead him to us. This is what Joe Loon says. Because I am the grandson of Joe Loon, I believe this as well."

"Because I am Joe Loon's friend, I will believe this as well."

❄ ❄ ❄

Kevin leaned against the bar as he talked with the owner of the Donegal pub where he'd met Brian so long ago. The publican told Kevin that there were a couple of stories told about the woman he was looking for, but she had not been seen for three years, maybe four. She had been a regular for a short while, Kevin learned, with the big man from Cong.

"One story says they got married, another that he beat a man senseless who later died so he's hidin' in London."

❄ ❄ ❄

Brian sat in the middle of Joe Loon's freight canoe, Albert in the bow, Joe Loon in the stern, all three with fishing poles jigging steep underwater shelves twenty yards off the rocky point that separated two quiet bays.

This Man stood knee-deep in the water, just around the point, a fish spear cocked above his ear. This Man was as motionless as the Great Blue Heron standing next to him, posed for common purpose, poised to the same intent.

Joe Loon and Albert were showing Brian that a day of fishing the River and its lakes with guests would best begin jigging or trolling for walleyes in the morning, and that the guests' lunch should be fixed on shore and built around filleting and frying the morning's catch.

Brian put his fishing pole aside to take a letter from his back pocket just as Albert reeled in another walleye. Albert removed the hook from the fat, flapping fish and Brian asked him if the hunters from Wiishkoonsing would come again in the winter.

"I was hopin' I could give you this letter to give to the hunters you guide."

Albert told Joe Loon of Brian's request. Joe Loon answered and Albert reported back to Brian.

"Yaway, that is a good idea. You are writing to ask them to tell their friends about this fishing camp."

"Yes. That's right. Good guess."

"No, I did not guess. Joe Loon told me."

"What a clever man."

"Last night he told me of his dream that the hunters from Wiishkoonsing would come fish the River and stay in our cabins."

❄ ❄ ❄

Dutch's Norseman landed and he taxied into the cove and over to the beach. There was a boat tied to the pontoon struts. Four cabins were completed and the walls were nearly done for a fifth, another of the smaller cabins. The men were happy to break from their labor and some stood in the water as others balanced on the pontoon to untie the brand new sixteen-foot fishing boat and lower it into the water. Then they unloaded a ten horsepower Johnson outboard from the plane.

Brian told Albert this was the boat and motor he planned to use the next summer. Each boat would be outfitted to carry two fishermen and their guide.

"What I'd like you an' Joe Loon to do is drive this boat up an' down the River the rest of the summer. I will buy five more of these boats for next summer if you tell me it is a good one."

※ ※ ※

A large movie camera on a tripod was set up next to the ancient and rough-hewn stone cross that split the village of Cong's quiet main street. The camera operator waved Kevin away when he stepped into his shot of the street. Kevin stepped aside, and then approached the camera man.

"Do you know where I might find Brian Burke? He's a big fellow, perhaps he's 30."

"Can't help ya there, buddy. I'm from the States, from Los Angeles, California. I'm just scouting some locations for a movie we're planning on shooting here next year. Sounds like you folks'll be hosting John Wayne in your little village."

"John Wayne? He's a cowboy actor."

"He's playing a son of Ireland in this one. This is one of the locations they're interested in."

※ ※ ※

Kevin knew an old Fenian radical living in Carrick, the village just to the west of Cong, and he traveled there next. After they spoke of old times and common friends, they turned to current events.

"I wasn't bettin' against your revival now, Kevin, but I wouldn't have placed a wager for you neither. First we're too friendly wit da feckin' Communists, an' then you go make a deal wit da feckin' Nazis an' those are big mistakes to overcome."

"I wasn't sure we'd make it back. And we've got Reds and Fascists among us still, no doubt. But some from before have come together to start charting a new course, and there's some good new blood coming in."

"I don't think I'm able to join you this time round, Kev."

"You'd be welcome to name your tune if you did, Seamus. You've done your part and some bit more. But I am in need of someone to be me eyes and ears, especially in Cong, so if not you, do you know of someone I should be talking to?"

"Cong? Nothin' has happened there worth notin' in two hundred years. Whatcha after?"

"A fellow who once lived there, Brian Burke."

"Sure, I know of him, and his cousin, Eamon. There was some trouble between them a few years back, and Brian was driven away, so I been told."

"Well, I'd like to find him. We think he may be able to lead us to someone we'd be very interested in talking to."

"There is a young fella I know, not much more 'an a boy, but his da knows some of me secrets an' has whispered his lad has a natural Fenian view."

"Can you put me in touch with him?"

"He's the local hurlin' hero. Marvelous midfielder. There's a match at our local pitch tomorrow. Can you stay 'til then?"

"Can you put me up?"

"Like it was the old times."

❄ ❄ ❄

The Norseman was tied to the brand-new dock that carried ten yards out into Innish Cove from the beach. Six log cabins had been built among the trees above the beach, a small log shed sat on the shore near the foot of the dock where supplies would be kept, and another small log building sat on a rocky ledge above the cove to serve as an ice house. Brian and Maureen stood on the dock with Joe Loon and Albert and Old George. Dutch was completing his pre-flight check. Simon and Mathew loaded Brian and Maureen's duffle bags into the plane's cargo door.

Brian shook Albert's hand. "It will be a happy day when I am standin' here with you again come spring."

"Joe Loon says he is honored you have asked him to be your number one guide."

"I will always give Joe Loon the number one guests."

"He says you must always place the most difficult white man in his boat."

Chapter 18

CUTTING ICE

IT WAS THE MIDDLE OF THE THIRD harsh Ontario winter. Albert broke a trail in the deep snow for Joe Loon, Old George, Louis Assiniboine, Simon, and Mathew as they snowshoed the deeply drifted snow that blanketed the River's frozen lake. Old George and Louis pulled small sleds carrying supplies. Axes and saws were tied on top of one bundle of blankets and cook gear; shovels and a pick and a kerosene lantern were tied on top of the other. They had been laying traps at opportune places along the way, and two traps were still part of their load. Louis stepped up to take Albert's place, and they continually changed duties to keep their steady pace.

Just before the early dusk turned to full nightfall, they arrived at the cabins they had built with Big Brian during the summer. They trudged up to the largest cabin, dug the snow away from the front of the door, and entered. Before they left the cabins at the end of the summer they had stocked this one with firewood, and Brian had Dutch fly in a load of canned goods. As soon as they arrived, Simon began building a fire in the stove and they heated beans and slices of canned ham.

After they ate, they built pallets of furs and blankets around the stove to sleep. Joe Loon settled in next to Albert. The lantern had been blown out, the room was dark, and in the darkest corner This Man sat with a blanket over his shoulders.

When Joe Loon spoke it was of a recent sadness to all lying in darkness.

"We must remember last spring. We must always remember that the sons of Adam Angeconeb did not come back from the white man's school."

This Man began a soft lament.

"We must not forget these two boys were beaten to death by a white man wearing the sign of Jesus the Christ. With a stick in his hand he beat these two boys until the Great Creator released them from their pain."

"I have been told their mother still mourns for them with her tears each night."

"The mother and father did not find out their sons were dead until the other children returned to Grassy Narrows from the school. Their sons were not with them. That is when they were told they were dead."

"Adam Angeconbeb is drinking all the whiskey. He has joined the people who sit by the side of the streets in Kenora and cry of their loss."

"The children knew what had happened to their sons because these brothers were beaten many times. They saw much bleeding from deep cuts on their backs and their legs."

"I have been told they were forced to watch these brothers get beaten."

"That is why none of our children will go to the white man's school."

"Before the ice leaves they will come looking for our children in the winter cabins. They must not find them."

They were quiet for some time, considering how they would protect the children from those who would carry them away to the white man's school.

After a while Mathew asked, "Grandfather. Even though I did not receive a vision, is it true I am no longer a child?"

"Without a vision you are a man who will decide his own fate."

❀ ❀ ❀

Their solicitor was reading a file. Brian and Maureen sat across the room from each other, reviewing copies of the incorporation document that would launch their float plane airline. They had been discussing how much of Northwest Ontario Airline Dutch should own. The general plan was to buy Dutch's plane from him at a fair price and guarantee him a salary equal to his best year's profit, along with an owners' interest in the business. They were working on his fair equity share of NOA.

The solicitor's assistant appeared at the door, knocking for his attention.

"Sir, Mr. Taylor says he needs you right now on the Dryden Pulp contract."

"Sorry folks, we've been trying to wrestle this one down for days now, our largest client and all, they're buying out a competitor, it's a big deal. I'll be just a moment, you carry on reviewing the contracts." And he was out the door.

NOA was created out of Maureen's vision. She had recruited Dutch's enthusiastic agreement that together they could expand the company many times larger than he would be able to on his own, and once he admitted to himself that he would rather be a pilot than a businessman, he listened closely.

Maureen's other recruitment ideas were taking much more time than she ever imagined, and when she finished reading the agreements she reached out her leg and nudged Brian with her foot.

"Wouldn't this all be so much easier if you'd just ask me to marry you? We'd get rid of the expense of maintainin' the partnership and just put everythin' in your name."

"I thought we agreed we'd only talk about that topic with a drink in hand, to cut the edge of me sayin' no again to the lovely woman's offer."

"I can't accept you don't want to marry me."

"We're preparin' our grand openin' of Eden, an' now we launch our bush plane operation in partnership with our Dutchman who seems true to his word an' a good man to be workin' with. We've got nearly thirty guest nights booked at camp. Why mess with what we got, is one way of lookin' at it. An' I never said I didn't want to, only I can't, is another."

"We could be havin' heroic fucks."

Brian sat up and Maureen smiled.

"Which I offer to you as a third way to be lookin' at it."

"Now look here, Lady Girl, you can't be talkin' like that in this man's office an' then be pushin' me away when—"

"I think I could just about guarantee our weddin' night would be sometin' very much like a heroic fuck."

The solicitor walked in, smiled, sat at his desk with his files, and returned to his study of them.

"An' so doesn't that mean we'd want to do it a lot?"

"It sure hain't my idea to be waitin' on that."

"As long as we're business partners, I'm tellin' you as long as *all* we are is business partners, I'm not riskin' my stake in what we are doin' here by becomin' your whore."

The solicitor's attention was pulled away from his study. He stole a quick glance at his two clients and saw them sharing a smile so he returned to his documents.

The Ojibway cleared the snow from a wide section of the frozen lake, close to camp. They chipped a hole in the thick ice sheet to allow them to insert first one saw, then another. Referencing the hole as the corner, Old George and Albert sawed away at a 90 degree angle.

They were cutting thick sheets of ice for the fishing camp's use in the summer.

Each of them would take a turn sawing the rock-hard ice, and while they waited they stood together in the bright sun, protecting each other from the cold wind.

As Joe Loon took the saw from Old George he turned to Simon and Mathew.

"If the men from the white man's school come before we have left Grassy Narrows, we must have places for the children all to hide. You show the children the best places you have found."

"Why is it we do not say no to these men, Grandfather?"

"They send men with guns who take the children if we say no."

"I have heard the boys on the Reserve talk of playing games at the schools."

Albert was the only one there who had spent time in a residential school.

"The games we played were not dances of joy. The games I

played with boys from White Dog and Red Lake were streaked with anger."

❄ ❄ ❄

As soon as the ice was gone in front of their dock and office on Lake of the Woods, Dutch would fly Maureen and Brian to Innish Cove to see what was to be seen there. They were at NOA's office on a sunny afternoon. Dutch and Brian were up on the roof, hammering the new NOA sign to the frame, and Maureen was smiling below.

"Hey Dutch, last week you predicted the ice would be gone before the week was out."

"You'll be surprised how fast it goes when it goes, especially if we have a few more days this warm. I said it would be Wednesday or Thursday, and I'm sticking with that... most times the waters up there are a couple of days behind us here anyway, so don't be surprised the day we can fly out here we still can't land there."

"I got a feelin' we'll find 'em waiting there for us, don't you, Bri?"

"I find myself eager to see Joe Loon."

Dutch started collecting the tools. "How do you do it, Brian?"

"Do what?"

"Get these Indians to work for you, for both of you. You see 'em dead drunk around town, beating their wives, kicking and fighting each other. Everyone knows you can never count on Indians to do what they say they're going to do; it's not nice to say it but plenty do, and worse, I know, but it's the truth. Yet they sure seem to enjoy working for you two."

"Best I can tell is we showed up at a time they seemed to be expectin' us."

Maureen called up to them.

"An' they see our camp as somehow honorin' their sacred place. It all ties together; I'm still tryin' to figure it out."

"Just know that when I tell folks about what I saw last summer, folks who only know Indians from what they see in town, they look at me with total disbelief. And they predict you are in for a big disappointment at some point."

Brian called down to Maureen.

"I was thinkin' about how Joe Loon handled our request to

build there and wondered what would happen if we brought him home to Ireland an' let him speak his peace to the lot of them thugs who claims to be IRA now."

"They ain't all thugs, Bri, an' I wish you'd stop sayin so."

Chapter 19

THE QUIET MEN

IT WAS EARLY IN THE MORNING, SPRING 1951. It was still dark when Eamon Burke awakened ten-year-old Patrick and told him to get dressed, then fixed him a cup of tea with plenty of cream and a slice of bread thick with butter. In the past year the boy had begun to grow out of the worst of his sickly and fragile childhood, but he was still slight, certainly less than robust, and still subject to incapacitating spells. Eamon got him out for long and steady walks every morning he could.

They headed down the road to Eamon's nearby field where he kept a few head of cattle. A calf had been born the night before. Eamon attended to the birth, returned to sleep a couple of hours, and was eager to show the newborn beauty of it to Patrick.

When they arrived, the calf was sleeping on a sweep of straw under the small shelter of stones and posts and sheets of tin. The cow was eating hay. Patrick approached the calf and Eamon stood behind him, then crouched down over him, and spoke soft and low, whispering to the boy that he should love the sight of her as the calf awoke.

"Look at her, lad. She's so new, so fresh."

"Her eyes look like they're liquid."

"Watch the gentle breath comin' in… an goin' out. Comin' in… an' goin' out. Feel my chest, breathin' in… an' breathin' out. Now you fill yourself up, nice an' easy but as full as you can… then let it out. Fill your lungs, make your chest work, lad, good, an' as you do, take the young strength of her into you with your breath an' hold it deep... before you let it out slow an' easy sayin' thanks be to God."

Eamon heard the car's roar from the road behind them and then the stone wall in front of them shone bright in the headlight beam. The calf tripped on her own legs as she jumped to her feet.

Eamon turned with a frown for the driver, and his frown became a scowl as the big black touring car roared in its approach, slowed as it passed, and then stopped to back up, and when it did Eamon took bold strides towards the rock wall between him and the road.

The man driving the car was the movie actor, Victor McLaglen. Next to him sat John Wayne. They had arrived in Cong the day before for the filming of *The Quiet Man* and were on the road early to spend a couple of days in Dublin engaged in a bit of publicity work and pub crawling while final production details were sorted out.

McLaglen had a great smile as he tapped his traveling companion on the shoulder and gestured towards Eamon.

"Jaysus, Johnny boy, there he is."

"There who is?"

"Well, there you are, Johnny boy, there you are. When I saw him I thought I'm sitting in a motorcar with Johnny Wayne but there he is walking across the field. He's your double, your body double. Your stand in."

"Ya think so? Well then, let's go check 'im out."

Eamon's fists tightened when he saw the car doors open, then relaxed when he recognized one of the two big men who got out was Victor McLaglen. He checked Patrick, who had a hand upon the calf's hind leg, studying her as she nursed eagerly.

When Eamon met the actor, they shook hands across the rock wall and then Eamon turned to point out the scene behind him.

"Now that's how you should open your film. Let everyone know we're not just raisin' sheep an' fightin' the Brits."

"That's the intention of this one, best I can tell, to show the pastoral splendor."

"We'd all heard the Magnificent McLaglen had arrived. I've seen a number of your filims, an' loved each one."

"Well, then, good morning to you, and how do your friends call you?"

"I'm Eamon Burke. Had a calf born last night, just checkin' on her. That's my nephew there, young Patrick. He's..." Eamon turned back to the actor. "Ah now, *The Informer*. What a grand bit of storytellin' that was."

"It was good work, and we've got us the same director for this one, Mr. John Ford himself."

"That's who you are then, Mr. Ford?"

"No, no. No. I'm John Wayne."

"John Wayne the actor? Of course you are, I can see it when I picture a cowboy hat an' a vest an' all... sorry, but it's English filims that mostly gets shown, if any."

Wayne punched McLaglen on the shoulder. "That's the third time since we arrived they've known you and not me." He turned to Eamon. "You see, we've got a little problem here with our Irish film, and we were thinking maybe you can solve it for us. Let's go sit in the car where it's warm and we'll tell you about it."

"Sure, of course. Let me grab my boy. He won't recognize either one of ya.'"

❄ ❄ ❄

Katie helped her aunt lay out the breakfast, and as the four of them settled in Eamon told his wife about meeting the movie actors.

"An' so as our American cousins say, they get right to it. They're lookin' for a body double for Mr. John Wayne to do his stunts for him an' his ridin', an' they figure I'm the man for the job."

"Ah, Eamon, how grand. I've been told they're payin' wonderful wages."

"We're to meet when they return from Dublin so they can introduce me to John Ford. He directed Victor in *The Informer*."

"Did you hear, Katie? Your uncle Eamon is callin' him Victor."

Eamon's wife slipped the last sausage off her plate and onto her husband's.

"Another servin' for the true quiet man."

He thanked her with a pat on her back and carved a piece.

"What I find interestin' about this..." Eamon was quiet as he chewed. He took another bite, and everyone at the table could see he was shaping his thoughts, so they ate in silence.

"I just think it's interestin'... It was two days ago that I found myself thinkin' about Brian. I don't know what it was that brought him to mind. Maybe I saw Jimmy earlier in the day an' that triggered my memories of bailin' Brian out of trouble. An' so I was thinkin' about whether he ever got his fishin' lodge built... the Great Lodge at Innish Cove, that's what came to me first actually, I just suddenly thought of the name an' then startin' considerin' if it was built, an' it must have been because earlier I had seen Jimmy at the market."

Katie moved her chair closer to Patrick at the mention of their father's name so she could put her arm around his shoulders.

"An' sure he's my cousin but ya' know when we was growin' up he as more like my little brother, yeah. So I do think about him from time to time... Not very often. It's a surprise of sorts that I don't think about him for months... But then somethin' from our past stirs up a memory an' I find I can't get him off my mind for days."

He ate another bite of sausage. That released his wife to get up to clear the table, and Katie led Patrick outside, told him to stay there, and then returned, standing inside the door. "Because you know, mostly the memories of him are good ones... So suddenly I have these thoughts of Innish Cove an' for the past two days I have been thinkin' about him an' now I am John Wayne's body double. He calls me his close companion."

As she worked his wife listened closely, and now showed confusion on her face.

"One of his best ideas, everyone thought so, was once he gets set up, once he knows he can operate a fishin' lodge, he would invite famous American outdoorsmen to come as his guests, for free. He always said he'd invite Ernest Hemmingway but the last time I heard him tell the story he swapped him out for John Wayne."

When he stopped they were all quiet in the face of what he might say next. He took the last bite of sausage and it was Katie who spoke next.

"Just don't let him get too close to Patrick."

"What's that?"

"If you invite him to come, if he returns, just don't let him hurt Patrick again."

※ ※ ※

Joe Loon was carrying one last bundle through dusk to the freight canoe outfitted with his 5-hp motor. This big canoe was beached on shore where it was just a thirty-yard walk from their winter camp cabins at Grassy Narrows Reserve. When his people first spent the winter on the Reserve four years earlier, they chose these cabins at the edge of the Reserve, right on the River, and the others honored their claim.

They loaded their belongings and supplies into the three big canoes and the fishing boat Brian left for their use. They kept Nigig free of supplies.

They planned to leave the Reserve early the next morning, to set up their village camp at Innish Cove.

Joe Loon froze when he heard the rifle shot echo through the trees. He imagined the rifleman working the bolt, ejecting the shell, chambering a second round, lifting the rifle to his shoulder to aim at the high trunk of a tree, and pulling the trigger. At that moment, he heard the second shot.

He pulled the bundle from the freight canoe and dropped it on the ground. He quickly shifted other bundles into the canoe and the fishing boat. He started one outboard, and then the other, looking towards the cabins in the forest, as if he expected someone.

At the second rifle shot, Simon bolted from his cabin to dash between trees to the neighboring cabins. He pounded on the doors and called to the people inside.

"All the children. To the River. Now. Run."

After he warned those closest, he headed further inland to the next cluster of cabins where Albert and Mathew and their family stayed that winter. He could hear voices, then shouting, but it was getting dark and the forests were thick there, and he couldn't see anyone.

As he drew closer, he could tell it was a white man's voice that he heard.

"Hold him. Hold him!"

Two young girls ran through the trees towards Simon and he urged them on to the River.

"Don't stop. The canoes are ready. Run."

He drew near to the cabins and crouched when he saw Albert was being held back by two men in bright-red Royal Canadian Mounted Police uniforms. An old grandmother beat on one uniformed back. Other women called out to the three Ojibway boys being led away by two more Mounties and a man in a suit.

Two of the boys were very young. The third was his cousin, his Big Brother, Mathew.

They disappeared in the forest. Albert was quiet. The women wailed.

Simon stayed low and circled the cabin clearing then headed into the trees in a quick trot. The path the Mounties followed led to an old logging track cut in the forest that led to a narrow paved road, but the path took many turns to get there, and they would have trouble navigating as night began to fall. Simon's course was direct through the forest.

More light penetrated the forest as he neared the paved road, and Simon got to it first. A small panel truck sat with its back doors open and two Mounties stood guard over the Ojibway children already inside. Two RCMP cars were parked behind the truck.

Simon removed his knife from its sheath and held it between his teeth. On his hands and knees he crawled to the edge of the thick underbrush of Juneberry bushes that grew closest to the road, near the front of the truck. The Mounties had their backs to him and were telling each other stories of chasing these children through the forest.

"It's the little girls that surprise me. I've never seen my daughter's friends run so fast."

"It's the looks on their faces. You'd think we were here to hurt them."

Simon crouched low and crawled out from under the bushes to the front of the truck. He dropped to his belly and snaked under the front of the truck. Underneath, he slowly inched his way to the back, without a sound, where he was in easy reach of both Mounties.

He took his knife in his hand, and one by one, practiced the cutting moves it would take to slice through their boots and sever an Achilles tendon of each one. He had used this knife to cut through plenty of tough moose and deer sinews and tendons, and he thought about how hard his cut must be to disable each Mountie, to cut through boot leather and tendon.

Then he practiced the motions again, faster this time, first the Mountie on his left, then the one to his right.

The Mounties stepped forward when shouts from the forest announced the approach of the next captives. Simon scooted back under the middle of the truck. He saw the feet of his friends and relatives and heard their footsteps above him as they were loaded into the truck. There was a crash of someone falling, and one of the Mounties laughed, and another cursed.

The truck doors slammed shut. Car doors squeaked open and slammed closed.

Simon inched over to the left rear tire and began to drill a hole in the rubber with the tip of his knife. When he heard the air escaping, he shifted over to the right rear tire as, one by one, the truck and car engines started. The two RCMP cars began to roll forward slowly. The knifepoint cut chips and curls of rubber tire, and Simon felt it penetrate. The blade stabbed deeper into the tire than he planned just as the truck began to move. The knife was ripped from his hands, stuck in the tire. He grabbed for the knife in the turning tire, and the blade cut his fingers just before he flattened himself for the truck to pass over him. As soon as it did, he jumped to his feet and dashed into the bushes. If the men saw him, they were satisfied with their full load and let him go on into the dark woods.

Simon hid behind a tree to pull off his shirt and wrap his hand tightly, for it was bleeding steadily. He watched the cars lead the truck holding the children. Their headlights came on all at once to glaze the trees with a brilliant edge. Once they were gone, he returned to the spot where he had laid and looked for his knife.

Inside the panel truck, in the dark, Mathew sat in a corner. A small boy leaned against him, a younger girl was nearly on his lap.

"Listen to me, my brothers and sisters. This is what I will do. I will tell my spirit to stay here. My spirit will wait for me here, for my spirit must live on the River, and in these forests. You will decide if that is what is best for your spirit. But I am telling my spirit to stay here with my people."

Simon trotted in the darkness back to the River. His hand was still bleeding and two of his fingers were growing numb when he tried to grip. He nearly stumbled over a young boy hiding under a bush. He took him by the hand and they headed down the slope to Joe Loon who stood silhouetted at the shore.

Joe Loon had loaded his canoe with five children and Old George took them to Three-Headed Rock. The fishing boat held three more children and Joe Loon had waited for more to emerge from the darkness but had just sent it off with Louis Assiniboine when Simon and the boy arrived.

"What did you see?"

"Men in uniforms with guns. They captured many of our children. Mathew was with them. They caught Stevie Angenconeb. They caught Louis Strong. I saw the daughters of John Fobister being led away."

"Your hand is bleeding."

Joe Loon opened a bundle to use the cloth that wrapped it. He examined his grandson's hand then rubbed some medicine from the bag around his neck on the wounds.

"Gitchi Manitou, you know of this brave son of the Keewatin People. We ask his hand to be strong when you have healed his wound." He tied the wrap around the wound.

"You will take Nigig. It will be dark when you get to Three-Headed Rock. I have told them no fires tonight, so you must watch carefully for them for there is no moonlight."

The boy climbed into the bow of Nigig and took up a paddle as Simon settled into the stern. The wounded fingers felt better pressed against the wood. Joe Loon held Nigig steady as they settled in, then pushed it from shore.

"We will be there tomorrow. Then we will travel together to Big Brian's cabins and wait for him."

❋ ❋ ❋

The pub had been crowded every night since the movie crew arrived, and tonight was more crowded still. John Ford just bought a round for his table, so John Wayne, Victor McLaglen, Barry Fitzgerald, and Eamon Burke turned for his toast.

"Here's to blue skies, to lovely women…" he lifted his eye patch just a bit and acted as if he was searching, "… and to more lovely women."

After they drank, he picked the conversation up again with Eamon.

"You can ride?"

"There's a two-mile horse race at some big sand dunes just north of here. They call it The Race to The Sea—"

A couple of old-timer pub regulars were seated so close at the next table that their chairs nearly touched, and one of them leaned over to interrupt, nodding at Eamon.

"This fella here, when he won the race last year, 'twas his third victory in five years. No man alive but Eamon Burke himself has had such a reign of success at the Race."

"We've got a big racing scene in our movie. I'd like to hear more about how your race is staged."

The other old-timer took his turn.

"Ah no, Mister Hollywood man, nothin' staged about it. He wins 'em on the square."

"And you can take a punch?"

The first old-timer spoke up again.

"No, now, there I gotta say no man 'round here has ever dared throw one his way."

John Wayne knew the outcome was assured.

"He's the man for the job, if you ask me, and it sure seems like my vote about my double should count for something."

"Welcome to the movie business, Eamon."

❋ ❋ ❋

As closing time approached, it was just Victor McLaglen, Barry Fitzgerald, and Eamon sitting at their table, but with the actors buying drinks for the house there were a number of locals at the other tables.

"Can I ask your opinion about somethin' here Victor?"

"Ah, I got lotsa opinions, bucko, which one ya want?"

"It's about a cousin of mine. His name is Brian Burke."

All night three local lads, one fifteen, one sixteen, one eighteen, had been working their way to a table closer to Eamon. They finally made their destination when the old-timers left.

The sixteen-year-old had spent the evening with an eye on

Eamon as he was shaping his new hurling stick with a small fine file. He tapped the table with the file to quiet the other two.

"He left here a couple a' years ago, yeah, with plans of buildin' a fishin' lodge somewhere in the wilds of Canada. He was thinkin' Ontario before he left."

Eamon gave a brief description of Brian's dream for the Canadian fishing camp, mindful of it being the first time he had told Brian's story, and he was pleased with his effort even before Victor spoke with such enthusiasm.

"Now that's the business we should be in, creating adventures, real adventures, every day treating your audiences as guests and your guests as audiences."

"You sound like my cousin talkin' about it."

"Somewhere I went astray and decided to make believe. Let's get into this with him, yes, sir. He's looking for investors is what I feel coming next, so I'm saying bring it on."

Eamon's smile didn't last long.

"I don't know anythin' at all about what he's up to. I'm sorry to say we haven't spoken since he left."

"A movie concept of the wayward one, going off to make good, and he's vanished until he does?"

"Which movie was that?

"I'm saying once you know the plot you can see it coming in scripts time and again."

"I suppose that's as good a summary for his life as another. I don't know if he's got the camp built, or if it is still bein' planned. Or even if he's in Chicago to stay. But if he built it, when he did, his plan was to send invitation letters to movie actors like you and John Wayne, invitin' you to come, for free, to stay as his guest. That's what I was goin' to ask you about, would you be interested in that sort of offer?"

"Ah, now what a grand gesture. That's marvelous, in fact. I know ol' Johnny boy is a true sporting man. I've seen him with a shotgun at his shoulder, shooting like he's John Wayne. He's likely to be interested. As for me, as soon as we're wrapped up with this picture, I'll be ready to go."

"Do you think with John bein' here, you bein' here—for the next two months is what Mr. Ford said I should set aside—do you think if I could track down my wayward Cos an' invited him to come see you, you two could meet with 'im?"

"Of course. We'll sit right here and toast his success and damn the rest."

❋ ❋ ❋

At closing, the pub emptied quickly. A horse and cart waited on the curb as two men climbed in, shouted good-byes, and clip-clopped down the street while Eamon reminded the actors how to find their accommodations.

The local lads who listened for Brian Burke's story stayed as close to Eamon as they dared. Finally, they were alone in the street. The eighteen-year-old, the biggest lad, implored the fellow spinning his hurling stick in his hands.

"I'm sayin' no, we don't tell him. I don't want to do nothin' could feck with this movie makin', anyone could see the reasonin' in that. They're payin' me da just to take pictures of his cottage for Christ's sake."

The younger lad was timid but clear.

"Tony's right, there's plenty makin' more the next couple of months than they do in two years of feckin' sod cuttin' or sellin' their wool."

Tony was certain. "Let's give 'em a feckin' chance here."

The hurling lad rested his stick on his shoulder.

"This woman's been disappeared for nearly ten years now, no one has a bead on where she went except maybe she ran off with Brian Burke. An' now we're handed important pieces of information to find her. An' you say don't tell Kevin?"

"At least wait 'til the filim is done."

"Not when others are lookin' for her as well as us. And on the chance Russell did get the 50,000 pounds he was after, Kevin is sayin' we should treat it as a race, not a search. Well, me boyo's, I know a winnin' edge when I see one, and our chances of winnin' the race just got a whole lot better."

He flipped his stick off his shoulder and twirled at his side. "An' I like winnin'." He hit an imaginary ball for a long looping ride with a good, full swing. They all felt the power in the whoosh of sound and air.

"So you can let me take all the credit when I visit Kevin tomorrow, or you can make a bus trip with me an' share the glory an' we'll have us a little fun in Dublintowne."

Chapter 20

SOMEONE'S COMING

TWO BOATS WERE TROLLING just above the wide falls that dropped straight down ten feet.

Joe Loon operated the outboard for the lead fishing boat with Brian in the middle and Albert in the bow seat. Albert was reeling in another walleye.

Each time they passed over the hole marked twenty yards off shore by the big rock with the scrubby stunted pine growing out of the rock's crack, they caught at least one walleye.

Simon guided the second boat along the same path to similar success. Maureen was the only fisherman with him.

A large, wooden box was tied in the bow of each boat. Both boxes were painted green, each with a distinct Ojibway pictograph of a walleye painted red on the lid.

The engines rumbled low in reverse, the boats piloted so their broad flat sterns' resistance maintained slow, steady trolling speeds.

The top of the falls was close and its sound was less a crashing roar and more a deep rumbling purr. Brian felt full of the purr, and as Albert netted a walleye he called to all who would hear him.

"All I gotta do is make sure the coffee's hot in the mornin' an' the steaks are cooked right for supper. If we do that, Lady Girl, an' you gentlemen of the forest bring our guests to places like this all day, they will have to agree they have found that bit a' Eden in the north woods we promise 'em. Them hard-edged Chicago businessmen will find a good fight in this action an' peace in this place an' it's great smiles an' grand stories they'll take home with 'em."

Brian turned to Albert.

"I hope Joe Loon understands your people have become my people. Anythin' he needs from me, he just has to ask."

"He asks you do you understand you are needed here."

Brian looked to see if Maureen was listening. Her head was cocked their way, but she was studying the shoreline, and rumbling water and coughing motor sounds filled the air.

"I am needed here?"

"We believe the white man who stay in the cabins will tell stories of this place to their children. We believe their children will come to see if the stories are true. They will fish here with their grandchildren. When their grandchildren have grown, they will tell their sons the stories of the first days they fished the River. Their stories will be filled with the spirits of this place. They will help us protect this place for our grandchildren."

"Protect it?"

"From the white man coming who would destroy the River."

"Why would anyone do that?"

"We do not know who they are. We know they are coming."

"This is what Joe Loon's dream is tellin' you?"

"It is telling us we must stop them. It is telling us you are here to help us stop them."

"Well, as soon as you see them, point 'em out to me."

"We are watching."

"I'll put my war paint on when you find them. Did your ancestors put paint on their faces when they went into battle?"

"Only when our enemy was worthy."

"Is this enemy worthy?"

"We have not met him yet."

❋ ❋ ❋

The small windows of the Mackintosh Residential School provided narrow views of the lovely spring-green countryside that surrounded the two-story brick building. Right behind the school a playground was defined by the large cinder-covered yard. Ojibway children laughed as they tossed balls and chased one another and lined up for the swings and the slide.

The boys wore uniforms of gray work shirts, thin denim pants, and canvas slipper shoes. The girls had similar shirts and shoes and denim skirts. Each item of clothing was numbered—on the back of the shirt, on the hip of the pants or skirt, and on the side of each shoe.

Each child had been assigned that number.

The cinder yard was surrounded by a three-inch high cement curb painted bright yellow. Beyond the curb the meadow was vibrating with emergent life. And beyond the meadow was a forest of birch and aspen where young leaves shimmered and quaked.

Mathew Loon was number fourteen. He stood alone in the far corner of the cinder yard, the tips of his shoes at the edge of the yellow curb. In just a moment he would sing the meadow lark's song back to the bird that had been teaching it to him. Mathew had never heard this lovely song before for they are indeed birds of the open fields, not found in the deep forests of the Keewatin Ojibway.

The school was run by the Jesuits, and two brothers stood together, arms folded, watching the children. One brother paid attention to Mathew.

"Watch number fourteen. Watch what happens. This is how it started yesterday."

Soon after Mathew began the meadow lark's song the children running closest to him slowed their step, then came to a stop, then drifted his way to stand with him. It didn't take long for three children, then five children, all from Grassy Narrows, to come to stand with him, watching the grasses dance with the wind, smiling at Mathew's song and at all the birds' songs.

The oldest girl, near Mathew's age, began to whistle the pine siskin's song.

Then two young boys answered with a redeye vireo duet, the long sequence handled as a round.

Another girl mimicked the black and white warbler, and as her call ended and the boy who sang to the song sparrow began, Mathew was compelled. He had to stand out in the meadow, in the midst of the songs and the wind and the sun and the purple and green grasses, to join the songs and the celebration. He stepped over the curb, one careful step followed by another, then one more, before he stopped.

He sang again, then took two more steps, his hands open to feel the tall grasses tickle his palms.

The brothers shook their heads, one smiling, the other frowning. The smiling brother said, "He did that yesterday."

"And you didn't strap him?"

"He came right back when I called him."

"And then you explained he's not to cross the curb again, eh?"

"That's right. He understood me. I thought so, anyway."

"That's why you have to strap them when they're new, so they understand the meaning of rules. Especially this one. The others look to him as their leader."

The leather strap unrolled as the brother removed it from his coat pocket and stepped towards Mathew. He called back over his shoulder.

"You have to be toughest on the oldest."

He approached number fourteen, the strap flapping at his side, the children scurrying out of his way.

❋ ❋ ❋

Brian and Maureen stood at the end of the dock and watched Dutch bank over the ridgeline in the freshly-painted bright yellow Norseman with the red NOA stencil on the tail. Dutch lined up his landing and sent a rooster tail of spray flashing silver when the pontoons broke the water's surface.

Joe Loon and Albert and Old George waited with Brian and Maureen on the dock, for in Dutch's plane were the first guests of the Great Lodge at Innish Cove. All of the Ojibway who lived there were watching—the women and youngest children from the village camp set up above the beach, the men and boys standing between dock and sheds.

Maureen waved when Dutch taxied up to the dock. Brian caught the wing strut and slowed the plane to stop dockside. Albert and Old George stepped forward to tie the pontoons. The cargo door opened, and out stepped Brian's first guests.

"Gentleman, welcome to the Great Lodge at Innish Cove."

The first man nearly shouted his delight. "What an extraordinary place!"

The second man smiled. "I'm Gary Dorn. The exuberant one is my good friend, Loran Fredrick. You must be Brian Burke."

"I am, an' me an' me partner here, Maureen O'Toole, together we are at your service an' humbly so."

"Why do I think there's absolutely nothing humble about either of you?"

"Wait 'til you get to know us, you'll discover we're shrinkin' violets. But for now…" Brian's gesture included Maureen and all the Ojibway men standing there, "…we all welcome you as our first guests."

Brian grabbed one of the guest's duffle bags, Albert and Old George grabbed the other bags and tackle boxes and rod cases, and they stepped from dock to beach to the path to the cabins.

"We're your first guests this season?"

"Indeed gentlemen this is our very first season of actual operations after years of dreamin' an' plannin' an' buildin'. So we're just open for business an' that makes you our first guests at the Great Lodge at Innish Cove. An' we intend to honor you for it."

Maureen spoke up. "We have a lovely little cottage, ah, that's the Irish in me, I mean that cabin ahead is all ready for you. These men here with us built all these cabins last summer while Brian an' I tried to help. That one right above yours, the biggest, we've set up as a lodge for meals, with a bit of a pub fixed up in the corner for your evenin' refreshment."

Then Brian said, "But most importantly, let me introduce you to this man, Joe Loon. He's the number one guide 'round here. He's been fishin' these waters his entire life, an' so too his father an' his grandfather's grandfather. If they didn't catch fish they wouldn't be eatin' or feedin' their young ones. So they know where the fish are as sure as the fish know where the fish are is what I am sayin' to you."

"Nice to meet you, Joe."

"He's called Joe Loon. An' you'll find he speaks no English."

"Won't that make it interesting? A guide who doesn't understand us."

"He'll understand what needs to be understood, and you'll understand him as he guides you on your fishin' adventures. Just follow his lead an' I promise you'll come back here this evenin' from the best fishin' you've ever had, an' if you're not toastin' the accuracy of that prediction with me at the pub tonight, well sir, the drinks will be on the house tomorrow night as well—bein' it was already determined our very first guests would drink free tonight."

❄ ❄ ❄

Two of the Irish lads who overheard Eamon's conversation in the pub took the bus into Dublin the next day. The eighteen-year-old, Tony, went with Kevin's recruit, the hurling lad, who carried his hurling stick with him everywhere he went. His da only had to mention once that the great Timmy McShay, the best hurler of his time, had carried his stick with him everywhere he went, and his son took up the practice immediately. The hurling lad loved the feel of his stick in his hands, the weight of it at his side.

A trip to Dublin was itself an adventure for these country boys—they'd each been there but once before—and as they walked the busy city street they felt like they were prancing.

The hurling lad led them onto a side commercial street lined with shops, and leaving Tony outside, he stepped into a music shop. From the window, Tony watched the hurling lad ask a clerk a question that elicited a serious reply with hands waving directions. The hurling lad dashed back outside and waved for Tony to follow him as he walked quickly, calling back over his shoulder.

"He says Kevin's home today with a bit of an ailment. Others were askin' after him as well, he says, just a bit earlier. There were three of 'em, an' he says they had the look a' toughs"

"The look a' toughs?"

"That's what he called 'em."

"An' he told you Kevin's street number?"

"He's just round this corner here."

The boys turned off the business street for one lined with modest townhouses. They dashed up the steps to Kevin's door, but before they could knock, they heard a crash from inside. They crouched low, listening at the door, and when all was quiet the hurling lad rose to peer through the door's window.

"I see half an empty room. There's a hall, but I can't see but a short length of it... no lights... no movement."

"What should we do?"

The hurling lad tried the door.

"It's not locked."

He pushed the door open a bit, holding it with his hurling stick. He peeked around the door and whispered back to Tony.

"Take it slow 'n take it easy."

"You sure we want to go in at all?"

"You don't start trouble in your own place, so I'm thinkin' these three must 'a brought it with them. We gotta see if Kevin is all right."

They opened the door and heard a cry of pain and another crash from down the short hall. The stick felt like a club in the hurling lad's hands now as the two walked quietly but quickly down the hall to an open door where they heard a voice roaring inside.

"Gettin' it yet, Kevin? It's us is real IRA. So it's us with the only claim on Clann na Gael."

The lads saw the broad backs of two men just inside the small room, and in front of them a third man stood over Kevin who was slumped on the floor, leaning against a narrow cot along the far wall of the otherwise empty room. His face was bruised, and his nose and his lip were bleeding.

"Not sure he gets it yet, J.P. Give him one more good measure of truth."

The third man grabbed Kevin by the front of his shirt and loaded another punch but sensed something and turned too late as the two lads dove into the backs of the closest two men. One man was knocked into the puncher, who turned swinging wildly, nearly hitting his own. The second man stumbled as the hurling lad raised his stick and followed up with a big blow. It was intended for his shoulder but the man moved and instead the stick hit him in the head, producing such a loud crack as it knocked the man to his knees that the hurling lad wondered if the stick was broken. There was such violence in the act that everyone felt it.

The two who were knocked into Kevin grabbed him and stood either side of him, fists cocked for Kevin's face.

The hurling lad had a full hold on the collar of his hostage and realized if he let go the fellow would fall flat on his face. Blood began flowing from his scalp, trickling down his neck.

Tony was looking for a move, saw none, and held his place next to the door. No more than four or five feet separated any one from another.

The lads were country strong. But the others were men.

Kevin spoke up, "Only smart move right now is to see how badly your man is in need of care. My lad's been smashing the ball across Connaught near all his life, and neither of you want a bit of what his club delivers. Take a look if that isn't clear already."

The hurling lad released his hold of the clubbed man's collar and they all watched the injured man's slow-motion roll from his knees to full spread out on the floor, nearly touching everyone in the room.

He lay motionless.

"Step back and we'll take him wit' us."

The club retreated and the two men released Kevin to cover each other's backs. They slowly worked their way to the door, supporting their fallen man between them.

Kevin rose to his feet and tried to sound strong.

"So we all know you heard me clear, tell Michael he should come talk with me himself, there's still time for you all to return."

The men stumbled as they dragged the injured man down the hall, and Kevin collapsed on the cot with a moan as soon as he heard the front door close. The hurling lad followed Kevin's attackers and locked the door.

When he returned to the room, he was staring at his club and frowning.

Tony handed Kevin a cloth for his cut lip, waiting for him to explain what just happened. When he didn't, and with the hurling lad standing stone faced and still, Tony told Kevin of their news about Maureen. By the time he finished, Kevin was sitting up.

"That's very promising, yes, quite a useful lead. Well done."

Tony checked back with his friend, who stood in the spot where he delivered the blow. He began to silently and slowly repeat the swing that had delivered that blow, shaking his head.

Kevin dabbed the cloth at his face one more time, then laid it aside. He was watching the hurling lad the whole time.

"There are some who want a statue of Sean Russell in Boston.

And some who don't."

"What?"

"I was attacked because we have yet another splinter group." He thought about that for a moment. "Aptly named. Splinters. Some things just can't be separated without the sharp pain caused by splinters. We grew up as one IRA. Each of us has a claim on that."

The hurling lad wasn't listening. He was playing what happened over and over in his head, repeating how he moved to understand what he did. Tony and Kevin broke away from studying him and Kevin went on. "As we've been reviving ourselves here, so has Clan na Gael in America, and there are plenty of rich American cousins eager to raise funds in Boston and New York and Chicago to support the new operations we're planning."

Now the hurling lad raised his club to study closely the point of impact. There was nothing to mark it, but he knew exactly where it was. He rubbed it once, then lowered the club.

"There's IRA who want some of that money to go to building a statue in Boston for Sean Russell. And some IRA don't."

Tony found he could listen only if he turned away from his fascination with his friend's state.

"Which are we?"

"We're in favor of the statue. Russell was a great man. But you have to understand it's no longer the issue, maybe it never really was. As I said, splinters hurt and so the fight turned to who gets the American assets in the first place; it's where most of our money has always come from. It's always about money, and so you've done us a good turn with the news you brought, for she just might be a link to plenty."

The hurling lad held his club in front of him and shook it repeatedly. He could feel the hit, and he could hear the crack, and he cried inside each time he did.

"If Russell died without speakin' to no one, how do they know there was money for her to take?"

"It was never more than a rumor. I'm not sure anyone considered it seriously. But if she and some broken-down ghillie have bought land in the New World and built a grand country lodge, you have to wonder if Russell hadn't handed her a small fortune. Where else does the money came from?"

"What do we do now?"

"I want to find her and get her back into our operations if I can. We can use her. And yes, we need to find out where her business capital came from, and if it was our money, of course we want it back. But some of the new boys, they talk like they want to punish her, to teach her some sort of lesson... So I need to find her first."

Tony had more news.

"I've been asked to be what's called an extra, in *The Quiet Man* filim. I'll be part of the scene an' hangin' 'round without suspicion. I can stay real close to Eamon Burke. They say I'll be in three or four scenes."

"Good. Keep a close listen."

Kevin had a pretty good idea what the hurling lad needed to hear.

"I'm thinking you knocked him out. He'll have a massive headache for a week. But he'll be fine. In any case, and I mean this, considering the circumstances that were facing me and what you walked in to, you did a brave thing, stepping in. And the right thing once you did. I'll make sure everyone knows you did this as a good deed to save me. That is how it was and how it will be seen."

The hurling lad found he could talk, but it came from somewhere outside of him. "I was swingin' for the back of his shoulder. I was goin' to hit him a good crack to knock him down... but he moved... I was swingin' for his shoulder... but I smashed his skull right above his ear ... I might have heard two cracks... Why did he have to move?"

"When's your next match?"

"My next match?"

"We play Saturday, against Sligo."

"Put your mind to that. He'll recover."

"I was just goin' to hit him on the shoulder, but he moved."

✳ ✳ ✳

New rituals took shape at this sacred place. The late afternoon Return of the Boats quickly became the most important. Brian saw it first; fishermen returning to a crowded dock filled with the excitement of other fishermen resulted in a greater celebration of the day for all. Maureen helped the guides orchestrate this happening by simply suggesting that when guides see a fishing boat heading back to camp at the end of the day, that unless the guides are finding fishing was spectacular in that moment, they should join them.

One late afternoon, a couple of weeks after the camp opened to its first guests, the dock was filled with the joy of a great day on the River. Two fishing boats had already returned, and Joe Loon's boat just rounded the point and entered Innish Cove.

The four American guests on the dock stretched and patted each other's backs and shoulders as they told Brian and Maureen all about their adventures. Albert and Old George walked past hauling shore lunch boxes to the big heavy-duty storage tent next to the log shed near the foot of the dock.

Behind the tent and the shed, farther up the beach, just at the edge of the forest, were the tents and birch bark wigwams of Joe Loon's clan. A woman stood in front of them behind two children, watching the action on the dock.

One of the guests had slapped down his big northern pike on the dock in front of Brian.

"So, Brian, what's your verdict?"

"It's a lovely fish. Just might be the biggest pike we've seen this summer."

"How big?"

"Seein' it makes me think about back home in the West of Ireland, before the war. The Brits came over to fish our River for trout an' some Germans did, too, but mostly the Germans were comin' to fish for pike in Lough Corrib. An' years went by before one as fine as this was caught."

"I was thinking it was 25 pounds."

"Maybe more, yeah."

Joe Loon's boat slowed as it approached within hailing distance, and the guest in the bow stood to call out greetings to all on the dock as they pulled up. The guest who had caught the big northern pike picked it up to feel its heft and show it to the new arrivals as he tried to keep Brian's attention on his story.

"But here's the most amazing thing. As I'm fighting this trophy, I can call it a trophy, right Brian?"

"I'd be proud to pay to send it into Kenora an' have it mounted with your name on a bit of brass, then hang it in the pub, if you would permit me."

Joe Loon was tying his boat to the dock.

"That's exactly what I'll do. Golly, yes. Hey, James, how'd you make out this afternoon?"

"We went after smallmouth bass off some islands west of here. We must have caught twenty before it slowed down."

"Take a look at this fellow here. I was just telling Brian that I hooked this baby..." he found his boat mate and waved him over, "... and the other boat is right close by, and we're all excited. They're calling out advice left and right and I'm fighting him and fighting him, but then I realize that no one is making a sound, and it takes me a second to check and see because I am kinda busy at the moment trying to catch this fish, but when I do look up I see no one is watching me anymore—"

His friend took over.

"Because Albert has noticed this osprey circling above us, a little off, but pretty much above us, and just as he taps me on my shoulder and points it out to me and I tell the guys to take a look, just then the osprey starts his dive. He folds his wings back and he just shoots, like an arrow, straight down. I mean, he must have been going a hundred miles an hour from about, gee what did we guess? Maybe 400 feet in the air? And he's diving closer and closer, and then he brakes and throws out his talons and *smack! bam!* He hits the water. There's a big splash, but just at the surface because he takes off right away and has this corkscrewing little pike in his grasp, a little one, about this big." He held his fingers ten inches apart.

"And then the osprey is flying away with his catch, he gets about a hundred feet above the water when we hear Albert saying something in Indian and out of the blue, and I mean it literally, just out of the blue, here comes this big old bald eagle. And the son of a bitch, he smashes into the osprey so hard you can see feathers flying off and the osprey makes sort of a shriek. But he drops his fish and flies away and the pike is flip flapping nose to tail as it's falling and the eagle now is streaking right behind it and just as the fish hits the water—"

A guest from the other boat had been listening and swooped in with his arm as he finished the story.

"The eagle scoops it up and flies away with it—"

"And then I finish reeling in this trophy and we get him in the boat... But I notice now we're all just quiet and I don't know, I just looked down at this fish... it even crossed my mind that maybe I ought to release him back in the water. "

"At that moment, I got to say it, at that moment, I was in awe. Of the world. And I'm proud to be saying it."

"I was just totally exhausted and couldn't say a thing."

"He's just sitting there smiling, for the next 30 minutes he's just smiling, staring out at the sky, looking at the fish, sipping his beer, staring out at the sky."

"I was thinking this was heaven... I kinda wish now I had thrown him back."

Maureen stepped up with her camera and took a snapshot unposed, and after another candid shot, the Americans all gathered with their guides to compose a pictorial signature of the day's adventure.

After the photo, as the guests gathered to go, the Ojibway guides and sons stood together on shore. This Man stood with them. As the guests passed, Joe Loon spoke the forest language of this place, and they all laughed softly.

The guests liked the sound of it, the peace of this native language, and their smiles grew deeper, for the ritual was complete.

❋ ❋ ❋

The Ojibway children's uniform numbers were tallied as they were led into the school's auditorium set up to show a movie. As a Jesuit brother shouted instructions the lights were dimmed, and the projected beam's flickering images came into sync on the title card.

It was a John Wayne film, and he and his men were about to kill a great number of Indians.

Mathew sat in the dark auditorium among sixty or seventy children with his eyes closed. The boys and girls closest to him closed their eyes as well. Still, the gunshots and the yelps of pain told them that John Wayne and his men were shooting more of the Ondaga Sioux and Cherokee.

The Jesuits showed these boys and girls movies of the white man killing Comanche and Dakota, Cheyenne and Shawnee, a couple of times a month during the school year. Sometimes it was cowboys doing the killing, sometimes it was blue-jacketed soldiers. The message the Jesuits were delivering was that aboriginal life was dead and that these children should accept the white man's ways.

The first time they showed a movie after Mathew arrived, when the children were back in the sleeping rooms, he waited until the dead of night, slipped past the rows of sleep-filled cots, checked the hall, came back to each cot to wake the children and bid others to do the same.

They had to gather close to him and listen carefully as he spoke softly.

"My grandfather is an elder of the Loon clan, honored by all of the People as a man of wisdom. He told me the true story of Geronimo, and I will tell it to you. Geronimo was a great Chiricahuas warrior. Geronimo fought many battles so his people could be free. Free to be People of the Great Spirit. Geronimo did all he could to save the People. This movie is a lie. Geronimo did not always lose."

This showing was the last night they would play this same movie, as school ended in three days and the children would be sent home for a short summer recess. Mathew had chosen this night for his moment of protest so the punishment inflicted would be visible to his clan when he returned.

The idea came to him the last time he was strapped by one of the men wearing the Cross of Jesus the Christ. The pain was so great he left his body. Before he returned, he had the vision of him fighting with Geronimo.

Sitting in the auditorium, Mathew waited for the moment Geronimo was going to be captured. Just before that moment occurred, he leaned his head back and called out loud to his spirit back on the River.

"I am Mathew Loon. I am here."

The children were surprised, for none knew this was coming, and then they were proud.

Mathew stood and called again.

"I am Mathew Loon. I am here."

The Jesuit brothers were stunned, and if one later realized he had been thrilled by Mathew's full-throated and deeply passionate yearning, three others stepped quickly to surround him. But before they could, Mathew called out in defiance, and as they grabbed him he assumed the exact position Geronimo had just taken on the screen as he was captured.

The brothers dragged Mathew from the auditorium.

After the rows of chairs were straightened again, the movie continued.

That night, Mathew did not wake the children to tell them of Geronimo, for his cot stayed empty all night.

❅ ❅ ❅

It was early morning at the NOA office, just a few days later. Dutch arrived to find two men waiting to talk about arranging a trip, the same two men who, years earlier, had purchased fish from Mathew and Simon while camping on Many Tall Women Island, though since then the boys called it Moon Bread Island.

Dutch sat behind his desk. The tall man unfolded a map across the desk top and began to outline a perimeter with his finger.

"So this map shows Grassy Narrows Reserve is there, and down the River here is White Dog Reserve, then the Hudson Bay Post is tucked here next to Grassy, and then that's it, in this whole quadrant, except for some isolated trappers' cabins. You figure that's about right?"

"It was until a year ago. As of last year, there's a fishing camp right here."

"Commercial fishermen?"

"No, it's a couple of Irishmen, a man and a woman, and they've got a fishing camp for sport fishermen, successful businessman, eh, from the States, mostly Chicago so far, for four days or five day trips fishing the River's lakes for walleye, smallmouth bass, big pike."

"How big is their operation?"

"They've got seven cabins now. Been slow this first year, but every guest I flew out was talking about returning."

"Seven cabins? Show me again."

"All around this cove here, on Rainbow Lake. He says he'll build another ten or fifteen in the next five years. I believe he'll do it."

Dutch noticed the disappointment on the men's faces.

"Why's that bad?"

The taller man was about to speak when the other interrupted.

"How far south do they fish?"

"I don't think they ever fish farther south than these rapids here. That's almost a half-day boat ride and then a lot of work to get above the rapids. There's about fifty yards of them. What are you fellas looking to do?"

Again the taller man was ready to answer but was cut off. He hid his surprise when the other said, "We're checking sites for a biology field study project. We intend to study how the populations of wolves and moose relate to each other. We're out of Queens University. Most of this quadrant is a ten-mile-wide natural bowl, so it makes a wonderful study area. We're valuing minimal disturbance."

"I've flown over all this maybe fifty times in the past five years, so I'm your man if you're scouting the area. There's more moose and wolves, and deer and black bear and all kinds—"

"Tell us about this fishing camp."

Dutch started to when the office door opened and a Western Union Canada delivery boy stepped in.

"Morning, son."

"Are you Dutch Acker?"

"That's me."

"They tell me I should see you if I got a telegram for Brian Burke?"

Dutch read the envelope.

"Excuse me a moment here, gentlemen."

Dutch turned to the two-way radio Maureen recently authorized NOA to purchase.

There was a radio in the Norseman and another base station on a table in the dining hall cabin at camp.

"Innish Cove, this is NOA. Innish Cove, this is NOA. Over."

❉ ❉ ❉

Brian was at the dock helping the guides prepare their boats for a day's fishing.

Maureen was attending the guests who were finishing their eggs and bacon and Red River cereal or enjoying last sips of coffee before they headed to the dock. She stepped away when she heard Dutch hailing them. With the radio placed close by, the guests could hear the conversation.

"This is Innish Cove. It's Maureen, Dutch, an' another grand mornin' in Eden. Over."

"Morning, Maureen. I just received a telegram for Brian marked urgent. It's from Ireland, from Eamon Burke. I was wondering if he'd want me to read it for him, since I'm not scheduled to be flying in 'til tomorrow. Over."

"He's down at the dock. I'll go get him. I'll call you right back. Over and out."

Dutch asked the strangers if they would step outside for a moment, then told the delivery boy to wait there with them for it was likely there would be a reply message.

※ ※ ※

Brian ran up onto the lodge's porch and through the door, Maureen behind him. The guests who overheard Dutch's transmission had left their last bits of breakfast behind, to provide privacy, their curiosity mixed with respect and concern.

Maureen rested her hand on Brian's shoulder as he sat in front of the microphone and hailed the NOA office.

"Dutch, it's Bri. Read it."

"It's a telegram from Eamon Burke. Marked urgent. Over."

"I said read it."

"Okay, here we go… Brian. Learned you built lodge. Stop. Two weeks to locate you. Stop. Hollywood movie being filmed in Cong. Stop. Set up meeting with John Wayne. Exclamation point. Come next two weeks. Question mark. Children are well. Stop. Send reply. Stop. Eamon Burke. Over."

"That's it?"

"That's it. Over."

"Read it again."

"He's talking about John Wayne the actor? Over."

"I guess, he must be—"

Maureen interrupted.

"Hey, Dutch, is the telegram boy still there? Over."

"He's just outside my door. Over."

"Tell him to hold close, we'll have a reply. Brian'll call you right back. Over an' out."

"I'll be here. Over and out."

Maureen leaned to hug Brian.

"My goodness, Brian. How grand!"

"An' I'm gonna see my children."

"You're gonna see your children. When will you go?"

"Last night you were complainin' about those six empty days between these guests leavin' an' the next guests arrivin'. We'll leave when these guests go, yeah."

"I'm not goin'. Someone has to stay behind an' take care."

"Sure you can come. No one needs you here as much as I need you there. We can site the number eight cabin before we leave, an' Albert can get it built while we're gone. I need you with me when I meet them Hollywood people an' all."

"I'm not goin'. This should be about you an' your children."

"From start to finish an' that's why I need you most of all. I want 'em to meet you, an' I want you to help me see the smart moves to be makin' with 'em."

"I'd be a distraction."

"Come on, let's go home."

"This is my home… An' our guests are gatherin' at the dock, an' if you're not there soon they'll be thinkin' the telegram was bad news. You need to go cheer 'em up."

❄ ❄ ❄

The next day Dutch flew the two lumbermen—still posing as field biologists—over the fishing camp to position it for them. Then he banked wide and easy to follow the River south. There was a canoe tied to the top of the Norseman's right pontoon, and camping supplies were piled in the rear of the plane. The taller man sat in back, the other was in the co-pilot's chair.

"The River flows north, and there's hardly nothing but wilderness between us all the way up to Hudson's Bay… North seems the direction most of their fishing parties head. I can't imagine Brian's guides would ever go any farther south than that far shore just ahead because, well, you'll see when we get there, those rapids on your map, they make a pretty formidable border."

The plane flew over the rapids and continued south, down the River, as the man made notes on his map.

※ ※ ※

The Norseman taxied away from the shore where Dutch had helped the two men untie their canoe and unload their gear. The men started right in to erecting their tent.

The tall man had a furrowed brow.

"Why does the board think we have to lie about what we're doing here?"

"It's not really a lie since I always wanted to manage a field study."

"I know you. We've been doing this work together for more than ten years. You've never lied before and wouldn't now unless you were told to."

"The way it's supposed to work is they'll just see it as a coincidence if they think about it at all."

"See what as a coincidence?"

"Where once there was our field biology camp, now they're building a pulp mill."

"So what if we can get away with it. I'm asking why hide it in the first place?"

"Because they're in no hurry to announce their plans."

"You're just telling me what I know. Tell me what's behind it."

"They're inviting me into some of those board meetings, with all the family, and I have heard them talking at length about their rationale for keeping this mill quiet for as long as possible. What they say, it makes sense to me, but I'm not the person to explain it to you, in any case. It's the sons running this one, the two brothers. It's their project, and I know I shouldn't say any more."

"Let me ask you this. We're not out here as pawns in the brothers' games, are we, just going through their paces for the Indian Affairs reports?"

"We're here because in our permit applications we emphasis the special care we would take protecting the Ojibway's sacred places. There's a burial ground back in there and a hilltop where they do that fasting and meditating-for-a-vision thing they do."

"Do we know where?"

"We have some indications, so you and I need to nail down the exact coordinates. We do want to avoid these sites, if we can."

❈ ❈ ❈

Since early morning Simon had paddled Nigig from the stern with Albert paddling from the bow. A bundle lay on the floor of the canoe between them.

They crossed two lakes to approach the great rock wall on the water's edge.

Simon began a song as they glided up to the wall to slowly drift around its broad face. As they approached the place where the pictographs began on the rock wall face the bundle moved and Mathew sat up.

Mathew had returned home from the residential school with the other children. The deep cuts and angry welts on his back and legs were still visible and angered his people. But it was the emptiness in his eyes that frightened them.

The canoe followed the characters and designs across the wall. There were dozens of images of spirits, and clans arriving, and great hunts, and all the animals of these forests, and all the fish of the River.

As Nigig continued, they came upon This Man painting a new image on the rock. His canoe bobbed slowly against the wall as This Man painted Simon praying for his vision.

They were quiet, the water lapping and the light playing on the face of the rock.

Mathew followed the ancient story told of Father Bear in the paintings as Simon spoke to Albert.

"Some say I have waited for too long."

"That is what some say. There is always someone who will say that."

"Others say I have my vision. That Grandfather's dreams have become my vision."

"Soon you will know if this is so."

As they passed, their canoe gently bumped This Man's canoe in the soft chop.

"I am afraid my vision will carry me away from Grandfather's dream."

Albert found the painting he had made of Mathew running with a leaping deer soon after his son was born.

"Were you afraid, Uncle?"

"The first night the spirits did not come. I was alone. My prayers were empty. That night my heart cried with my fear. The next night the spirits came to comfort me."

"I am ready for my new life to begin."

Mathew turned from the drawings to his father.

"Simon's new life will bring my spirit back to me."

❋ ❋ ❋

Tommy was called to Father John's office after supper and was surprised to see his uncle Eamon waiting there as well.

"Is it Patrick?"

"He's fine, so's everyone else. How about yerself?"

Once Tommy's fears were relieved, his suspicion carried anger.

"So he's built his fishing lodge, and you've decided all is forgiven."

"Your father is returnin' to Cong next week for just a couple of days. To do some business for his lodge. It's not wrong to want him to succeed."

"He can't return without your permission."

"I've invited him."

"You've invited him? What did Katie say?"

"She said 'Keep him away from Patrick.'"

"I'll be there."

"You want to see him?"

"No, but I need to help Katie protect Patrick."

"Tommy. Your da—"

"We don't call him that."

"Your father, he misses ya, Tommy. He asked me if I thought you might see him so he could apologize."

"Why is it that as soon as you find out he's buildin' his lodge, you want to act like everything's all right? You want to play the Quiet Man there, too?"

Father John spoke sternly, "Thomas Anthony Burke. You're to

obey the Commandments and show the proper respect."

"Sure, Father. Course, no one knows better than you how I have prayed to find forgiveness for Brian Burke."

Father John nodded his head. "I've prayed with you at times of great despair. And more than once, so yes, I know."

"And I've confessed to you the source of that despair... It comes when your prayers go unanswered."

Chapter 21
ON THE RIVER

BRIAN DROVE THE BOAT and Maureen sat just in front of him, facing him. They called out over the engine's roar as the wind whipped her hair in an ever-changing frame about her face.

"I don't just want you there, I need you there."

"It seems like somethin' a wife would do. Don't know if it's somethin' a business partner should do."

"Come on now, Lady Girl, who's business partners? We've never just been business partners."

"So what are we then?"

"We're a couple traveled far from where we started out, livin' a grand adventure an' makin' our way together, yeah."

"A couple?"

"A couple that needs each other, an' that's for sure now, isn't it? A couple that does things for each other to take care of each other. Everyone thinks we're lovers."

"I've kept you out of my bed."

"An' I never say different to anyone. I would tell you I love you is what I meant by that 'cept I know you want more."

"An' isn't that how we wound up so far from where we started? We're both ever after wantin' more."

Brian throttled back as he approached the shore lunch spot. The guests were surprised and delighted to see them coming. Brian had told their guides, Albert and Old George, that they intended to drop by, so they had added extra supplies to their shore lunch boxes and filleted and fried extra fish.

Brian grabbed a half bottle of brandy before he left, and when he and Maureen arrived at the shore lunch, he invited all the guests to take a bit with their coffee as they talked about his trip to Cong to meet the Hollywood stars.

"I'll put John Wayne himself in Cabin Three, that's the one you and Tom are in, Phil. An' Maureen will take a picture of him standin' in front and send you a copy. We'll name it John's Cabin an' you'll be able to tell your boys back home ol' John Wayne slept in your bed."

"When's he coming?"

"We haven't nailed that down yet. It seems by the time they finish with their movie our season will be over, so I'm guessin' it will be next year."

"You have family in Ireland?"

"Well, there's my cousin, who is makin' the introductions, an' he's been takin' care of the children until I get things such that I can bring 'em over."

One of the guests turned to Maureen. "You have children? You must miss them."

"Oh, no, they're Brian's children. We're not married, we're just business partners."

❄ ❄ ❄

The lumbermen traveled upstream, farther south, their canoe's three horsepower Viking outboard making slow progress against the strong current in this section of the River channel. The River soon opened broad and shallow as the bottom of a wide bowl and the forests slowly sloped up on both sides of the River in a slow and easy rise to distant ridges. The forest was fir and spruce and pine with groves of birch and waves of maple.

The men passed smaller channels of the River and many streams, some large enough to float logs to the main channel.

The tall man was at the throttle, the other was making notes and looking at maps. The tall man wouldn't stop pressing for openness.

"It's as if God just laid this out for us. He cupped these trees in his hands and said here, here's the easiest place you'll ever find to cut trees to make paper. And when that paper is needed for all those new jobs in all those growing companies in Toronto and Minneapolis and Chicago, supporting all those families growing happy and growing healthy since they won the war against evil, well, you tell me what anyone could say against that?"

"I don't enjoy having to repeat it to you, and I can tell you don't like hearing it, so maybe this can be the last time. I am invited now into some meetings you aren't asked to attend, and I have been told some things in those meeting that you haven't been told, and if that's what's bothering you, all I can say is—that's just too bad."

"Of course that's not it. The way I have always looked at it is the more time spent in meetings, the less time spent out here."

"Sure, okay, but there's things the two brothers aren't ready to talk about. About how this mill will be the first of its kind producing the new paper the future is demanding. That's what they keep saying, just like that, the new paper the future is demanding. And if they are right, they will be the first with this new process. So that's all I need to know when they ask me to keep this one quiet as long as we can."

He made a mark on one of his maps.

"I think the right site is that shoreline where the channel opens up just south of our campsite. That's as close as we'll get to that existing logging road, and we'll only have to cut a three or four mile spur."

They rounded a bend where the broad River fully opened up into a shallow, reedy lake. In the nearby bay they spooked a moose cow and her calf and watched them splash out of the water and back into the bush.

The tall man couldn't hide his disdain. "So record that in your journal and you'll be running a moose and wolf field study and you can save your lies for the next time."

"That's a bit harsh."

"I'll apologize for being harsh if you'll acknowledge it was also true."

Chapter 22

HORSE RACING

AFTER THE DETAILS OF BRIAN'S TRIP were finalized there were changes in the movie schedule requiring Eamon to be on the set in Newport Bay for the horse race scenes when Brian arrived at the airport in Dublin. These scenes were Eamon's most important contribution to the film, so he arranged for Aidan to borrow a car to pick up Brian at the airport and drive his cousin cross-country to where the action was.

When Aidan and Brian arrived, Eamon was galloping a powerful race horse up the sand dunes ahead of a pack of race horses, the open ocean sky as backdrop, horse and rider cutting down hard between two grassy hillocks, two horses right behind, many more strung out after them, all the horses breathing hard, hooves pounding, sand spraying, one horse and rider spilling, clusters of film crew watching, two cameras filming, John Ford directing.

This was one of the long shots, so Eamon galloped hard for another 50 yards, saw the mark, then reined in his ride.

But Brian wasn't watching his cousin winning the Race to the Sea as Sean Thornton. He had spied a boy standing with the crowd behind the crew and was wondering if that might be his son, Patrick.

Brian was on the verge, and he stepped down into the sand

slope and walked slowly, hesitantly, towards the boy.

As the crowd shifted with the end of the shot, Brian saw a teenage girl and young man who had the look of a young priest, and he knew they were his children. He stopped, still at a distance.

Tommy had been looking for their father and that's when he spied him. He called him out to Katie. He took Patrick's shoulder and pulled him to his side and planned their retreat if their father came closer. Just then, John Wayne stepped in to take Katie's hand and he twirled her around, then bowed to her.

"Didn't know I was such a great rider, did you, Katie darling? I'm thinking about challenging your Uncle Eamon in next year's race and was wondering who you'd give your scarf to."

Katie turned to keep her eyes on her father, who had stopped dead in his tracks. Tommy's hand slid from Patrick's shoulder to his elbow and with a slight pull he did his exaggerated John Wayne imitation.

"I say we mosey on over to Uncle Eamon and tell him we need to be aheadin' to the bunkhouse about now."

The actor laughed and led the children past the director and cameraman comparing notes and continued to where the horses were being cared for. Some of the riders were laughing, some were complaining, and they were all saddling fresh mounts as they refined their tactics for the next take, everyone determined to make it the last.

"Nice riding there, Uncle Eamon. You make me look strong in the saddle."

"Rabbit took quite a tumble."

Tommy stepped close enough to his uncle for a private word.

"Your cousin has arrived. He's over by the lunch table. We're ready to find a ride home."

"They're callin' for one more take. No one will be leavin' 'til it's done."

"So then you go tell him to keep his distance."

John Wayne overheard that last of it.

"Is there something wrong?"

Eamon nodded at Brian to hold him in his place, and Brian's gesture acknowledged the message.

"Brian's arrived. An' it's been a long time since they've seen their father."

"Your cousin Brian? The man with the fishing lodge in Ontario?"

"That's right."

"Brian is their father?"

"My cousin is their da."

"Who left his children with you to raise so he could go build his fishing lodge?"

Tommy answered.

"He didn't leave us. He was told to stay away. An' he has, until now."

❉ ❉ ❉

Inside the pub, the corner of the room where two small tables were pushed together was overflowing with Brian, Eamon, John Wayne, Victor McLaglen, and Barry Fitzgerald. Next to them were tables filled with crewmembers and extras.

Tony, the big lad who helped rescue Kevin, was one of them.

Brian quickly described the building of the fishing camp to everyone. They were delighted to hear stories of Joe Loon's clan. Then he turned his attention to John Wayne.

"What I'm proud to be offerin' you is a trip of your own design. You say when you want to come, an' how long you want to stay, an' I say yes to whatever you say on the matter. Bring the friend you'd like to spend all day with in a boat, an' if ya' bring three friends we'll outfit two boats for ya'. An' you'll be there as my guest an' at my expense."

"Sounds like quite a place."

"An' the same offer is extended to you other gentlemen as well. All our cabins are nice, but we'll put you up in the best of the lot. You pay your way there and tip your guides, an' I'll take care of the rest of the expense."

"You're a generous man."

"Just eager to share this Eden with those who would appreciate it. One tradition we've already started is takin' a picture of all the guests, so I'd be takin' one of you an' your friends. It won't be seen anywhere but in the photo album we keep in the lodge."

"We'd be clear about that before I came up, sure."

"I'd love to hang it up, maybe in the cabin you stay in, or in the Great Lodge Hall I'm goin' to build after I stockpile enough of the biggest logs I can find. That's the next big project, to build a showplace of a lodge right in the middle of the cabins with an Irish pub and a dinin' hall. I'll cover its walls with moose an' bear heads, an' trophy fish mounts, an' maybe you'd like your picture in an honored spot."

"Where everyone could see it... Listen here, I told Eamon I'd hear your offer through, and I have. So let me think about it for a while, how's that? Eamon, can you set your cousin and me up for a meeting in the next couple of days? When do you head back?"

"Friday."

"Okay, by Friday. We'll find the time by Friday to finish the discussion. Now we need to open this evening to other voices."

❄❄❄

The next day Eamon wasn't needed on the set, so he was tending his cattle when Tommy walked up. He asked his uncle a few questions about the herd then abruptly changed the subject.

"So, tell me why you had to invite him back."

"An' then you'll tell me why you won't ever forgive him?"

"For Christ's sake, Uncle Eamon, because of the bruises. From his lower back down the backs of his legs to his knees, it was one solid bruise. I know you saw it."

"Of course, I saw."

"Well, later that night when no one was around, I touched it. I couldn't help it, I had to touch it, it didn't look real. His body's recoil... The bruised flesh, it moved... It seemed like its own kind of life... It looked evil... I can't ever forget the bruises, so I can't forgive his deed."

"I remember the bruises an' counted the days 'til they finally disappeared. It was twenty-three days before the last spoiled spot was gone, but it was clear the damage ran deep, for he weren't gettin' any better as they vanished. An' I know about the nightmares an' the spells, an' I told you to go back to seminary once, an' I told you to go back twice, an' you were smart to do as I said, but it was me an' your aunt who came awake to his screams an' cared for him all those months he was afraid to sleep."

"An' I could only go back knowing you'd take care of him. I've thanked Christ for you every day."

"But has Katie told you Patrick's spells haven't gone away, an' her own nightmares just keep gettin' worse, or is she protectin' her brother from that sorry bit of news?"

"You're not making much of a case for your cousin, reminding me of the damage he's done."

"All I'm makin' a case for is maybe, you think on it an' pray on it, but maybe they'll always be afraid of him as long as we treat him as somethin' monstrous."

"So you've forgiven him?"

Eamon was quiet for a few moments. "Don't know if I will ever forgive him, Tommy. Any one of us who was there, I don't know, I would never expect it unless some act of grace shows me the way, but I do need to get reconciled with him."

"Reconciled?"

"I get tired bein' angry with him. Your da was a brother to me. So many of the best memories of my life include him. It's hard work stayin' angry at such a big part of yourself so much of the time. I'm not sure but it's wearin' us all out."

"What he did was evil."

"He knows that. An' he knows it can never be like it didn't happen. But how can it stay like this? I'll tell you, it can't. He's not an evil man, he did an evil thing... He's my brother who one day, long ago, did an evil thing and has paid for it ever since."

"By your actions so shall ye be known."

"So then you might want to keep an eye on how often you find yourself actin' like one of them feckin' priests that acts just like a feckin' priest."

"What?"

"I'm sure Father John is remindin' ya we're all sinners. Most Catholics are all too ready to believe that. You should consider it."

"Thanks for the advice."

"Here's some more. You don't have to forgive or even be reconciled with him to have a little sit down so he can get a good look at what a fine man you're becomin'. An' so you can hear a bit about what your da's been doin' livin' with the red men in the forests. It's really all quite remarkable."

"Not yet."

"He's only here two more days."

"I don't think I'll be letting go of the hate of him until he's had a chance to see how deep it goes."

❅ ❅ ❅

When Kevin got the news Brian had arrived in Cong, he prepared to leave immediately. He closed his music shop and returned to his new apartment to pack a small travel bag. Before he left his apartment for the bus station, he heard a knock on the door. It was Timmy.

"Bad news, Kev. The man yer lad clubbed with his hurling stick? He's never regained consciousness. They're saying his head got stove in real bad and he's gettin' weaker. We just foun' out."

"What should I tell the boy?"

"To hide for now while we talk a bit."

❅ ❅ ❅

When Kevin arrived in Cong, he found Brian down on the banks of the River with a small crowd of spectators gathered for the rehearsal of an important sequence in the big fight scene between Sean Thornton and Squire "Red" Will Danaher.

Eamon and Victor McLaglen's double were being choreographed as Kevin caught Brian's eye and thought he detected some recognition.

"You're Brian Burke?"

"Yes, an' you... Are you Maureen's London friend?"

"London? No. It was a pub in Donegal where we met. I'm Kevin Coogan. We spent some time talking over a pint."

"I remember."

"You look very well, indeed."

"We're grand. Just came back to enjoy this circus. We're in Canada now, me an' Maureen. We've gone into business together, in Ontario."

"Since I arrived here it does seem I've been hearing as much talk of your fishing lodge adventures among the red men as I have of the film. I've been looking for you since I heard you were here. I've some business I'd like to discuss with you and Maureen."

"She stayed behind. 'Tendin' to our holdin's' is how she put it."

"She's well?"

"She's great."

"You've gotten married?"

"No… we're engaged."

"Congratulations to both of you."

"I'll tell her you said so."

"I can do that myself when I see her."

"I said she didn't come."

"I've been hearing so much about your wilderness lodge… what do we call it?"

"The Great Lodge at Innish Cove."

"We take our Irish souls around the world with us and make it a better place for it. I've often thought about that night I heard you telling us your dream. It seemed real enough even then."

"An' how is it you'll be seein' Maureen?"

"Yes, you see, I'm a bit of a sporting man myself, and when I heard of your place, I thought I'd find you so we could talk about me booking a trip for me and some of the boyo's. I'm sure you'd be quoting us your friendliest rates."

"You want to book a trip to Innish Cove? That's grand. How many in your party?"

"It would most likely be me and two others."

"You want to be thinkin' even numbers, you see, for our fishing boats are set up to take two fishermen each."

"Yes, well then, that should have been my first question. Are you just a fishing lodge? We would love to fish. But I was thinking these boyo's would be even more interested in going over for some hunting."

"We've not booked a huntin' trip yet. The season's still to come in the fall. But I have guides who would make it a grand adventure for you. Is it black bear, or moose?"

"Both. What else you got?"

"Lovely white-tailed deer. An' wolves, but I think I'm figurin' it out that the Ojibway don't like to see wolves hunted."

"So we won't shoot a wolf. How do I go about making arrangements?"

"We pick the dates, an' I've got a paper with all the information you'll need in my suitcase. I'll give it to you tonight at the pub."

"We'll need rifles."

"You want me to get rifles for you?"

"We're wing shooters here. We've just got shotguns."

"We'll get you rifles an' have 'em sighted an' ready for you."

They were prepared for the first take of the fight sequence, and the director called for quiet. Kevin took a half step back so he could keep his eye on Brian as Sean Thornton and "Red" Will Danaher knocked each other into the River.

❄ ❄ ❄

The day's filming ended as the afternoon sun began its descent. The technical crews stored equipment. The cast and village extras and village spectators collected into groups of friends and began to walk away from the movie location at the River. Some headed home, others headed towards the village center.

Eamon and Katie walked down the street. Eamon's hair was wet after spending hours in the River faking throwing and taking punches, but he'd changed into a dry set of clothes. One punch inadvertently landed and there was a good sized bruise just below his right eye.

At the shout of alarm, the crowd of movie crew jumped back, for a horse pulling a cart had been frightened and suddenly bolted with a little girl alone in the cart, screaming her fear. Katie was in harm's way, and when Eamon pulled her back, he lost any opportunity he might have had to stop the horse and cart from dashing into town.

Brian and Kevin leaned forward as they walked up the short, steep section of street that led from the River up into town to the pub. From the street above they heard shouts of warning and the hard clash of hooves on stone and then around the corner galloped the out-of-control horse pulling a cart tipping on one wheel as it turned the corner nearly tossing the young girl who held on tightly, filling the air with sounds of her terror as the horse raced down the street toward them.

As the cart slammed back on both wheels and jolted the horse to slow for a step Brian jumped into its path and grabbed at the harness to try to gain control, but the horse swerved and knocked Brian back with a fully weighted shoulder. Brian was sent flying back past Kevin who was dashing forward as Brian crash landed on the street, thrown hard against the curb.

Kevin found Brian's action had slowed the cart so he yelled, "Jump!," and the little girl did, right into Kevin's outstretched arms. As he caught her, the wheel of the cart crashed into him and knocked him down to the street where he rolled to protect the girl under him.

The galloping horse and cart clattered away, down the hill and out of sight. Brian lay still on his back, his legs on the road, his torso on the sidewalk. Kevin sat up and checked on the little girl as her crying mother, other villagers, and movie crew came running.

After Eamon had pulled Katie to safety he ran after the cart and she followed the crowd following the horse. She caught up with the scene in time to see her uncle kneel over her father.

She ran to her uncle's side. Most of the crowd had gathered around Kevin and the girl, making sure she was all right, then making sure he was all right.

Brian was not responding to his name, and Eamon leaned closer to check his breathing.

Katie leaned against her uncle to get a closer look at her father. "Is he hurt? What happened to him?"

Kevin got to his feet with the little girl in his arms and handed her into her mother's care. He joined Eamon standing over Brian, and he placed his hand on Katie's shoulder.

"He helped save this little girl from the cart. He threw himself into the horse to slow it enough for the girl to jump."

"Get the doctor. Get some water."

Brian opened his eyes. It took a moment to realize where he was.

"What happened?"

"The horse knocked you to the curb."

"The little girl?"

"Kevin saved her."

Brian turned to find Kevin, but it hurt to move his head. He closed his eyes again.

"Kevin saved her?"

"When you collided with the horse, it slowed the cart so she could jump out. I caught her when she did."

Eamon was carefully examining his cousin's head for evidence of injury. "How badly hurt are ya?"

Brian opened his eyes again, moved his legs, then his arms.

"It's my bum shoulder throbbin' an' my head." He closed his eyes again. "Do I see Katie standin' here?"

Katie didn't respond.

"She's here."

"I'm okay, Katie dear. Don't worry about me. I'm fine. This bump on my head has got the world spinnin' when I open my eyes, that's all. I'll be right in a moment."

Someone arrived with a cup of water, another with a water bowl and towel. After Brian sipped the water, Eamon wet the towel and washed Brian's face.

"That's all I need. I'm feelin' better already. I am."

He sat up, took the cup again, and smiled at Katie before he drank.

The word reached the crowd that the runaway horse was reined in, and since Brian seemed fine the movie people began to disperse. The villagers stayed, for this was the first time Brian Burke and one of his children were together since Brian's exile.

Brian pulled himself up to sit on the curb, Eamon sat next to his cousin, Katie stood behind her uncle. Kevin was sitting on the other side of Brian. Someone draped the damp towel over Brian's neck and he took another drink of water, noticed all the folks still at hand, and found Aidan among them.

"Aidan, do me a favor. Tell Gus I'll buy the first pint for each of you in honor of this man's deeds." He nodded in pain to Kevin. "Help the hero Kevin to the pub an' let him tell you how his exploits was even trickier with me in his way."

Aidan helped Kevin back to his feet, and they moved as quickly as his sore back allowed, up the street and into the pub.

The street was quiet. Brian sat still on the edge of the curb where moments before he had hit his head. In the soft dusk light he studied his daughter's face as she looked back at him. Brian had never seen how much his daughter was looking like Deirdre and he enjoyed sitting there looking at her.

Eamon put his hand on Brian's shoulder. Her father's first tears were met by Katie's sad smile.

Eamon stood.

"You could go for a walk. Down Main Street an' back. I'll just follow along."

Katie shook her head no, without knowing she had, as she took one step back. Brian saw it.

"No, I think I need to sit here a bit."

The pain in his head caused him to clench his hands and that was when he discovered the sharp burn where two of his fingers had been twisted and sprained when he grabbed the horse's harness.

Brian was as startled by his behavior as Katie was when, after staring at his damaged fingers, he placed his head in his hands and began to sob.

Katie stepped closer to place her hand on her father's shoulder, but she couldn't.

"My Katie. My sweet, sweet Katie. Hate me if you must, but please, please don't be afraid of me."

He wiped his tears on his sleeve before he looked up again. His head was pounding.

"If you would let me try... if I could show you... how sorry I am... I love you. I miss you, an' Patrick... an' Tommy."

His pain was making him sick.

"I was afraid for Patrick when I heard you were comin' back."

"Yes... It's a strong, brave girl you've become, who knows how to take care for people you love. I want to show you I have learned how to do that, to take care of the people I love. Like you do."

"When I saw you lying there, I was afraid you were hurt." She said 'hurt' so quietly no one heard.

"Can I give you a hug?"

Katie stepped back, closer to Uncle Eamon.

"He wants to give me a hug."

"Don't you want to give your da a hug, too?"

Before she could answer, the horse and cart and driver came

around the corner, the mother sitting at the driver's side, holding her daughter in her arms. The driver stopped close by.

"You going to be all right?"

"Yes. How's the little girl?"

"Still scared, but she's not hurt. Thanks for saving her."

"The man named Kevin Coogan was the man who saved her."

"We were told you had a part and we thank you for riskin' yourself to play it."

While Brian was talking with the man in the cart, Katie whispered to her uncle, "I don't want him to hug me." Eamon asked the driver, "He says he's not hurt, but if you could give him a ride to my cottage, we'll come along behind and get him bandaged."

The mother and daughter slipped to the back of the cart and Brian climbed in next to the driver. The horse pulled them up the street and out of town to Eamon's cottage.

❈ ❈ ❈

After a rest his head cleared, so Brian and Eamon headed into town to join the second half of what grew into a great celebration of riotous laughter around Eamon and Brian and Kevin, as the Quiet Man, the Fishing Camp Owner, and the Little Girl's Hero each had their best stories to tell.

The whole audience was fully captivated by each one of them.

That night the movie stars were elsewhere, and the rest of the Hollywood crowd must have gone with them. That allowed the locals the room for full-throated merriment as they played themselves.

But then Kevin noticed that the stranger standing at the bar was Timmy. Five minutes after Timmy left the pub Kevin slipped away, saw him up the street, and followed him to a dark corner.

Timmy had come from Dublin with bad news for Kevin.

"Eddie Gallagher died yesterday mornin', an' I gotta tell you they're threatenin' us in all seriousness. For starters, they want your lad. We tried to talk this out with them, since, after all, it was them who came after you, but they won't give us time. Gallagher was a senior commander, Kevin, an' your lad... he's just a lad."

"Our lad. Start saying he's our lad."

"Yeah, well, it hain't me callin 'im your lad, it's them. An' they know who he is. An' they say they want your lad punished now, and fully, or they're threatenin' things could get bad between us."

"He had no idea he was getting himself into this sort of thing, Timmy. He was bringing me the news we're using to locate Maureen O'Toole, and he came to my rescue."

"No disputin' he's done us a good turn, Kevin, just as there's no disputin' it was his blow killed Gallagher. It's bad there's been the splinter there's been, but it would be a whole 'nother thing if we started killin' each other, so."

"The people of Ireland would never stand for that, and surely they see that as clearly as we do. It's their own interest to settle this reasonably."

"Seems to us who's been talkin' with 'em that it may be they don't put as much stock in how the people might think as we always have. It's this new set who sees things different, and da feckin' scary thing is, sometimes they see things a lot different. It's the effect of the war. Seems killin' is easier for some since the war."

"He's my lad, so it falls to me?"

"I'm here to take it on. 'Cause if it don't get done right an' right now, they say they'll be comin' after you, Kevin."

"You don't know where he is."

"So tell me."

Kevin stepped back deeper into shadows when he heard footsteps that passed by unaware.

"I'll take care of it."

"You'll do it?"

"I'll tell him it's resolved and he can come home now. We'll let him spend a couple of days with his mum. His innocence earns him that at least. I'll wait round here and then ask him to drive with me to Dublin. And I'll take care of business."

❋ ❋ ❋

Aidan prepared to drive Brian back to Dublin to catch his plane home. As he waited outside Eamon's cottage, he had the car's bonnet pulled back to pour water in the radiator.

Eamon leaned against the car, and Brian loaded his suitcase in the back seat. Katie stood back, near the cottage door, and looked at photos of Ojibway girls her father had given to her uncle to give to her.

"Thanks for the chance, Cos, but I'd say it hain't better than a one in ten that your, what did you call him, your close companion Johnny Wayne, will take me up wit' any part of the offer if he wouldn't even find time to meet again."

"At least you booked your first huntin' trip."

"They arrive two days after we was figurin' to shut down, an' for what we're chargin' 'em, I figured we'll be cuttin' our first year losses almost in half."

Brian motioned to Katie.

"You gave her the photos."

"And I gave Patrick his as well."

"Did he take them?"

"Not yet. But he knows they're there for him when he wants them."

"Thanks."

Katie looked up from the pictures and called out across the yard to her uncle.

"What are their names?"

Her father answered.

"The older girl is Marie Loon. The younger one is her sister, Ruthie."

"They don't have Indian names?"

"Sure they do, Katie."

"Do you know them?"

"I don't remember, but I can have them write to you an' tell you."

Katie smiled and waved, and as she turned to enter Eamon's cottage she said, "Tell them to send me more pictures when they write."

When she was gone, Brian got into the car with Aidan. He rolled down the window, and Eamon leaned against the door to speak with him.

"He was interested until the moment you arrived. That's when he heard me an' Tommy talkin' about what happened an' that I'd made you leave."

"He heard about me beatin' Patrick?"

"None of that. But he did become suspicious of you."

"I guess for what I did, I should be servin' penance still."

"I'll look for a chance to talk with 'im again. An' Victor might still be interested. You tell your lady Maureen I look forward to meetin' her someday and good luck to you both."

"An' congratulations."

"An' congratulations?"

"When I get back, I'm goin' to ask her to marry me."

"Congratulations!"

"If I can't get her to come here for a weddin' this winter, we'll plan it when you come visitin' next summer."

"Can I tell folks?"

"Take some a' the money I left in your chest drawer an' buy a round of drinks on your announcement of it."

Brian and Aidan drove away.

Chapter 23
THIS MAN AND THE ENGLISH

THE FIRST FUR TRADER OUTPOST was far beyond the edge of European settlement when it was built by the French voyageur. It was a simple cabin on high ground, above the River, and it served him well for many years.

Soon after the British occupied the post they added two more buildings and constructed a rough stockade surrounding them. The original cabin—the smallest—was the living quarters for the factor. A larger cabin was a bunkhouse for trading company employees with extra beds for trappers in need of one for the night and the senior officers of the patrols of soldiers who showed up at infrequent intervals. The troops would stake their tents inside the stockade.

The largest cabin was the commercial building where trading goods and furs were stored, secured, exchanged, recorded, and shipped, and where a small office was set up in a corner.

The new factor was sitting at the office table that looked out over the room. As he marked in his ledger, two employees—an Englishman and an Ottawa—called out the inventory of the trading supplies they had transported across the wilderness to the post. Suddenly, another Englishman burst through the door, looking back over his shoulder with deep concern.

"Mister Ellis, you need to—"

He interrupted himself to step aside as the Ojibway chief strode in, and then the chief stepped aside as his warriors, each one displaying his full battle dress, entered the room.

One after the other, they entered. They wore many feathers. Their faces were painted, red and yellow and black and white. Each carried a spear or a war club or a battle axe. Some had bows over one shoulder, quivers filled with arrows over the other. A dozen Ojibway warriors stood stone quiet along the walls and still more came. Their chests were bare or covered with breastplates of beads and quills.

Three carried muskets, loaded and primed.

The only sound was the whisper of their moccasins and one employee's, "Oh, my God" of a gasp followed by his hard breathing.

This Man entered last, after nearly twenty warriors had filled the room.

The English factor had looked up from his record book when the procession began but stayed seated. The other Englishmen sidled over to the table. The Ottawa stood behind the factor. Because the Ottawa and Ojibway spoke similar dialects of the Algonquin tongue, the Hudson Bay Trading Company had assigned him here from an eastern post.

The chief stepped forward, holding a few beaded strings in one hand, his war club in the other. The Ottawa translated the words of the Ojibway chief for the English factor, and because there were differences in their native languages the Ottawa sometimes interpreted.

"This English must be brave and not afraid of death to come among your enemies. Our French Father treats us as we treat our favored children. We promise our French Father our friendship for him. This friendship is strong even when he is chased away by you English. We come to tell you English we keep the friendship with the French Father. It is you who have brought war to our French Father. It is you who steal from him. You may have defeated the French. You have not defeat us. Do not look at us as weak. If you have brought war with you here, you will be destroyed. I can hear the French Father waking. I know he is rising from his bed to gather his best warriors to strike you hard."

The Ottawa then translated the factor's calm words.

"I have heard there is no one who speaks as eloquently as Ka-ka-ke. These must be the words of the great chief of his tribe."

"I am Ka-ka-ke. But it is Omig-aun-dib who is the chief. He is my father."

"I am honored the favored son of such a great chief would come to greet me. I am honored you call me a brave man who is not afraid of death. I ask you to honor me as a man of peace who is not afraid to tell you I do not like war. I love this land and respect your people. I wish to help you. To bring you great riches. You see I have come unarmed. You see there are no red coats in the fort. Let us agree we do not need them."

"I see you have come unarmed. But you have many red coats you can call. The French did not bring their warriors with them."

"There are many red coats who carry many firearms for the English King. To defeat an enemy as great as the French, these red coats must be very powerful. The red coats can hear my call if I need protection. But when the red coats come, they steal my best trading goods. I would rather trade these goods with the great Ka-ka-ke and his people for many beaver furs."

"We will listen to what you say. We will watch what you do."

Ka-ka-ke held out his war club to the factor.

"Everyone knows this is the war club of Ka-ka-ke. As long as you hold it, no

Ojibway will harm you. If your red coats come with their rifles to harm my people, I will return for my club, and I will use it to kill many English. You will be first."

"I understand. Let me show you the fine treasures I have brought with me now. I would like to give the great Ka-ka-ke a gift so he will learn the British will be great friends."

Chapter 24

SIMON FOBISTER

THE DAYS BRIAN SPENT IN CONG were the days of Simon's vision quest. Simon sat at the highest point for many miles in every direction. He sat on a beaver fur near the edge of the cliff that marked that highest spot. He was wearing the moccasins his grandmother had made for him. He wore the necklace the men placed around his neck when they left him alone at this cliff.

As the sun rose, he looked out over the eastern sky and soon shed the blanket that kept him warm while he sat there through the night. He had tried to stay awake but dozed off occasionally.

A narrow, yellow stripe of paint cut diagonally across his cheeks from below each eye to each corner of his jaw.

Simon had been on the mountaintop for two days and two nights.

He had water to drink, and he ate a handful of blueberries and a little bit of venison jerky each morning.

He was praying, and he was fasting for his vision.

This Man stood just at the clearing's perimeter.

Simon sat before the only tree on the cliff, an old cedar gnarled and twisted from fighting the winds and clinging to thin soil. Feathers and strings of beads had been tied with rawhide from some of the cedar's branches, and they hung down behind him, the feathers riding the slightest breezes.

Enough of the sun emerged now that he closed his eyes to the brighter intensity of it as he breathed in air full of the cedar's deep red heartwood. He closed his eyes tighter and watched the lights dancing just inside his eyelids. One of those lights began to take a shape so he followed it as it grew and split and added color at the edges.

This Man spread his arms and closed his eyes and chanted what the spirits spoke of, softly, to the wind.

❄ ❄ ❄

When Simon and This Man opened their eyes again, hours had gone by. Each checked the sun and saw it had passed its midday height.

Simon had clear pictures dancing in his head from the first day he spent on the mountain top, and they returned, in new versions, and always telling the same story. But since they were the familiar pictures he hoped to see he was confused, for he knew of no one whose vision was exactly what he prayed it would be.

Ever since the white man they call Big Brian had arrived to help them guard the River as Joe Loon's dreams had foretold, Simon watched for the white man who might be the River's destroyer, as the dreams had also prophesied. Joe Loon invited all the people of his clan to see Simon as a guardian of the River. Whenever the spirits and the ancestors were called for in ceremony, Simon showed himself to the spirits as a boy with this purpose.

Simon stood to fetch his water bottle from the small birch bark lean-to behind the cedar at the back of the small clearing.

This Man made a warning sound.

They stood quietly, listening. From far down the path below Simon heard muffled voices. It was still two days before his people would come for him, so he knew it was not members of his village.

The voices grew louder. It had the sounds of white man talk and Simon knew it must be since all the Keewatin people would know Simon was there and would never interrupt a young man's vision quest.

Simon wondered if he was acting in a dream as he dashed back to the cliff side to grab his beaver pelt, then began stuffing the feathers and beads up in the cedar boughs to hide them. The voices were excited and the sound of them told Simon they would soon arrive.

He dashed behind the first big tree and then looked to find his next point of retreat.

As the two pulp-mill men followed their voices up the last length of the path and into the clearing, Simon stayed just long enough to see them, still uncertain of the reality of it all, then he slipped into the forest and settled down behind a large boulder. When he hit his knee on the edge of the big rock, he considered the sharp pain to be evidence he was in the natural world, that this wasn't his dream vision. But he wasn't sure.

The men stopped on the spot Simon was sitting as it afforded a completely spectacular view. The tall man was delighted to have found this place.

"I was right. The highest peak around with a view looking out to the Eastern sky."

The shorter man was also taken by the sweep of the forests and lakes below.

"That's where we were when you saw this, right there, on that lake right there, just off that point, eh?"

"I looked up and said, 'I'll bet that's the place'."

"You found it."

The tall man reached into his rucksack for the map and studied the high ground to the north.

"Their burial ground is out of sight from here. It behind where two ridgelines meet. Just tucked behind on that branch of the River, eh?"

"Yeah, yeah, I think so."

"Well, if it's just these two sites we have to worry about, then we got nothing to worry about. We just shift the whole operation southwest, which lengthens the road cut a little, but that lets us stay off this ridge... And if we stay off this ridge we wouldn't want to log anywhere near that ridge wall so that should be plenty of protection for the burial site."

The men turned away from a sudden, strong gust of wind that kicked up a bit of fresh ash from the fire pit. With the next gust, the feathers and beads fluttered down.

"Someone was up here last night."

The tall man let the feathers dance on his open palms.

"I'd like to do that. I'd like to spend a night here examining and wondering about my life, about my role in my life... I wonder if they'd let me."

The short man noticed the lean-to and saw its meager rations.

"I think there's someone here right now."

"We should leave. We might be interrupting some sort of something."

They looked around quickly, then headed back down the path. After just a moment's hesitation to create a safe distance, Simon followed them. They made it easy, their voices amplified by their excited spirits. Simon was still not certain this wasn't part of his vision. He had to find out who these white men were and why they were here, and why they were so interested in the most sacred places of his people. This would help him understand if this was his vision or if these were the white men coming to destroy the River.

❋ ❋ ❋

When the two lumbermen got to their canoe, Simon was back in the trees on a small knoll, watching them push off from shore, start their motor, then turn upstream. He stayed back off the shore and followed the sound of the outboard as he dogtrotted the ridgeline where he could see the River between the trees. He wasn't worried when the outboard motor's last echo faded for he was certain he'd come to their camp soon enough.

From the top of the steep slope he could see over the trees below, and he could see a great length of the River before the rapids and he knew their camp would be on this side of them.

Before dusk settled and as the ridge grade became more severe, Simon left the slope and walked along the bank of the River where there was more light; shadows spread and met and darkened the forest, but along the bank he was able to maintain a steady pace.

In the last light he saw the canoe pulled up on shore, just above the rapids, and he left the River to come to the camp from the deepest forest.

❋ ❋ ❋

The two lumbermen sat at the fire on their campstools. Between them and their tent a table sat under the glow of a kerosene lantern.

Earlier, they had eaten at the table while they recorded the day's findings in journals and on maps they kept in a briefcase. When they finished, they took a bottle of whiskey from the briefcase and the tall man poured a couple of fingers of whiskey in two glasses as they settled in around the fire.

The short man pushed and poked at the fire with a stick.

"They say they've got a new job for me. It's an extra $50 a month, but it's in an office in Dryden. I told my wife there's no better job for me than this one I'm doing now, but I'd let her think about the money and tell me what it would mean to the family."

"So then how can you hide the work you love so much? Aren't they telling us to hire as lumberjacks every one of the Indians who want the work? And don't the Indians want these jobs so they can live out in the forests still with some steady money in their pockets? And now, now that we're learning to keep away from their sacred sites, I say there is no better job than this, and I'm proud to be doing it."

Simon moved quietly in the dark. He had scraped the paint from his face so nothing reflected the campfire's light. When he got down on his hands and knees to approach the camp, he discovered how tired he was from running and how weak he was from fasting for two days. He leaned against a tree to rest and gathered his spirits as he plotted a course to the edge of the camp.

The short man sipped his whiskey and smiled.

"It's possible we were the first white men up there on that cliff. To be making your life in the forests where there's Indians still living their ancient ways, that's what makes this job special."

"That's why I just don't understand you."

"What?"

"That you can talk that way one moment and then consider sitting behind a desk."

Simon crawled on his belly up to a fallen tree and realized that if he could get to the cluster of low-brush bushes just ahead, he would have a full view of the camp. He slid over the tree trunk and inched his way under the bushes. He made no sound that didn't belong in the forest's nighttime symphony and the rapids' rumbling undertone.

He peeked from under the bushes and a second later This Man crawled up next to him.

Seeing this white man camp helped Simon remember. He and Mathew had traded with these two men at their camp, when they had first tasted moon breads, years ago.

He had liked those men. Simon learned that white traders usually gave less than he expected. These men had wrapped up such large portions of batter and butter and syrup to take back to their camp that Nokomis made them moon breads for two days. The second day had seemed like an extra gift to Simon and Mathew.

The fire burned low. The men kicked the last flame out and gathered their papers and charts and stuffed them back in the briefcase. One carried the lantern, the other carried the case as they retreated to their tent.

Simon watched their silhouette shadows on the tent walls as the men settled into their cots. The lantern's flame was soon extinguished, all was dark, and a few last muffled words were spoken.

Simon waited a long time, resting under the bush. He listened to the night sounds, and he waited longer.

For a short time he slept.

When he awakened, he listened through the nighttime forest music for the sound of deep, peaceful sleep. He crept out from under the bush to crawl to the table, then to the tent. He lay quietly just outside the tent flap, listening to their sounds. He had never been close to a sleeping white man, and they sounded like his own people. Slowly, he pulled back the tent flap.

The briefcase was right there, in arm's length, so he slipped it out and carried it to the fire ring. He gathered up pine needles and twigs and carefully tended a last hot coal until he was able to start a small flame.

He removed a chart from the briefcase and he burned it, carefully, allowing just enough flame for the fire to keep itself going, positioning his body between the flame and the tent to block the light.

Then he removed a map and slowly burned it.

One by one, he removed the papers and the maps and the

charts from the briefcase and burned them, slowly, watching their demarcations and specifications curl and darken and disappear in burnt black ash flakes.

He protected an occasional corner of a document so the white man could identify the source of the mound of ashes they would discover in the middle of their fire pit in the morning.

The last two documents he removed were a map and a sealed envelope that he tore open to find a thick report with big, bold, bright red letters on its cover. He set the map and report aside but burned the envelope, leaving a reminder of it in the ash.

Then he returned the case to the tent and vanished into the trees, carrying the last documents as his coup, and so he would know when the sun came up if this had been real and what it might mean for his vision.

※ ※ ※

In the morning, the pulp-mill men were quite surprised and very confused to find the briefcase empty, then angry to discover someone had come into their camp at night and burned all their papers.

The short man was especially angry with himself for leaving his copy of the confidential report in the briefcase but he felt somewhat relieved when he discovered the evidence that the report had been burned.

The tall man conjectured that it was probably some Indian boys who had stumbled upon their camp during the day, then came back to practice their warrior skills in the night. Since neither could think of a better explanation they decided that was what had happened.

※ ※ ※

Simon sat under the cedar and waited for his grandfather and the others to come for him. His hand rested on his coup. This Man stood to honor him. Soon, Joe Loon appeared at the end of the path followed by the other men of the clan.

Simon sat next to Joe Loon and the other men formed a half circle, looking out over the cliff. After Simon told his story of the strange visitors and showed his coup, they praised his bravery and his craft.

While the men passed the map around and located many familiar places marked in the white man's pen, Joe Loon picked up the report. For a long time he looked at the large red markings stamped on the cover, moving his fingers along them again and again. Then he opened the report and carefully studied every page, following every line.

When he completed his examination of the last page he looked up.

"This is Simon's purpose. It is shown to us all. Simon will learn all about the white man. He will learn how they use their language as the weapon that gets them what they want. This is what he will do to help us protect the River."

Joe Loon listened as others offered agreement.

"It is time to bring Big Brian into our council. We will ask him to tell us what these markings mean. Then I will tell him that Simon will no longer sleep in my wigwam. Now he must live with Big Brian and Raven Hair Woman. They will teach him how the white man thinks about these things they do."

Again, the men told Joe Loon why this was a good idea. And Simon wondered what this would mean for him, to leave his family's wigwam to sleep in a bed in a white man's cabin.

Chapter 25

THE COMMITMENTS

BRIAN WAS IN BED THE MORNING after Dutch flew him back to camp. It was a long trip from Ireland, and he had been waking slowly. Knowing he had arrived to an empty camp, he allowed himself the extra sleep his body and soul needed.

Maureen called from the porch that she was coming in and then appeared at his bedroom door. They each had a bedroom in this two-bedroom cabin, but the first season's low occupancy rate permitted Maureen the privacy of her own cabin for most of the summer.

She brought him a cup of coffee.

"Good afternoon."

He sat up with a grin.

"Ah, right with the tease." Brian stretched. "I slept like a feckin' baby."

"You've been in the pubs."

"Every night."

"You don't say feckin' to me, or the guests, an' most certainly not the Ojibway. That's the way you talk in the pub with your lads."

"It was a feckin' great trip."

Maureen crossed the room and handed him the cup, then stepped back. They had each seen the other in bedclothes before, but neither had been in bed at the time.

"An' full of surprises."

"An' full of surprises." He took a drink. "The day I caused that look a' terror on Katie's face, I figured she'd be the last who'd be able to forgive me, poor, poor Katie. Plenty a' time I fell asleep prayin' for her to be able to find some peace about that night... not for me, for her. What she must a' heard, on the other side of that door."

"She forgave you?"

"Oh no, no, after her first approach she kept me at a distance, but she didn't run an' hide. She did ask if we would send her more pictures of Innish Cove an' the girls."

Maureen sat on the foot of the bed, for the room had no other furniture.

"So now can you see a path to havin' 'em back in your life?"

"I'm not sayin' we're on it, but see it? Yeah, maybe I see it."

"Wouldn't they love it here? Ah, it would be grand. We'd set a cabin up special for them. I say we put a plan in place that has 'em comin' over for a visit next year."

Their mindfulness that this was the first time they were on a bed together was growing.

"So you go back over this winter to keep workin' on 'em."

"An' you'll come with me this next time."

Maureen feigned admonishment to break the growing tension as she stood and stepped back to the middle of the room, away from the bed, her hands on her hips. Brian put the cup aside.

"Let's not have this discussion every time you're headed back over."

"As I recall, last time, your point was it wasn't somethin' a business partner would do."

"It's somethin' a wife would do."

"So, this time the discussion is—would you go back with me if it was to become my wife?"

Maureen's arms dropped to her side.

"Become your wife? You need to be clearer than that when it's as important as this."

She took a step closer to the bedside.

"So then, I'm askin' you to marry me, back home, in Derry with your people or in Cong with mine, I don't care. Let's get married."

"When?"

"This winter, an' it's time ya answered me."

"Of course I will, yes. Haven't I been sayin' yes every day since we got reacquainted?"

Brian rose in the bed and Maureen moved to be embraced, but instead he swung his legs around her and dropped to the floor on his way to retrieve something from his trousers tossed in the far corner.

She sat on the edge of the bed when he returned, opening a dark blue velvet jeweler's box.

"I got it durin' my layover in New York. I nearly missed the flight to Toronto. I went into the nearest jewelers, an' comin' back I got caught up in more traffic than I imagined." He removed the simple gold ring from the box and she held out her hand for him to slip it on her finger.

"It'll do for an engagement, an' we'll make it up with a nice weddin' ring."

"It's perfect."

They embraced on the edge of the bed.

"What changed yer mind?"

"It was seein' Katie lookin' down at me when I was lyin' there on the street, an' she had this look about her, might have been but a moment, but I saw it; she looked like she cared—about me, if only was I hurt or not. My head was spinnin' still, an' my old shoulder pain was throbbin', but Lady Girl, I'm tellin' you, my spirits soared when I saw she cared. An' I must have had another dream, for from lofty heights I could feel you there next to me an' I knew if you were standin' there with me life would be grand."

"We'll get 'em back. An' I'd like to talk about us havin' some of our own."

"Is that what you want? I never figured you as one who wanted such."

Maureen pulled away slightly.

"Of course. It's what every woman wants."

"Even after you know what I am capable of."

She pulled back the rest of the way and stood before him.

"I know who you are. I may never understand what you did, how you came to a place where you were beatin' your own child. But I know you could never do anythin' like that again."

"I know that's so. I do. I know I have changed. There's hot temper there still. But it won't ever hurt anyone else again."

Maureen began to unbutton her blouse.

"Here's what every lovin' couple wants, an we're a pledged couple now for sure."

She unbuttoned her jeans.

"Mind you, I'm savin' our heroic feck for our weddin' night."

"That's fine. All I want in the world right now is to make love with you."

❊ ❊ ❊

Kevin had met with the most senior IRA leaders, some old, many new, for two days in a row after he first shared the news leading to his ideas for finding and approaching Maureen. He wanted her back, and active, and at first thought the others felt the same. He didn't like how this third meeting was going.

"So if you're saying you're taking over now, of course, that's your prerogative. I'm just asking if you'll explain why when I seem to be putting us in a preferred position with her, and all in good time."

"A fair question has an easy answer. Maureen O'Toole is your girl. You recruited her, you trained her, you sent her to Germany to get the money in the first place."

"No, it was Russell who approved of O'Brien's recommendation; you'd do well to keep that in mind about her. None other than Russell picked her to give him support on what he thought was the most important mission of his life."

"Just the same, there's those who think you two weren't just *acting* as sweethearts."

"We were close. I was recruited myself by her father. But there were never any passions or dalliances, and no one will ever say so in my earshot."

"But you can't deny you cared for her."

"It was my role to care for her."

One man had stayed silent until now, one of the new bloods. "An' so I have to say it, I know others are thinkin' it, why doesn't it surprise that you are the one who found her? And as you say, all in good time. Almost like, I don't know, you knew where she was."

Kevin looked from him to the others.

"I'm not sure I like that very much."

"He's not speakin' for me, but we are in one mind in bein' concerned that your closeness could tend to limit your... imagination about what we might want to do, or have to do, once you get to Canada, to get our 50,000 pounds back."

Kevin knew who his closest ally was in the room and directed his comment to him.

"And we still want to recruit her in again, because she wasn't just the lovely decoy some of you want to think. She starts smart and gets smarter under pressure. And she cares about the Cause."

"That's what we mean, that your care for her could cloud your judgment."

"I respect her. An' you need do is remind yourself of what they did to her da if you have doubts about how deeply she believes in the Cause. And I'll say it again if I need to—it was Russell himself who picked her."

New blood barked, "Russell's dead. He's no help to her now."

"If you can bring her back in, Kevin, all's the better, every one of us here is in favor of that. But what if she says no? What if she's grown soft out there away from the struggles? Then I'm with you to point out other options."

"Like what?"

"Like statin' plainly we need our money back and we want it right now."

"As far as any evidence I've seen, it's still not conclusive she ever had the money. The rumor I've been hearing is that when Russell died, he had the money with him and the Germans kept it."

"So I want to be there when she answers the question, where did they get the money to build the camp?"

"What if it was the money she got from Russell they used to build their camp? Are you going to make them sell it?"

"No, we've decided we want to own it."

"The IRA is going to own a fishing camp in Canada?"

"Of course. First, the profits are ours. And then, name a better business to cover us buying guns and ammunition? And an occasional purchase of dynamite as well, I would imagine."

"An' picture us bringin' in wealthy Irish businessmen from Chicago for a little holiday, so they enjoy themselves while we're telling 'em all about our needs to support the boyos back home."

"So I'll be comin' with you to make sure all these options are placed before her with sufficient vigor and import."

Kevin saw the logic to all of it.

"If you have it all figured out, how do you figure to play Brian? We've never strong-armed anyone across the Atlantic. That's a bit of legacy can't be changed."

"Seems she wouldn't want her husband to know."

"They're not married, just engaged."

"Our luck just keeps gettin' better and better on this one, Mac. If they're not married yet, won't she be all-the-more interested in keepin' our story away from himself."

"Guaranteed compliance… seems smugglin' guns might be the exact place to start with her as we decide if we want to keep it hid from Brian or demand he accept it."

"We won't know 'til we get there, so Kevin'll finish makin' the arrangements for our huntin' trip."

"I'm workin' on it. But let me hear you say it clear, we're going to start with the idea we've come to invite her back in."

"Sure. That's where we'll start."

The meeting ended. Kevin hung back to be the last to leave, then left through the back door, walked two blocks quickly to force anyone following to have to match his speed, and when he was confident he wasn't being followed, he hailed a taxi.

"Take the next left."

A two block drive down the side streets assured him no one was following, so he told the driver to head to the airport.

❈ ❈ ❈

Kevin had a cup of tea in a shop off the Dublin airport lobby, waiting to be certain he wasn't being followed, then lined up at the Pan Am ticket counter.

"How much for a ticket to New York on tomorrow morning's flight?"

"Sorry, sir. We're fully booked on that flight. Thursday mornin' we'd be lookin' at now, I'm afraid."

"Let's do that then. One way."

Over the next two days Kevin mentioned in passing to agents and associates that he was planning on doing a bit of travel, including a trip to Cong to recruit a new field agent to replace that unfortunate hurling lad.

❊ ❊ ❊

It was early afternoon the day Brian proposed. Dutch was flying into camp with four new guests. Brian and Maureen were lying in bed together when they heard the engine's roar and set themselves right to head out together down the path between the cabins and past the sandy beach to the dock.

"Lady Girl, I've forgotten to mention another notable occurrence of the trip. Guess whose comin' huntin'?"

"We hadn't yet decided we were takin' hunters."

"It was too good to pass on. You see, your Kevin's arrivin' two days after we figured to close for fishin', so we'll stay open another week at the healthiest of profit at what I quoted him."

"Who?"

"Your friend, Kevin Coogan."

"Kevin… you visited with Kevin?"

"He was in Cong."

"What was Kevin doin' in Cong?"

"He came to town to see the Hollywood circus. A great part of Ireland has traveled to Cong to join the circus. That's what they were callin' themselves, the national amusement. He arrived just before I got there, an' when he heard I was visitin' he tracked me down. Innish Cove was gettin' our share of the pub talk every night."

"The very same Kevin I was with the night we met?"

"Lookin' much older. Seems the war years were rough on him. There will be two or three joinin' him. He's still got to give me the final count, but we have dates nailed down. He's goin' to wire half the fee in the next few days."

"Kevin's comin' here with a huntin' party?"

"He sent his good wishes, an' he's lookin forward to seein' you, yeah."

At the dock they met Joe Loon and Albert, distracting Brian so he didn't notice when Maureen turned to walk back to her cabin.

As the Norseman taxied across the lake, he asked Albert to tell Joe Loon about the hunting party and his need for rifles, and then told them what he knew about the guests on this plane. It was not until the guests stepped out of the plane and into Brian's introductions that he realized Maureen was gone.

❄ ❄ ❄

The newly arrived guests were settling into their cabins so Brian returned to his to check on Maureen. She wasn't there, but he found her buried in the pillows and covers in bed in her own cabin.

"How 'bout that for a total transformation. I looked for you in my bed first."

"It came on me all of a sudden, a sickness of some sort. I needed to sit down, then I needed a lie down…"

"I turned an' you were gone."

"I was just fadin' to sleep when you stepped in. I think the best is a good rest. I'm quite tired. Why don't we just assume I'll sleep the night an' hope I'm feeling better come mornin'."

"I'll check in on you?"

"That'd be nice."

❄ ❄ ❄

Brian said good-night to his guests after sharing a drink with them in their cabin, and before he returned to his own he checked on Maureen. She feigned sleep as he entered.

Brian tucked the covers around her, and she awakened enough for a kiss and a good-night, then Brian left.

As he approached his cabin he saw Joe Loon holding a lantern, waiting at his door. Simon and Albert were captured in the illumination.

"Simon has something to show Big Brian."

"Well, come on in."

Inside Simon told Brian about the strange visitors he had followed, what they said and what they did, and then handed him the map. Brian spread it open on his bed, noticed the Abitibi Lumber Company's Crown Corporation seal on the corner, and discovered his fishing camp on the map, "Irish Cove F C" written in small, neat blue-inked letters next to an X that marked the spot. When he tried to determine the key that identified the other markings the code was confusing, the patterns beyond his recognition, and he wasn't aware of what was located in any of those places to begin with. Most of the markings, nearly all of them, were to the south, well above the rapids, and quite a distance from Innish Cove. Brian was happy to note that, and the anger that was growing since he saw the inaccurate identification of Innish Cove relaxed a bit.

Albert translated for Brian as Joe Loon explained the map, pointing to the sacred places as he described them. Two of them were marked in the same small, blue-ink letters, I. B. G., and VSITE and Brian learned about the centuries-old burial ground and the place where Simon had been on a vision quest.

Then Joe Loon unfolded the full map and spoke of the whole expanse captured by its boundary markings.

"This is the white man's picture of the River and the forests of the Keewatin clans. The white man's treaties left this land for our people so we can live like our ancestors taught us. Because we have been happy to live the true life of the River, it took us a long time to learn what the white man means with these treaties. Our ancestors did not know. When our grandfathers signed the treaties, we were told the treaty words meant our People would allow the white man to live in these forests with us in peace. Later, we found these treaty words meant we must surrender these forests to the white man whenever they decide to take them. This is the forest we have not surrendered. This is where the Keewatin clans trap. There are many other clans north of this lake we call Gaawaandag. Here there are Métis families living in the bush. None of these people have surrendered to move to Grassy Narrows or White Dog. We will not surrender. Now we come to ask for your help."

"I can tell you this—when someone's tryin' to hide somethin' from us, that's never a sign of good intention. Dutch flew 'em in a few days before I left for Ireland, an' they said they were scientists, men who study animals, from some university. I don't remember if Dutch said which one. They said they were lookin' for a good site to observe wolves an' moose."

"For many years we have worked as lumberjacks for the lumber companies. There are many times they say cruel things to us there.

Some of the men treat us like dogs. But we ignore these things for these are jobs many of our young men enjoy doing. The ancestors smile at this work."

"This time it looks as if the plan is to cut a loggin' road that connects this paved road with the River here, and then build a pulp mill on that site... You imagine we'd ever want to fish that far south of the rapids?"

Albert and Joe Loon concluded they would not, that they saw no reason to fish the other side of the rapids at all. Albert translated Joe Loon's direction. "There are days we will take the White Man who Fish to the River below the Mamangashkaa. There are many bass feeding among the rocks there. And they will see the great beauty in the spirits that gather all around Mamangashkaa and it will fill their hearts with a great happiness. But there is no reason to fish above the rapids."

"I was thinkin' the same. Say again what you call those rapids?"

"Mamangashkaa."

"It looks like they're plannin' on buildin' their mill about ten or so kilometers south of Maman gashkaa, an' that's over twenty kilometers from Innish Cove. I'd rather they were downstream of us, but nearly twenty-five kilometers upstream with the nearly-insurmountable Mamang ashkaa between, they shouldn't be a problem for us... So what's to hide?"

"The answer to that question is in this."

Simon handed Brian the report.

"What do we have here? Yes, this was meant to be kept secret. These big red letters, they spell the word 'Confidential', meanin' they don't want anyone to know what's in here but them who needs to know. An' from now on that includes your people an' mine."

"You will learn their big secret?"

"After the boats go out in the mornin', I'll set down with Maureen to go over it together. She's better 'an me at gleanin' meanin' from things like this, at knowin' what to pay mind to. We should have some idea by the time you get back from guidin'."

Albert took Simon by the shoulders and stood him tall in front of Brian.

"Joe Loon asks that Big Brian give him a special gift. He asks that you make a place in your cabin for Simon. He asked that he stay in the cabin of Big Brian to live with you. He must learn how the white man thinks. Simon will stay with you so you will teach him how to do this. Then we will know if they are the men from Joe Loon's dream who will harm us."

"You want him to stay with me?"

"You will treat him like he is a son to be taught the ways of the world he is to live in."

"I am honored you ask this of me. Tell Joe Loon that I obey him as if he were my father."

Joe Loon reached out to take Brian by the arm.

"He calls you his son and says Albert Loon and Big Brian are brothers."

"We will always be brothers."

Chapter 26
SECRETS REVISITED

THE NEXT MORNING BRIAN GAVE SIMON a canvas and cloth shoulder bag to carry the map and report. They headed to the lodge to make sure someone had started the fire for the cook stove to prepare guests' breakfasts. Joe Loon and Albert were waiting for them outside their cabin.

"Naomi and Marie are boiling water to make coffee for Big Brian's guests. They will make Red River cereal and fry the eggs and bacon. We will go with you to see Maureen."

"She was not feelin' well last night."

"We will go there with you."

❀ ❀ ❀

Maureen and Brian sat at a table in her cabin. The Ojibway stood around them as Maureen had the document open at two places at once, checking from one page to another. Brian looked up and scratched his head as he turned to Albert.

"Maureen will keep studyin' it. The rest of us need to get down to the dock an' get boats ready. Simon will stay here with Maureen."

Brian gave Maureen a pat on her shoulder and led the Ojibway out to work.

❀ ❀ ❀

The fishing boats had all departed for the day. Brian and a young Ojibway boy collected the stray floatation cushions and an extra gas can and carried them to the dockside shed. Maureen emerged from the trees, heading down the path to the beach, the report open in her hands.

Simon was right behind her.

She stole another glance at what she had just found as she approached Brian at the shed.

"I've seen this sorta thing before. You say it, but you bury it. Then later, if things go wrong, you can claim you did your duty, you warned of risks to come, the point being whoever wrote this thinks there might be risks to come."

"Ya've seen this sorta thing before, you say?"

Maureen stood in front of Brian and with her finger drew a circle around the middle portion of a page.

"This here was prepared to be filed as part of two permit requests. One is for loggin' an' another for buildin' a pulp mill on the River."

"An' still I see no reason to hide that. I'd rather they were farther south or downstream. But still there's nothin'—"

She flipped to another page.

"Well, it's the fact that they're plannin' to build a new sort of pulp mill, with some new process none have used before. It's right here, 'a process that must be seen as fundamentally experimental in its nature, in that it is still bein' 'tested and refined' it says here, but no place else. It's all about tryin' to create a new sort of paper."

"Paper is paper."

"No, actually. Feel this last page; it's much smoother and almost shiny. They're sayin' this is the sort of new paper that big businesses will need soon because 'we're beginning to view a great range of new office automation machines that increase organizational efficiency.' That's what this front part says, there's new sorts of machines bein' developed that will make copies of documents for an office, and these machines require smoother paper, without this heavy pulp content, so it will glide more smoothly through these automation devices. A harder paper, so no paper pulp residue is caught up in the office machines. They want to be offerin' it first out of this new mill. Right here it says 'It's the future of the paper business,' this new process makin' this new paper."

"So where's our concern in that?"

She turned to the last page she'd marked.

"This new process, or some piece of it, it seems there's someone thinks it just might be a threat to the River. They have asked in this application to be permitted to dump 'processed residual by-products' right into the River. That's where they start makin' it hard to decipher what they're up to."

She turned the page again when Brian said, "It's a great big River; they're so far away. How could dumpin' wood bits left over from makin' paper into the River be in any way dangerous to us?"

"I'm thinkin' it's somethin' else they'll be dumpin', but I can't tell 'cause they are hidin' it well. But they have attached this scientific study that concludes this mill will be of little risk to River life in closest proximity, and no risk after that."

"So then."

"But it's noted here, in a dense page of equations an' footnotes, that a previous study came back with a minority dissent by someone who says that if this waste they'd be dumpin' would somehow become concentrated in fish life, then a diet of contaminated fish might have 'the potential for a range of debilitating impacts on fetal development to a population that consume the River's downstream fish as a regular part of their diet' are the words he uses."

"Babies in the womb?"

"Exactly. It took me all mornin' to tease it out, and I'm still not sure it's anythin' once I did, because he goes on to say this is a 'worst-situation speculation with minimal scientific exploration,' but I'm guessing this has somethin' to do with why they are tryin' to keep all this secret."

"For shiny paper they'd even consider puttin' the River at risk?"

"Keep in mind it's just one dissent against three other scientists who declare any risk is minimal, and only local. And the dissenter backtracks as soon as he states his concern. But it is there."

"Here's a guess. Not a one of them lives on the River."

"The permits have already been granted an' a good deal faster than it took our partnership to get our land lease."

"Is the dissenter identified in the report?"

"That study came from Queens University, in Kingston, near Toronto. Only name given is their lead scientist, Dr. Tobin Williams, and he's on record as sayin' the risks are negligible."

"So we need to find this fellow, this dissenter, an' find out what it is that concerns him."

Brian asked Simon, "What's your understandin' of what you're hearin'?"

"We need to quickly learn if we have a good reason to stop this pulp mill."

"Our solicitor does a lot of work with lumber companies. I'll get Dutch to fly me an' Simon into Kenora tomorrow an' see what he thinks about all this... seems the government needs to be protectin' her lease holders."

※ ※ ※

The next day Brian was in the co-pilot's chair, flying back to Kenora with Dutch, with Simon in Maureen's usual place, standing between the two seats. The young Ojibway had only flown twice before, and his delight was clear in his broad smile.

When Brian radioed Dutch to come get them he hadn't told him why, not trusting the security of radio communications. He explained his suspicions as they flew back, and Dutch told all he knew about the two men.

"When I flew them out they said some Indian boys had vandalized their camp, that they had burned all their maps and records."

"So they have no idea we've got their report."

"That's what it sounds like to me."

"Did they say anythin' about comin' back?"

"In fact, they said their job was done, that the site wasn't any good for a field study after all."

※ ※ ※

As soon as the Norseman disappeared over the horizon, Maureen began outfitting a boat. When she was finished, she entered the Ojibway camp and found Albert in front of his wigwam on all fours on the ground playing with a toddler.

This Man sat under the nearest tree, adding to the designs he'd been carving in his pipe.

"Who is this young fella?"

"This is John Baptiste. His father is Adam Baptiste. He's Métis."

"Well he's a darlin' child... Albert, I'm here askin' you to take care of things while I go to the Hudson Bay Post. I need to check out the rifles we need to purchase for the Irish hunters and was wonderin' if there were any shortcuts or tips to make sure I'd find it."

She offered her map and Albert located the mouth of a narrow Riverside channel for her.

"This can be hard to see. You look for three tree stumps at the back of this bay. And there are rocks in this channel. When the water is low, these rocks could break a prop."

"How long a boat ride is it?"

"Oh, it takes between two and three hours, I reckon. You will need two tanks of gas to get there and back. You don't want to buy gas from the Post, oh gee they charge a lot for gas."

"I'll plan on bein' back in time for the guests' supper. But in case I'm a bit late, can the ladies cook up some steaks an' potatoes for them?"

"We will take care of the guests."

❄ ❄ ❄

After a brief stop at the NOA office at the Lake of the Woods docks, Brian led Simon from the docks up the street into downtown Kenora. As they turned onto Main Street, Brian walked right past but Simon stopped frozen at the sight of an Ojibway man, a drunk in an unrecognizable shambles, sitting on the corner, leaning against a lamp post, head bowed, a low grumble rumbling from him. It was a chant.

Since Brian continued walking Simon finally pulled away, looking back while he caught up. He realized it was Adam Angeconbeb when he heard the chanting was about the man's dead sons.

❄ ❄ ❄

Maureen navigated the narrow River channel while standing in the back of the boat, one boot on the back bench, the other on the engine's throttle. She set the throttle at quarter speed as she stood tall for the best view to slalom between rocks and logs. Tall ridges on both sides of the River gave it a canyon effect.

Lily pads and rushes grew in the shallows.

She flushed a pair of blue-winged teals around one turn, a pair of mallards around another. A flock of coots exploded off the water, and then a great blue heron slowly rose with deep and strong wing strokes from its fishing in shallows chocked with grassy reeds.

❄ ❄ ❄

Brian sat across the desk from his solicitor. Simon had never been in a white man's house or office. He wandered the room, listening to the conversation as he touched all the books and the pictures and the odds and ends on shelves and windowsills that fill up a lived-in office.

Brian placed the report in the center of the desk, explained where it came from, and the nature of their suspicions. As he spoke his solicitor grew increasingly anxious, and after the quickest glance at the cover, he didn't look at it again. When Brian finished his story, the solicitor pushed the document back to Brian's side of the desk.

"I do hope you'll understand when I say working for you and Maureen is extremely interesting, you're both quite delightful as clients, in fact. But I need to be careful here, Brian, I'm sorry. Your business is important and I've told many I expect you and Maureen to become business leaders here in Kenora before too long, but last year over 70 percent of my billings came from the lumber industry, and there's years it's been even higher."

"That's why I figured you could help, you know the industry so well."

"I do know the industry quite well. And I best represent your business interests by helping you understand something, Brian. Every town around here is a lumber town, built by the lumber companies. We like to see businesses like yours flourish, but for this corner of the world, timber rules. And we need them to grow."

"Does that mean you won't help me on this?"

"I'm saying I need to think about it very carefully and you should, too... The Bureau of Indian Affairs is where you want to go first, I can tell you that. You won't get any other Ministry taking your concerns seriously on something of this nature unless you can get Indian Affairs on your side. But if this report is the smokescreen you think it is, and if they are hiding something, I'm not sure you do any good to be known as the man that brought this to light."

"If it's nothin', then it's nothin', an' nothing will come of it. But if it's bad for the River, I'd be proud to be the one who stopped it here."

"Stopped it? If they've got their permits, you won't be able to stop it. Once the government has made a ruling, I can tell you getting them to say they made a mistake, especially when it means opposing something the timber interests want, well that will be a long and expensive fool's errand."

"If you feel that way, I doubt you can help. But I'm not givin' up on your say so an' you've taught me enough to know this is a privileged conversation we're havin', an' so you can't be tellin' anyone I've shown this to you, yeah."

"That's right."

"Was a day I was ready to lay down a threat without a second thought about it, an' if it sounds like one now I don't mean it to necessarily, but I better not find out comin' to you first ever works against me later."

"It will suit me just fine if no one ever knows I've talked with you about this."

❅ ❅ ❅

Kevin deplaned in New York. He entered a phone booth at the airport, made a call to a Clan na Gael contact, and wrote down an address given him. He handed it to a cabbie who took him to a corner bar at the Queens address. One of the men waiting inside came out to pay the driver.

A half-dozen men were already gathered and a couple of more were due. Two of the men wore firemen's uniforms, two wore suits and ties, the others were blue collar in their appearance.

The bartender joined them.

The new arrivals handed tens and twenties to the bartender who stuffed them in an envelope already loaded as Kevin brought them all up to date on important IRA activities.

The envelope was handed to him and he folded it into his pocket.

"I can't say where I'm headed or to what specific purpose,

there's a secrecy about it we need to protect. But if you've ever hoped of finding a hidden treasure, well, I tell you I'm on a journey to see if I've found us one."

Kevin took a deep drink of the beer someone had put in front of him. He wiped his mouth with the back of his hand. "And I ask you to pray I retrieve it peacefully."

The firemen and others crossed themselves, one of the men in a suit reached across the table to shake Kevin's hand. Then they all did, as they got up to leave, and Kevin accepted the invitation to sleep for a couple of hours on a cot in the back room before he returned to the airport for his flight to Toronto.

❄ ❄ ❄

Maureen stood at the Hudson Bay Post counter nearest the wall where their inventory of firearms was displayed. The clerk assisting her held the bolt-action Winchester Model 70, a 30/06 caliber rifle she'd just examined, while next she studied the Colt .45 pistol.

"I'd have been happy just servin' fishermen at our camp."

The clerk nodded. "Ah but the hunters, they're the high rollers, eh?"

"It's what I've been told. I just don't know if I need to see a dead moose lyin' on the dock, or a lovely black bear shot dead. But they've asked us to outfit them with proper rifles, so I'll take that one there if you can get me five more just like it in two weeks."

"Three weeks to be safe."

"It's a month before they arrive, but I need to be sure."

"I'll radio you when they come in."

"Let's do that. Where do you get your rifles from?" She held the pistol and looked to aim it, moving off her first target, a moose head mounted above the door, to site on the British sailor in the center of the Player's Navy Cut cigarette sign on the wall.

"We get all our goods from the Company warehouses. And the Company, they buy enough they get them direct from the manufactures."

"With all Brian's talk about offerin' some evenin' entertainment for our guests, I think a little target practice might be fun. I want five of these Colt revolvers as well. The guests will have fun target shootin'."

"I only have one more in stock, so I can sell you two now and add three more Colt's to your order of rifles."

"I guess, yes, let's do that. Now let's look at ammunition."

❋ ❋ ❋

When Maureen returned to camp, she found Albert and gave him the rifle.

"I've ordered five more. If you'd sight them for us, make them ready, that would be grand."

She carried the two pistols in a small duffel bag to her cabin, pulled the trunk out from under her bed, removed her winter coat and wrapped it around the duffle bag, buried the coat under her clothes in the bottom of the trunk, and pushed it back under the bed.

❋ ❋ ❋

In Cong Tommy led his sister and brother to the Monk's Fish House. The abandoned small stone hut was built in the 12th century and sat over the River just below the monastery ruins. A slit in the flagstone floor allowed the monks to let out their lines and fish the River for trout in dry warmth when it was raining and cold. The roof had been gone for ages, but the walls were solid, and the three of them sat on benches along the walls, the lantern light shimmering gold on their faces and stone walls.

Tommy had come home for Patrick's eleventh birthday.

Katie had the stack of photos Brian sent her, and Tommy had just examined the picture of the two Ojibway girls who had written Katie a letter inviting her to come visit them the next summer. She looked him in the eye and she said, "I'm not saying I want to go. And I'm not speaking for Patrick, just myself. I'm only asking you to not get angry with me if I ask why we can't even talk about it."

Patrick couldn't look at his brother but did speak for himself.

"It could be an experiment. Do the spells go away, or do they get worse, if I start thinkin' of Katie goin' over to visit the Indians and see the wilderness?"

"What's the result so far?"

"Too soon to tell. I was all right when she first told me, but then I did get a spell right before you arrived."

Katie studied Tommy in the lamplight as Patrick spoke. She decided it was time to tell him the truth.

"Uncle Eamon always told us we had to be true to each other."

Tommy nodded. "We will always be true to each other."

"I see a pattern to them."

"What's that?"

"Patrick's spells. There's a pattern to them. They usually get worse, he has more of them, and they seem more severe, when he knows you're comin' home."

"What?"

"He loves you too much to say it to you, Tommy, and I told Uncle Eamon I love you both too much not to."

They were quiet. The River rushed under them, gurgling around the stone pilings. Tommy stared at the fishing hole in the middle of the floor.

Patrick wiped at his eyes. Katie let her tears roll down her cheeks. She got up and sat right at Tommy's side, hugging him. Patrick slid over to lean into Tommy's other side.

"How long have you known you get worse when I'm coming home?"

"A couple of years ago is when I first noticed."

"Do you know why?"

"I'm afraid I'm not as angry as you want me to be, with him. When you aren't around I have learned to not think about any of it at all, and that helps me feel better. But when you come home you expect us all to still be so upset with what he did... to me... so I pretend to be angry, like you, an' I think that sets 'em off."

"You pretend to be angry so I won't be mad?" Tommy was quiet. His brother and sister waited for him to speak. "I've been failing you as a brother and my Lord as His servant."

They all listened to the River's music. Katie leaned back so she could look Tommy in the eye.

"So you won't be angry if I just talk about makin' a visit?"

Tommy was quiet much longer this time. He put his arms around his brother and his sister, and they waited patiently for his response.

"I think I should go first. Father John's been urging me to

an' has offered for the Church to pay for my flight if it was a trip attempting reconciliation. I'll go, and when I come back I'll tell you what I've found, and you can decide for yourself. If you go, your trip will have my blessing."

"I'll start measurin' my spells, so."

❄ ❄ ❄

The next morning Tommy waited for the bus back to seminary. Eamon, Patrick, and Katie waited with him. Tommy turned to Eamon.

"I'll ring you as soon as I work out arrangements."

"Brian'll pay for the tickets when you let him know you're comin'."

"I'd rather not take his money. Father John has said many times the Church will cover it if ever I was ready for a trip of reconciliation."

"That's what you're callin' this?"

"I'm praying without ceasing that it will be."

The bus chugged down the road into the center of the village. Tommy asked Patrick and Katie to walk with him for a moment, leaving his bag with his uncle.

"All this anger I've got, I need to confess why it burns so hot. It's because, the way I've always figured it... Well, it should have been me was beat that night. It shouldn't have been me baby brother, it should have been me."

"Oh no, Tommy. You tried to stop him. We both did, but we couldn't. He was too strong for us. So you did the only thing we could do to save him. You ran to get Uncle Eamon."

"I should 'a sent you to get Uncle Eamon, Katie. I should have stayed and put myself between... Instead I ran out into the night, scared of what was happening and left you both with a madman."

Katie was crying.

"Ah, Tommy, I never thought that way, not one time, and if you are askin' me to now, I say you're wrong as you can be."

They were quiet. The bus unloaded one passenger. Eamon stood at the door chatting with the driver but then he waved Tommy back.

Patrick took his brother's hand.

"I never thought I ever had to forgive you."

They hugged and then Tommy looped Katie in with one arm for each.

"Blessings on you both."

"And on you and your safe travels."

❋ ❋ ❋

Brian and Simon stayed the night at the Hotel Kenora. The next day they waited for nearly two hours in the Indian Affairs Regional office until the first agent was made available. Brian was barely into his story when the agent interrupted him, excused himself, and hurried from the room.

Brian joined Simon's examination of a wall of photographs of Ojibway and Cree taken from the late 1800's and early 1900's. There were portraits of posed warriors and chiefs, of their people tapping maple trees, of a man and woman building a wigwam, of two men paddling a birch bark canoe.

Brian examined the chiefs.

"Look here, lad. Doesn't this fella look so like Joe Loon? What was his father's name?"

"They called him Waubishgaugauge."

"Does that by any chance mean White Crow?"

"I hear the name as Wise White Crow."

"Then this must be Joe Loon's father."

When the agent returned, Simon composed his look like a warrior from one of the photos, the shoulder bag strap across his chest like a warrior's sash. Brian and Simon were ushered down the hall to a meeting room where four men and a woman waited. The men were introduced as the senior staff of this regional office of the Bureau of Indian Affairs, the woman as their secretary.

Brian was surprised they were all white. One of the men stood to direct Brian and Simon to their chairs. Simon removed the shoulder bag and placed it on the table in front of him and sat up in his chair, resting one hand on the bag, maintaining his warrior pose. The staff turned to the regional manager at the head of the table.

"Mr. Lerner thought your story seemed important. We'd all like to hear it, Mr. Burke, if you don't mind, from the beginning, please. Mrs. Parker is here to take notes."

As Brian told them the story, they asked few questions. Once the secretary asked Brian to repeat his answer, after the regional manager asked her to make a special note of it. When Brian finished, the regional manager tapped the table twice with his pen.

"Do we have any further questions for Mr. Burke?"

Each of the others said no.

He tapped the table again.

"Fine, then, fine. We thank you, Mr. Burke, for bringing this to our attention. Here's how we proceed on a matter such as the one you present to us today. You can leave the report you mention with us." The regional manager nodded at the bag in front of Simon for he'd assumed the report was there. Neither Simon nor Brian acknowledged the nod. "We will conduct our own examination. And when we have, and we are clear on the nature of the threat, if indeed there is a threat at all... If you would note, Mrs. Parker, that we can't possibly assume, just on Mr. Burke's say so, that there is a threat to life on the River at all, of course, just so we're all clear about that. But if upon our examination, we consider the evidence indicates further action, we'll arrange for a follow-up meeting and notify you once it is scheduled."

"You're askin' me to give you the report?"

"That's right."

"I can't."

"Why?"

"Because it doesn't belong to me."

"Yes, that's right. Mrs. Parker, let's note that Mr. Burke agrees on a key point of fact here and that is this report, in fact, belongs to the Abitibi Lumber Company, doesn't it?"

Brian smiled at Mrs. Parker. "Mrs. Parker, if you please, note that what I am agreein' to is that the report may have Abitibi's name on it an' their information inside, but in point of fact, it belongs to Simon Fobister."

"Then let me address myself to you, young Simon Fobister, yes, I should, you are the Indian boy at the center of this, who took these items. It seems I am speaking to a boy who thinks it's just fine to sneak into a camp at night to steal the possessions from the representatives of a very highly-regarded Crown corporation." He looked at his staff. "Let's keep that in mind as we proceed here." He looked away from Brian's gaze when he saw the strength behind the controlled anger.

"Listen, son, if you'll let us keep your report for a few days, we'll have a good study of it and decide how we can be of best service to your people. If you cooperate, we'll overlook any punishment that may be warranted for your taking another man's property."

"My name is Simon Fobister, and I will keep this report until I burn it."

One of the staffers said, "Until you burn it? What is it about you people that you can't figure out how to live in a civilized manner?"

It was Brian's respect for Maureen's last words to control his anger that had slowed his burn but only delayed combustion. Finally, it ignited and he pounded the table once, hard, and had everyone's immediate attention.

"Have you no Ojibway workin' in yer office?"

"I beg your pardon? Are you questioning me?"

Brian hit the table again, to the same effect.

"I'm just expressin' my surprise. I figured I'd surely find a number of Ojibway or Cree workin' here. Wouldn't it be the best job a red man could have, wouldn't ya think, workin' to help his people, usin' the might and power of government to do good for his people? I was thinkin' so many Ojibway would want to work here there'd be two or three applyin' for work every day."

"Well, for your information they don't apply at all."

"I hear your answer as a confessin' to somethin' about what is goin' on here that you don't want to be confessin'."

"What's that?"

"That the people you're supposed to be servin' see no reason nor benefit to what you're doin', or they'd be here lookin' to help you do it."

"Maybe they don't understand our purpose."

Brian couldn't hold back the disdainful laugh. "Sure, let's hear your purpose."

"Our purpose is to assist our native peoples in their assimilation into mainstream Canadian society."

"Now how would I translate that? That your job is to get 'em all livin' on one of your reserves? I think that's what I hear you sayin'. I think the Keewatin Ojibway, I think they understand your purpose quite well. An' they reject it."

"There's no doubt we're better equipped to help them when they all move to a reserve."

"An there's no doubt it's so much easier to take the rest of their land from them if you move 'em off of it first, if you got 'em herded all together."

"Your insolence does not serve your cause, sir."

"It's your cause, an' I hain't no feckin' sir. Two of your reserves, yeah, Grassy Narrows an' White Dog, they're both on branches of the River downstream from the site of this new mill. If this process dumps anythin' poisonous into the River, well, that won't be good for reserve Ojibway nor the wilderness clans."

"I am trying to take into consideration your outsider status, Mr. Burke, but even so, you have now gone too far when you start insulting my staff here by suggesting we would assume a cavalier attitude about a chance these people might be poisoned."

"Then I will apologize for my rudeness, but if Mrs. Parker would be clear in her notes that what I'm sayin' now is you an' your staff will not stand by an' let someone poison this last lovely Eden."

"I was told you came for our help."

"I'm ready for all the help I can get. I'm makin' it clear to what end your help is to be directed if you decide to make any effort."

"Ah, I see. Now you're telling us how to do our jobs."

"I'm sayin' the buildin' of this mill needs to be slowed down long enough to take a further look at what it is that concerns the dissenter. He may be but one man, but he's a scientist an' there's plenty of times it's the one fellow on his own who gets it right. An' sure, we'll turn over the report to you, an' I will sit with you all day to allow you to examine it an' copy any information out of it you want, so you can execute your duty to determine if there's a threat, but when we leave, it leaves with Simon Fobister."

"If we decide that step is called for, we'll call for it."

Brian stood. Simon looped the shoulder bag over his head and stood with him.

"When you decide you want to read it, you should come callin'.

You should come visit our fishin' lodge an' Joe Loon's village, or we will meet you at Grassy Narrows an' then we will gladly hand over the report for your examination."

The regional manager and his staff stayed seated.

"Thank you. Yes. We're finished here. You may go."

Brian saw Simon's stoic control, and it helped him leave without another word.

❋ ❋ ❋

After a good nap and a meal, Kevin caught a plane from New York to Toronto where he barely made the last connection to Winnipeg. He spent the night at a cheap hotel near the bus station, then took the first bus to Kenora the next morning, arriving a bit before noon.

While he shopped at an outdoor supply store, purchasing a couple of shirts, some trousers, boots, and then a small duffel bag to carry his traveling clothes, he asked where the NOA office was.

❋ ❋ ❋

Brian and Simon arrived at the NOA offices just as Dutch and an Ojibway were loading the Norseman with supplies going into camp on a flight scheduled to bring four guests back to town.

"The way I'm figurin' it, Dutch, is by the time you're ready to return with the guests I'll be ready to come back with you. I'll talk it over with Maureen to see if she don't agree but my argument seems a good one. I need to find the report's dissenter as fast as possible now that this is all in motion. I need to find out what he thinks of the mill's threat, an' I need to start now, for I'm thinkin' findin' him is just the first step."

"Don't be surprised if, when you do find him, he's already been turned. When you spend any time on the frontier you know Abitibi can play rough out in the bush, but others say it's nothing to how the family operates in the boardroom."

"It's clear them bastards at Indian Affairs are goin' to need some other source of evidence, since they're seein' the document itself as poisoned. They wouldn't even study it, bein' it's stolen property."

"You've got two days of mail at the office; I'll grab it, and we're off."

Brian and Simon settled in the Norseman while Dutch retrieved the mail and was locking the NOA office door when he turned to see who was crossing the dock behind him.

"You must be Dutch," Kevin said as he held out his hand.

"That's right." Dutch took it.

"I'm Kevin Coogan, a friend of Brian and Maureen's."

"Nice to meet you."

"And the same. I don't know if Brian mentioned he and I met up during his trip to Cong. I booked a hunting party with him for later in the year, and then good fortune brought me to Toronto to look after some business interests, so I thought it's just one more short step at the end of many to come out and see the famous Innish Cove myself. I've come to finish off making arrangements."

"So then welcome to Kenora. Brian's down there, at the yellow Norseman. He must be aboard."

"With Maureen?"

"No, with an Indian boy who works at the camp."

"The honor of flying in to the Great Lodge at Innish Cove with Brian Burke himself, and I get to meet my first red man. I've just arrived and the trip's already a success."

"How long you staying?"

"I'm afraid no more than a day or two. I'm leaving business that needs attending as it is."

"The fish are always biting somewhere on the River."

Brian turned in the co-pilot's chair when the side cargo door opened behind him. Figuring Dutch found something more to load, he was getting up to help. But Kevin stepped in, and Brian was shocked to a standstill.

"Kevin?"

"Hello Brian. Sorry if I've given you a surprise."

"Simon, this fellow here keeps poppin' up in the most unexpected places, includin' bein' the very hero I was tellin' you about who saved that little girl from the runaway horse cart back in my village. So welcome, an' if you don't mind, just what in blazes are ya doin' in Kenora?"

Dutch climbed in the pilot's chair and worked through the last steps of his flight check.

"I was telling Dutch, I needed to make a business trip to Toronto, and before I headed back to Ireland, I thought I'd come look your place over, see what I've gotten myself into. Tend to final arrangements."

"Maureen will be surprised to see you."

"She's back at the lodge?"

"She'll be waitin' at the dock."

Dutch interrupted for he was ready to take off.

"After we get up in the air, you can slide back with your buddy if you'd like. If you haven't buckled in back there, Kevin, Simon there can show you how."

❄ ❄ ❄

In the kitchen at the lodge, Maureen was fixing her midday meal. The radio in the dining room squealed and squawked, calling her. She dried her hands as she approached the small table where the radio sat, the microphone in front.

"NOA-1 to Innish Cove. NOA-1 to Innish Cove. It's Dutch. Over."

She sat at the desk, the microphone before her.

"This is Innish Cove. Good day to ya Dutch. On your way back? Over."

"I've got all the supplies on your list, and a few surprises. Brian and Simon are with me. Let me give the microphone to Brian. Over."

Maureen sat back and smiled at the sound of Brian's voice.

"Hey, Lady Girl. We've got such stuff to talk about, we need to huddle up as soon as I arrive. But someone else here wants to say hello."

Kevin was standing behind Dutch and Brian and the microphone cord was stretched tight to reach him.

"Hello, Maureen, it's Kevin. So I say *Over*?"

Maureen shot to her feet, the chair falling over behind her, and she nearly fell when she took a step back and tripped over it. The fear around her eyes was momentary, and she collected herself, setting the chair back in place.

"Can you repeat that transmission NOA-1? I had so much static my end I didn't hear clearly. It sounded like an old family friend, Kevin Coogan a callin', but that's too good to be true. Over."

"It's me. Over."

"How wonderful of you to pay us a visit! Over."

She stood over the microphone.

"I found myself in the area and thought I'd drop by for a cup of tea. Over."

"I'll start brewin'. I hope you're plannin' on stayin' awhile. Over."

"Just a day or two. Over."

"I'll get a cabin set up for you. Over."

Brian reached for the mike.

"We've been airborne about a half hour, but we're flyin' into some strong head winds, so the Dutchman figures we're still an hour an' thirty out. The departin' guests are still on the River?"

"Their guides will have 'em back by half three. I told them we'd get them to town for supper. Dutch has rooms for 'em at the Kenora Hotel, and their flight home is first thing in the morning. Over."

"That's what happens when you run things. It all goes accordin' to plan. I'll sign off, Lady Girl."

"Over and out."

❊❊❊

Maureen sat on the floor of her cabin next to her bed, rewrapping one Colt pistol in her coat, then returning the coat to the bottom of her trunk. She stood and held the kept pistol at her side, then turned suddenly to thrust the gun out in front of her. When she found she was pointing it at her image in the mirror, she quickly lowered the pistol.

She opened a box of ammunition and loaded six bullets into the cylinder. She held the pistol out in front of her again, this time aiming it at a tree trunk through the window. Then she slipped a small handful of bullets in her pocket and stepped outside.

After a side trip to the kitchen to collect targets, Maureen headed to the far edge of the fishing camp, away from the cabins, where a big tree had fallen over a rock outcropping. She placed an empty bean can on the rock's top edge so the massive trunk was a backstop. She stepped off ten paces and turned and sighted the can with the pistol in her right hand.

She'd never fired a gun before. She felt its weight and found she held steadiest at the first. Maureen slowly cocked the hammer, then slowly released it back to rest.

She lowered her gun hand and took a couple of deep breaths. She had wondered for years if they'd ever come after her, if too many breadcrumbs were left to lead them to her. The IRA had rules about physical force, and one of the most honored was that no violence occurred in the new world. She knew the rule, yet still she wondered.

She aimed again, cocked the hammer, and squeezed the trigger. The blast of the shot was louder than anticipated and the pistol nearly jumped out of her hand as the ricochet whine and an explosion of dust told her she had shot the rock, well below her target and to the right.

Maureen took her next shot with her right hand cupped in the palm of her left. She aimed, and fired. The rip in the bark was high and to the left, and closer to the can, but still nearly a foot away.

❉ ❉ ❉

The interior of the Norseman vibrated with the engine's rumble, and the wind was loud. Brian sat next to Simon, both of them across from Kevin, and as Brian leaned forward to hear better, Kevin leaned to meet him.

"I never heard you talk about makin' musical instruments before."

"I don't make them; I sell them. I represent craftsmen, artisans, from all over Ireland who are making the traditional instruments. I've kept shop in Dublin for some years now and have started calling on stores this side of the ocean. Exporting is the future, it seems. I have a few stores carrying our goods in the cities you'd expect, like Chicago, Boston, New York. I was in Toronto scouting opportunities there."

"And business is good?"

"Ah, Bri, that's the question I've pondered since I set out on this trip. It's never seemed a business before, you see. It was more a mission. Or if you allow me to say so, it's a calling that chose me. But it's changing. It all went stone-cold dead during the war, of course, and was so slow starting up after. But the last year or two, well there's new blood, and no doubt they see it as a business, which has brought great demands on some of my finest craftsmen an' a whole lot more competition."

Kevin leaned back and talked louder.

"I spend too much time wishing old days were back again and not enough time figuring out the new business end of things."

※ ※ ※

Joe Loon emerged from the trees and found Maureen standing fifteen paces from the can. He found the pistol he had been looking for since he heard the first shot in her hand, at her side.

She stood still, unaware Joe Loon was behind her, watching.

She stood still, breathing deeply, steadily, easily.

Then quickly, she raised the pistol in her right hand and cocked the trigger in the same instant, and just as quickly she raised her left arm to provide support, cupped her right hand in her left, took aim, and fired.

The shot was just short but so close the can was flipped spinning into the air.

"*Yaway.* Raven Hair Woman is a good shot. Her enemies must be afraid."

Maureen turned at his voice and answered what sounded like a compliment with a sheepish smile.

※ ※ ※

Simon found Brian's hand on his shoulder naturally comforting. Brian's voice easily boomed over the rattling, buzzing sounds of flight.

"His grandfather is Joe Loon. When I call Joe Loon the camp's number one guide, I do him a disservice. He's so much more than that. He's what we would think of as a chief. We'll make sure you get out on the River with him. This is one of the last places on earth you can be out in wilderness like this with a native born to it. Best I've figured, Joe Loon was born a couple of years before the turn of the century, somewhere around 1895 or '96, an' I'm startin' to see how life then was not much different than it was 100 years before that."

"You're lucky to have him as a guide."

"The actual fact is we wouldn't be where we are without him takin' it on like it was his own. All the Keewatin Ojibway have done us a great turn. Maureen's just come up with the idea we need to offer his clan some part ownership of Innish Cove."

They sat quiet for a time, dozing off, each looking up to see the other looking back.

After a ten minute nap, Kevin awoke to find Brian staring at him.

"You spend much time in Kenora?"

"We come in occasionally. This trip was for some meetin's with our solicitor an' with some government ministry types. We're not all together sure, but it seems we might have a threat to what we've just started buildin' here. Sorry, my mistake, the true threat is to the life him an' his people have been livin' on the River and in these forests for centuries."

"What kind of a threat?"

"We're not exactly sure. That's what we need to find out right away."

❄ ❄ ❄

Maureen pulled the trunk from under her bed, opened it, and placed her pistol, fully loaded, on the top of her clothes, just under the lid. After she pushed the trunk back under the bed she stood at the mirror, hairbrush in hand, and worked on her curl. She put a touch of red on her cheekbones. Just the slightest bit worked best for her.

She returned to the trunk, removed the loaded gun, placed it on top of the closed lid, and pushed the trunk back under the bed.

When she heard the far-off echoing rumble of the Norseman she gave her hair one more stroke, then headed down to the dock, smiling.

❄ ❄ ❄

Because Simon was returning after being away from his people overnight, all of the Ojibway gathered at the dock, or on the beach nearby, to greet him on his return from his adventure. One little girl, Sweet Mary, had become very fond of Maureen, and when Maureen noticed her, she scooped her up and hugged her tightly.

Sweet Mary rode Maureen's hip as the Norseman taxied in to be met by Albert and Mathew who caught the plane's struts and absorbed the last momentum of its glide to slow it to a stop at dockside. When Mathew caught the strut at his chest, he was a bit off balance. As he stepped backwards with the plane, he tripped over a gas can that shouldn't have been there, that someone left out of place. He stumbled and fell, arms and legs flailing as he tumbled off the dock and splashed into the cove.

As became his habit, Brian had climbed out of the plane as it taxied into the cove and was standing on the dockside pontoon as the plane approached. When he saw Mathew's spill, he jumped to the dock and ran to kneel down to reach his arm out to Mathew. He had learned that, just like most Irish fishermen, many Ojibway hadn't learned to swim.

When she saw Brian poke his head out of the bush plane, Maureen handed Sweet Mary back to the little girl's mother so her arms were ready to embrace him. Instead she ran to grab him by the waist of his pants as he bent over to help Mathew out of the water and onto the dock.

Mathew heard the laughter of his people and once he was on the dock, he joined them.

Maureen picked up the gas can. She hid her anger but spoke forcefully.

"Who left this there is who tripped Mathew into the River, and he owes Mathew an apology. He's just wet, but he could have gotten hurt, or it coulda been a guest who tripped. This area is always kept clear so we can load an' unload."

Joe Loon nodded once and that was enough for those who had watched for it.

Mathew began to shudder and held himself tight-shouldered as he fast walked down the dock up the shore to head up to his wigwam, and the young boy who had left the gas can ran after him to apologize.

Simon was followed by Kevin out of the Norseman's cargo door and down the ladder. Kevin didn't see Mathew's fall, but Simon always looked first for his Big Brother and saw his shivering wet departure and headed after him.

"How 'bout it, Maureen? An old friend of yours, a new friend of mine."

"Hello Kevin, it's good to see you."

"Once the prettiest girl in all the Six Counties, you're the prettiest in Ontario, I'm sure."

Kevin and Maureen hugged briefly, then Brian remembered he was looking forward to one himself and he took Maureen into his arms.

"And congratulations on your engagement. To both of you."

"Thanks, Kevin. An' I know you and Maureen have plenty of stories to tell, but some of my business with her is urgent. We'll get you set up in your cabin straightaway an' let you settle in."

"Of course, when a friend drops by unexpected everything you do is a most gracious acceptance of my intrusion."

Chapter 27
SWEAT LODGE

SIMON STOOD IN FRONT OF HIS VILLAGE CAMP, surrounded by all of Joe Loon's clan except the two men who were still out on the River with guests. Joe Loon stood beside him, and Mathew, in dry clothes and a blanket draped over his shoulders, was on the other side.

Simon took Mathew's arm, just above the wrist, and held him as he spoke about his trip.

"Big Brian took me to a place where we met with a big, important white man who is afraid of the lumber companies. The next day we met with many men from Indian Affairs. They are like the men from Indian Affairs who visit us when we are at Grassy Narrows." He waited while each of them remembered their time with these strange white men.

"They all got very angry when Big Brian told them about these papers."

Simon removed the document from his bag. He turned to the pages where the dissent was noted, and he placed his finger there.

"Big Brian says we will leave again, to search for this man who is afraid of what the pulp mill will do to our River. We will ask this man how to stop this. Big Brian says this man is far away in a place called Kings Town. He has asked me to go to this place with him. We will be gone three or four days, he says."

"When do you leave?"

"Big Brian wanted to leave today with the guests flying back to Kenora. Then this friend arrived who has been on a very long journey to come here. Now I do not know when we will leave."

"What lessons are you learning of the white man?"

"I am watching carefully. I examine all the things they place about them. I see that Big Brian is also Big Brian in the white man's world. I see he is the only one who is not afraid of the lumbermen. That is one thing I understand. Most of the white man world is still a mystery."

Mathew had heard Joe Loon speak of Maureen's skills as a marksman and had seen for himself her determination as she was coming to understand the pulp mill document's meaning.

"Raven Hair Woman is also a warrior," he added.

Joe Loon stood on the other side of Mathew. "There will be a sweat lodge tonight for Mathew. I will ask my son Brian to wait until the new day before he begins his journey so his son Simon may join us."

❄ ❄ ❄

Maureen led Brian out of Kevin's cabin and entered his behind him.

Brian turned to take her elbows.

"If there is or if there ever was anythin' between you two, please tell me right now."

"Let go."

He let go of her arms as she pulled away.

"Yes, of course, you're right. I'm sorry."

Brian took a seat, a deep breath, and looked up at Maureen standing boldly in front of him.

"I will tell you one more time. I nearly said one *last* time, but that's a dangerous thing to say, but yes, if you grab me with anger again, it will be the last time."

"I didn't hurt you, did I?"

"More than you should, an' the only reason I am forgivin' you is that there is somethin' between Kevin an' me, an' it is a deep love, but not in any romantic way. It's a long family friendship; it's more like you an' Joe Loon, an' you need to accept that right now."

"Can I ask one more question?"

"We said if you accepted the money, you accepted the past unquestioned from then on. Here's the first real test of your promise, and rules don't change because we are marryin'."

"But why does he keep showin' up, an' when he does, why does he seem to be lookin' for you?"

Maureen relaxed, smiled down at him, then knelt at his feet and looked up at him.

"An' you should be happy he does, or we'd never a' met in the first place."

"One more question."

"We agreed none."

"I said before I thought it seemed very strange to bump into him in Cong—"

"Where he saved a little girl."

"An' now he shows up here unannounced an' for the whole plane ride, I could tell Simon was made nervous by him."

"You're makin' me feel like I have to defend myself for Kevin bein' Kevin. Tell me what you're sayin', an' I'll tell you what I know, an' if that hain't enough, I have to declare all engagements an' partnerships as null an' void because I won't be livin' with suspicion. I can't."

"I'm sayin'…" Brian shook his head. "I'm sayin' I'm confused an' I need help unravelin' this mess I've made with Indian Affairs. I'm so tangled an' don't want to make it worse."

Maureen stood, pulled up a chair, and sat and waited for Brian to collect his thoughts.

"Our solicitor is sayin' that except for what you an' I own, all the rest of everythin' else in Kenora, all the businesses are either owned by one or another of these lumber an' pulp mill companies or they depend on them. He's even suggestin' that in this part of Ontario the government ministries are owned by the lumber companies as well. He says to see Indian Affairs first, we won't make any progress gettin' Forestry to reconsider the permit unless Indian Affairs files a protest, but the folks I met with care as much about these people as IRA cares about the cottages in Connemarra."

"But IRA does care about the cottages all over Ireland. Everyone benefits when we are one country again."

"I'm sorry Lady Girl, I'm not lookin' to bring IRA into this. I'm sayin' I probably mishandled our chance of gettin' Indian Affairs on our side by gettin' so angry at their mousey attitudes."

Maureen slid from her chair into Brian's lap.

"Then I've somethin' for you to consider. About the trip to Kingston an' about Kevin's arrival."

"Let me hear it."

"You've told everyone I'm understandin' what's in the report better than yourself. If so, then just maybe I should be the one lookin' after the dissenter."

"I was plannin' on headin' back to Kenora with the Dutchman today, dependin' on how you was thinkin' about it. I'm fearful I've riled the Indian Affeckers enough they might even tell Abitibi what I'm up to, just to spite me. So I'm thinkin' someone's got to go find this fellow an' talk to him before the lumber company does. Scientists like money, too, an' Dutch was wonderin' if he isn't already been bought off."

"So Dutch takes our guests back to Kenora as planned, an' we have him come back first thing in the mornin'. You an' I are here together hostin' Kevin at the lodge tonight, an' after we say good-night to him we'll come back here and decide who leaves in the mornin' with Dutch."

Brian stood with Maureen in his arms and he finished the plan.

"I'll go tell Dutch, an' then I'll see if Joe Loon can take me an' your man Kevin out for some bass fishin' before supper."

He tossed her on to the bed; she caught herself and rolled and opened her arms and legs to him.

"If you're goin' fishin', we've only got us a few minutes."

"So we'll do what we can with the few minutes we've got."

❈ ❈ ❈

In the Ojibway village camp, a great fire was blazing in the pit dug to heat the sweat lodge stones. Round, smooth hunks of granite called the Grandfathers, each one bigger than a two-handed hold of them, were collected over many years for their shape and size by Ojibway men as they traveled along the shores of the River and its lakes.

There were nearly twenty Grandfathers in the fire pit.

A traveling medicine man tended the fire with a pitchfork, maintaining its furious blaze. He was an old Mediwiwin, hair white and silver and grey in a long thick braid down his back.

This medicine man told himself his favorite stories as he stoked the hottest fire.

Men settled at the edge of the fire's heat, holding sacred bags or an ancestor's beaded belt. They told themselves their favorite stories, gave the bags an occasional shake, and rolled beads between their fingers.

This Man stood behind Simon and Mathew.

This Man knew these stories and many more.

The boys stared into the fire, watching the Grandfathers glowing so hot the center of each stone seemed the source of its brilliantly pulsing red.

Again, Simon held Mathew's arm, just above the wrist.

"My prayer tonight is you see how your wounds will heal."

"Ah, Little Brother. My wounds heal. But I am not the same as before."

"What does that mean?"

"When I was taken away from here, I called out to my spirit to stay behind. To wait for me here. When I came back from the white man's school, my spirit was not waiting for me. I am afraid it is hiding from me. The spirit that is in me now is a visitor. It is a stranger to me. I know when it arrived. I do not know where it came from. It will not leave."

Simon put his hand on his cousin's shoulder and rested his head on it, and they watched the fire. When Mathew finally spoke again, Simon heard and felt his sorrow.

"My prayer tonight is that I find out what I am becoming."

❋ ❋ ❋

The cabin that had been outfitted as the lodge was equipped with a small kitchen and all three of the Irish were jammed in together making supper and sipping whiskey.

None of the Ojibway would leave the sweat lodge preparation, so before supper Brian had taken Kevin for a boat ride and a bit of fishing and they returned just at dark.

The overriding goal now, both Kevin and Maureen understood and knew the other did too, was for Brian's suspicions to be fully deflated. Only then would they find a chance for a private conversation.

As they prepared the food, they spoke of all the crazy happenings in Brian's village back home in Cong.

"It was your man here who told them to call me a hero, and they treated me as such all night."

"You saved that girl's life."

"It was nothing more than being in the right place, just letting her jump into my arms. Truth is, I'm not sure I didn't trip you when I stepped forward."

"Naw, t'was the horse an' his riggin', got me 'cross my shoulders to knock me flyin' into the street. I got a pain there still."

"A hero among heroes is what Bri was callin' you when he returned."

The sweat lodge was low and round and covered with blankets and furs to be even tighter than a wigwam's birch bark walls. Its door faced the northwest, for as it was first being framed Joe Loon had been standing there when a loon's cry told him that was where the door must be.

Gathered between the sweat lodge and the fire pit were Joe Loon, Albert, Mathew, Old George, Simon, and three more Ojibway men preparing with prayer to process into the sweat lodge.

Some wore breastplates. They all wore thick bandanas that would soon be used to mop their sweat. Many had worn beaded and painted moccasins when they were sitting at the fire, but all were barefooted as they approached the Mediwiwin who held chest high the bowl of smoking cedar boughs. Each man stood before him, tossed a pinch of tobacco into the smoldering fire, scooped the cedar smoke into his face, again, and again, and again, then stooped to enter the sweat lodge.

The three Irish made a Canadian version of Irish breakfast for supper. Each plate held a mound of beans, thick slices of Canadian bacon, and a couple of biscuits. Kevin ladled the poached eggs onto each plate.

"When I consider all the Irish immigrants who live in my

business territories, and when I see how determined they are to remaining Irish, I have become convinced that in every English settled land in the new worlds it's the Irish who have the stronger and longer lasting influence."

"One of our guests, called himself Southside Irish, from Chicago, he was sayin' somethin' just like that. The way he put it we all agreed, that when the Brits became American they stopped bein' Brits, but our cousins in Chicago are still Irish when they become American."

Maureen had heard IRA leaders talking this way. "We can win in the world-stakes but can't claim victory in our own county."

"It creates a great export business for the bits of Ireland they still want around them, and the sounds of genuine Irish instruments, playing the old tunes, that sound is in our blood."

They filed out of the kitchen to a table set for a meal. As they settled, Kevin pulled out a chair for Maureen. Brian noticed.

"Kevin, I don't think I ever got the story where you two met."

Kevin knew to let Maureen handle this, since he didn't know how this had been answered before.

She started by taking Kevin by the hand.

"Me da helped Kevin get into the music business. Da was one of the finest fiddle makers around and was lookin' for someone to sell his fiddles and Kevin was lookin' for a business venture. Kevin was so young then that the other craftsmen, they were slow to warm up to him, but me da's support, it signaled to the other craftsmen in the area they should join as well. Then, after me da... died... Kevin came callin' on the family, offerin' his sympathy an' care, an' when I was showin' such a deep, lastin' grief, Mum asked him to divert me, to try to lift my spirits."

Brian waited for more.

Maureen and Kevin knew how to let silence work, knowing the quiet made Brian uncomfortable and that he would fill it.

"An' within your territory you go round callin' on, who, store owners?"

"That's right. I'm looking to find more shops to carry more of our instruments."

❋ ❋ ❋

In Dryden, a hundred miles east of Kenora, in the boardroom of the Abitibi Lumber Company on that same night, just two men sat at the end of the massive table, making the large room seem cavernous.

They were brothers. Their grandfather was the founder and chairman of Abitibi Lumber, their father was managing director.

The pulp mill brothers had worked for the family business as jacks in their teens and early twenties. They served in the British forces during the war and when they came home they first managed logging crews and then increasingly larger parts of the business operations.

It was still a couple of years before their grandfather intended to hand the chairman's position to their father, but it had been talked about. Their father had stated he wouldn't announce his successor until he assumed the chairman's role.

The brothers had led the initiative to build the new experimental mill, and it wasn't easy. Their grandfather didn't like the risk involved in investing so much in what was still an experimental process that would only pay off if a future market emerged. Their father believed the idea was a good one but thought the market was still five or six years away, so he felt there was no hurry. He wanted to see his boys struggle to prove their case.

There was a woodsman's hat sitting upside down on the table between the two brothers and a note pad next to it.

The oldest brother, James Miller, reached for the pad.

"I'll fold, you pick."

The younger brother, Stephen Miller, grabbed the pad first.

"I picked last time, eh?"

"Sure, you fold, I'll pick."

"Here's the obvious one. We need to find out as much about this Brian Burke fellow as we can."

Stephen wrote it down, tore off the page, folded it, and dropped it in the hat as James offered the next task.

"Check if any of his Indians ever worked for us as jacks, if they caused any problems, with alcohol, or any safety issues, any sort of attitude problems. Just write 'Problems with Indians' and we'll know what I mean."

Stephen tore the page, folded it, and dropped it into the hat, then prepared to write again as his brother kept talking.

"Which leaves the tough one, this asshole biology professor at Queens University. All he's got is conjecture and a big ego. This is starting to be more than a nuisance. Someone needs to visit him again."

Stephen looked up at James.

"Do I even pretend to write that one down, or do you want to go ahead and claim it?"

"What, you want me to go to Kingston to see if the muzzle is still in place?"

"What if I told you I know you're already packed and ready to go."

"And how would you know that?"

"Because that young Métis mistress of yours next door in Toronto sounds like paradise."

"What are you talking about?"

"You're not going to deny it, are you?"

"How did you find out?"

"What should concern you is that I didn't go looking for this news, it found me."

Stephen picked up the hat and offered it to his brother to pick his assignment.

"Does anyone else in the family know about her?"

"The place where I was when this news came to me, well, let's just say it's not where the old man hangs out."

❋ ❋ ❋

The Ojibway filled the sweat lodge, their hunched backs pressed into the heavy blanketed hides draped over the frame of strong, supple saplings. They sat under the tensed curve, cross-legged, knees just inches from one another.

Dangling from the saplings used to frame the sweat lodge were strings of cowry shells and figurines carved from antlers. Four white ribbons marking the Four Directions hung down from the centered top of the lodge.

The shallow fire pit in the center of the sweat lodge had been dug first and the lodge built around and over it. A bit of cedar bough was placed in the center of the pit and it was crackling sparks as the first bright and red-hot glowing Grandfather was laid on top of it by the pitchfork-wielding Mediwiwin who called on this Grandfather's spirit to be present with them.

The men answered with quiet calls to familiar spirits, for their presence, for their memory, for their story, for their honor.

The Mediwiwin brought another round stone, and another, filling the pit with glowing balls of fiercely-radiant heat and filling the lodge with the Grandfathers' spirits.

The first sweat appeared as beads on the first brows of the men.

After the seventh red-hot stone, the Mediwiwin sat at the door and closed the flap behind him.

It was full dark.

It was very hot.

The Grandfathers' glowed red in their deepest cores.

Simon couldn't resist; he always held his hand right at the tip of his nose to re-discover he could not see it as he felt the water rising in his body.

The stones were glowing, then all at once they sizzled and sparkled and snapped as the Mediwiwin ladled water on them. The steam rose and quickly disappeared in the dark.

The medicine man began a prayer chant to Gitchi Manitou.

The dry heat was filling up with hot steam.

Simon looked up and saw the four white ribbons glow in the dark.

The Mediwiwin was beating the drum now, to tell Gitchi Manitou that they have come to give thanks to him, and to hear him speak his wisdoms. Then he stopped and handed the drum to his right. Albert reached out in the dark, felt for it, and took it.

He drummed his prayers to the spirits and asked that they lead Mathew's spirit back to him again, then handed the drum to continue its journey around the circle.

❀ ❀ ❀

They were finishing their meal when Maureen and Kevin turned to listen to Brian.

"If the dissenter is prepared to speak out, I don't see we have a problem. No one could proceed as planned in face of expert evidence to the contrary."

Kevin stood to get the whiskey bottle from the bar as Maureen answered him.

"We don't have to look far to find examples of a British government doin' what was good for the powerful few even when it was wrong for the many whose life came from a little piece of land. An' last I checked, the British Queen is on the Canada dollar."

Brian held his glass for Kevin to pour him a shot.

"I guess you're right, now that I think about sittin' there with Indian Affeckers."

Maureen touched Brian's arm.

"Are you goin' to call 'em that from now on?"

"It's who they are."

❀ ❀ ❀

Twice during the sweat-lodge ceremony there was a brief pause to refresh. Both times the Mediwiwin opened the flap and the men all leaned forward to stretch their backs and to breathe deeply the cool air that rushed in.

At the second pause, Simon studied Mathew's face in the bit of light and smiled when Mathew looked at him.

Joe Loon was speaking to Albert.

"Maureen will take Simon Fobister to this place where the dissenter is found. This time my son Big Brian will stay here."

"I will tell Big Brian you must speak to him."

❀ ❀ ❀

No smart play had presented itself, so Maureen and Kevin still hadn't huddled for even the briefest private moment by the time Brian declared his night was over. He took one lantern and Kevin another, and they walked through the trees on a path just being worn.

Except for the lanterns, the stars were the only light. They could hear the soft lapping water on shore, the insects' buzz and chirp and hum.

Maureen followed behind Brian, Kevin followed behind her.

They were nearly to Kevin's cabin when Albert and Simon

stepped from the darkness. Albert told Brian that his father Joe Loon had invited him to his wigwam for a council fire. When Kevin heard that, he smiled.

"Your father?"

"I told you on the plane Joe Loon's people see me as a father to Simon. I've been honored to be called Joe Loon's son as well, an' Albert's brother."

"You certainly have gone native, haven't you? A feather would look good in your hair, Maureen."

"We show the respect they show us is all it really is. Where will you be when I return, Lady Girl?"

"I'll be in my cabin, waitin' for ya."

"Good night, Kevin."

"Good night."

They left Kevin at his door. Brian handed the lantern to Simon so he could use it to lead Maureen to her cabin, and then Albert and Brian followed him through the dark trees past empty cabins, along the beach, past the dock, and over a slight rise to the Ojibway village camp at the edge of the forest.

All of the people—the men and women, their children and the elders—sat around the fire where the Grandfathers had been prepared. The fire was burning low, steady for a long night. Some sang and others laughed at the stories the Mediwiwin told.

Old George taught a young boy a drum beat his grandfather had taught him when he was a boy.

Mathew watched Simon lead Brian and Albert into Joe Loon's wigwam and followed.

❄ ❄ ❄

Maureen lit her lantern before Simon left with his. She placed in on the floor next to her while she retrieved the pistol. She tucked the loaded gun in her jacket pocket, left the lantern on the table at her window, and stepped out into the dark night. She moved slowly while her eyes adjusted, then stepped gracefully towards the bright light coming from Kevin's lantern, shining through his cabin window.

When she drew close she called out, but softly.

"Kevin?"

He was waiting for her.

"I'm here."

"Kill your lamp."

A deep darkness enveloped them as she slipped into his cabin. They stood just inside his door, feeling close yet barely able to see each other, their expressions hidden.

"And so, Lady Girl, the question I have to ask is how much of our money is left?"

"Your money?"

"IRA money. The money Russell gave you."

"I told you, I never met up with Russell."

"I believed you when you first said it. Most did. But after you disappeared, then showed up here, hiding—"

"If I was hidin', would Brian have gone to Cong to tell everyone what we are doin' here?"

"And so you are building a fishing lodge, and an airline it seems, and these sorts of businesses, well, they take capital. Lots of it. Perhaps twenty or 30 or even as much as 50,000 pounds? So unless you can convince the others by showing us the source of that capital, and we know it didn't come from Brian, and I know it didn't come from your family, so unless you can show them where it came from, they will conclude it's their money you're using."

"We haven't invested anywhere close to 50,000 pounds to build this place."

"That's great news. So you are saying most of our money is still available."

Maureen looked out the window to check on Brian's return.

"Can I still count on you as a friend?"

"I have always looked out after you, Lady Girl. I've put myself at risk to come now. If you want my support to continue, you have to tell me right now where the money came from to build this camp. Surely you can see that's necessary."

"Brian was right when he said it wouldn't take much money to get this built. We didn't have to buy the land, we wanted to, but they would only lease it to us, an' I negotiated a very favorable payment for the first five years of the lease... An' with the Indians providin' knowledge and muscle, the cabins mostly come from the forest."

Maureen had circled Kevin a bit to position herself so the cabin's window opened out in the direction of the Ojibway camp, and she kept an eye cocked to the dark for a returning lantern. As Kevin turned with her the previously shadowed moonlight revealed more of their faces.

"What is Brian going to tell me when I ask him about the source of the money you've invested in your airline? In all those motors and boats, and the appliances in the kitchen? They didn't come from the forest."

Maureen didn't answer.

"Because when my huntin' party arrives, that's what they're huntin' for, the answer to that question."

They stood in the quiet and the dark.

❈ ❈ ❈

Brian knew the ceremony Joe Loon performed to bring together in his wigwam the clan elders, the spirits of their ancestors, the spirits of the animals, and the Great Creator. He took the pipe handed to him by Old George, raised it to the Four Sacred Points, took a puff, and then held the pipe so smoke rolled over his face.

He handed the pipe to Albert.

Sitting across from the men, Simon and Mathew listened to Albert explain Joe Loon's reasons for Simon and Maureen to take the next leg of this journey to learn about the threat to the River. This Man sat down behind Joe Loon and Albert.

"It is Maureen who told us what the words on the paper mean. She will be best at speaking to the man who wrote these words. The man named Dissenter."

Mathew sat with his head rested on Simon's shoulder. In a quiet moment, Mathew spoke softly.

"My spirit calls to me now. It is far away so I do not hear everything it is saying. But it offers us a warning. We must be careful. Danger comes closer. "

❈ ❈ ❈

Maureen took a deep breath, exhaled slowly, then spoke.

"Russell was a broken man when I saw him. He was wrapped in sadness. He was failin', the trip was failin', an' there was such a disappointment to him—I reckon it's what killed him. That's how it looked to me, an' I was the last countryman to see him alive, if you haven't realized that yet. He had concluded he had no chance gettin' the Nazis interested in attackin' the Brits in the North, an' I watched as he begged them for money. Gettin' British pounds wasn't provin' to be easy with the war ragin', that was the excuse they told him."

"You were the last to be with Russell."

"We can't ever tell anyone, Kevin, but he said he felt we were defeated."

"But he did give you some money to bring back to Ireland."

"He had a satchel with some pound notes in it, an' it was so few he seemed embarrassed to hand it to me."

"How much?"

"It sure wasn't 50,000. It was barely 2,000 pounds, an' when he gave it to me his last words were for me to hide it for him, an' to deny it existed, to deny we'd even met, that was his idea, until he came an' he got it from me himself, so."

"You should have told us this when you learned he died."

"When first you told me, well, I wasn't sure he was dead. No one had seen his body. An' until I was sure, I needed to be true to his directive. Then I went to every meetin' point we used, for months, for years, lookin' an' not findin' any of you. So then who should I have given the money to? If anyone's claim at that point was strongest, it was the Nazis."

"So even if you're given all the doubt on all your points, even if you can convince them the IRA abandoned you just as you say, and you were left with the money, then what? They'll take one look at this place and be quite pleased to conclude there had to be more money than you're saying, and that IRA has the prevailing claim on it all. A claim on all that money, and a claim on all that money has created."

"Innish Cove must be left untouched by this."

"Does Brian know?"

"Of course not... How can you help me, Kevin? What can you tell me that gives me a view to the right move?"

"It's the reason I came, to do just that. To find that move that helps make the IRA stronger and to keep you safe."

"Keep me safe? The IRA doesn't go after the New World. It's one of the first lessons you taught me, Kev. We keep Irish eyes smilin' in Boston so their money keeps flowin' to the boys in Dublin by makin' certain no whiff of actual bloody violence ever threatens the New Worlds. If Clan na Gael have to stare killin' in the face, they'll stop payin' for it."

"Some lessons that were true when I taught you aren't seen the same by many now. There's splintering left and right, and one of the new organizations is nearly as strong as us and claiming to be the real IRA. Hagan and Malone, they just left us to join them, and so have a couple of Hagan's toughs. It's mostly new lads, and those who fought in the war, and I have to say that war changed them, for they think differently about using physical force."

"That glow up in the trees, if that spreads, it's Brian's lantern crestin' the rise. We got just a minute. Let me show you this."

She removed the pistol from her jacket.

"It's loaded."

"You brought a loaded pistol."

"You're a good teacher." She handed it to him. "I've started stockpilin' pistols an' rifles. And plenty of ammunition, rememberin' times the boys had guns but no bullets."

"An interesting element to add to the discussions. Guns are always an achievement. How do we get them back home?"

The light was moving towards the guest cabins.

"That's Brian for sure. I haven't figured transport yet, beyond the notion that if I got them on a fishin' boat out of Nova Scotia, I'll bet you could figure out how to link up an' get them home. But understand this, Kevin. I'm prepared to send you guns or I'm prepared to use them on anyone who comes to this place intendin' to harm its existence in any way."

"I believe you."

"I may be leavin' in the mornin' for a few days. One of us needs to visit the dissenter an' it's best if I go."

"We'll try to find a moment in the morning before you do."

Maureen gave Kevin a familiar touch and navigated back to her cabin by the lantern in her window.

Brian knocked on her cabin door and burst in, filled with the joy he found whenever he was with his new family.

"When you an' Joe Loon…"

The lantern was on the table, but the room was empty.

"I'm in the bedroom."

Brian continued to the bedroom door.

"When you both have the same idea about what it is I should do next…"

In the candle's glow he saw Maureen stretched out on the bed in a white cotton nightgown, cut deep at the bosom, and open.

"I'll bet you know what you should do next."

"An' we have more 'an just a few minutes."

"So let's take our time."

"Are we workin' our way to that heroic feck you keep promisin' me, or is it makin' love we're after?"

"The heroic feck'll be me weddin' gift, an' thanks for askin'."

Chapter 28
THIS MAN AND THE WOLVES

THE ANNISHINABE AND THE DAKOTA fought hundreds of small skirmishes between their great battles for control of these forests for over a century. And just as the Iroquois tribes had driven the Annishinabe west, the Annishinabe slowly drove the Dakota from the forest to the plains.

It was the dead of winter, near the end of their war. A small Dakota village sat in front of a cluster of trees in a valley where the dense forests of the northeast thinned at the first rough edges of the great central plains. The village of nine teepees looked east over a vast expanse of frozen lake. The only movement was the smoke drifting from each teepee.

It was the moment of first light and no one was outside until a man emerged from his warmth, wrapped in a thick buffalo robe. He stood in front of his teepee and chanted a brief welcome to the rising sun, thanking the Great Creator for a new day.

It was cold so he hurried and was ducking to return to his warm bed when he stopped, for he could just make out two, no, three dark shapes at the far end of the lake, the sun's first red bright glint behind them, distorting them.

He called to his brother's teepee. He called a second time. The brother emerged, also wrapped in a buffalo robe.

From so far away, in the horizon's dazzle of half-light and reflecting snow, they couldn't tell if it was men approaching or beasts crossing the frozen lake.

The shapes weren't coming directly towards the village but perhaps were angling closer. One brother thought the figures were larger and thought they were far away, the other wondered if they were closer and smaller.

"They are men. Then they are wolves."

They called out to others in their teepees. First an older boy emerged, then two more men. They were five big brown humps wrapped in their great thick buffalo-hide robes.

"First they are wolves. Then they are men."

Each of the men returned to his teepee and came back wearing snow shoes, some carrying spears and clubs, others a bow in one hand and a couple of arrows in the other.

The shapes came closer.

"They are wolves."

The snow on the lake was deep and freshly fallen, so even with their wide paws it appeared the wolves were struggling as they crossed the lake.

A grin broke out on the face of the older boy, and he gave a soft morning whoop. He shifted his buffalo robe up over his head and stumbled through the snow as an old dying buffalo might, moving across the lake towards the wolves, his short spear hidden at his side, his breath frosting the air.

The wolves stopped.

The boy moved closer, excited the wolves hadn't retreated, hoping to get close enough to create a show, expecting they would turn and run when they realized they were approaching a village.

Instead the wolves jumped up into the air and tossed their wolf hides aside and three Annishinabe warriors were revealed. One was cocking his flintlock, the others held theirs ready but watched as the first took aim at the Dakota who had flung off his buffalo robe.

As soon as the wolf disguises were discarded, the men of the Dakota village were in action. One man ran to the teepees to alert everyone. The others threw aside their robes and ran out on the lake to rescue their own.

Those running to rescue lost but a half step as the musket barked and the shot struck the Dakota in the stomach, knocking him on his back, his arms and legs flailing, the explosion rolling through the valley and back again. The first from the village ran on as an Annishinabe raised and aimed his flintlock, but there was no more than a flash in the pan and he flipped the misfired gun to use it as a club when the Dakota rushed in behind his battle ax.

Another shot was fired wild, and as the echoes died the chilling yells of attacking Annishinabe were heard from behind the Dakota from their village. They turned to the cries of their families telling them they'd been lured from the main thrust of the attack and ran back to their village and families.

An Annishinabe had reloaded his flintlock, aimed at the closest Dakota running back to his family, and fired. The Dakota was hit between the shoulder blades and fell forward in a spray of snow, his legs kicking up over his head.

The Annishinabe gave chase to the two Dakota men running back to their village where now their teepees were burning.

The raid was already over as quickly as it began. Dakota women and their children ran from danger into the woods as the fires set to flush them from their teepees and then destroy the village grew stronger.

The leader of the raid called to his two companions to stop. He saw that the fire's heat was so fierce now that the rest of his raiding party was already retreating.

Soon the whole village was consumed in flames.

When they returned to the two Dakota, bleeding out the last of their lives in the snow, This Man watched as the Annishinabe kneeled next to them. "We have spoken our claim. These hunting lands are ours. Now you will believe us." Their scalps were cut from their skulls, their magic snatched from their necks.

The Annishinabe warriors gathered their wolf hides and crossed the lake into the trees where they met the rest of the raiding party to head back to their village in the forests in the east.

This Man went with them.

Chapter 29

THE DISSENTER

DUTCH HAD TAXIED THE NORSEMAN out of the cove and was readying for takeoff, Maureen in the co-pilot's chair, and Simon on a bench seat in the fuselage.

"Hold on a second, Dutch."

Maureen unfastened her seat belt and stepped back between the two seats, smiling at Simon.

"Go sit up there with Dutch. You'll get the best view of what we're tryin' to save."

"No, not the best view."

"A lovely view then."

"Yes, a lovely view."

❆ ❆ ❆

Maureen had been reading the report over and again since she first got it, and she was reading it when Dutch called her forward. He was flying over the rapids and heading south, down the River channel.

"Around this bend, there's a bit of a point, then there will be a shallow cove… Right there, that little cove, that's where they camped. And it won't take long before you can see the new highway. It's off to the south and to the east, that's where they plan on connecting. You'll see it's really quite a good distance from Innish Cove."

❄ ❄ ❄

Joe Loon took Kevin and Brian trolling for walleyes off a sharp rocky point. They caught a few, though nothing bigger than a couple of pounds. Kevin missed a strike, reeled in to check his bait, then turned to Brian to continue their conversation about running a fishing camp.

"So with a substantial capital investment up front, it becomes all about occupancy rates."

"We figured it would be at best 30 percent this year, an' it hasn't been, it's just over 20 percent. So even if it improves fast, we figure we don't have the capital for anymore improvements for a season or two." Brian felt a nibble, waited for another, and set the hook. "Everythin' costs more than you'd expect. I sure never expected solicitor's fees could mount up so."

"So along with investing capital to build, you're needing capital to cover running the place at a loss the first year or two, until occupancy rates do move up."

"The good news is every guest reserved a trip for next summer before they left, an' most of 'em say they'll be talkin' it up with friends, so they may be addin' even more to their groups over the winter. Maureen projects it out a couple of years an' shows how your growth creates more growth. It compounds itself, she said. It'll be a tight financial situation for us next year still, yeah, but I think we got it workin' right if we can keep the mill from feckin' it up."

❄ ❄ ❄

They were unloading at the dock at the end of the day's fishing when Kevin said, "I'd love to stay another day, but I do have to return to selling fiddles. What's my chances of getting out of here very first thing in the morning?"

"We've guests comin' in by ten. We'll send you back with Dutch."

❄ ❄ ❄

The next morning, Brian and Kevin waited on the dock as the Norseman taxied up. Brian and Albert caught her and tied her down. They unloaded the guests, four fishing companions, and Albert led them to their cabins. Brian promised to meet them there as soon as he saw the plane off. Kevin put his hand on Brian's shoulder as they shook hands.

"That bit of Eden you promised us that night we all met, Brian; I believe you are making it come true."

"Celtic Christians say we're on the earth to help complete God's creation. Don't know I'm altogether interested in what the Romans have to say in the general course of a day, but the Irish Church, she got that one right, best I can tell."

"I'm already looking forward to my return."

"We'll be ready for you. Joe Loon an' Albert here will be scoutin' game the week before you come an' them rifles Maureen ordered should be here in another week, so they'll be sighted an' primed an' loaded for bear."

Dutch climbed down from the plane, asked Kevin if he'd enjoyed his trip, then handed Brian a telegram.

"This came just as I was loading up."

It was from Ireland. Brian tore it open.

"Speakin' of the Roman Church, it's from me eldest, the seminarian."

"And good news, I hope."

"Well, now listen to this. 'Brian. Am plannin' a visit. Stop. Please call St. Michael's for arrangements', and he gives me a number to call."

Knowing all but the worst details of Brian's exile and estrangement from his children, Dutch understood a visit from any one of Brian's children would be a great occasion, a cause for celebration.

"That's great news, Brian. Kevin's becoming a bit of a good luck piece for you, eh?"

Kevin smiled. "You'll be bringing half of Ireland over here before you're through."

"Dutch, can you plan on placin' the call in the mornin' an' then patchin' me in?"

"Let me write down the number."

"Safe travels home, Kevin, an' Maureen an' I will be ready for you an' your boyos."

❊ ❊ ❊

When Maureen and Simon arrived in Kingston, they searched out the offices of the biology department at the university. They found the secretary alone, and after a hushed conversation she agreed to talk again. On the second day, to Maureen's surprise, information was promised for the exchange of money. A dinner meeting was set up where the exchange would take place. Then Maureen took Simon shopping for new clothes.

He stood on a tailor's footstool, nearly surrounded by the three-sided mirror and Maureen and the old tailor who was marking the blue suit Maureen picked out for Simon to wear.

"We need it tonight."

"Alterations take three days."

"I started makin' my own clothes at ten. What I see needs to be done can be done in an hour."

"But I won't have that hour until Wednesday, or Tuesday at the earliest."

Maureen had the bill folded and ready, and she tucked it in the tailor's shirt pocket while he marked the cuffs.

"I'm reckonin' on that bein' enough to help you find that hour today, even if it means stayin' over a bit. We have a dinner at eight, an' my friend here needs this suit for an important meetin' takin' place durin' the dinner."

The tailor pulled open his pocket to see the size of the bill, took a fresh look at his customer and his patron then smiled while he returned to marking with a chalk.

"You can pick it up at six."

❊ ❊ ❊

Maureen and Simon sat at a center table in the finest French restaurant in Kingston. Most of the patrons took a moment or two to look their way and some found it hard to look away. Some noticed Maureen's black hair and made the same initial mistake often made when Maureen was with the Ojibway, that she was aboriginal. Or, when they then noticed her bright blue eyes, that she was partly so. At more than one table they were the new topic of conversation, the beautiful woman and her handsome young Indian companion.

Simon wore the dark blue suit with a fresh white dress shirt and silver tie. Before they returned to the hotel to dress, they found a store where Maureen bought Simon the blue paint he had requested. He painted a broad blue diagonal stripe across the tie.

Before they left the fishing camp, Mathew gave Simon the head dressing he made for the trip. It was a single great grey owl feather, tagged by a ring of quill bits, and he was wearing it near the top of his head, just off center to the right.

Maureen wore a blue evening dress with her mother's lace collar pinned in place.

They had menus and water and were being served dinner rolls. Maureen showed Simon where the menu was in French and where it was in English, then touched his arm to get his attention, directing it to the woman across the room being led to their table by the *maitre d'*.

The woman was showing her awe at her surroundings, and Maureen spoke softly to Simon.

"That's her, and in the white man's world, a man of honor stands when a woman approaches his table. And wait for her to offer her hand to shake it... now... Good evenin' Doris, my that's a lovely color on you."

"Hello, Maureen. Is this Simon Fobister?"

"Yes, mam. I thank you for joining us."

"Now isn't he the polite one?"

It was a slightly-skewed smile that came to Doris' middle-aged face as she was cared for and attended to by the *maitre d'* who held her chair for her, then called over staff to fill her water glass while he unfolded her napkin.

"Now that was just as lovely as you said it would be, Maureen..." Doris leaned forward and whispered, "... I'm surprised you have us sitting right out in the open like this."

"Don't lean over and whisper like that. I intend everythin' to be right out in the open."

Doris sat up straight but looked around nervously.

"But what you have asked of me, if I were to do it, well you can see it's something I need to hide."

"First, sit back and relax and let's enjoy the loveliness about us. And then when you're comfortable I want you to scan the room, don't hurry, take your time, an' as you do, consider this. Some of these people have noticed us, an' some shoot a glance or two our way, an' some even study us. But none has a suspicious thought about us unless we give them one."

She gave Doris time to do as directed while she studied the menu.

"However, when someone sees you whisperin', well you see, then they might decide it would be interestin' to try to hear what it is you are sayin'. Long ago, I came to an understandin' that the best place to hide somethin' is right out in the open where no one expects it to be."

Doris had been checking out the room, peeking out over her menu.

"My goodness, you sound so practiced."

"You don't see anyone from the university."

"I don't, no."

"I wouldn't think so; this place is too expensive for professors' salaries, I'm sure."

Doris relaxed and began to read the menu. "The menu is in French."

Simon reached over to turn the page for her.

"It's in English on the next page."

And Doris blushed.

"I see... I've heard about this restaurant for years." Doris took another glance around the room. "Some of them *are* looking at us, or at the two of you, anyway."

"Many consider this as fine as any of the French restaurants you'll find in Montreal."

Doris looked over her menu at Maureen.

"It really is quite lovely."

"Then let's enjoy our evenin', shall we? How far you venture will always be your choice to make, but you are in the right place to do some defenseless people a great service, an' I could see that was important to you the first time I mentioned it."

Doris returned to her menu.

"My Lord, it is expensive."

"No. It's very expensive."

"And this is what you're offering me, if I do what you ask. Slices of this?"

"Ah, I'll bake you a whole loaf of it, if that's your heart's delight. Sometimes life does offer you adventure, Doris, an' I'm invitin' you to join me in this one."

"Me, living an adventurous life. I never thought."

Simon turned to Doris again.

"Long ago, the French asked my ancestors if they could live with us on the River. If they could live with us in our forests. When we said yes, they showed us ways to make our lives better. When they traded with us, it was good trade for our People. We were Brothers. Then the British drove the French away so they could take from us what is ours."

"Hear that, Doris? An' in all the movies isn't that the most romantic part, the one given to the French character? You give me the name of the dissenter, an' where he lives, or where I can approach him alone, an' it's like you're the romantic French hero carin' for Simon's people."

"He's a young professor, still new in the department. But I'm afraid you might be too late. The men from Abitibi, the men who contracted this research project, they were waiting in his office for him when he came back from lunch yesterday."

"What's his name?"

Doris looked around the room again. She opened her purse in her lap, and under cover of the tablecloth removed an envelope. She tingled as she placed it in Simon's lap.

"You'll find his name, his home address, and his direct phone number at the school. But also a copy of a department memo where he now states he has no scientific proof for his previous opinion... 'a line of speculation fueled by my curiosity' is what he called it in the memo."

"He wrote the memo?"

"No, Dr. Harris, the department chair, wrote it, but Dr. Harris quotes him saying he was wrong."

Maureen had passed the breadbasket to Doris; she had slipped an envelope between the rolls, and Doris retrieved it.

"He now says he has no scientific proof?"

"That's right."

"That's his current position?"

"Well, I'm betting the current position is that he's not permitted to have a public position on this, beyond what's in this memo."

"When was it written?"

"Yesterday afternoon. I typed it right after the men from Abitibi left."

"Doris, you've done a good deed here tonight. It might even turn out to have been a noble thing. So let's enjoy our dinner, yeah. I've already taken a peek at the desserts an' they look grand."

They all studied the menus for a moment in quiet.

"After we've had our dinner, I'd like a few minutes of your time. Maybe you can join me for a drink in our hotel; it's just round the corner."

"Everything I can tell you is in that envelope."

"I was hopin' you might be interested in discussin' a new job."

"A new job?"

"Helpin' me, workin' for me. I may be settin' up a new export enterprise."

❊ ❊ ❊

After the radio patch into the international operator failed repeatedly, Dutch flew into Innish Cove to retrieve Brian and returned with him to the NOA offices. During their first call, they discovered the best time for Tommy to travel was right away, then they lost the connection again.

Finally, they got Tommy on the phone to hear him say, "I'll be there in three days."

Brian asked, "What do I do when I see you?"

"What?"

"I don't want even a moment that goes wrong. So should I shake your hand? I'm sure I'll want to hug you, but I don't know if you'd want that."

"Let's shake hands."

"Sure."

"I've got to hang up now. I'll see you Thursday."

❈ ❈ ❈

An early morning fog floated over the River. Skirting the edge of a dense cloud bank, Mathew was alone paddling Nigig with a soft, easy stroke and he let the canoe's glide come to a stop before he paddled again.

Just inside the cloud bank This Man paddled his canoe, keeping pace.

For an instant Mathew caught a glimpse of This Man through the fog, and he turned Nigig into the cloudbank, paddling more steadily, trying to discover what he saw.

❈ ❈ ❈

An early morning fog lay easy over the lough. Tommy knelt beside a Celtic cross on a small knoll above the shore where he looked out over the waves of fog. He held his arms out at his side, assuming the position of the cross.

He closed his eyes, and he prayed for forgiveness. Tears came to his eyes then began to roll down his cheeks.

A flock of yellow wagtails landed in the tree branches just above him, a dozen small birds with bright yellow and soft green bodies and black wings. They flitted from branch to branch, often no more than a foot from Tommy's head as he knelt below them, still.

The yellow wagtails sang to each other and groomed themselves.

A great convulsion shook Tommy's chest and he collapsed on the ground, crying out loud, scattering the birds. He sobbed deeply, lying at the base of the cross. He pushed himself up into a sitting position, leaning against the cross, and cried and cried, and cried still more.

❈ ❈ ❈

The fellow outside the office door in Dublin let another in and that meant four from the IRA Executive Military Council had arrived for the meeting. There was a lookout stationed down the hall, another on the street. Kevin was the only one missing.

"He's been in the West these last few days."

"He told me he'd be back for this meetin'."

"I haven't heard from him since the day he left."

"Not a phone call?"

"Me neither."

"That's not good."

"Which way do you mean that's not good?"

"Do ya think others got to him?"

"Which way do you mean, killed him, or flipped him?"

"Flip Kevin? I was wonderin' if they might have done him in."

"What makes ya think they could flip him?"

"I wasn't sayin' they could, I was askin' if you thought they did."

"Are we ready to handle this as an urgency?"

There was a knock at the door, then again, and Kevin stepped in.

"Ah, grand, it's Kevin himself."

"Evening. Everything all right?"

"We was just getting' a bit agitated when we realized none had seen nor heard from ya since ya left for the West."

"We lost two good lads when word got out what we did to their hurling champion. It's going to take some serious recruiting to replace those who quit us. At least they didn't go over to the others."

❊ ❊ ❊

Maureen had been taught that two o'clock in the morning was when the world was quietest. In the darkest first hours of morning on the side street of a nice old neighborhood in Kingston, very near Queens University campus, the glow of the street light on the corner barely carried to the second house.

Maureen and Simon had parked her rented car and walked the sidewalk for a couple of blocks, passed through the light, and used trees and fences to melt away and reappear at the back door of the third house down.

Maureen checked the door, found it secure, them discovered a window she could shimmy open. As she slipped inside, Simon faded back into the shadows.

No more than a minute later, Maureen climbed back out. She joined Simon standing in the bushes.

"Yes, it's just the right thing to do."

"I will carry the next one."

A block over, a few minutes later, Simon was in a kitchen, paper in his hand. He left it on the table then left through the back door.

And in another house, just two blocks down from the second, still dark, Maureen took a knife to stab a photo in place on the pantry door. The photo was framed by the piece of paper behind it. Hearing noises, and then footsteps above her, Maureen quickly retreated back out the window.

A moment later a man flipped on the lights as he came down the stairs cautiously. He took the candlestick from the mantle as he passed through the living room and slowly peeked into the kitchen. He turned on the kitchen lights. It was empty.

As he turned to flip the lights off he noticed something on his pantry door. A knife, and the blade frightened him into readying the candlestick for use. It *took* him a moment to approach it, but when he did he realized the knife held in place a photo of an old Indian woman holding a baby in front of a wigwam.

In any photos he had seen of Indians they all looked serious. This grandmother was smiling.

He pulled out the knife to examine the picture more closely and to read the paper behind it. "Naomi Loon. Born on the River 1898. Her grandson Little Stevie born this year, 1951. Are you asking this child to take on a risk you wouldn't?"

❀ ❀ ❀

It was another house like the others, but the sun had been up for thirty minutes. Maureen and Simon walked up the sidewalk to the front door in the early morning light.

The man inside was in his bathrobe and pajamas and he pulled back a corner of the curtain to see who was knocking on his door before he'd even had his breakfast.

It was a splendid if confusing sight. A handsome Indian man-child stood next to a lovely woman, Indian he thought, before he realized she was a white woman. The Indian handed something to the woman. The man adjusted and retied his robe before he opened the door.

Before he or Maureen could speak, Simon began.

"We have come to help you."

The man's surprise grew and he could only sputter, "Good morning."

"We gave the others pictures of my people. Next time they will listen to you about your fears for the River. So you will speak with them again. You will continue your dissent."

"What are you talking about? Who are you?"

"I'm Maureen O'Toole, an' this is Simon Fobister. Before we knew your name we called you the Dissenter."

"You call me what?"

"The Dissenter."

The man's wife, after peering out the window, had stepped up behind him, fully fascinated, but her husband was beginning to see direction to this and he was stepping back to bring the door half-way closed.

"Who are they?"

"We were just sitting down for breakfast, so why don't you just tell me what this is all about."

It was the report the Dissenter had seen Simon handing to Maureen, and she opened it to the page where his dissent was noted.

"This is you. You say there are reasons to believe this new paper-makin' process will poison our River. All by yourself, your concerns weren't sufficient to stop the project until more study can be done." Maureen shifted her gaze to the man's wife. "Your husband is a brave man, ma'me. We're here to thank him." She returned her attention to the husband. "An' we are here to offer you our help."

"Where did you get that? You aren't supposed to have that. And what does he mean, he gave them pictures? What pictures?"

"Ask him."

"Pictures of what?"

Simon had removed two more photographs from his shoulder bag, one of Mathew paddling Nigig across the river, the other of children wading in the River. He stepped right up to the door and held the photos high over the man's shoulder so his wife could see them, too.

"The River gives us our life."

The man's wife peeked over her husband's shoulder to see the photos as her husband snatched them from Simon's hand.

"We're through here, and I am asking you to leave right now."

"No, please. Let's at least talk. Just invite us in for a bit of tea an' let us ask you a couple of questions so we can understand better what we're up—"

"I'm telling you to leave now. Good-bye."

He closed the door, so Maureen raised her voice.

"What was it that scared you so you had to speak out?"

There was no sound from the other side.

"If you don't answer that question, I'm afraid your wife won't like the consequences."

The door opened fast and wide, the dissenter stepped forward, and he closed the door behind him.

"You're threatenin' my wife?"

"No. But if there *is* a threat to your wife, it will come from livin' with her shame of you because you didn't do all you could to stop it."

"I wrote that nearly a year ago. I've had time for further consultation with my colleagues, and I amended the report in a recent memo. I acknowledge my earlier statement was an untested hypothesis and that I have absolutely no evidence of any kind that the mercury will have the effect I initially modeled."

"It's *mercury* that they'll be dumpin' in the River."

"Ah, yes, that's right."

"An' now your position is that you have no evidence to suggest dumpin' mercury in the River will cause harm."

"Indeed, if you were ever to swallow a large drop of it, why it would simply roll down into your stomach then pass through your bowels and out of your body without any effect at all which, I might add, happens with some regularity, as thermometers do break."

"What?"

"We put mercury in our mouths all the time, in thermometers. You've more danger from the broken glass of a thermometer than the mercury inside it."

"But surely you knew that all along, while you was testin' your ideas that suggested mercury could poison our River. Let me ask, what convinced you that you were wrong?"

"I've said all I have to say. Any further attempt to speak with me will be reported as harassment."

"Be ready for your colleagues to bring all this up again with you, for we did share some pictures with them. An' if you decide it does need to be stopped, you can contact me at the Northwest Ontario Airlines office, in Kenora. I'm Maureen O'Toole."

Chapter 30
COME A' CALLING

KEVIN CLOSED HIS MUSIC SHOP in the early afternoon, packed an overnight bag, and drove the road that followed the Royal Canal out of Dublin due west. When he got to Mullingar he headed northwest, past Longford, into the River valley, and on towards Lough Arrow. He stopped in front of a small cottage that sat just above the shore.

An old man came walking up from the lough at the sound of the motor car and rounded the cottage as Kevin stepped from his car. Kevin greeted him with a bag filled with goods from the market.

The old man accepted the goods and offered disappointing news in return.

"He's left."

"He's left? I told him to stay here 'til I was ready to move him."

"'Twas but two days after you left he lit out fer Sligo. I was remindin' 'im you was hidin' him to keep from havin' to take his life, but he was sayin' if he's got to hide he's gonna hide wit' his friends an' not wit' an ol' sod like me."

"The fecking idiot needs to be hiding from friends. Did he mention any names?"

"Lads on the Sligo Hurling Club. I got two names outta him by conversin'.

"So he's been gone a week?"

"An' 'is lucky if'n he tain't been dead most of it. So if you find him alive, you need to do what was called for in the first place, Kevin, or he's bringin' danger to yourself."

"I'll stop on my way back and let you know it's done."

❉ ❉ ❉

Maureen and Simon returned to the Great Lodge at Innish Cove from their trip to Kingston and the next day, after getting three boats of guests out on the River for the day, Brian, Maureen, and Simon flew into Kenora with Dutch.

They had a second appointment with their new solicitor, Tom Hall, recently hired to help them stop the mill. He was to report on the success of his preliminary conversations with government officials.

After dropping off the others at the dock in Kenora, Dutch flew on to Winnipeg. Tommy would soon arrive there on a flight from Toronto, and Dutch would fly him back to Kenora later that afternoon.

Maureen told Tom Hall all she had learned, most importantly that the element causing concern was mercury. The report had studiously avoided naming it.

When she first described the break-ins to Brian, Simon's role was described fully and he was there to add details. When Maureen told the stories in the solicitor's office, she acted alone.

As soon as she finished, Brian spoke up.

"I've been tellin' her she went too far, bringin' a knife into it, escalatin', threatenin' violence. But I'm watchin' you listenin' to her rationale, an' it doesn't seem to have bothered you nearly as much as it bothers me. Unless you're just keepin' a professional openness to your client's angles an' ideas."

"I am intrigued. I want to hear more."

Maureen was insistent. "It was clear to me standin' there that the Dissenter has not changed his belief. He's taken it back to keep his standing at the university. Or they paid him off. But I could see it in his eyes an' I could hear it in his voice. He still believes whatever it was that caused him such concerns. He fears what the mercury could do to the River. In front of his wife I made him acknowledge he had just given up. When he did, I knew for sure. I've been around a man who had given up on somethin' that he knew was important. I know what it looks like."

Tom liked to pace when he was thinking and did so now. He was a young solicitor, still building a practice, and he knew the risk of going against timber interests yet had taken this on enthusiastically. Even the disappointing results of his first discussions with the Indian Affairs and Timber agency counsels couldn't temper his determination.

He walked from the window on one side of his office with its obstructed view of Lake of the Woods to the other window looking out fully on Main Street. He was smiling when he turned and said, "You and Simon Fobister broke into three houses?"

"It was just me. Simon was on the trip with me, as he is here with us now. But he did not participate in any way in my house calls."

"It would be best if we were to remember that, in fact, Simon was in his hotel room at the time."

"That is my recollection. He was in bed. It was two in the mornin', after all."

After Maureen and Simon told Brian about their break-ins, she then insisted that the story she would tell to everyone else was a version that kept Simon out of it, free from anything that might come of it. He didn't understand the reasoning but agreed to follow her lead.

Maureen enjoyed watching the activity on Kenora's Main Street during her first visit to this office so she stood at that window, collecting her thoughts while watching a mother holding hands with her young daughter as they walked down the sidewalk and entered a clothing store. When the door closed behind them, she turned to the room.

"So my overall strategy I am workin' here, an' this is as simple as I can see it, is that the cards have been dealt an' if this hand plays out, they win. This pulp mill gets built. So our slim advantage is to show them we are prepared to change the game; we have a play we can make that knocks them off the path they want to be on. An' more importantly, we're prepared to make that play, an' more."

"That's it?"

"One thing more. They'll take all kinds of disruption before they want to call us on it."

The office wasn't large enough for two folks to be moving

around in it, so Tom sat back down behind his desk. "I can tell you we need something besides the formal political process. After meeting with the Ministry it's clear they will be much too slow. They started talking about how filled their calendars are, that it will be at least six months and up to a year before the preliminary hearings could begin. They can bury this in so many committee meetings. And when we could ever meet if we don't have the full support of Indian Affairs by then we won't make any progress." He directed his next comment to Brian. "And as I am sure you can guess, they are none too happy with you right now."

"I tried, but their... I guess I have to call it their silliness, they wore me down with their silliness 'til I had to call them on... bein' silly."

"So I'll be insistent and steady with the Ministries without stealing your money with very little expectation. Now that this memo is written and the dissenter recants everything, that direction is working against us."

Brian said, "We got money to pay you."

"It's the waste of time that's most costly, for they'll be moving forward every day with their plans while we're fighting just for permission to speak to someone about it. I mean it when I say they can put this off for years, the sort of public hearing we need."

Maureen nodded. "You stay attentive there, at the Ministries, probe an' look for high leverage plays. An' I'll play this out with Abitibi. They don't want any illegal proceedin' of any sort in any way related to this project. That's when we could go after 'em about why they are hidin' what they are doin'. So they keep absorbin' my provocation, I keep raisin' the stakes, at some point the only choice they have is to ask us to stop. Then we deal."

Both Brian and Tom Hall nodded in understanding. Maureen went on. "Who's the ambitious journalist at the newspaper who wants the insider view of the biggest story of the year as it unfolds?"

"You've never wondered why the newspaper is called *The Kenora Timbermen*? The publisher's money came from his father's lumber company, Dryden Paper and Pulp."

"I'll show them a story that's too big to keep under wraps. An' if I can't find one, I'll create one. An' sooner than later I will make them beg to sit down with us an' talk."

✳ ✳ ✳

Simon walked just ahead of Brian and Maureen to the diner nearest the floatplane dock. He stopped and turned.

"I must know how I would stand today in your world without you. I need to know where I am on this journey." He entered the diner, and Brian and Maureen waited a few moments before they followed him in. He was standing inside the door, but they walked by without a word, and a waitress quickly cleaned and set their regular booth and gave them a friendly smile. Their habit was to sit on the same side of the table at the window that looked out onto Lake of the Woods. They could see the bay where Dutch would land when he returned with Tommy. Maureen leaned into Brian's chest, a position that had quickly become a favorite part of sitting there for both of them.

Simon stood at the door. He didn't know to claim a table. He was ignored by the staff, the target of frowns from customers.

Brian hugged Maureen's waist. "When you got back from Kingston I was really concerned we were goin' too far too fast, escalatin' the violence."

"There's been no actual violence, only a feel of it. The River must be protected, an' there are circumstances when physical force is the most effective means of accomplishin' a mission. Suggestin' it helps as well."

"I don't have the same faith Joe Loon's people have in his dream, or that you have. If I *knew* it, the way they seem to *know* it, that the River *is* threatened by this pulp mill, well then I might find what you are sayin' now becomes somethin' we should be talkin' about."

An empty table, a small one just at hand, came open. Simon sat in the empty chair. Customers' frowns turned to loud whispers of displeasure. The head waitress called the owner at home.

Maureen was talking with Brian, but taking it all in.

"Pre-emptive moves have leverage. Now Abitibi is off balance. Then we keep them off balance. Then we sit down an' talk about restorin' balance."

"But if you weren't *knowin'* about this dream of his... Without the dream, you're talkin' about such slim threads of evidence that there's even a threat at all. Most of the scientists say it ain't."

"At every turn, Joe Loon's dreams have power an' truth. It always seemed to me it was your dreams that brought us here, but it was his dreams that led us right to Innish Cove."

"Yes. Sure, I've believed somethin' like that, before, when we were just happy to be accepted an' life was openin' up everywhere. But now the cost of bein' wrong about actually believin' in a dream seems to be growin' and growin'."

She leaned away so she could look him in the eye.

"Will I now hear Big Brian Burke, owner and proprietor of the Great Lodge at Innish Cove and the son of Joe Loon, say it's just a dream?"

The diner owner didn't answer the phone, the two waitresses agreed to ignore the Indian boy as long as no one asked for his removal. Simon knew it was time to stand and leave, and before he did, he called out to them all in his forest language. "You people do not want us to live in your world. I must do all I can to keep you from destroying the world of my People."

He returned to the dock where he would find a friend.

❀ ❀ ❀

Dutch helped Tommy make out the first traces of Kenora on the far horizon and Tommy, dressed in his work cassock and white tab collar, couldn't make it out yet and returned his attention to a his great appreciation of the beauty all around.

"It's a grand place, what magnificent country. You explore this wilderness every day?"

"Most days, anyway. Not so much during the winters but just about every day the rest of the year. I was a pilot in the Royal Canadian Air Corps, and when the war ended I bought this lady, used and worn, but there's no aircraft as rugged and reliable and perfectly designed for what we are asking her to do. So I fixed her up and I flew her into Lake of the Woods one day and have been here ever since."

"You must have one of the more wondrous jobs a man can have."

"Brian says those exact words."

Dutch set himself before he spoke again.

"There's something I wanted to say, but I figured it is such grand country, I'd wait til the trip had ended, in case I said it wrong, I didn't want to spoil the flight for you."

Then he was quiet long enough for Tommy to wonder if that was all he had to say. So Tommy was quiet, too, and began to discern the town's details as they flew closer to the far outskirts. Then the massive Lake of the Woods taking over the world ahead of them captured his attention.

"I've never heard what it was your father did to you. As terrible as he feels about it, it must have been serious and grave."

Tommy studied the lake.

"But I can tell you this. Your father loves you and your brother and sister every day."

❀ ❀ ❀

Brian, Maureen, and Simon waited at the end of the NOA dock for Dutch and Tommy. With the toe of his boot, Brian was knocking stray cigarette butts between the slats of the dock and into the lake to wash away.

"Tommy's got 'im a handsome mind. You could see it when he was still in nappies. Was my doin' that put this hard edge to him an' it would be oh so grand if this was the place that might take some of that hard edge off 'im again."

"Simon should take him out on the River. With Mathew."

"The three of 'em out on the River for a day a' fishin', yeah."

"I was thinkin' an overnight camp, let the boys show him their world, let him see it's becomin' our world."

Simon agreed. "Yes. I will talk with Mathew about this."

❀ ❀ ❀

Dutch steered the Norseman's glide to the dock so precisely that first Brian, then Maureen, and finally Simon simply stepped from the dock onto the pontoon as it passed. Brian took one step up the ladder, opened the cargo door, and one after the other they climbed inside.

Tommy unbuckled his seat belt and was ready to give up the co-pilot's chair to his father.

"Hello, Brian. You sit up here with Dutch, I imagine."

"No, Tommy, you keep the seat." He approached with his hand out and Tommy shook it, feeling awkward from the getting up and sitting down and reaching back in tight quarters.

"Seein' you sittin' up there next to Dutch, that's a sight I've been prayin' for. You get the best views, an' we'll be flying over land an' water even lovelier than what you've seen."

"Thank you."

Brian and Tommy stood inches close but felt distant. Brian broke the tension by turning to open a view to Maureen and Simon behind him in the fuselage.

"Tommy, let me introduce you to Maureen O'Toole, my business partner, but soon to be Maureen Burke, my wife. Here's my son the Father, Tommy Burke."

"Pleased to meet you but no, I'm not a priest yet."

Maureen bent past Brian to extend her hand to Tommy.

"I've been lookin' forward to meetin' you."

"Nice to meet you."

Brian and Maureen settled back on one of the fuselage benches across from Simon.

"An' this is Simon."

"Pleased to meet ya, Simon."

"You are Big Brian's oldest son."

"Big Brian? Yes, I am his eldest son. So when's the wedding?"

"We've decided to get married this winter back home. Maureen's people are in Derry, so it'll be there, or Cong; we won't tend to the plannin' til the season is over."

Dutch taxied his Norseman back out into the bay and lined up his take off.

"As soon as everyone is strapped in, I'll be ready to go."

❋ ❋ ❋

It was a Norseman of a different color that circled over Innish Cove, this one forest green with the words Abitibi Lumber Company captured in the gold seal painted on the tail. James, the older brother, piloted the plane, Stephen, the youngest, was in the co-pilot's chair. Three of their biggest lumberjacks sat on the bench seats behind them.

The youngest brother had radioed their approach and received no answer from Innish Cove.

"Is that an Indian camp down there as well?"

"I saw it."

❄ ❄ ❄

Mathew was sitting before his wigwam, surrounded by the village's children, telling them about the white man's school and how to avoid going. And what to do, and what not to do, if forced to go.

The men of the village were guiding, or scouting trap lines, or visiting other forest clans, so Mathew was the oldest male in camp.

"The story they tell of Geronimo at this school is not true. They will trick you by making it look real in their movies. But it is not true. If they catch you to send you to their school, you must not believe the picture they show of Geronimo. Then you must wonder if the story they tell of Geronimo is not true, what other lies do they tell us?"

When Mathew first heard the distant sound of a bush plane's approach, he listened to identify it. It sounded like Dutch's plane. He stood when the plane came into sight across the far horizon, but he could tell immediately it was not the bright yellow of Dutch's Norseman. Perhaps it was green, or blue, but it was not Dutch's plane. As it came closer, he saw it was green, and when the plane banked to line up a landing, he studied the gold mark on the plane's tail.

Only after the plane taxied around the point and into the cove did Mathew realize the tail marking was the lumber company mark on the map and report, the symbol used by the Atibiti Lumber Company. He called out to the women.

"Take the children to South Ridge Rocks. Stay there until I send someone for you."

In a few moments Mathew was alone in the camp. He sat at the fire ring to wait for what was to come.

When This Man emerged from the forest, Mathew moved over so that This Man could sit down next to him.

❄ ❄ ❄

The dock was empty as the jacks tied down the Atibiti

Norseman.

Stephen had his army pistol, a Browning 9mm, holstered at his hip, the standard officer issue he had brought home from the war. When his older brother James saw him strapping it on, he said, "You're bringing your pistol?" and Stephen replied, "She used a knife." Quickly, the older brother realized he wouldn't mind how foolish the pistol made his brother look, maybe not now to the jacks, but certainly later and much more importantly to their father and grandfather, so he didn't say anything more about it.

From where they stood on the dock they could see much of the operation and there were no signs of anyone about.

The older brother had been composing a letter in his head that he'd write and leave if they discovered everyone was gone. Now that it seemed clear they'd arrived to an empty camp, he turned to Stephen and said so only his brother could hear, "If you don't show me how you are keeping track of these blunders of yours, I'm going to start keeping track of them for you."

"What are you talking about?"

"I said no. When you suggested we just drop in on them, I said no, that we get no advantage from surprise like you claimed. She used it because it's all she has. We have nothing to hide or slink around about. But you made the decision, and here we are, and they aren't here, so once again your judgment was—"

The youngest brother turned and started down the dock to shore.

"I saw Indians. We'll start there."

When the two pulp mill brothers followed by their jacks crested the short rise from the shore to the village camp, they saw a teenage Ojibway sitting alone in front of the cluster of tents and wigwams they'd seen from the sky.

The pistol was strapped to the youngest brother's left hip. During the war his habit was to walk with his left fist resting on the pistol stock, his arm slightly bowed, and he walked that way again as he approached Mathew.

"The kid should speak some English," the older brother said.

"Hey, kid, you speak English?" the youngest brother barked.

Mathew stayed seated, and answered in his native tongue.

"Come and sit with us."

Stephen shook his head at the Indian boy.

"I don't understand that mouthful-of-shit talk. You don't speak the white man's tongue?"

Mathew spoke of this white man who was kneeling down next to him. He was speaking to the spirits of the ancestors who lived in the cove so he spoke the forest language.

"This is where our journeys gather on the same path."

James looked at the Indian boy at eye level.

"Brian Burke? You tell me where I can find Brian Burke."

Mathew looked past this white man and studied the younger brother's pistol. "In the movies, a white man with a gun in his holster will take it out to shoot my people. I will take that gun away from you so you do not shoot my people with it."

Stephen turned to the jacks. "How the hell do they expect to survive in the world today if they won't even learn English?"

James turned and headed back to their plane. "I'm going to try the radio one more time. If we don't raise anyone, we're leaving." The youngest brother and the jacks followed him.

As soon as they stepped back down out of the forest onto the beach, Mathew entered his wigwam. When he reappeared, he was wearing a small buckskin pouch around his neck. It rested next to his heart. It held his magic. He stopped at the fire pit to scoop ashes with two fingers, then streaked them across his cheekbones.

As he marked himself, This Man emerged from the wigwam, carrying all of Mathew's possessions.

He held Mathew's blanket out in front of him, folded and draped over his arms like an offering.

In the middle of the blanket was a wooden bowl. In the bowl was a necklace of quill. Next to the bowl, a beaver trap.

Balanced across his arms, This Man carried Mathew's bow and a quiver of arrows that he had made when he was a boy.

Mathew disappeared into the forest. This Man set the possessions on the ground, arranging them carefully next to the fire pit.

❊ ❊ ❊

No one responded to James' radio call.

"If I can't raise them, they won't be returning anytime soon."

"Maybe they're behind a ridge line."

"I'll write them a letter that we were here, and then we're gone."

"One more thing first. I was thinking, maybe we should show them we can violate their private space as easy they can ours."

"You mean check out their cabins?"

Stephen had already turned to again lead the jacks down the dock to shore. This time he headed across the beach into the forest where the cabins sat among the trees. After a moment, James followed.

The cabin set up to serve as a lodge was identified readily by its oversized front porch and the wooden door propped open. Stephen led them there, pausing long enough to send one of the jacks back to the plane.

Mathew was nowhere to be seen.

❄ ❄ ❄

Early in the flight Dutch had suggested and then a few minutes later he urged Tommy to sit in back with the others, and he did. He sat down next to Simon, across from Maureen.

Maureen told Tommy about Joe Loon's dreams, the pulp mill's threat, and their solicitor's certainty that fighting through the legal system to reverse the permit would take so long that the mill would be in operation before they could stop it. Brian leaned in closer to hear Tommy and Maureen continue the debate started when Maureen introduced physical force as a legitimate step.

"Most of the students in seminary got angry with me about this, you see, but I would insist on Gandhi as a model Ireland needs to look to now. No, he's not Christian, let alone Catholic, but surely conditions the British left in India an' Ireland are similar."

"They split countries in two parts for their own advantage."

"So, sure, Christ should be enough, but you have to consider Gandhi's relevance to our cause, to our need."

"It was a sin against humanity what they did, usin' ancient grievances, inflamin' them, pittin' Hindus against Muslims, Proddies against Catholics."

Brian chose his words for his son carefully.

"I imagine you've come to a profoundly spiritual understandin' of violence."

Tommy stood to return to the co-pilot's chair. "There's times I think so."

"So maybe you've a destiny... Ireland's Gandhi?"

Tommy looked back before he sat down. "If you want to think on it in such terms at all, yeah, I've been seein' me as the Irish Gandhi's John the Baptister."

❋ ❋ ❋

The jack sent to the plane had returned with an ax over his shoulder, and he joined the other two waiting on the porch of the lodge cabin.

Just behind the lodge cabin, Mathew was hidden in the trees, working his way to a protected view of the front door, the porch, and the visitors. This Man stood back in the trees, watching.

The two brothers entered the lodge cabin, the screen door slamming behind them.

The older brother was impressed. "Looks to me like they've got the makings of a nice little business here. We should talk to them about us bringing some of our customers here. I'm thinking Mark Vincent and Jake Preston, Erik Edwards and Robert Martin. And Fredrick Fulbright. They're all big customers and all serious fishermen."

"You're still not seeing this right. She came in after us in the middle of the night, while we were sleeping, with a knife in her hand. Most would call that an attack."

"She didn't come after us. It was a bunch of college professors. And the knife was nothing more than a prop for dramatic effect. It wasn't a threat. But now we pay a surprise visit with a gun and an ax. Interesting logic. How does it continue?"

The youngest brother called to the jack with the ax, and the others followed him inside. James stood at the bar and poured himself two fingers of whiskey.

When the men entered the cabin, Mathew dashed from the forest to crouch below the front porch, a bench and the open door providing cover, as the screen door slammed behind the last jack.

"But before you set these fellows loose here, let's imagine two scenarios at the next board meeting. The first one, well, let's say it's me, and I'm explaining to Father and Grandfather how all of a sudden the micks said everything was all right when I offered to bring some of our best customers here to fish. Let's say I promised ten customers for four days, forty nights of business, and that was that, eh, we get happy customers, we got happy neighbors."

He paused to sip his drink.

"Or there's a second scenario, why don't you be thinking of a name for it, since it's the one where I get to watch you telling them something altogether different. That you waved your old army pistol at them after your man there chopped up the radio and then, what, they apologize for daring to be downstream of us and decide to leave?"

The youngest brother waved the jacks back outside. "Let me talk to my brother."

The jacks left.

By this time Mathew had climbed up on the porch to cram his body tight between the open door and the cabin wall, so tight the slashes of ash on his cheeks had smudged against the logs and the door. Mathew could smell the white man smells on them as they passed shuffled back out onto the porch.

The youngest brother poured his own drink.

"Nice move on your part, waiting 'til I called them in before you made me look like a fool."

"Stephen, what you don't understand is that when you came walking down the dock this morning with that holster strapped to your hip, that's when you looked like a fool."

"It's great to know I have a brother who enjoys letting my errors play full out for everyone to see before you show 'em to me."

"You need to understand that it comes from my fierce loyalty to the company."

"Loyalty to the company? What's that Irish saying... oh yeah, what a load of shite."

"Study my logic. First, I am convinced that I'm the right one to take over next. But I also know I need you helping me if I'm going to lead this company to something well beyond what Father has ever imagined. So I need to make sure everyone, and especially you, see as clearly as I do that I'm the right man for this job."

A bit softer this time, the youngest brother repeated, "What a load of shite."

"And if I was helping you along, if I was saying to you, hey little brother I think the pistol might be a mistake, you wouldn't see it's these sorts of errors of judgment you make that could really damage us. And you'd begin to think you were actually making good decisions."

And softer still, "You've always been a cold bastard, James."

"It wasn't me put us in this place, it was Father. And just remember later that I was clear with you about what I am up to. Nothing behind your back."

Mathew heard it first, then one of the jacks called back to the cabin through the screen door, but by then the brothers heard it as well and were on their way to the door.

It was the echoed faint rumble of an approaching bush plane, still at a distance.

The pulp mill brothers stepped outside onto the porch where the jacks were waiting.

Mathew was wedged in tightly just behind the door.

The older brother directed the jacks.

"Go on down and pull the plane around so they can pull up. We'll be right behind you."

The brothers found the place on the porch affording the best view of the sky in the direction of the plane's sound. The youngest brother stood in front of Mathew with his back to him. His arms were folded across his chest as he listened to his older brother's directions.

"Here's the slant. We're here to start over. To show we want to be good neighbors, to assure them the finest scientists have given their endorsement to all safety issues and we should have been more forthright with what we are doing and that's what we are doing now. We're here to talk, so let's talk about doing some business, maybe a lot of business, as the beginning of an era of neighborly behavior."

The pistol may have been army issue, but the holster was not; it was uncovered, without a strap to secure the pistol. The older brother remembered it.

"You need to get down there and put that pistol away before

they get here."

The pistol's handle pointed right at Mathew and he raised his hand towards it and didn't stop reaching for it. He stepped forward and with his right hand pushed the door out hard, with the left hand he grabbed the pistol out of the holster. The door smashed into the older brother and he staggered two steps.

After Mathew grabbed the pistol clean, he hesitated, looking for the eyes of the youngest brother who had turned and was reaching to regain his gun.

When Mathew hesitated, Stephen had time for his Army training to guide his instinct and he grabbed the pistol in one hand and Mathew's wrist in the other, turning them against each other so Mathew's grip would weaken and he'd be forced to release the gun.

As the move was executed Mathew found Stephen's eyes and spoke to him in the forest language.

"To fight your poison I bring my strongest medicine."

The confusion in Stephen's eyes turned to surprise when Mathew gave way to the move so easily that the pistol turned clear around to point at Mathew's chest as they fought for control of the gun, and then Stephen's eyes showed panic when a finger found the trigger and the shot exploded Mathew's magic pouch as it made a hole in his chest, knocking him off the porch and into a tree before he landed flat on his back.

The pistol fell to the porch at the youngest brother's feet.

The older brother jumped from the porch to stand next to Mathew, staring down at him; his body lay still though his head turned back and forth and his lips moved without a sound.

"You shot him? You stupid son of a bitch... Stephen... why did you shoot him?"

"I didn't mean to... No, James, no, I didn't do it... He shot himself! He did, he shot himself. He said something to me and then he shot himself."

The youngest brother stooped to pick up his pistol and his older brother said sharply, "Don't touch it until I figure out what we need to do."

"I was fighting to get my pistol back from him. When he hit you with the door, he grabbed my pistol from the holster. He must have been hiding there, behind the door, waiting for us. My first thought was he intended on using it on me, on you, on both of us.... So I was disarming him, and I thought I had. Then I was struggling to keep him from turning the pistol back at himself because that's what it felt like he was doing and he said something and then... I don't know, but he must have pulled the trigger because I didn't."

The jacks had dashed back when they heard the shot, and the first to arrive called from the path. "He's right. The boy grabbed the gun and then he turned it on himself. We all saw it. We were standing right there and we all saw it."

❀ ❀ ❀

Tommy was back in the co-pilot's seat, so Dutch took a wider approach that would provide him with the best view of the full scope of the forests and the River of Lakes and a most dramatic introduction to the Great Lodge at Innish Cove with the ridges behind it.

When Dutch saw the plane at the dock he called to Brian and Maureen. "You've got company. There's an Abitibi Norseman sitting at your dock."

❀ ❀ ❀

James knelt over Mathew whose shirt was soaking blood. His pouch had been ripped open by the slug and flecks of his sacred herb floated in the edge of the blood. His eyes were open, but he looked far far away as he slowly, barely, rocked his head back and forth. A last bit of ash dusted his face.

This Man came from the forest and began to sing a mournful cry.

Mathew's breathing was weaker, then weaker, with first just a sputter of blood then quickly more blood streaming from the corner of his mouth.

Soon his head was still.

His heart skipped and convulsed, he closed his eyes, and This Man changed his song.

"He's dead, you god damn—"

"I didn't shoot him."

"All that matters now, you got to understand this, all that

matters now is that it was your pistol, a loaded pistol you brought to their home, it was your pistol that killed him."

Before the older brother stood, he wiped the bit of blood from his hand on the ground.

"Everyone gather around me right now. Each of you has a part in this, and we got to get this right the first time and each and every time from now on."

They formed around him.

"The three of you, that's easy, you were half way down the path and so, even though you came running at the shooting, it was all over before you got here, so you didn't see a thing. Since you didn't see a thing, they leave you out of this, all you have to do is stick to that, which is true after all, you didn't see a thing. Now then, me and my brother. We had gone in to see if anyone was here, and when we stepped out, the Indian boy jumped my little brother from behind and stole your army pistol from you, Stephen.

"Before we knew what was going on, the Indian raised the gun and... and he shot at me and I fell away... So then I didn't see a thing after that... By the time I got back up, it was over... So now you're the only one who knows how brave you must have been, Stephen, after he shot at me, to go after him to get the pistol away, in self-defense, to save us, and as you fought to get the gun back... Well, it was a struggle for a loaded gun, and it went off, and he got shot."

"I'm telling you, James, and you're not listening to me—he shot himself. The crazy son of a bitch god damn Indian boy grabbed my gun and said some words and then he shot himself."

"He was shot with your gun. That's the one thing for sure. This boy, he's the son and brother of the people who live here and you, a stranger, maybe an adversary, you flew in here carrying a loaded gun and this Indian was shot with it. So we have to give them a story about how it happened, or the story they'll figure out for themselves, Stephen, is that you shot him."

"The pistol has only been shot once. You say he shot at you. They'll know that's not right."

The older brother had already slipped a work glove on his right hand and retrieved the pistol from where it lay on the porch, looked at his brother, then the jacks said, "Goddamn you Stephen". He quickly cocked the pistol, pointed it at his own thigh, and shot through the fleshly edge. In searing, ripping pain, he leaned against the open door, cursing and spitting.

The shock of the second shot compounded the first, and the youngest brother and the jacks were so stunned they didn't know what to do next. James was ready to tell them. He gestured towards the pistol and through clenched teeth directed Stephen.

"Toss the pistol there next to him, toss it at his feet, centered, we don't know if he's left or right handed... You two run ahead and get the first aid kit ready, there's a tourniquet there. You lend me your shoulder. And you get rid of that ax."

The youngest brother and one jack helped support the older brother who called out to the jacks running down the path ahead of them.

"You didn't see a thing, goddamn it, you didn't see a thing."

As they made their way slowly down the path, the NOA Norseman was approaching its landing, and a break in the trees allowed them to see past the cove, past the point, to the open lake as the bush plane's pontoons bounced off the water once, then grabbed and landed in a spray.

"My wound means I have to leave here fast. So you'll need to volunteer to stay behind, you want to... god damn this hurts... you feel badly about what happened and since they'll insist you stay to answer their questions, you volunteer before they do, out of sympathy. Their pilot can fly you out after you've shown them what happened."

"Who'll fly you home?"

"Jerry has plenty of hours. I trust him."

"Goddamn it. Tell me again why we were here in the first place."

"To assure them the scientific evidence supports the safety of what we are doing and to invite them to find the foundation for a friendly relationship. You can use my ideas for bringing them business as examples of what we hoped to be talking about. Have a long list of names ready so it seems real."

"So why did I have my pistol?"

"Someday maybe you'll understand, and when you do, I'm

guessing you won't carry it anymore. But if they press hard on that, you can see what happens if you do suggest it's because the woman came after us with a knife and we were taking precautions."

❋ ❋ ❋

Brian was standing on the pontoon as Dutch taxied into the cove. He was balanced behind the wing strut but from there he could show himself to the men gathered on his dock.

Two jacks caught the Norsemen's wing strut to guide it in next to their own plane, and Brian jumped onto the dock and approached the strangers waiting for him. He checked, he always did, and found he was the biggest among them, but these men were large enough and more than hard. One man was leaning against another, as if he was injured, and it was this injured man who spoke to Brian.

"There's been a shooting accident. Just now, I was shot..." He winced to show how dreadful was his pain. "... In the leg, by one of your Indians. I'm bleeding rather badly, I'm afraid, so you'll understand that I must be off."

Maureen was right behind Brian coming onto the dock, and Tommy followed her. They stood on either side of Brian when he stopped to consider this man's claim, which he supported by pointing to his tourniquet and bloody bandage. Maureen studied the wounded man's face.

"Tell me what happened."

"It happened fast. We had just been inside the big cabin. An Indian boy was waiting for us outside. He shot me, then was shot himself when my brother tried to disarm him."

"Who shot you?"

"He didn't give us his name... What I know is I have been shot in the leg by your Indian boy."

Simon ran down the dock, heading to the cabins.

"I have to get to the hospital right now. My name is James Miller and this is my brother Stephen Miller and he's offered to stay behind to help you sort out why your Indian would have attacked me."

Maureen called to Simon to wait, then turned to the youngest brother.

"Where did it happen?"

"He jumped me outside your big cabin, the one with the porch. He hit me from behind and stole my pistol."

"He stole your pistol? Why did you bring a... Show me what happened."

Maureen turned to go, the older brother nodded to direct the youngest to follow her. As they headed down the dock, the older brother began limping his way closer to his plane. Tommy could see the rage building in his father so he stayed close at hand.

"James Miller? Millers are the owners of Atibiti."

"That's right."

"I've got one last question for you before you go."

The older brother stopped and turned for it.

"Can I see the bullet wound?"

"Show you the bullet wound. Your Indian—"

Brian's body became tense and he commanded, "Don't say that again."

The jacks were ready, Tommy was frightened, but he stood at Brian's side.

"Don't say what?"

"Don't say 'Your Indian.' If it's the young man it must be, I love him like he's my son, but he's not 'My Indian,' not the way you mean it."

"I came calling to talk about some of my customers being your guests here, but instead I get shot by an Indian that works for you, and now you're preventing my prompt return for medical care."

"An' you send your employees into the bush pretendin' to be field biologists an' what the feck did you need a pistol for unless you intended to use it."

The older brother motioned for the jacks to help him up the ladder into the plane. Brian stepped forward again, but Tommy grabbed his arm. Brian pulled away and shot a look at Tommy that Tommy had seen before, and he stepped back. The shock of arriving to find violent death waiting was now quickly enveloped in fear. He tried to stay calm, but his heart was racing.

As James stepped into the plane he called out over his shoulder. "It's my brother's army pistol, he has a habit of wearing it, you'll have to ask *him* why. And if you need to see a bullet hole oozing blood, you can follow me onto the plane and check it out as we're flying to Kenora."

Brian's anger grew again when he was dismissed. Tommy fought to collect himself, knowing Brian was close to losing control, and stepped between his father and the plane, sweat streaming down his sides, his priestly dress, he hoped, his shield. When Brian hesitated, Tommy turned so he could see into the cabin where the older brother was settling. He wondered if he would be able to control his voice.

"Let's do this instead. Why don't you expect we'll be calling the hospital tomorrow to check up on you?"

"What neighborly concern."

"Something like that."

❊ ❊ ❊

After the youngest brother told Maureen what had happened, she told him to repeat it for Brian when he and Tommy joined them.

Simon was kneeling over Mathew's body and Tommy stood next to him. They both were whispering prayers and fighting tears.

The younger pulp mill brother waited a moment to collect his thoughts before he turned to Brian.

"We went inside the cabin looking for you. We figured by then you weren't here or you would have shown yourself, but this seemed like a building open to the public, so my brother figured it was the best place to leave a note or a letter that we'd been here to talk with you. To mend fences."

He climbed onto the porch and began to act the behavior he spoke of.

"And so we heard a plane and figured it was you, and when we came out the boy must have been waiting behind the door for us, because we're just standing here watching your plane come over the ridge when *wham!*, from behind, the door slams into me and my brother, both of us, and we go falling, but he had grabbed my pistol—"

"What the feck are you doin' bringin' a pistol with you to Innish Cove?"

"I always wear one when I'm back in the bush and there's plenty of lumbermen who do."

"So there's a bunch 'a idiots we have to worry about, is that what you're tellin' me?"

"Look, Burke, I didn't shoot anyone. Your Indian—"

"His name is Mathew Loon."

"He jumped us from behind, and he took my pistol and shot my brother. Then when I tried to disarm him, and we were fighting over the gun, I tell you, I wasn't turning it on him, I was trying to take it away from him to keep him from shooting me, well, that's when he got shot, accidentally, and it was his finger on the trigger when it happened, not mine."

❋ ❋ ❋

Mathew's body had to be moved right away. Everyone gathered round him understood that guests couldn't see a dead Ojibway lying in a pool of blood in front of the lodge cabin. That wouldn't be good for anyone.

The women and children had come down from their hiding place to join them, and with Simon interpreting for Naomi, Brian and Maureen learned that all of Mathew's possessions were laid out next to the fire circle in the Ojibway village, as if waiting for the return of his body, as if preparing for the beginning of a journey along the Path of Souls.

Tommy stayed kneeling at Mathew's side, praying in the name of the Father, the Son, and the Holy Ghost.

This Man stood at Mathew's head, his arms raised to the sky, singing of the boy's life in these forests so all the ancestors and the Great Creator would hear.

Brian hooked his arms under Mathew's arms and lifted his torso off the ground; Naomi and Simon each grabbed one of his legs. Maureen was right behind Brian, followed by the other women, and then Dutch, Tommy, and the children.

This Man preceded them as they headed through the forest across the open beach where they could hear faint rumblings of distant boats returning. They were silent now.

The youngest brother waited for a moment, examining the scene one more time, then followed at a distance.

They laid Mathew in the middle of his things, his head on his blanket, his bow and arrows on one side, his trap on the other.

carl nordgren

Naomi folded Mathew's arms across his chest. The other women sat close by and began a chant to call Mathew Loon's spirit to rest.

The children stood back and some joined in the chant.

This Man was silently waiting.

Maureen had been fighting tears since she learned of Mathew's death. Seeing him lying there in his blood-soaked clothes, she was suddenly knifed by the guilt of having set this all in motion and she fell to her knees and sobbed.

Brian put his hands on her shoulders then turned to the youngest lumber mill brother, who stood back from the scene.

"Whatever it was actually happened, you had your hand in the death of this boy. Now what are you goin' to do about it?"

"What do you expect me to do about it?"

"For now, I expect you to be civilized an' show some respect."

Brian knelt to pray beside Maureen, and the youngest brother came up closer to stand behind Brian, bowing his head.

❄ ❄ ❄

The guests and guides had returned from fishing the River and its lakes. Brian met the guests at the dock and quickly led them to their cabins where he told them that a young Ojibway boy had been killed in a shooting accident. The guests were left stunned.

The Ojibway continued to pray and chant over Mathew's body, and Tommy prayed without ceasing.

Maureen exiled herself to her cabin. She was lying on her bed, crying into her pillow.

The youngest brother and Dutch were in Brian's cabin, silently awaiting the next move.

❄ ❄ ❄

Some of the Ojibway men returned from their wigwams and tents with their rattles and drums, wearing feathers or a bit of buckskin or fur. Joe Loon listened closely to what the spirits might say about what it was that happened here.

This Man stood with his head bowed in honor of a fallen warrior.

Brian quickly visited all the guests again in their cabins, apologizing for supper being delayed. He left them drinking quietly

284

from personal stocks, watching the light leave the sky, first above the forests, then above the River, and wondering at the saddest sounds they had ever heard coming from the Ojibway village camp.

Then Brian checked on Maureen. They were alone for the first time since they returned from Kenora to find the dock filled with five strange men. Brian sat on Maureen's bed and held her in his arms.

"It is not your doin'. Why does this fool bring his gun into our home?"

"It's because I brought a knife into their home."

"Jesus, Maureen, you were miles away in a bush plane when the gun was fired."

The mourning song from the Ojibway camp cried a new grief.

"I'll be hearin' their sad song all my life, Brian… Was me called this down on us."

"I won't rest until I convince you otherwise but I need you to set it all aside for I am in need of you here. I need to hear your thinkin' about how we proceed in this important moment in our life together. I need you to guide me through it."

Her sobs subsided.

"I've given it a look from a couple of angles an' have a first idea or two."

❀ ❀ ❀

The youngest brother looked out the cabin window to the east, then turned back to Dutch.

"If they have any more questions, you know where I am."

"Right."

"So we need to leave now."

"Brian'll tell us when he's ready for us to go."

"The sun'll be setting soon."

"Our window to leave ended about thirty minutes ago. So settle back, they'll make up a cabin for you to stay the night, serve us a nice breakfast, and I'll have you on the float plane docks in Kenora in the morning."

"You're holding me against my will."

"Don't you understand how suspicious this all is?"

"It was an accident. Or he killed himself."

"We have an interest in considerin' all possibilities. Seems you need to be here for that."

✻ ✻ ✻

Brian got up at the knock on the door and Albert entered. Albert touched Brian's arm.

"Mathew Loon's spirit has returned. My son's spirit has spoken to me. All of his people have heard it."

"What does it say?"

"His spirit says my son gave his life. To protect the River. The white man with the gun did not take my son's life. Mathew Loon gave his life. This is so his spirit will be a fierce warrior spirit protecting the River."

"What do you mean, Mathew gave his life?"

"Now the white man will know the power of this great spirit protecting the River. When they know what my son did here today, they will not poison our River. That is why my son gave his life."

Maureen listened from the bedroom, then came to the door.

"Are you sayin' that man didn't kill Mathew?"

"That white man did not kill my son."

"Mathew wanted to die, to save the River?"

"No young man wants to die. But to protect the River for his people, my son gladly gave his life."

Maureen began to cry again, and Brian took her in his arms, speaking over her head to Albert.

"Tell me what you would like us to do for you, my brother."

"At sunrise we load our canoes and boats and take my son's body to the burial grounds. You will join us."

Maureen turned back into the bedroom and cried softly as she wondered still about her role in Mathew's death.

✻ ✻ ✻

Kevin spent the day in Sligo, listening at the pubs, asking a few questions that would identify any lads from the local hurling clubs. He found four of them at the third pub he visited. He sat close by, sipping his pint, waiting for the next reference to the sport.

"You lads play the Irish game?"

"Aren't ya lookin' at the heart an' soul of the Sligo club, mister?"

"An' Sligo Hurling A.C. has won the Regional Cup two years running."

"I've heard it said on the streets in Dublin and pubs in Cork that the fellows 'round here are known for the quality of their midfield play."

"We're strong up and down that line an' none says different around here."

"So let me ask you about a young fellow, quite good at the game himself, yeah. He's from a small farm outside of Cong, quite a stick man."

❄ ❄ ❄

The procession of canoes on the River's lake spread all the way across it, from Albert paddling Nigig to the channel at the far shore. Mathew lay on a pallet on the floor of the birch bark canoe.

He had been dressed in the pieces of traditional clothing that he owned. He was wearing the moccasins his grandmother had made for him. He wore the cowry-shell necklace his grandfather had handed down to him. Above his left ear he wore the eagle feather with a beaded crest that Albert had made for him when he became a man of the clan.

Around him were his possessions.

Just behind Nigig, Joe Loon paddled his square-end canoe, the motor removed and left behind; Simon paddled from the bow, Naomi added strokes from the middle, and two young children, a boy and a girl, sat behind her.

Their canoe carried some of the supplies needed for a three-night camp as did most of the dozen canoes that followed.

The canoes of Joe Loon's clan were closest behind Albert and Mathew.

This Man paddled his canoe among them.

Then came the canoes of other Keewatin River clans and camps. One canoe was paddled by a hermit trapper, an old Ojibway only ever seen by anyone when he visited the Hudson Bay Post trading his furs. At the far edge of the lake appeared the first mourners from Grassy Narrows Reserve. They traveled in outboard motor boats for theirs was the greatest distance. They throttled down as they approached the line of canoes.

Up and down the River's channels and across connecting lakes more Ojibway were coming in canoes and boats.

With Brian at the stern, Tommy a priestly presence at the bow, and Maureen amid, their canoe traveled with Joe Loon's people. They were quiet, the only sound the paddles' splash, then a raven's echoed call. As the canoes formed a single file to paddle up a narrow River channel to the burial ground, they began a lament.

❄ ❄ ❄

Nigig was beached on shore and many canoes and boats lined up on either side, covering the open River bank. Mathew's pallet was set down under a grove of aspen. He had been propped up in a sitting position and was being wrapped in birch bark.

Behind the grove was the opening in the forest where the Keewatin clans had buried their dead since the first days they came to the river. Totem posts and wooden Christian crosses marked generations of graves. Grasses and wildflowers covered the low earthen mounds. There were gifts left to honor ancestors' spirits— pots and pans, a rusty rifle barrel, and a broken fishing pole. A plastic baby doll marked one grave. There were strings of shells and necklaces of beads, and on older graves soft circles of each remained where the rawhide cords were lost to many years of weather and rodents. A shiny ceramic northern pike leaping into a fighting pose sat at the base of one cross.

The two men who had been digging Mathew's grave were finishing as more people arrived to set up camp, pitching tents, making shelters, greeting old friends solemnly, saying little as they set up cook fires.

They waited for a man of a Red Lake clan, a Fourth Order Midewiwin. He would lead the burial ceremonies. The ceremonies would last two days, and many people would stay for three.

❄ ❄ ❄

As Brian, Maureen, and Tommy pitched a tent, Maureen told them her decision.

"I am goin' to Ireland... After we've laid our young hero to rest, I'm goin'."

"Sounds like you're sayin' you're goin' alone."

"I need to stand away and see what it is I just did here."

"Then I should go with you. You might need remindin' of what actually occurred."

"You tell me how being alone when you were banished from your village was the only way to see honestly what you'd done."

Tommy looked at his father to see his response and noted his acceptance.

"This ain't a place nor time for debate," Maureen added, "I just thought once I was certain I was goin', alone, I should tell you."

"It don't take a debate to be clear what I did deserved bein' banished an' is nothin' like any role you're claimin' for yourself here. I had intent." Brian looked at Tommy. "I meant to strike Patrick, an' I had control over each blow." Tommy's eyes began to tear, so he walked away a few steps. Brian turned back to Maureen. "But it was that lumber man, an' it was Mathew, that's who acted here, not you, an' if you try to say otherwise you empty his action of any of the meanin' his people are askin' we give to it."

"That's your say on the matter, an' it brings some comfort when I think upon your distinction. I will keep it in mind."

❄ ❄ ❄

Kevin pulled his car in front of the cottage on Lough Arrow.

The old man stepped out to meet him.

"So it's done?"

"He'd left town before I could find him."

"How's that?"

"He told his lads he was going to Derry, and listen to this now. He has a cousin in the Royal Irish Fusiliers at Ebrington Barracks. He's planning on enlisting."

The two men looked at each other a moment, then began to laugh.

"It don't usually make me smile to hear of an Irish lad fightin' for the British crown, but that just might be the safest place for him."

"I've got to return to Dublin tonight, so it's a loose end dangling for now."

"Ah, no, see loose ends, they just make you stumble. I'm afraid your hurlin' lad here, he could still bring you down so hard you hain't gettin' to your feet thereafter."

❈ ❈ ❈

After the old women had lined the bottom of Mathew's grave with a mat of woven rushes and wrapped his body in birch bark, the men slowly lowered him into his grave to rest on the mat. They chanted their prayers and cried their grief.

The body had been placed so Mathew faced west. On his right side Albert laid his son's bow and arrows and a trap. At his left side his other possessions were stacked.

The Midewiwin chanted above the rest.

"Our Brother, you leave us now. Our Brother, see it there before you. See the Path of Souls before you. You see it. Do not stumble. Our Brother, the River will sing to the People of the courage of Mathew Loon. The River will sing this song of the warrior Mathew Loon as long as the People are here to listen."

As the Midewiwin chanted, each of the men took a handful of soil and, one at a time, stepped to the edge of the grave and tossed the dirt, calling out a sharp cry or releasing a low moan when the dirt bounced off the birch cover.

The first to step up to the graveside were drummers, and after they attended to the grave they started a steady beat on the drums.

Soon the women rose and began the Burial Dance.

When Tommy saw that crosses were also used to mark graves he was glad he'd brought his Bible, and when the Midewiwin ended his chant Tommy held his Bible to his chest while he spoke.

"These words I speak to you are from the Gospel according to Matthew. When Jesus the Christ saw the crowds He went up into the mountains, and His disciples came to Him so He could teach them… This was what He said to them. He said the Good Lord blessed the poor in spirit and would prepare a special place for them in his Heaven. He told them those who mourn will be comforted. And Jesus told them blessed are the meek, for they will inherit the earth. Blessed are those who hunger an' thirst for righteousness, for they will be satisfied. And blessed are the merciful, for they will be shown mercy. Blessed are the pure a' heart, for they will know the Great Creator. Blessed are peacemakers, for the world will see they are children of the Great Creator. And blessed are those persecuted for the sake of righteousness, for theirs is the kingdom of Heaven."

Many of the Ojibway crossed themselves as Tommy finished, and Maureen and Brian and others said, "Amen".

Then Brian heard an Ojibway cry that sounded out his own pain, and he shouted a Gaelic echo. The drumming started again, and the Burial Dance continued.

Soon fires were started, for meals and for dancing, and the River bank was aglow.

❄ ❄ ❄

Many of the Ojibway prayed and danced and feasted in honor of Mathew Loon's brave spirit for three days, but after two, Brian and Maureen returned to Innish Cove to prepare for the arrival of guests. Joe Loon promised he would send some of the men back to Innish Cove to guide the next day.

Maureen and Brian were in the bedroom of her cabin. Dutch was headed in to camp with guests, and Maureen was packing her suitcase to head out with him. Brian had been sitting on the bed watching her, but when they heard the plane approach, she slowed her preparation enough that he had to head down to the dock without her yet ready. He kissed her on the head as he walked past.

"When you've packed, leave your bag here an' I'll come back for it."

"I'll just be a few more minutes."

She waited until Brian was well down the path before she pulled the trunk out from under her bed and quickly retrieved five Colt pistols and six boxes of .45 caliber shells. She unloaded the Colt she kept at the ready, then wrapped the guns in dresses and sweaters at the bottom of her suitcase, folded two nightgowns over them, and finally covered it all under her bras and panties.

She closed the suitcase, picked it up to shake it a couple of times, then left it at the front door when she headed down the path to the dock where Brian was welcoming their guests.

After the guests were settled, Dutch told them that on his way in he'd received a radio call from the Chairman of Abitibi himself. He wanted to speak with Brian and Maureen.

❄ ❄ ❄

Tommy had stayed behind when Brian and Maureen left the

burial ground. He found that if he kept close to Simon he would translate for him, explaining in whispers what was said and helping him understand the meaning of the ceremony.

The grave fire and the cook fires were burning.

Albert stood at his son's grave, silently. He had left the site for only a few moments since Mathew's body had been covered. He placed his sleeping mat there and slept at the side of his son's grave.

It was the evening of the last night the Ojibway would spend at Mathew's grave for his spirit was ready for his journey on the Path of Souls.

Simon and Tommy filled their plates with fish and *manoomin*. Simon nodded for Tommy to follow him, and they sat on a log at the River bank.

The only canoes left were from Joe Loon's clan.

"We leave tomorrow. The others will go home. I will take a journey to honor Big Brother. You may come with me."

"Yes, I will."

The next morning, Tommy and Simon pushed off in Nigig and headed down the River.

❄ ❄ ❄

In the Abitibi boardroom the two brothers sat on one side of the table, their father on the other, their grandfather at the head.

The grandfather had the trace of an accent that spoke of a birth and adolescence in England's Midlands, for he had come to Canada with his family when he was in his early teens.

"What's most important to the family is that these Irish and Indians together have taken the position, yes, it is their view, that this young fellow, Mathew Loon is the young man's name, well apparently, this aboriginal actually intended to shoot himself."

The youngest brother hit the table in excited relief, right in front of his older brother.

"It's what I've been saying all along!"

"And it's a most unexpected explanation they're offering up, you see. They say it wasn't an accident at all, nor suicide per se, nothing like an act of despair, but rather some sort of act of self-sacrifice. They say Mathew Loon gave his life, and he did this for the express purpose of stopping the two of you from building your mill on the

River."

The youngest brother laughed.

"Then he's well named, eh, because that's just crazy. Why stop a pulp mill that'll provide jobs for his people? For that he'd shoot himself dead?"

"No, no, you must understand the following, and take it to heart, for it appears your adversaries have, you see. They seem to believe that if your mill opens and begins to use this new process of yours, well, you see, they believe the one scientist got it right, the dissenter they call him, and that the mercury you're dumping will poison their River and will be the end of their way of life."

The older brother made a point of keeping the mercury safety research file close at hand when he came to the boardroom and at that comment he began to open it.

"We've gone through the research five times; I've marked the dates you've asked me to—"

"But if I am going to have to deal with them, and you two have certainly fixed it so I must deal with them, then I am going to understand their fear, and accept it as their fear, and not deny it."

The older brother pulled out a paper.

"Mercury's so heavy it'll sink right to the River bottom, and their camp is 27.7 kilometers away." He turned to another page. "And you can swallow—"

"Yes, yes, I really don't need you to take me through all that again, you see, for right now is not the time to win an argument with them. Now's the time to calm the waters."

"So what are you proposing?"

"I'm past proposing. Your father and I are not asking your opinions here, you see, we're simply doing you the courtesy of keeping you informed of a deal already accepted by all the parties. I've decided that to keep there from being any formal investigation, to keep your names clear of this, and, of course, by that I mean keep my name clear of this... And yes, let's not forget, out of sorrow for the loss of this young Loon's life, I have promised the Burkes we will postpone the construction of your mill."

"What?"

"And when we do start the construction, when we begin again

next year, we will not be incorporating the new process as part of operations."

"Why? After all the work I've done to get the permits?"

"After all the work I've done for 40 years to build this business! You can wait your turn before you double its size or crash it trying. We will hold off and take the next couple of years to fully explore this new process. We don't want this little skirmish of yours to grow into an ongoing conflict. You know how the Irish get hungry for revenge. So I am declaring it history, and if your study is right there will be plenty of time to take your new process operational before the market demand really grows."

The pain in the older brother's leg was sometimes relieved by standing and stretching it out to the side, and he did that now.

"Whether you want my opinion or not, it seems to me you're giving up an awful lot out of sympathy for someone who they admit shot himself."

"Yes, well, you bring up a very interesting subject, this topic of shooting yourself. It appears there were Indian women in the village when you arrived, who took the children into hiding when the gun carrying white men attacked their camp." The younger brother started to interrupt, but his father stopped him with a look. "Of course, these women are each of them in agreement with your statement that two shots were fired. However, they are also all in agreement in insisting that these two shots were fired approximately five minutes apart, and most certainly not three or four seconds as your story insists."

The youngest brother blurted, "So they say!"

"Yes, that's right, so they say. But I can't think of what they have to gain from saying so, and it is no more than their innocent observation of what they heard before they had a sense of the significance of it, apparently. Hard to confuse it, five seconds with five minutes. So, Mr. Burke isn't changing his story about this aboriginal self-sacrifice, no, as I said, that's held in high esteem. But he did wonder what I thought might have been going on during those five minutes between the shots, and he has suggested, quite reasonably it seemed to me at the time, and after further reflection it seems quite reasonable still, that the Provincial Police might be interested in learning more about the whole thing. That's the moment I made my proposal to put off construction in honor of the boy."

Chapter 31
BACK HOME

THIS MAN WAS STANDING IN HIS CANOE, painting on the great rock wall, his canoe bobbing gently, scraping softly against the rock face. It was a picture of Mathew standing above the River with his arms out, raised up, receiving great power.

Tommy and Simon paddled Nigig up to the painted wall. As they got close, Tommy turned to Simon.

"There's many places in Ireland where the Celts carved their images into rock walls. These are similar in many ways. Simple, but the natural lines seem filled with stories... and spirits."

"Maureen has told stories of Celtic Indians."

"Celtic Indians? I guess that's about right."

They studied the images in silence. This Man began a soft chant.

"When Mathew returned from the white man's school, he could not find his true spirit. When we came here he thought he caught sight of it again."

"I believe it was with him when he died."

"Yes, it returned to him before he died."

❋ ❋ ❋

Simon and Tommy sat at their campfire, a small tent pitched behind them next to a small wigwam.

"We camped here before Mathew prayed for his vision. My Big Brother was afraid of his vision."

They were quiet. Tommy stirred the fire and released sparks to the stars.

"Can I ask what Mathew's vision was?"

"He never had one. Not everyone receives their vision. Sometimes the message from Gitchi Manitou is that your life is yours. You will decide what your story will be. Some take that as a freedom. But that was a message that gave no comfort to Mathew."

❄ ❄ ❄

The next morning, in Dublin, while in the backroom of his music shop, Kevin heard the front door open. He came out to find a woman standing with her back to him, studying the high wall covered with fiddles and dulcimers, bodhrans and mandolins.

Kevin recognized Maureen before she turned, and as she did, he retreated to the back corner of the shop so she would follow him and be out of sight from the shop window.

"I need your help, Kevin."

"There's times I know the shop is under surveillance and of late it's often. Your best move now is to leave and make sure no one tails you. If you're sure you're clean, meet me at the Plumbridge rendezvous."

"Let 'em grab me. That's why I've come, to meet with them and explain the situation… to explain everythin'."

"Some who might grab you don't waste much time meeting. The others, it's best we meet with them when we're ready, and if you're saying you need my help, then I'm saying we're not ready."

Maureen gave Kevin's arm a squeeze before she left his shop and crossed the street to the café that offered a backdoor to a side street. By the time she turned a second corner she was certain no one was following her. She continued to where she had parked the hired car and after visiting her mother she would head to Plumbridge.

❄ ❄ ❄

Kevin had a part-time assistant who kept the shop open during his extended trips, and when the hurling lad entered the shop later that day, it was this clerk who greeted him.

As on that tragic day the hurling lad had crushed an IRA brigade leader's skull he was given directions, to Kevin's new apartment, and was told to hurry. Kevin was leaving town that day.

❄ ❄ ❄

Kevin tossed his overnight bag in the Morris Minor and was starting the engine when he saw the hurling lad cross the far end of the street. Kevin rolled the window down as the lad approached and called out to him to get in.

"Get on the floor, keep your head down, lower, and stay down 'til I tell you otherwise."

Kevin pulled away from the curb. There were just a few cars parked ahead of him and only one behind him on this residential street. They all appeared empty, and none moved as Kevin turned onto a side street.

"Just how foolish are you?"

The hurling lad sat on the floorboards, leaning over the seat, looking up at Kevin, and he smiled.

"If I've made the discovery I think I've made, I knew you'd want me to come tell you about it."

"And just what have you discovered?"

"I've been to Derry."

"Enlisting in the Royal Irish Fusiliers is what I hear."

"You know everythin'?"

Kevin checked his mirror as he made a quick turn.

"No, but I try… Tell me your discovery."

"I'm hopin' it keeps me alive an' safe."

"It's going to have to be a most extraordinary discovery to accomplish that for you now, I'm afraid."

"I got a cousin who got me a recruitin' visit an' a tour of Ebrington Barracks. When they was leadin' us past the armory, well, the doors was propped wide open, an' I'm tellin' ya, Kevin, I never imagined so many Brens an Stens, an' rifles, an' mortars all in one place."

"When that place is called an armory, it's what you'd expect."

"But listen to this. As they were escortin' us recruits past it again, later in the day, I saw where they put the keys for the lock on the armory door."

"You got nothing."

"I remembered the advice you gave me, that if I see one thin' leadin' to an advantage, start lookin' for the next thing, so I kept sharp attention to the surroundin's an' realized the most extraordinary thing. You just sort of expect a soldier to be armed, yeah; when you picture a soldier in your head you seem him carryin' a gun, so it took me a few minutes before I noticed that none of the men in the barracks, none of the men in the offices, none of the men in the mess, not a single soldier was carryin' even so much as a pistol on him. Not a one. They was all walkin' 'round unarmed."

"Now I'm interested."

"So I'm sayin' good-bye to my cousin and I ask him about what I saw, and he says it's always so. That unless the men are drillin', the guns are all locked away in the armory, and he's been there six months, and it's been true each an' every day, yeah. All exceptin' for one, he says. The sentry at the main gate, he's got one of dem Sten machine guns."

"One Sten's plenty."

"But the day I was there, yeah, he didn't have the magazine loaded in it."

"And the next day?"

"An' so I walk by the next day, an' it's a different sentry, wit' a Sten, without a magazine loaded. And yesterday, the first sentry's back, no magazine in his machine gun, that's three days runnin'. That's when I figured I should come tell you what I've found."

"What's your cousin's sentiments?"

"A ticket for each of us to Chicago where we got family an' we're both in. If I get word to him, he'll make sure the keys are where I expect them to be."

"You can get up now. I'm headed to meet someone tonight in Plumbridge." He made one last evasive turn before he headed on his true course. "She might be very interested in your discovery."

❋ ❋ ❋

The priest of a local parish, an old family friend, drove Maureen's hired car up to the cottage where she was born and raised. It was one of a cluster of small cottages just outside Carrowkeel on a spur off the main road that headed south to Derry.

The priest found Maureen's mother ready. She got in the car, and they drove away.

❋ ❋ ❋

An old road crested the ridge overlooking Lough Foyle, and Maureen waited there for her mother. When she got out of the car they took each other by the hands, facing each other, but when Maureen saw her mother's tears begin, she dropped one hand and led her to the shore.

They walked a slow pace around the lough while Maureen described the Great Lodge at Innish Cove and told her of their Ojibway friends.

They sat on the rocks at the shore and she told her mother about the events that led up to Mathew's death.

She stole glances at her mother to study the deep wrinkles around her eyes.

Her mother had known Maureen was an IRA sympathizer. There had even been times she suspected she had followed her father and become a volunteer. But she was afraid as she listened to Maureen tell of the Nazis' money and the factions that appeared to be after her now.

She saw the lines and scars of a tired daughter.

"Was Mathew's death sent me here, Mum, but to do what, I'm still not sure. It was my moves that led to his death, my desires to set things right that turned them wrong, an' I'm tired of bein' the schemer. If I could return their money, I would, but it's all been spent buildin' Innish Cove."

"Sounds like you have given them more than most. Shouldn't they see that an' release any claim on you?"

"I think there might be some from past days could see a fair logic to that, but Kevin says these new lads jump to the gun. I've got Kevin on me side, or at least it feels that way now. We're meetin' tonight to talk about how we can make this all end as best it can."

❋ ❋ ❋

Simon and Tommy paddled Nigig across the middle of a great lake on their way back to Innish Cove. They paddled silently. They had been approaching a loon floating calmly in the middle of the lake. As they drew near, the loon swam in a quick circle then dove underwater. Tommy counted to 74 before the loon resurfaced at a safe distance away.

❁ ❁ ❁

The rendezvous was just outside Plumbridge, at the Cruckaclady farmhouse. It was late into the evening. Kevin and the hurling lad were talking with the farmer when Maureen drove up. The farmer left them, and Kevin made the introductions.

"Meet the lady of the legends, Maureen O'Toole."

"Yes 'um, you're just as beautiful as everyone says."

"Sure, of course, an' so show us a favor an' leave Kevin an' me alone, an' don't be offended by my request."

"I'll go see if there's a stew pot on the stove."

Kevin's plans needed the hurling lad to stay close by.

"No, just go wait under that tree until I call you in."

As he walked away Maureen followed Kevin into the widow's cottage just down the lane from the farmhouse. While the old Maimeo sat at the hearth smoking her pipe, Kevin and Maureen settled in at the table.

"I need the end of this now, Kevin, an' I won't be leavin' 'til I'm assured all claims are settled."

"So then, how much money did you bring?"

"Ah Kevin, I told you, it's all tied up in the camp. This is all I've brought with me."

She placed the old valise that Russell had given her on the table, opened it, and showed him the four Colt pistols and boxes of ammunition. She kept one Colt in her jacket pocket, loaded, along with a handful of bullets.

"An' I'm dry of any desire to be makin' plans."

"What have you decided so far?"

"I got an objective, just no play to make it so."

"And your objective is?"

"First and last, to protect Innish Cove. An' that includes Brian and Joe Loon's people. I'm here to protect them. At all cost. At any cost. What's most important to me now is they be left alone."

"But without the money, some are thinking the camp is theirs."

"I'm tired, Kevin. I need you to tell me what I should do to get Innish Cove clear an' clean of all I've done."

"You were offering more guns than this if I remember a conversation in a dark forest one night."

"My front for buyin' them would have to be Innish Cove an' I'm prayin' we can find a way to keep it free from that."

"So if I had a plan that would get the camp free and clear, you're in?"

"With that assurance locked down tight, I'm in."

"Time to call in the lad and we'll see if we don't have an idea that can save both of you and Innish Cove."

❄ ❄ ❄

The lad explained the situation he'd found at the Ebrington Barracks to Maureen while the Maimeo nodded by the fire. While he worked on a map of the layout Maureen asked for, she helped the old lady to her bed. By the time they heard her snoring, Maureen had begun to outline the approach.

❄ ❄ ❄

The next morning, Kevin drove to Dublin to make a proposal to the Executive Council while Maureen drove to Derry with the hurling lad to reconnoiter. Kevin was able to meet with four senior members of the Executive Council that night.

"So, first off, she claims Russell didn't raise 50,000 pounds, that is was barely 2,000, and it was his deep disappointment that the trip was a failure that broke him. Additionally, it was his orders to deny they met that she was acting on. She insists all the money's in the business, along with a good bit of debt. And then she tells me that between the shooting death of this poor Indian boy and the pulp mill threatening their River, they may not even open again next season, and if they don't she's not sure they'll ever open again."

"And we're supposed to believe her because that's what she says?"

"What I know independent of her supports what she says."

"She's got to be offerin' us sometin', she must know that."

"We are offering something. Something astounding."

"You're standin' wit' her?"

"I stand where I always stand, and she's standing where she always stands, and that's against the British occupation of our homeland and with all others who believe the Brits need to be driven out of all corners of our island. And I'm here to tell you, we've got a plan. A plan to pull off a raid on a British military target that would be the biggest in our history. It not only triples our armaments, it's got a boldness to it that will get the hearts of the people beating again. We'll be needing the guns because recruits will be streaming in when people see what we can do to the Brits."

"So you're tellin' us that she's standin' with us again."

"It's her plan, and mine, but it's her thinking smart for us, like before the war. And we have the advantaged position to pull it off and fast. Four days from now we're going to walk in to one of their fortresses and take all their guns away from them."

"It's Omagh or Ebrington, if you're talkin' the biggest depots they've got. And we've been watching both of 'em for months."

"And what you've seen is too big a risk to move. I've heard the debate, and its conclusion is the same each time. So now you've heard me say we'll be leaving tomorrow, and when we return in four days it will be with more armaments than we ever imagined."

"An' so yer bargain is ya' pull it off, an' we say she's paid in full?"

"She leaves knowing there's never a chance anyone drops by their fishing lodge unless she made the invitation."

"That's a lot to ask for by someone in no position to be askin' for much."

"I'm not sure. There's many among us still who argue we must always stay true to leaving the New World alone. I'm not the only one sitting in this room who knows how our American cousins would fret if IRA violence reached their shores. And if you try to take over their fishing operation, she promises there will be violence."

"It's the right rule until somebody steals somethin' from us and runs there to hide."

"This woman lost her father to the Black an' Tans. This woman has carried bombs strapped between her legs. And now she's ready to risk her life to arm us again."

"An' she stole our money."

"That money's gone, there wasn't much, and we never had it anyway. I'm saying we have the chance to be reborn with this move. And not just new recruits, think what happens to the splinters when word gets out what we've done. Flanagan's crew will come running back first and others will drift in soon enough."

One of the men nodded in agreement.

"He's right. But one of us goes with him."

Another said, "I'll go."

"Thanks Charlie, we can use your help as it seems we could be taking over two hundred rifles and nearly a hundred machine guns, Brens and Stens. And there's mortars and mines. Just tell us what you want, we'll get it for you."

"So it is Ebrington."

"I'll let you know when it's time to let you know. But you need to pull back anyone you have who's close to either Ebrington or Omagh. We can't have anybody stepping into something they don't know about. You need to do that now."

❄ ❄ ❄

As Tommy and Simon Fobister paddled across the lake on their return to the Great Lodge at Innish Cove, two fishing boats with guests and guides passed them at the end of a day's fishing. They waved.

Nigig slowly bobbed in one boat's wake and then the other. When they rounded the point into the cove, Tommy saw his father standing on the dock, patting his guests' backs as they showed him the day's catch. His father leaned back with laughter that rolled over the water.

Tommy rested his paddle on his knees, then pointed it to shore.

"We could build a chapel, right there, between your village camp an' the guests' cabins on that shelf of land behind those birch trees."

"That is where Nokomis built her wigwam as the fires burned."

"I was thinking the chapel would be built to honor Mathew's sacrifice."

"You will talk with Big Brian and Joe Loon tonight to receive their blessing, then I will show you which trees to cut."

"We'll get started tomorrow?"

"Or the next day."

❄ ❄ ❄

Three days later, in the middle of the afternoon, Maureen sat at a table in the café just across the street from the ten-foot-high brick wall enclosing the Ebrington Barracks. It was the only table affording a view of the main gate, but at such an acute angle all she could see was that the gate doors, as expected, were wide open.

The yellow scarf she had worn on the boat to Copenhagen was wrapped around her neck.

※ ※ ※

A few blocks away on a commercial side street, Kevin and the hurling lad were loading masonry tools and equipment into the back of a truck. "O'Hearn and Son, Masonry Repair" was spelled out in big red letters on canvas signs lashed to both sides of the truck.

They each wore work overalls. Kevin carried the last kit of tools to the truck. After he loaded them he checked that the heap of canvas signs inside the truck were high enough to hide the four men from the Derry unit Charlie had recruited for Kevin when they returned from Dublin.

※ ※ ※

There were six guests at Innish Cove. Louis Angeconeb, Joe Loon, and Old George were guiding them, leaving Brian, Simon, Tommy, and Albert to work on the log chapel.

The walls were five logs high. Two sturdy pole pines were propped against the top log, and the men pushed the next log up this ramp.

This Man stood in the middle of the chapel and called for the blessings of Ningaabi'Anong, Waabanong, Giiwedinong, and Zhaawanong, the spirits Gitchi Manitou created to protect each of the Four Directions.

The log dropped into place, notched ends fitting notched ends.

As Albert trimmed one end and Simon the other for a tighter fit, Brian took a deep drink from the water bottle then handed it to Tommy.

"Not many priests as young as you has already built his first church."

"I'm just a candidate."

"Just makes it more impressive... I'll bet I could get the bishop to fly in for a couple days fishing to bless this when we're through."

"Maybe."

"It's the Catholic way."

"Don't know it needs to be a Catholic chapel. Maybe it's a place where all us sinners go to find peace, not just the Catholic variety."

❀ ❀ ❀

Maureen was served her tea. She looked up as the sentry stepped out on the sidewalk, took a last puff on his cigarette, then flicked it into the street. When he turned to go back to his post, she could see the Sten strapped over his shoulder, but she couldn't tell if the magazine was in place.

She sipped her tea, wiped her mouth, then removed her Colt pistol from the pocket of her jacket and checked one more time that it was loaded and ready. She replaced it in her pocket.

She mumbled low. "Lord, forgive me for what I am about to do. May you keep as many safe as you can. May you welcome the innocents to your heavenly kingdom."

❀ ❀ ❀

Kevin climbed behind the wheel of the truck, the hurling lad settled in next to him, and they drove the streets of Derry towards Ebrington Barracks.

"It was a bad turn of luck your blow killed a man. With a bit of good luck and cool heads all 'round, you and your cousin will be on your way to Chicago within the week."

❀ ❀ ❀

Maureen checked her watch. Precisely at two o'clock she laid some coins on the table, crossed herself, and stepped outside into the street.

Charlie watched her from his car, parked across the street and a few doors down from the main gate.

❀ ❀ ❀

An Ojibway girl, no more than nine or ten, carried a baby boy on her hip when she came to check the work site.

Tommy smiled at her, rubbed the baby's chin with the back of his hand, and continued his story.

"We took a ferry out to Inis Mor last year, some of my friends from seminary. There's a place where St. Edna built the first church on the island, 1,500 years ago, where people have been prayin' together for peace an' love an' grace in their lives ever since. An' just down the road from the ruin of his church is another church with an old sculpture just inside the door. It's a wood carving, about so tall." He held his hand just above his waist. "It's a worn, but wonderful, image of Joseph, and he's holding an infant Jesus up on his shoulder. Jesus is no more than two or three, an you can feel Joseph trying to collect him, to hold him safe as Jesus is climbing Joseph like he's a ladder. Details of faces are worn, but I picture 'em both laughing."

"That's exactly what we need here in this chapel."

❀ ❀ ❀

Maureen approached the main gate, stopping short of the opening, distracted for a moment by two children passing by.

Charlie stepped out of his car. He was wearing a full-length oilcloth rain slicker.

The truck Kevin was driving pulled up to the corner but waited there, the engine idling.

When Maureen took her next step, it was with a heavy limp. She made it to the open gate then leaned against the wall, demonstrating her obvious pain, checking that all was consistent with their reconnaissance of the past days. She confirmed that once again the sentry's Sten had no magazine and, as the hurling lad's cousin had assured them, the soldiers were in the barracks or offices and none were out and about in the open grounds beyond the gate.

Maureen tried to walk but her ankle hurt too much. The sentry noticed.

"Can I 'elp you, miss?"

Maureen removed her scarf and began to bandage her ankle with it, and Charlie relayed the go sign to Kevin. The raid began.

"Could you now? I've just stepped off the curb an' twisted me ankle an' it's hurtin' just to stand on it… Maybe I can just rest here for a moment."

"There's a chair inside the guardhouse. Let me give you a hand."

He smiled when the lovely woman put her arm over his shoulder, and he carefully supported her weight as they entered the one-room guardhouse. She slumped into the chair.

"Would you like a drink of water?"

"Water would be grand."

He turned and Maureen slipped the pistol from her pocket as she stood and pressed the point of the barrel against the sentry's head just behind his temple as the truck pulled off the street and entered the gate.

"Sit down an' shut the feck up or you're dead. I know that Sten hain't loaded, so place it on the floor at your feet."

Kevin stopped the truck at the guardhouse.

Charlie walked in behind the truck, whispered encouragement to the men hiding, and entered the guardhouse where Maureen stood over the sentry.

Charlie removed his raincoat. He was dressed in a British uniform. He had concealed a coil of rope under his slicker and tossed it to Maureen. He picked up the Sten, looped it over his shoulder, put on the guard's hat, then stepped outside to assume the guard's role and position.

The truck drove on, across the empty and open grounds, past the offices and mess hall, past the barracks, to the far corner where the storage buildings and armory sat side by side. There were no soldiers to be seen.

Maureen hammered the pistol handle hard against the sentry's head and he slumped down out of the chair to the floor—out cold. She tied his arms and legs and gagged him with the yellow scarf. She pushed him behind the small desk in the corner and covered him with Charlie's rain slicker.

She stepped back outside, crossed the street, and sat behind the wheel of Charlie's car.

❋ ❋ ❋

Tommy was notching the next log by cutting a sharp groove on the bottom of each end. Then he cut a sharp ridge on the top of each end.

Albert examined his work as Brian watched them both.

"Your son does his work well."

"My son does his work very well."

✳ ✳ ✳

Kevin parked the truck between the storehouse and the armory. The cousin had told them of a crack in the foundation of a wall in the storehouse and they planned to fix it. There was one soldier sitting on the steps. Kevin grabbed a clipboard from the front seat, stuck a pencil behind his ear, and held his pistol concealed behind the clipboard. He hopped down from the truck to come around to the rear as the soldier nodded to him.

"You're repairing that bit of a crack?"

"That's right. It's a small job now, could be a big one later."

The soldier stood and headed to the truck.

"My father is a stone mason in Manchester. Wants me to join him when my soldierin' days 'r done. He don't know I enlisted to keep from joinin' the trade."

"It's good honest work."

Kevin pulled back the canvas flap covering the back of the truck. As the soldier stepped up to check out the tools, Kevin knocked him hard with his pistol and the soldier slumped over a toolbox. Two Derry men grabbed him and pulled him into the truck, tied and gagged him, and stashed him behind the canvas.

The hurling lad pulled off his overalls to reveal his British uniform, and he dashed to get the armory keys while two of the Derry men dressed as laborers helped Kevin unload their tools and set up to repair the foundation crack. Kevin repositioned the truck to stay close to the repair site and closer to the armory door.

Kevin emerged from the cab of the truck in British khaki as the two Derry men dressed as day laborers began to repair the crack and the other two, in uniform, followed Kevin to the armory door. The hurling lad handed the keys to Kevin, then assumed his post as lookout.

Kevin found the proper key and the armory door swung open to reveal the largest cache of British arms in all of Northern Ireland. Kevin headed straight to the Brens, grabbed two, and carried them to the truck. He directed the men. "You and I grab weapons, you grab ammunition for the weapons we grab."

✳ ✳ ✳

The men pushed the next log into place, Tommy at one end,

Albert at the other, Brian and Simon in the middle. Tommy was tired, and his end was lagging, so Brian shifted his hands towards Tommy's end and pushed harder.

The log slid up and into place, bringing the walls to shoulder height.

"If you thought there was any chance of Katie an' Patrick comin', we could have the weddin' here. Right here, at the chapel. That is, unless Maureen has been makin' plans there that we can't get out of."

※ ※ ※

Maureen started Charlie's car but stayed parked at the curb. Charlie kept his post, walking back and forth from the open main gate to the guardhouse, keeping his face hidden as best he could, watching for anyone headed towards the armory.

The Derry men and Kevin carried load after load to the truck, pausing only to cover the growing piles of rifles and machine guns and ammunition with the canvas signs.

When the hurling lad saw two soldiers coming towards the storage buildings, he scooted around the truck and told the crew.

The laborers slapped some fresh cement against the foundation wall.

Kevin swung the armory door shut, the four of them inside, and they continued to stack weapons and ammunition just inside the door.

"When we get this stack loaded, we've got plenty."

When the repair men saw the soldiers walking by, they called them over.

"Someone around here is lookin' smart. An easy repair today, could have been a problem soon enough."

"I don't know about that, mate. But I do know Captain Barkley, an' he won't be happy with your lorry parked 'ere. You need to park it over behind the guardhouse."

"We're just finishin' up now... by the time we'd move it we'd be done with the job. We'll be out of here before you know it."

"No skin off mine, mate. Just lettin' you know Barkley can blow pretty hot."

The soldiers moved on, the laborers tapped out an all clear on the armory door, and the men quickly loaded their last stockpile into the truck, covering it with canvas.

Maureen spotted the British army lorry as it rounded the corner and headed their way, towards the barracks. She pulled the car out into the street at an angle that blocked passage and then applied full choke to flood the engine. The car stalled in the path of the army lorry, stopping it ten yards short of the main gate.

She got out of the car and began to pound on the hood in exasperation.

The driver had stopped just a few yards short of the car. The passenger upfront was a sergeant and he got out to see what the problem was.

"You 'avin a bit of motor troubles, miss?"

"My husband will be furious. He's told me keep me hands off his Vauxhall."

"Maybe ya could listen to him then. She's stalled out, is she?"

"I'm afraid so."

"Let me give 'er a try."

❄ ❄ ❄

Albert took the baby boy from the girl and set him up on his shoulder, and they walked back to their camp for a midday meal followed by Simon.

Brian and Tommy stood side by side, examining their work.

"I took so much away from you an' Katie an' poor little Patrick. I will never pretend otherwise."

"When I return, I will tell them what I have found here. All of it. The beauty, yes. The lovely people, yes. But I must also tell Patrick and Katie about Mathew's death. They are so afraid of violence in your world, I don't know how else to say it, so it's hard to predict how they will react."

"I understand."

❄ ❄ ❄

One Derry man dressed as a laborer was driving, the other sat in the cab with him, and Kevin and the others sat in the back amongst the piles of weapons and the bound British soldier. The truck drove across the open yard, stopping at the guardhouse. Charlie checked that the sentry's ropes were holding then returned in time to climb into the back of the truck.

The truck driver exited through the main gate. To his left, he saw two soldiers pushing the Vauxhall back into its parking place, the sergeant inside steering the car.

The driver of the army lorry was still sitting at the wheel.

Maureen stood on the sidewalk, thanking them for their help.

The Derry driver pulled out onto the road, turning right, and accelerated hard. His passenger pulled the pin from a Mills grenade, leaned out the window, and threw it at the army lorry so it bounced then rolled under its cab.

There was no part of the plan that called for this, but as soon as Maureen saw the Derry man toss the grenade, she was moving fast.

One British soldier saw the man tossing something at their lorry and he called out his warning as he dropped to the street behind the Vauxhall.

"Grenade! Cover!"

The sergeant dove to the floor of the motorcar, the other soldier jumped over the hood and landed on top of his fellow soldier.

The army lorry driver froze in fear.

Maureen saw a short brick wall in front of the house behind her and dashed behind it.

In the back of the truck Kevin was so close to the engine's revving he wasn't sure if he'd heard a warning shout from the street, but when the Derry men and Charlie crouched and covered he was guessing a grenade had been thrown at their truck, and he covered as best he could.

In two seconds the grenade exploded, the front of the army lorry reared up into the air, then slammed into a motor car parked in front of the Vauxhall as shattering glass and metal fragments riddled the cars. Then a second whoosh of a blast from the truck's fuel tank quickly enveloped the entire chassis in flames.

Kevin realized they weren't the target but rather someone from their truck had tossed the grenade and found Charlie grinning confidently.

"Who did that?"

"We figured if we were successful, walking in and taking so

many guns, that they'd be so embarrassed they'd do all they could to keep it quiet. Now they can't."

"But Maureen's out there."

"If she's the great soldier you say she is, she'll be waitin' for us in the alley."

"She might be killed back there or captured. This was my operation, mine and hers."

Charlie pulled back an edge of canvas and revealed the stacks of rifles and machine guns and ammunition.

"An' you managed your end of it well. We just put our stamp on it."

"What else is altered?"

"Nothin' else. If your girl is safe, she's free. Her camp is free. Your boy can leave safely for the States."

❄ ❄ ❄

Maureen was confused. This wasn't the getaway planned. She peeked around the wall to see the soldiers running into the barracks and others running out. She quickly walked down the sidewalk and when she got to the corner, she ran.

And as she ran, she began to cry.

❄ ❄ ❄

Tommy sat at a table in the lodge cabin. Brian placed a plate of fish and beans in front of his son, then sat down at his own place.

"I've wanted a lot from life."

"You've got a good bit from it, best I can see."

"What I want most of all, now, is for my son to bless our meal."

"Heavenly Father. Give us grateful hearts. For this food. For this place. For all your tender mercies. Amen."

"Watch over Maureen in her travels, an' bring her safely home. Amen."

❄ ❄ ❄

The truck pulled half-way down an alley, next to a row of trash bins, where the men tossed their uniforms. The truck's signs were removed and replaced with new signs that read "Manus and Canning, Drayage". The old canvas signs were used to re-cover the pile of guns.

At the end of the alley a car was parked. Kevin and the hurling lad would wait there for Maureen.

The hurling lad had been studying Kevin closely. "You trust 'em?"

"I can't deny there was something to their play there at the end. Everyone will know about this now. Everyone will know we've got our legs set strong again."

"You think she made it out of there?"

"You never bet against her."

"I'd stay if they'd let me."

"You can do so much more for us in Chicago. As soon as you get set up, find the lads that are interested in our fight."

Kevin pulled the armory key ring from his pocket, removed one of the keys, and handed it to the hurling lad.

"Tell them about today. Show them this key. Tell them you're giving the Ebrington Amory key to the one who can raise us the most money."

"After I send you the money, we'll wait a little while, then you can send me a second key, and I'll tell them you just found it, and that it's the key that opened the second lock on the Amory door."

"I've always known how to spot talent."

Charlie drove the truck down the alley towards Kevin's car. When they drew next to it, the truck stopped. Charlie leaned out the window.

"Half the load we deliver to Kenny, half goes to the Farm. The truck is left on the streets in Belfast with the soldier and your note."

"I'll be back in my shop Wednesday. Take care."

When the truck passed and drove away, Kevin could see the length of the alley again.

Maureen was coming.

❊ ❊ ❊

Everyone in camp was at the dock, or on the beach, as Maureen climbed down from the Norseman. Brian reached for her hand as she stepped from the ladder to the pontoon, then pulled her into his arms when she stepped onto the dock.

He held her close as Simon called out in Ojibway.

"If Big Brian is a wise man, he will not ever let this Raven Hair

Woman go."

When they heard a natural love in the laughter, Brian and Maureen held each other a moment longer.

"We've got something to show you, Lady Girl. Follow me."

The whole crowd followed.

When they got to the chapel Tommy entered first, then Maureen and Brian, then one by one all of the Ojibway entered the chapel, filling the space.

"So I hope you haven't made any plans for a weddin' in Derry that can't be changed."

"Let's get married right here."

"Next summer. We'll pick a week when we won't book any guests. We'll fly everyone over."

"Me ma would love to visit."

"If she likes it once she's here an' decides she'd like to stay, she's welcome."

"It wouldn't surprise me if she did exactly that."

❉ ❉ ❉

That evening after supper when it was very near dark in the forest and red-gold over the water, Brian was called to the Ojibway village camp by Joe Loon, his father.

When Maureen walked from her cabin to Brian's, she saw Tommy standing at the chapel, and she headed his way. "Tommy," she called as she drew close, and when he turned, she could see his eyes smiled.

She walked past him to the chapel door.

"I need you to hear my confession."

"I'm sorry, Maureen. I can't hear it. Not 'til I'm ordained."

She stopped.

"Oh."

"I wouldn't be but an intermediary, anyway. Those folks over there, they got it right. They talk directly to our Creator every day."

Maureen entered the chapel. Tommy stayed outside. In the middle of the empty room she fell to her knees.

"Forgive me Father, for I have sinned..." She prayed silently for a long time before she said, "And God bless the Innocents," then crossed herself and found Tommy and Brian waiting for her outside.

※ ※ ※

Outside in the near dark, out in the open River, This Man rode the moose. The great animal approached the far shore, and as it found its footing in the shallows This Man slipped from his back and splashed into the water while the moose kicked and bucked. The moose stopped as it reached land, shook once, and then disappeared into the dark forest.

AUTHOR'S NOTE

THIS NOVEL IS CRAFTED WITH RESPECT for the large historical events that advance our stories. So while I have fictionalized these events, I have not distorted them.

That respect extends to my use of labels and names for the First Nations Ojibway and in my presentation of their customs.

My guide on this matter is my good friend Steve Fobister. Steve and I worked together at Delaney Lake Lodge and Ball Lake Lodge in Northwestern Ontario back in the mid to late 60's. He went on to be an elected chief of the Grassy Narrows First Nation, serving his people at a crucial time.

Steve is an Ojibway. Others spell the tribal name Ojibwa (which is how I always have pronounced the name because it is how Steve pronounces it) or Ojibwe, and both seem to be increasingly popular. Back in the 60's I don't think I saw it spelled any way other than Ojibway, and the last gift Steve gave me was a T-shirt with "Ojibway Nation" on the front.

In this novel the Irish of the 30's call First Nations aboriginals "red men." I believe the novel benefits from that historical reference, and Steve agrees.

The label "Indian" is used most frequently, as it would have been at the time. Steve and many men I worked with never indicated that they considered Indian to be offensive, only inaccurate.

When a disposed people re-claim the authority to determine how they will be known, we all support that, we even celebrate it on our way to further victories for expressions of aboriginal justice. The First Nations people of Canada, the Native Americans in the US, those self-determined names will be used when the story catches up to them.

The representation of Ojibway customs and habits are accurate and only occasionally embellished for the story's purpose. Steve and I became good friends the four summers we worked together. He led me to Ojibway burial sites. He took me on my first expedition to a Hudson Bay Post. He invited me to sweat lodge ceremonies. He was born in a wigwam and didn't move to the reserve until he was nine, and it is my good fortune that he loves to tell stories as much as I do. He approves of the stories I tell of his people.

You might find this an interesting note about Steve Fobister's name. There are many Fobister's living at Grassy Narrows Reserve. It seems that when the government officials approached the Ojibway living in that area and told them they needed to adopt an English name for the official census records, the man leading that effort was named Fobister. Many of the Ojibway thought they were being told that was the last name they should choose.

ABOUT THE AUTHOR

CARL NORDGREN WAS BORN in Greenville, Mississippi where his great grandmother's house was across the street from the boyhood home of author Walker Percy. Carl has worked as a fishing guide on the English River in Northwestern Ontario and on the White River in the Arkansas Ozarks, as a bartender, a foundry man, and an entrepreneur. He lived with his family in Ireland for a year where he researched the IRA, and he currently teaches courses in Creativity to undergraduate students at Duke University. His first book, Welcome to the Creative Populist Revolution, was written to help us all grow our creative capacity and develop our entrepreneurial instincts. He graduated from Knox College and lives in Durham, North Carolina with his wife Marie where they have raised three daughters.

CPSIA information can be obtained
at www.ICGtesting.com
Printed in the USA
LVOW12s1533281016

510723LV00002B/174/P